HOMICIDE AT HOME

Melissa Craig was nearly home. She always enjoyed the moment when, rounding a curve, she saw the valley open out ahead with the cottages, hers and Iris's, snuggling cosily at the foot of the bank.

There was nothing cosy about the setting on this occasion. Two police cars were parked outside Iris's cottage.

Iris was standing by her garden gate where a woman police officer seemed to be trying to reason with her. There was something unnatural and disturbing about Iris's appearance. She was rigid, her thin hands were locked together against her mouth and her eyes were wild, as if some hideous image was trapped inside them. Her face was the colour of clay. Melissa hurried over to her.

"What in the world is going on?" she exclaimed.

At the sound of her voice, Iris unfroze as if a switch had been pressed. She reached out with both hands. "I found it . . . I dug it up . . . oh my God!"

"She's had a rather nasty shock," said the policewoman. "It seems she came across the remains of a body in the woods."

"A nicely rendered English-village setting, a well-rounded cast of characters and suspects, and a genuinely puzzling mystery. Fans of the 'cozy' English mystery should grab this one up immediately."

—Dean James, Manager, Murder by the Book

A MELISSA CRAIG MYSTERY

A Little Gentle Sleuthing

BETTY ROWLANDS

JOVE BOOKS, NEW YORK

The villages of Upper and Lower Benbury are not to be found on any map of the Cotswolds. They, as well as all the characters and events portrayed in this work, are fictitious.

This Jove Book contains the complete
text of the original hardcover edition.
It has been completely reset in a typeface
designed for easy reading, and was printed
from new film.

A LITTLE GENTLE SLEUTHING

A Jove Book / published by arrangement with
Walker and Company

PRINTING HISTORY
Walker and Company edition published 1991
Jove edition / July 1992

ISBN: 0-515-10878-2

Jove Books are published by The Berkley Publishing Group,
200 Madison Avenue, New York, New York 10016.
The name "JOVE" and the "J" logo
are trademarks belonging to Jove Publications, Inc.

PRINTED IN THE UNITED STATES OF AMERICA

10   9   8   7   6   5   4   3   2

ONE

EARLY IN MARCH, MELISSA CRAIG PARCELLED UP
the manuscript of her latest crime novel and sent it to her agent
with a covering letter.

Dear Joe,
Don't expect to hear from me again for a few weeks as I'll
be getting ready to move house. Everything's a bit fraught
at the moment but I'm looking forward more than I can tell
you to a peaceful country existence. The cottage is a dream.
It's just outside a village called Upper Benbury, one of a pair
wedged into the side of a valley with a brook running along
the bottom. Idyllic! I've only got one near neighbour—in the
adjoining cottage—but I haven't met her yet. I'm told she's
an artist who winters abroad. She sounds interesting.

Yours,
Melissa

As an afterthought, she added:

PS There's a disused shepherd's hut about a quarter of a
mile along the valley. It's tumbledown, rather smelly and a
bit spooky when the wind blows in a certain direction and
howls through the holes in the roof. An ideal location for the
discovery of a corpse, don't you think?

Finding the cottage had been a piece of serendipity, the result
of stooping to pick up a fallen glove outside the window of an
estate agent in Bristol where she had been doing some research.
As she straightened up, her eye fell on a photograph, taken on

1

a bright winter's morning when snow hid the broken tiles and the shadows were tinted with the blue of the sky. There was a bird-bath on the lawn and a nesting-box nailed to an apple tree. Add a robin and a sentimental message, she remembered thinking, and you have a Christmas card.

There was no bright sunlight and no snow that grey December afternoon but she had finished her research, had a couple of hours to spare and, on impulse, asked to view the property. It lay at the end of a rough track in which potholes had been crudely repaired with rubble and it slumped against its well-maintained partner like a drunk leaning on a friendly shoulder. The nesting-box had slewed sideways and the many weeds and a few unhappy-looking plants in the garden lay flattened and soggy on the saturated earth. The interior was even more dilapidated—peeling plaster, a smell of damp and only the most basic amenities. But Melissa did not need the assurances of the agent—young, enthusiastic and full of plans for what he called 'tasteful renovation'—to realize the possibilities. By the time she returned to London she had taken the first tentative steps to becoming the owner.

It was a blue and gold April morning when she took possession. Having spent the night in a nearby inn, she arrived at the cottage a good hour before the furniture van was due. Just as well, she reflected, noting the clutch of empty paint tins in the kitchen, the scattering of loose nails over unswept floors and the dusty huddle of discarded packing material in the grate. The builder had prom-ised to send in a cleaner the day before. He had also promised to arrange for a delivery of oil for the central heating boiler. Melissa went outside and rapped the bottom of the oil tank with her knuck-les. Its echoing emptiness proclaimed a further broken promise.

At least the telephone had been installed. She rang the builder to draw his attention to the deficiencies.

'Thought it was the twelfth you were moving in,' he said cheerfully.

'Today *is* the twelfth,' Melissa pointed out.

'What? Oh—so it is. Sorry about that. Want me to send some-one up later on?'

'Later on will be too late—my furniture will be here in an hour,' said Melissa frostily. 'It's just as well I brought some cleaning materials with me. Now, what about the oil?'

'What oil?' He sounded nonplussed, as if expecting to hear that a drilling rig had appeared overnight in the garden.

'The heating oil you were going to have delivered yesterday.'

'Oh, that oil. Hasn't it come?'

'It has not. When was it ordered?'

'Er—have to ask the girl. She's not in at the moment. I'll call you back.'

'Don't bother!' Melissa slammed down the telephone in a fury. Fortunately she remembered the name of the oil merchant. She reached for the directory, brushed off the layer of gritty dust, checked the number and was about to pick up the receiver when the bell started ringing. The sound echoed in the empty room, making her jump.

'Hello!' she said, half-expecting to hear the voice of the builder.

For a moment, no one answered. She could hear faint sounds of movement, as if the hand holding the receiver the other end was shifting its grip.

'Hello!' she said sharply. 'Who's there?'

'Babs?' It was a man's voice, low and urgent. 'Babs, I must see you!'

'I think you've got . . .' Melissa began but the caller hurried on, ignoring her interruption.

'Tonight . . . I'll come to the usual place. Be there, please!' Halfway through, the voice began to waver. On the final word it cracked altogether.

'Just a minute!' Melissa raised her own voice in an effort to stem the tide of grief spilling from the instrument. 'I'm not Babs . . . you have the wrong number . . . hello!' But the man had hung up.

The receiver rested in Melissa's hand, gently purring where a moment ago it had sobbed out a man's anguish. It was a disturbing start to the day. First a series of blunders by the builder, now a stranger beseeching her to meet him. It troubled her to think that somewhere that evening a distraught lover would wait in vain for his Babs to turn up. If he had stopped to listen, she could at least have spared him that.

She glanced at her watch. It was nearly nine fifteen and the removal men were supposed to be here by ten. The place was a shambles, unfit to receive furniture. The oil would have to wait.

It was nearly ten thirty when the van came bumping along the track leading to the cottage. By that time, Melissa had managed to get most of the builder's rubbish into plastic sacks outside the back door, sweep the floors and wipe the worst of the dust from shelves and window-sills. The immersion heater had provided plenty of hot water and she had brought with her in the car a supply of detergent and teacloths. At least she was ready to wash and put away the unbelievable quantity of crockery, glassware and kitchen utensils that would soon have to be disinterred from newspaper-filled tea-chests. She thought with nostalgia of her orderly London flat and wondered what had possessed her to leave it.

'Sorry we're late—had a job to find it,' apologised the foreman. He took a quick look round, raising his eyebrows at the sight of the bare boards.

'It would have been nice to get the carpets fitted before I moved in,' agreed Melissa, reading his thoughts. 'But the building work was delayed and anyway the shop couldn't deliver the carpet in time.'

The foreman scratched his head and grinned. 'Usual story,' he commented. He cast an experienced eye around him and added, 'at least they left it clean.'

'*They* did nothing of the kind!' snorted Melissa. 'You should have seen it an hour ago!'

The man chuckled. 'DIY job, eh? Well, let's get on with it then—if you'll just tell us where everything's to go.'

By three o'clock the van had left. Melissa sank wearily into an armchair in the sitting-room and contemplated the surrounding chaos. There was so much to do, so much of it needing to be done before life could become anything like normal. She remembered the day she first viewed the cottage. She had stood in this room, with its stone fireplace and wooden beams, its low ceilings and its unspoilt view across the valley, imagining herself living there with her own belongings around her. In her enthusiasm, her almost superstitious certainty that she had been meant to find this place, it had been easy to see beyond the crumbling plaster, the festoons of bare wires and the rotting floorboards and window-frames. On her second visit, so much had been done that she was impatient to take possession. She had measured for curtains and planned where she would arrange her furniture. Bookshelves in the alcoves on either side of the chimney, her desk by the window. Deep soft cushions on the window-seats and a standard lamp behind her favourite chair by the fire. Pictures on the walls.

Now she was faced with the reality. The furniture was arranged, more or less as she had envisaged, but of course it would all have to be pushed around when the carpet fitters came. The books were still in boxes and couldn't be unpacked until the shelves were fitted. There were no hooks for the pictures and anyway the walls would need another coat of emulsion where the painters had skimped their task. Melissa tried not to think of the stack of unwashed kitchen items littering every available surface, nor the bags and boxes waiting to be unpacked. She felt grubby, longed for a shower but felt unable to face the task of making the bathroom fit to use. And she was hungry, having had nothing since breakfast but a cheese sandwich and countless mugs of watery coffee.

She was pulled back from the edge of self-pity by a knock at the door. The visitor was a woman of about fifty and even before she introduced herself, Melissa had no doubt who she was. With her bobbed mouse-brown hair held in place by tortoiseshell slides and her shapeless plaid pinafore dress worn over a close-fitting sweater, she was the archetypical 'arty' character of an amateur stage production. But she had fine features and a clear, tanned skin, her grey eyes were intelligent and humorous and there was genuine friendliness in her smile.

'Iris Ash,' said the newcomer, holding out a thin brown hand. 'Next door,' she explained with a jerk of the head. 'Just popped in to say hello. Expect you're in a pickle.' Her glance, sliding over Melissa's shoulder and back, seemed to encompass the entire chaotic interior of the cottage and her mouth formed a sympathetic grimace. 'Beastly business, moving house.'

'It certainly is!' Iris's handclasp was firm, strong, and immensely comforting in its warmth. 'I'm Melissa Craig, I'm so pleased to meet you. Won't you come in?'

Iris shook her head. 'Not now. Only be in the way. Came to ask if you'd care to have supper with me.'

'That's very kind of you.' Melissa had a steak in the refrigerator but had already been dreading the prospect of preparing her own meal at the end of a hard day. 'I'd like that, thank you very much.'

'Vegetarian,' Iris explained. 'Nuts and beans. Things from the garden. Lots of roughage.'

'Oh, er, that's fine,' said Melissa, trying to sound as if she meant it. She was committed now and there was always cheese and biscuits if she felt hungry later on.

'About six thirty, then.' Iris turned on her heel and marched back to her own cottage. Her walk was stiff and erect and she swung her arms like a child playing at soldiers.

'Nice,' said Melissa to herself as she closed the door and set about her tasks with renewed optimism. 'Eccentric but nice.'

Two

By half past five, Melissa had finished the washing-up and put everything away. She unpacked and stowed her groceries, adding yet another empty cardboard carton to the growing pile outside the back door. She hung the cream curtains, sprigged with blue and yellow flowers and chosen to blend with her crockery and the new vinyl floor tiles. She set a pot plant on the window-sill and stood in the doorway for a few moments to admire the effect.

The window looked out over the long strip of garden at the side of the cottage. The little plot had once been laid out with a lawn, flower-beds and fruit bushes but now it was badly overgrown, mutely begging for someone to care for it. Well, there would be time for that in the weeks to come. A large, fluffy cat was picking its way along a mossy path, ears pricked and tail twitching, while a blackbird piped an alarm from among the tight pink buds on the apple tree. Melissa gave a contented sigh. This was her home. Here, she could put down roots, get everyone off her back and be herself.

It was time to tackle the bathroom. She decided to treat herself to a good long soak instead of a hasty shower and hummed a tune as she rinsed away the ubiquitous dust before filling the bath and lowering herself with thankfulness into the steaming water.

A little before half past six she emerged from her front door and stood for a moment looking across the valley, which lay sunning itself in the warm golden light of evening. On the opposite slope, in the path of the slowly advancing shadow of a clump of trees, a flock of sheep nibbled at the grass while their young pranced and played around them. Some children in bright sweaters and gumboots were prodding with sticks at something in the stream,

7

their high young voices cutting through the clear air.

A gravelled track ran from the lane as far as the end of Melissa's garden. It widened out at the end and became a turning space, roughly reinforced with broken bricks and rubble. Beyond was a hawthorn hedge, green with new growth, through which a stile gave access to a path running down to the valley bottom. She strolled up to it and turned back to look at Hawthorn Cottage, indulging for a few moments in the pride of ownership. Not a rented flat belonging to some faceless landlord but her property. Created, like its fellow, from two minuscule labourers' dwellings, it was the first piece of real-estate that she had ever possessed in her forty-four . . . no, nearly forty-five years.

Behind the cottages rose a steep, sheltering bank dotted with brambles. There would be blackberries in the autumn, and apples from her garden. She would try her hand at making bramble jelly. No doubt Iris would give her some hints. Birds would move into the nesting-box that she had beguiled the carpenter to repair and refix.

The sun gleamed on the brass knocker on the newly painted front door and on the windows that still bore the smears and puttied fingermarks left by the glaziers. Another job that the builder had promised—and failed—to take care of. If Aubrey were here they wouldn't have got away with so much . . . but this wasn't the time to think about Aubrey.

'Hello!' called a voice. Iris was leaning over her garden fence and waving a bunch of greenery. 'Just been cutting a few herbs. Nothing like fresh herbs. Come on in!' She indicated a white-painted wooden gate and led the way along a gravel path to the rear of the cottage.

'Your back yard's a lot tidier than mine!' remarked Melissa, surveying with some envy the trim space enclosed by white-washed walls. 'The builders have left an awful lot of rubbish for me to get rid of.'

'Make 'em come and clear it away,' Iris advised.

Outside the back door was a small lobby of brick and glass where shelves were stacked with scrubbed flowerpots and garden tools. Iris kicked off her muddy shoes and shoved her bony feet into wooden sandals. She still wore the plaid pinafore dress, which was not long enough to conceal the ladder in her tights.

'Hope you don't mind coming through the kitchen,' she said.

'Not a bit,' said Melissa. 'My kitchen's the only room I'd care for anyone to see at the moment.' She turned to close the door and the fluffy-haired cat slid through just in time. 'Oh, is he yours?'

'That's my Binkie!' said Iris in an infantile voice as the cat, purring vigorously, wound itself in a figure of eight round her legs. 'Who's a greedy boy then, he's had his tea!' The cat regarded her with expressionless yellow eyes, then stalked away and disappeared through a half-open door leading out of the kitchen. Resuming her normal voice and expression, Iris threw her bouquet of herbs into a colander and turned on the tap. 'Just wash these off before chopping 'em,' she explained. 'Drink before we eat?'

'Thank you,' said Melissa, curious to know what kind of brew she was going to be offered. She scanned the little kitchen with interest and some surprise. She had half-expected a cluttered and slightly old-world interior but it seemed to contain every imaginable modern fitting and piece of equipment, all spanking new. If, as the estate agent had asserted, Iris was an artist, she would seem to be a successful one.

She certainly knew how to make food look attractive. On the table were dishes of salads and a selection of cheeses laid out on a tray, all garnished as if prepared for a cookery feature in a magazine. A simmering casserole on the Aga was releasing a spicy, appetising aroma. It was all very promising.

Iris took a heavy green bottle from the refrigerator and released a wired-in cork. There was a loud explosion and an eruption of white froth.

'Elderflower champagne!' said Iris proudly, filling two glasses. 'Last season's brew—should have quite a kick. If you're too squiffy to stagger home you can sleep on the couch. Cheers!' She quaffed deeply and reached for a knife and chopping-board.

Melissa sipped cautiously at first, then with relish.

'It's nectar!' she declared. 'Did you make it yourself?'

'Of course. Make all sorts of wine. And jelly. Blackberry, rowan, rosehip. Live from the garden and the hedgerows. Hungry?'

'I am rather.' If the food was as good as the wine, there would be no hankering after steak. Iris chopped her herbs and scattered them thickly over the salads. Their sharpness mingled tantalisingly with the steam from the cooking-pot. Melissa inhaled with enthusiasm. 'It smells divine!' she declared.

'Good. Ready to eat, then?' Iris lifted the bubbling casserole from the hotplate and led the way out of the kitchen. 'Give me a hand with the other stuff,' she commanded over her shoulder.

In the dining-room she ladled a steaming concoction of spiced vegetables into earthenware bowls of brown rice and handed one to Melissa.

'Help yourself to bread.' She waved a hand at a plaited basket full of what looked like fossilized gastropods. 'Bake my own,' she added. It was a simple act of information, without vanity.

'Thanks.' Wondering if her teeth were strong enough, Melissa broke open one of the rolls. It was crisp and delicious and she felt ashamed of her misgivings. Iris might be eccentric but she was a superb cook.

'You from London?' asked her hostess between forkfuls.

'Yes.' Iris had obviously made her deduction from the name and address on the removal van and was curious about her new neighbour. Melissa suspected that she was about to be quizzed. It might have been the elderflower champagne that prompted her to respond with unusual candour. 'I've always had a yen to live in the country but somehow I've been stuck in towns,' she explained. 'This is the first chance I've had to break away.'

'Hope you'll like it here.'

'I'm sure I shall. I had a feeling about this cottage the moment I saw it.'

'A feeling it was about to fall down?' Iris gave a sardonic chuckle. 'Me too. Used to be afraid it'd take this one with it. Great relief to see it done up.'

'You must have felt rather isolated while it was standing empty,' commented Melissa. 'That reminds me, who lived in my cottage before me? Was it a woman called Babs?'

Iris shook her head. 'Old man, near-recluse. Died about nine months ago. Cottage a pigsty, no woman'd live in it. Why?'

'A man phoned this morning and thought I was Babs.' Melissa repeated the conversation. 'He's probably been hanging about waiting for her all evening. He sounded quite distracted and didn't give me a chance to explain his mistake.'

'Poor chap!' Iris considered for a moment with furrowed brow. 'Jacko was there for years. Never had a phone. More rice?'

'Thanks.'

'Salad? Help yourself.' Iris shuffled dishes around on the battered gate-legged table and brought more from the kitchen. Her keen eyes took in Melissa's left hand. 'You a widow, then?'

'Yes.' As she normally did with strangers, Melissa left it at that. It was no one's business but her own that Guy had been killed before he'd had time to make an honest woman of her—always supposing that he would have wanted to, knowing that she was pregnant. She had never really known Guy except through his son. Simon's intensity, his ruthless search for perfection in everything he did, his bouts of irritability that alternated with an irresistible charm, were all inherited from his father. This she knew from Guy's parents, who had cared for her and Simon when her own mother and father had rejected them both. Their only condition had been that she take their name for herself and their grandson, and put on a wedding-ring for the sake of appearances.

Iris persevered with her interrogation.

'Children?'

'One son.' Maternal pride took over. 'He's twenty-five, he's an engineer, working for an oil company in Texas and doing very well indeed.'

'So you're on your own?'

'At the moment.'

Once again, Melissa could feel the elderflower champagne dissolving her shell of reticence. She began to tell Iris about Aubrey.

'He was becoming just too protective!' she complained. 'Not possessive . . . he's never tried to organize my life or been jealous of my friends or anything like that . . . he's just convinced himself I can't get along without him to take care of me. It was lovely at first . . . and I suppose I sound unappreciative . . . but lately I've been feeling absolutely stifled. If he had his way I'd never so much as change a light bulb, let alone mend a fuse. Anyway, he's married and his wife wants him back although he keeps insisting he loves me and not her.'

'So he's not too pleased at your move?' Iris observed.

'Not particularly, although one of the last things he said before I left London was that it'd soon teach me how much he meant to me and how much I needed him.'

'Conceited creatures, men,' observed Iris. 'More rhubarb yoghurt?'

'It was absolutely delicious but I couldn't manage another morsel!' declared Melissa with genuine regret. 'You've probably heard this before, but I had no idea vegetarian food could be so good.'

Iris accepted the compliment with a matter-of-fact nod. 'Healthiest way to eat!' she asserted. 'No need for it to be boring.'

'Did you grow all those vegetables yourself?'

'Most of 'em. Spend a lot of time in the garden. Freeze a lot.'

'When do you find time to do your painting?'

'Who said I painted?' Iris looked both amused and irritated.

'The estate agent said you were an artist and that you spent the winter abroad,' Melissa explained. 'I apologise if I misunderstood.'

Iris shrugged and pulled a face. 'He said "artist" and you thought "painter",' she mocked. 'There are other art forms, you know!'

'Yes, of course,' said Melissa, a shade pettishly. There was no reason for the woman to be so superior—the mistake had been a natural one. She finished her elderflower champagne and tried to think of a way to break the edgy silence. Iris picked up the bottle and reached across to refill the glasses. Melissa shook her head. 'No more for me, thanks—tomorrow's going to be a heavy day.'

'Just as you like. Coffee?'

'Yes, please.'

'Decaffeinated beans. Tried dandelion root but didn't like it.' Iris vanished into the kitchen. Melissa began clearing the table but was checked by the command: 'Leave those. Go through to the sitting-room.'

As in Melissa's own cottage, the sitting-room and the dining-room were interconnected. Originally, they had been the living-rooms of two adjacent dwellings and there was a fireplace in each, back-to-back with a common chimney. Melissa guessed that, when on her own, Iris ate her meals in the kitchen. The dining-room, with its bare walls and minimal furniture, had an air of being seldom used. There were few ornaments or pictures and the plain curtains and dull, faded carpet were not what one would expect in the home of an artist, of whatever sort.

To her surprise, the sitting-room was equally plain and sparsely furnished. A green glass jug of daffodils and a few patchwork cushions provided the only splashes of colour. Beige curtains, a dowdy brown carpet and a couch covered with what seemed to be a regulation army blanket gave a sombre, depressing effect only partially relieved by the log fire glowing in the grate. When Melissa entered, Binkie raised his head from a prime position on the hearth-rug, blinking at her with topaz eyes half-buried in fur.

'Fabric design,' said Iris unexpectedly, appearing with pottery mugs of coffee on a tray.

'Sorry?'

'I'm a fabric designer.' She pulled up a low table with a stained top and set the tray down. 'Seat?' She indicated a fireside chair covered in khaki linen and handed Melissa a mug. 'Sugar? Milk?'

'Er . . . no, thank you.' Melissa stared around her, trying to reconcile what she heard with what she saw. She sipped at her coffee, which was far too hot, and watched in fascination as her hostess, mug in hand, sank with surprising ease into a cross-legged position in front of the fire.

'Don't like chairs. Always sit on the floor,' she commented. She reached out to fondle the cat which sat erect, yawned, and after several seconds of careful consideration stepped into her lap. Iris put down her mug and encircled the animal with both arms, scooping it into the well between her thighs and leaning forward to lay her cheek against its head. Her features blurred into a doting expression and the cat purred in a throbbing crescendo, its eyes half-closed as if in ecstasy. The effect bordered on the erotic. Feeling unaccountably embarrassed, Melissa played with her too-hot coffee, stared into the fire and wondered how soon she could decently go home.

'My studio's upstairs,' Iris remarked suddenly, the light of intelligence returning to her face. 'Show you some time if you like.' She glanced around the room while Melissa made polite murmurs of interest. 'My background.' She made a circular gesture with her mug and a splash of coffee landed on the carpet. 'Never mind. Doesn't show.' She fished a paper handkerchief from her pocket, dabbed at the spot and threw the paper on the fire. 'Always keep a neutral background. Helps with new ideas. No distractions. What do you do?'

'I write.'

'What?'

'Novels, mostly.'

'What sort?'

'Crime, detection, that sort of thing.'

'Not much material among the folks round here. Deadly dull, most of them. Shouldn't let it get around though.'

'Sorry, let what get around?'

'That you write, of course. They'll have you contributing to the parish magazine and the Garden Society newsletter before you can turn round. Tried to get me designing new curtains for the village hall before I'd been here six months, cheeky lot!'

'Have you lived here long?' Melissa felt reassured by Iris's switch to a near-normal style of speech but it proved to be a flash in the pan.

'About ten years. Eleven next August. Only here March to October. Cotswold winters too cold and damp.'

'Do you have someone to look after the house while you're away?'

'Village girl comes in every day. Checks the boiler and feeds Binkie. You want help in the house? Gloria might do you. Little tart, thick as a board but a good worker.' She had been caressing the cat with increasingly vigorous strokes as she spoke. On the final words he ejected from her lap as if his threshold of tolerance had been finally overstepped. He settled at the far end of the hearth-rug where he sat staring icily at his mistress, tail twitching, front paws marking time.

'Binkie boy!' pleaded Iris inanely. 'Did Mummie upset him then?'

Melissa got to her feet, murmuring that it was time to be getting along.

'I'm really grateful to you for inviting me, and the meal was lovely,' she said as they moved towards the door. 'And I could do with some help once or twice a week. If you'd mention it to Gloria I'd be grateful.'

'Will do. Enjoyed your company. Come again,' said Iris. She was back to normal and obviously meant what she said.

'I hope you'll come and have a meal with me when I'm settled,' said Melissa.

'Love to,' said Iris. 'No meat though, remember!'

'I'll remember,' promised Melissa, wondering if macaroni cheese would do.

THREE

AS MELISSA REACHED HER FRONT DOOR AND PUT HER
key in the lock, Iris called out 'Goodnight' and turned off her
porch light.

There was no moon, no glow of streetlamps or lighted windows,
not even a sparkling of stars to relieve the awesome blackness.
Melissa, a lifelong city-dweller, was unaccustomed to the enve-
loping darkness and silence of the country at night. Disoriented
and confused, she slammed the door and scrabbled along the
living-room wall in search of the light switch. She had no idea
where it was; her mind was a blank. She should have brought a
torch. How ridiculous to be lost in one's own home! Not home,
not yet. This place, immured in inky isolation at the end of a
nameless track, was unknown territory. She was an intruder in
a strange house where an old man named Jacko had lived and
died in solitude.

Aubrey would have thought of the torch. Aubrey thought of
everything. But Aubrey was a hundred miles away and that
distance between them was of her own making. Oh, God, she
thought, where is that bloody switch!

At last she found it. In the harsh glare of a single bulb her
furniture looked unfamiliar, almost hostile in this alien setting.
Still, any room would look ghastly under a naked light. First
thing tomorrow she would unpack the box of lampshades. The
place needed ventilating too, to get rid of the smell of paint and
new plaster.

It was chilly as well as cheerless. An urgent telephone call had
brought a delivery of oil during the afternoon but the service
engineer who would light the boiler and commission the heating could not attend until tomorrow. The carpets, she had been

assured, would arrive by the end of the week and the fitters—all being well—the following Monday. There was a two-page list of defects noted during the day that the builder must be made to deal with. The settling-in period unrolled into the future like a road disappearing over the brow of a hill.

The blackness outside pressed against the uncurtained windows like fog, threatening to seep in through any available crack. Melissa had checked all the windows before going out but now she checked them again. The glass panes gave back a distorted reflection of her oval face, white under the sickly light, dark brown hair drawn back so that nothing but a skull-like head stared in at her with huge glittering eyes. Aubrey had wanted her to have safety catches fitted before moving in but she hadn't bothered. She should have listened to Aubrey instead of dismissing all his advice and suggestions as 'fussing'. She should have found the time to hang all the curtains before going out. Curtains would have been a comforting barrier against the night. Pursued by the echo of her own footsteps she made for the kitchen. She had almost reached it when the telephone rang.

If it was him again, demanding why she hadn't turned up, it would be the last straw. Perhaps if she let it ring he'd give up. But the sound continued, crescendo, fortissimo, as if someone was turning up the volume. Reluctantly, she went back and snatched up the receiver.

'Hello!'

'Lissie? Is that you?'

'Oh, Aubrey!'

'I thought you'd like me to call!' She could picture him looking self-satisfied, no doubt reading pleasure at hearing from him into the relief that her voice had betrayed.

'How did you get my number? I didn't know it myself until today.'

'I rang directory enquiries, of course. Darling girl, are you all right? You sounded strange when you answered.'

She gritted her teeth at the endearment that had recently begun to irritate her beyond words but she kept her voice even. 'I was afraid for a moment it was someone else.'

'Who did you expect it to be?'

'I had a strange phone call earlier in the day and I thought . . .'

'Oh, God, not one of those perverts who . . .'

'No, nothing like that. It was some man who thought he was

talking to his girlfriend. He was very agitated and didn't seem to understand when I told him he'd got the wrong number.'

'What have you done about it?' Aubrey's voice had become clipped and urgent, as if he were back in the army and had just been informed that the enemy was about to attack. 'You should report it if you think . . .'

'Oh, for goodness' sake, Aubrey, stop making such a fuss! I told you, it was a wrong number.'

'You can't be too careful. It's obviously upset you.'

Oh, God, give me patience. 'It didn't upset me, I just didn't want to be bothered a second time. I'm tired and I was just going to bed.' Take the hint, can't you? I'm not in the mood for any more. But Aubrey hadn't finished yet.

'You're sure everything's all right? I've been trying to get you all evening!' he complained.

'Of course it's all right. I've been out to supper with my next-door neighbour and I've only just got in.'

'You're sure?' At least he wasn't quizzing her about the neighbour but no doubt he would, sooner or later.

'I'm sure.'

'Well, mind you lock up everywhere before you go to bed.'

'I already have. Thanks for calling.'

'Darling girl, I miss you.'

'Aubrey, I've asked you before not to call me that.'

'I'm sorry.'

'It doesn't matter. Goodnight.' She put the phone down while he was still saying his farewells. It was ungracious of her; he was kind and considerate and he cared for her. That was the trouble; he cared too much. He enveloped her in his caring and kindness until she felt like a fly in the web of a well-meaning spider. That was one of the reasons why she was here. But she hadn't entirely escaped; the telephone wires had become part of the web. She toyed briefly with the idea of changing her number and going ex-directory as she went into the kitchen.

At least that wore a welcoming aspect. The refrigerator was gently humming and the digital clock on the cooker winked at her like a friendly eye. It was warmer in here than in the living-room and behind its diffuser the fluorescent light had a softer glow. Melissa drew her new curtains, made a cup of tea and drank it from one of her new yellow mugs, sitting at her new pine kitchen table. It made her feel a lot better. She was dog-tired though. A good night's sleep was what she needed.

*   *   *

She awoke to a world brimming over with sunlight and birdsong. Last night's fears seemed childish and absurd and she thought of how Aubrey would laugh if he knew. Not unkindly—she had never known him to be unkind—but with indulgence, as if such an endearing weakness was only natural. Also, and she had to admit this was true, he would fondly claim that in his protective presence it would not have occurred to her to be afraid. He had, in an oddly perverse way, rallied her spirits; the irritation aroused by his call had settled her jumpy nerves so that she had gone calmly to bed, dropped off almost immediately and slept through the night like a child. Of course, Iris's elderflower champagne might have helped as well.

She ate her breakfast looking out of the kitchen window. Beyond the hedge that enclosed her garden, the valley stretched away to the north, its flanks scored with narrow sheep-tracks along their grassy slopes. The brook, catching the morning sun, crooked a glistening finger into the distance. Just where it curved out of sight behind a steep, projecting bank, Melissa could make out the roof of the shepherd's hut. At the moment it was in shadow; presently, when the sun rose higher, it would stand out more clearly.

Melissa nibbled her toast, turning over in her head some details of the plot of her next novel. The postscript to her letter to her agent had been written in jest but from it had grown an idea that had been steadily taking shape over recent weeks, despite her preoccupation with the move. She took a pad out of a drawer and made a few notes before bringing her mind back to the business of the day.

The first job was to call the builder.

'Morning, Mrs Craig!' he said breezily. 'Lovely morning!'

'Lovely,' agreed Melissa.

'Nice to move house in good weather,' he continued. 'Makes settling in much easier.'

'It does indeed.'

'You'll soon be able to make a start on the garden.'

'There are a few other things to see to first.'

'Yes, of course. Takes a day or two to get straight.' Plainly, he was in no hurry to know the reason for her call.

'Quite a few other things, in fact.' Melissa read from her list. 'Cracked cistern cover in downstairs toilet. Taps in bathroom hand-basin not as specified. Only one thin coat of emulsion on living-room walls. Dining-room window . . .'

'Hang on a minute,' protested the builder. 'The foreman told me he'd checked everything personally.'

'Then he's either talking about another property or he needs glasses!' said Melissa in what she hoped was the right mixture of firmness and jocularity. 'If you can spare the time to come and have a look for yourself I'd be most grateful. My carpets are due to be laid any day and I don't want workmen in after they're down.'

'No . . . er . . . no, of course not,' said the builder, waking up at last to the fact that she meant business. 'I'll pop round later on this morning, okay?'

'Not too much later, please,' said Melissa. 'I have to do some shopping.'

'Right-ho,' said the builder. 'About half past ten?'

'That'll be fine.' Feeling that she had handled that rather well, Melissa put the phone down. Almost immediately, it started to ring. It was the carpet fitter.

'Mrs Craig? Have your carpets been delivered yet?'

'No . . . they said they'd be here by the end of the week.'

'We've had a cancellation. We could come to you on Friday if that's convenient.'

'That would be wonderful, but suppose the carpets haven't come?'

'We'll do what we can this end to chase them up. We'll call you back if there's a problem.'

'Thank you very much.'

Things were looking up. The sun was shining, she had slept well and felt full of energy to tackle the tasks ahead. Maybe by the weekend she'd be something like straight.

The telephone rang again.

'Hello!'

She knew it was him, even before he spoke. There were the same sounds as if someone was fumbling with the instrument, the same hoarse, urgent voice.

'Babs, we must talk—please!'

'I'm sorry, you've got the wrong . . .'

'This evening, Babs. I'll be at the usual place!'

'But this isn't Babs!' Melissa almost shrieked into the telephone. 'Please listen . . . you've got . . .'

But already the caller had hung up and there was nothing but dialling tone coming from the receiver. Angrily, she put it down. Drat the man, why couldn't he listen? He sounded distraught, almost hysterical. She returned to the kitchen, torn between pity and exasperation.

The postman brought cards, some comic, some artistic, all hoping she'd be happy in her new home. Aubrey, she noted wryly, had not expressed any such hope. There was also a long letter from Simon that she put aside to read presently. The milkman, jolly-faced and whistling, appeared shortly afterwards, his boots crunching on the gravel and his bottles jingling. While he was explaining that he could supply eggs, yoghurt and cream as well as milk, that he only delivered three times a week and called for his money on Saturdays, a man from the oil company arrived to commission the boiler. Just as he was leaving, the builder's bright red BMW came tearing along the track and nose-dived to a halt in a fusillade of loose stones.

Mr Allenby was a big, heavy-jowled man who looked as if he had been pumped up to fill his bulky sheepskin coat. He wore a tweed hat which he kept on as he stepped inside the cottage, sniffing the air like a bloodhound.

'Lovely smell of coffee!' he commented breezily.

'Is there?' Melissa looked blank. 'That must be from breakfast.' The man's face fell and she glanced at her watch. 'Goodness, is that the time? Would you like some coffee?'

'That's very kind of you!' He managed to sound surprised, as if it was the last thing he expected.

'I'll make some as soon as we've gone through this list,' promised Melissa, making a great effort to sound businesslike. 'We'll start in this room. Look at the emulsion on these walls— you can see through to the plaster!'

Mr Allenby pushed back his hat and scrutinised the offending paintwork, blowing softly through pursed lips.

'Mm, yes, there are one or two holidays,' he admitted. 'Easily done in a bad light.' He wrote on a pad. 'Can't get anyone along until next week—got an outside job to finish while the weather holds.'

'But I want it done before Friday!' pleaded Melissa. 'The carpets are being laid then.'

'Sorry, no can do. Anything else in here?'

Melissa felt herself losing ground. If I were a man, she thought, this is where I'd start putting my foot down. She made an effort.

'It was supposed to be done properly before I took possession,' she pointed out, trying to iron out the tremolo in her voice. 'I don't want paint stains on my new carpets.'

'Don't worry,' said Mr Allenby with a patronizing smile. 'They'll put down dustsheets.'

Melissa saw red. 'Did they put down dustsheets while they painted the kitchen?' she demanded.

The builder stretched his eyebrows. 'Sorry—don't follow you!'

Melissa turned over the pages of her list. 'Kitchen floor tiles spattered with paint,' she read out. 'There are several other things to see to in the kitchen but we'll come to them later. We haven't finished in here yet.'

'What else is there?' Into his swagger had crept a hint of the defensive that made him appear a shade smaller. Melissa stood up straight, making the most of her five feet five inches.

'Cracked cover on electric power point, plain instead of rising hinges on doors, windows covered with paint and putty marks,' she read.

He made more notes, his eyes moving warily to and fro between his pad and Melissa's face. 'That all?'

'That's all in here. We'll do the dining-room next.' She marched ahead of him, pointing out the window that stuck, the loose floor-board and the unpainted radiator.

'Just wait till I get my hands on that bloody foreman!' muttered Mr Allenby, scribbling furiously.

Melissa left the kitchen until last. She filled the kettle for coffee and pointed out defects while waiting for it to boil. Mr Allenby, stony-faced, started a third page on his pad. He brightened up at the sight of a steaming mug and a plate of fruit-cake.

'Now, when are we going to get all this done?' Melissa demanded.

He swigged his coffee and munched his way through a large slice of cake before consulting his Filofax.

'I'll send Mrs Parkin round first thing tomorrow to clean up. Charlie can come on Friday morning to attend to the carpentry jobs,' he said at length. 'I'll get everything else seen to as soon as I can.' He stuffed the Filofax inside his sheepskin and stood up. 'Thanks for the coffee and cake. Must go now—I'm sup-posed to be in Gloucester in fifteen minutes.' The multiple chins compressed beneath a jaunty smile as he began edging towards the door.

'Just a minute,' said Melissa. 'What about the painting?'

The smile faded and the chins quivered defensively. Out came the Filofax again. 'Monday or Tuesday be all right?'

'No, it will not.' She was quaking inside but she wasn't going to let herself be outmanoeuvered. 'The painting jobs must be done before the carpets are laid.'

Mr Allenby gave a sigh of resignation. 'Oh, very well—I'll send Pete round this afternoon about half past four,' he said grudgingly. 'You realize I'll have to pay him overtime?'

'If he's the one who did it in the first place, you should jolly well make him do it in his own time,' said Melissa, smiling to show that there were no hard feelings now that she had won the day.

The builder gave a hoarse chuckle. 'I could do with a tough lady like you in my office!' he told her. 'Let me know if you want a job!'

They parted the best of friends and Melissa closed the door behind him in the knowledge that she had called up reserves of which she had been unaware. Aubrey, she thought, you'd have been proud of me! On second thought, she felt that Aubrey might have been not entirely pleased at her display of assertiveness. It was an agreeable notion.

Four

AT NINE O'CLOCK ON THURSDAY MORNING A STURDY, moon-faced young woman appeared on Melissa's doorstep. She had a spiky halo of bright yellow hair and large eyes the colour of treacle toffee. She was like a sunflower on an abnormally short thick stem.

'Mrs Craig? Mr Allenby sent me to clean up after his men.'

'Oh, yes, do come in! You must be Mrs Parkin.'

'You can call me Gloria,' said the newcomer, unzipping her anorak and releasing a generous gust of perfume. She cast an appraising eye around her as she followed Melissa to the kitchen. 'My, they makes a fine old mess, doesn't they?' she remarked, her tone suggesting that this was no bad thing since it made employment for the likes of herself.

'Are you the same Gloria who works . . . er, helps my neighbour?' asked Melissa.

The yellow spikes nodded assent. 'Miss Ash? That's right. I goes to her every Tuesday morning after I takes the kids to school.'

'She said you might be willing to come to me,' said Melissa.

The spikes danced with enthusiasm. 'I'd be glad to. Would Wednesday morning be all right, nine till twelve? I goes to the Rectory on Monday and I likes to keep Thursday and Friday free.'

'Wednesday morning would be fine,' said Melissa warmly. She was fascinated by Gloria's speech patterns and couldn't wait to note them for future use.

'Wednesday it is. Now, let's get started on this little lot.'

Gloria hung her anorak over the back of a chair, produced a plastic apron and rubber gloves from a shopping-bag, rolled up the sleeves of her flowered polyester blouse and fell to work with an energy and efficiency that left Melissa gasping. Windows sparkled and paint stains vanished before her assault.

At eleven o'clock Melissa made coffee. Gloria clamped her mug in two plump hands that were heavy with rings and wandered over to the kitchen window.

'Why, you can see old Daniel's hut,' she remarked.

'You mean that old shepherd's hut?'

'That's right.'

'Why do you call it Daniel's hut?'

'An old man called Daniel died there, didn't he?' Gloria sucked noisily at her mug. 'A long time ago it were. He were going home to Lower Benbury from the Woolpack one January night in the snow. They reckon he stopped by for a pee and just passed out and died of cold. It were several days before they found him, lying flat on his back with his flies still undone!'

Her burst of uninhibited laughter set the sunflower head rocking on its stem. She was outrageous, yet there was warmth and good-humour in her vulgarity. The swell of her breasts inside the polyester blouse, the broad hips and curving stomach crammed into tight red slacks, all clamoured for attention. She had a compelling, earthy sexuality that many men would find irresistible.

'Poor man, how dreadful!' murmured Melissa. She felt obliged to show concern for the fate of the unfortunate Daniel but it took all her will-power to keep a straight face.

'They all thinks it's haunted,' Gloria went on with a jerk of her head in the direction of the village. 'They says that on winter nights you can hear old Daniel hollerin'. There's some that won't walk that way in the dark! Chicken, that's what they are!'

'That will be the wind howling through the holes in the roof, I suppose,' said Melissa.

Gloria shrugged, her mug upended as she swallowed the last mouthful. Her throat was creamy white and voluptuously rounded; between the buttons, the front of her blouse strained open in a series of little half-moons.

'I reckon,' she said carelessly. She drew the back of her hand across her mouth, took the two mugs to the sink and washed them. Her eyes flicked over to the clock. 'I've got just over half an hour. What else is there to do?'

'We could have a go at the spare bedroom.' Melissa led the way upstairs. 'I haven't even had time to sweep up and all sorts of stuff was just dumped in here.'

'Coo, look at all they books!' There was a note of awe in Gloria's voice. She picked up one that lay on top of a bulging cardboard box and examined it. '*Death with a Doornail* by Mel Craig.' She read slowly, brows puckered like a child's. Her toffee-brown eyes rolled in Melissa's direction. 'Relation of yours?'

'N . . . no . . .' Remembering Iris's warning, Melissa was reluctant to admit that the book in question was one of her own. It had been her agent's idea to shorten Melissa to Mel because he felt it would have more appeal on the American market. She didn't really like it and had no idea whether it made any difference. There were times when she failed to follow the logic of Joe's arguments but in this case, as in so many things, she had allowed herself to be overruled.

Gloria was rummaging eagerly among the piles of books. She pounced on another which had Melissa's photograph on its dust-jacket and her eyes saucered in wonderment. 'This is you?' she breathed.

Melissa nodded resignedly.

Gloria's eyes moved to and fro, comparing the picture with the original. 'I likes the hairstyle you've got now better than that one.'

'Ah . . . that was taken some time ago.'

Gloria put the book down almost reverently. 'The Rector, he likes a good meaty thriller—when his wife's not looking!' She gave a hoarse chuckle that set her bosom bouncing. 'I likes a nice love story myself. You write any of they?'

'No, I'm afraid not.'

Gloria's face fell.

'But I've got a stack of them somewhere.' At one time Melissa had thought of trying her hand at romantic fiction and researched the genre at some length before turning to crime. 'I'll find them once I get all this lot unpacked. You can borrow them if you like.'

'Ooh, my, thanks ever so!' The moon face shone with anticipation, totally won over. Melissa felt she had made a friend.

At five minutes to midday, Gloria switched off the vacuum cleaner and carried it downstairs. She put everything tidily away in the broom cupboard and removed her apron and gloves.

'I has to leave at twelve o'clock sharp to get the kids from school,' she explained. 'They won't eat school dinners so I has to get them something at home.' She had three children and with very little prompting recited their names and ages: Wayne, Darren and Charlene, all under eight years old.

'Quite a handful,' remarked Melissa. 'Does your husband work in the village?'

The sunflower executed an emphatic and slightly indignant denial. 'He's got his own business in Gloucester!' Gloria zipped up her anorak and thrust her apron and gloves into the shopping-bag. Melissa let her out and watched her climb into a red Ford Escort with the driver's seat pulled well forward to accommodate her short legs, an arrangement which brought the steering wheel dangerously close to her chest. She rolled down the window, called out, 'See you next Wednesday, then!', executed a hesitant three-point turn and drove off.

'Yoo-hoo!' called a voice. Iris was clambering over the stile from the field, a plastic bucket swinging from one hand. 'That Gloria's car just gone?'

'Yes, the builder sent her to clean up. It was supposed to have been done before I moved in.'

Iris grunted. 'Inefficient lot, builders!' she commented.

'She's coming to me on Wednesday mornings. I told her what you said. She's quite a character, isn't she?'

Iris sniffed. 'No better than she should be!'

'She told me her husband has his own business. Do you know what he does?'

'Second-hand car dealer. All crooks, one jump ahead of the law. Get caught one day. So will she. Serve 'em right!'

'Are you saying they're up to some fiddle?' It was not unlikely; par for the course, so to speak, if one believed what one heard about the motor trade. Gloria's rings looked genuine and she was lavish in her use of expensive perfume.

'They?' Sly malevolence gleamed in Iris's sharp grey eyes. 'He's the one on the fiddle, she's on the game if you ask me! Works in a fancy club a couple of nights a week and we know what type goes to places like that, don't we?' The unusually long sentence seemed to reflect the depth of Iris's feelings on the matter.

By way of changing the subject, Melissa peered into the plastic bucket. 'Dandelions!' she remarked. 'More wine?'

'Right. Ever tried it?'

'I don't think I have.'

'Come and have a tot before lunch.' Without waiting for a reply, Iris marched off towards her own cottage.

They sat in her spotless, ultra-modern kitchen sipping a sweetish pale yellow concoction and nibbling home-made nut biscuits. Melissa recounted with relish some of the choicest tit-bits from Gloria while Iris, who plainly had a different sense of humour, muttered derogatory asides. As they were chatting, someone passed the window and tapped on the back door. Iris's sharp features fused into a glow of pleasure as she ushered in her visitor.

'Mr Calloway! Do come in!' She turned to Melissa with a hint of a blush on her cheek, a trace of archness in her smile. 'Our Rector . . . Mrs Craig, my new neighbour.'

He was tall with sparse fair hair, a round, pink face and the innocent expression of a well-scrubbed choirboy. He beamed at Melissa and encased her hand in plump, slightly damp fingers.

'I can't tell you how excited I am to meet you!' he declared with sparkling eyes, like a child gazing at Father Christmas. 'We don't get many famous authors in our quiet part of the county!'

Melissa stared at him. 'How did you . . . ?' she began.

He chuckled and wagged a finger at her. 'I met Gloria . . . Mrs Parkin, that is, as I was walking down from the village and she stopped to tell me. She said you tried to deny it!'

Melissa shook her head, smiling.

'Oh, yes, you did . . . she told me!' The finger continued to wag in benevolent reproof.

'She asked me if Mel Craig was a relation of mine, and I said "no", which is perfectly true,' protested Melissa. 'Then she spotted my photograph on the dust-jacket.'

'Aha!' His smile became roguish. 'Little Mrs Parkin isn't just a pretty face!' From the corner of her eye, Melissa observed Iris's mouth screwed up in distaste. 'She knows I've read all your books and she couldn't wait to tell me. I'm afraid,' he confessed, looking as if he had been caught with a comic concealed in his hymnbook, 'that I get them from the library . . . I'd like to buy them but . . . the fact is,' his voice dropped to a comically conspiratorial whisper, 'my wife doesn't really approve, so I hope you'll keep my little secret!'

'That's all right,' said Melissa cheerfully. 'We have Public Lending Right now, you know, so it's all grist to the mill! And I promise not to split on you if you don't split on me!'

'Ah . . . I'm afraid it's bound to get out without my saying anything. The penalty of fame, you know!'

Melissa shrugged. She might have known that keeping a secret in a village was a non-starter. 'Oh well, it'll be a nine-days' wonder, no doubt,' she said.

'Sit down, Mr Calloway. Have a tot!' urged Iris, pouring dandelion wine into a third glass. She plonked it on the table, her mouth still signalling disapproval.

The Rector, one hand hooked in readiness over the back of a chair, expressed just the right degree of surprise and appreciation before drawing it back and lowering his plump rear on to the seat. He had brought with him a plastic carrier which he propped against the leg of the table.

'Here's your copy of the parish monthly,' he said to Iris, extracting a flimsy magazine with a line drawing of the village church on its cover. She took it from him as if it were a rare and precious gift. 'I'm afraid it's very late this month. The printers have been extra busy. They charge us a special rate, you see,' he explained, turning to Melissa, 'so if any urgent jobs come in, our poor little mag goes to the bottom of the list.' He dived into the carrier again and hesitantly withdrew another copy. 'I don't suppose you would care to subscribe? Only twenty-five pence a month.'

'Of course!' Melissa accepted the magazine and was rewarded by a smile of gratitude that was almost saintly in its simplicity. 'I'll have to pop home for the money . . . I haven't got my purse with me.'

'That's quite all right—you can give it me any time. I'll just make a note.' He drew out a small black pocket-book and wrote. 'Mrs Craig, Hawthorn Cottage—there! I'll see you get your copy every month.' He beamed at her again. His eyes were clear, wide and trustful under a smooth high forehead. It was difficult to tell his age; he could have been anything between forty-five and sixty for he had the clear, fine skin that often goes with very fair hair and stays firm and unlined for many years. He lifted his glass first to Melissa, then to Iris and once again to Melissa. 'Your very good health, ladies, and welcome to Upper Benbury, Mrs Craig!' He drained the glass and set it down. Iris promptly refilled it, ignoring his token protest. 'An excellent year, Miss Ash, if I may say so!'

'Glad you think so!' simpered Iris.

'I wonder . . . ?' The Rector turned his grey-green eyes on Melissa and cleared his throat. 'Shall we be seeing you in church on Sunday, Mrs Craig?'

'Er . . . yes, I expect so.' It was several years since she had regularly attended church but to say 'no' would have seemed churlish, like refusing a personal invitation. 'What time are the services?'

'All the details are in here!' He patted the magazine lying on the table. 'We're not very High . . . I hope you're not too High?' He looked anxious, as if wondering what could be done to accommodate her if she proved to be High.

'No, I'm not at all High,' she assured him and he looked relieved. 'I really must be going. Iris, thank you so much for the wine, and it's been a great pleasure to meet you, Mr Calloway.'

'A great pleasure for me, and a great honour!' he assured her, scrambling to his feet as she got up. 'I must be getting along too. Thank you for the dandelion wine, Miss Ash. I'll see you both on Sunday then, ladies?'

The ladies assured him that he would indeed see them on Sunday. At the gate, he turned in the direction of Melissa's cottage instead of walking back towards the road.

'I take a short cut just past Daniel's hut,' he explained. "There's a footpath leading up the bank straight into the churchyard. It's rather steep and a bit tricky when it's been raining—muddy, you know, and slippery—but it saves quite a distance over going by road.'

'I must stroll along there some time and find it,' said Melissa, adding impulsively, 'I'm going to be using that hut in my next novel.'

'Really?' He stopped short outside her door and turned on her an expression of mingled amazement and delight. 'How very exciting! May one enquire how it is . . . er . . . going to feature in your story?'

'I don't usually discuss my plots with anyone except my agent,' said Melissa. He looked so disappointed that she hastened to add, 'But I might be very grateful for your help when I come to do the research . . . local customs, bits of country lore, that kind of thing. I always try to make my backgrounds authentic.'

The Rector nodded eagerly. 'I shall be delighted to help in any way I can . . . delighted and honoured!' He rubbed his hands together and chuckled. There was a gleam in his eye that his wife, Melissa suspected, would not have approved. 'To think I shall be working with a real crime novelist!' he gloated. 'Do please call on me at any time . . . except, well, perhaps it would be better if we kept this a secret between ourselves, eh? Otherwise they'll all want to join in, haha!'

'I shall be the soul of discretion!' Melissa assured him. She found him a delightful character, simply asking to be written into a novel himself. Saintly, unworldly country cleric with a secret weakness for the crime novel becomes embroiled in murder and mayhem in sleepy rural parish. She wondered how it would look on a dust-jacket. Joe would probably laugh it out of court.

Mr Calloway was standing a little way back from her cottage, rocking on his heels and appraising the clean, newly pointed stonework and the restored roof of genuine Cotswold tiles.

'Mr Allenby has made quite a good job of the old place,' he observed. 'It really was in a dreadful state—I used to get quite nervous when I visited poor old Jacko . . . afraid the roof might fall on my head, don't you know, haha! I expect you've made it look a bit different inside . . . ?' He finished the sentence on a questioning note whose meaning was unmistakable.

'You must come and see it when I've got everything straight,' said Melissa. 'Perhaps you'd care to call in for a cup of tea one afternoon when you're passing?'

'That is *most* kind of you!' He was at pains to convey the impression that such an invitation was the last thing he had in mind.

When, eventually, he said goodbye and clambered, rather awkwardly, over the stile, Melissa went indoors, got out her pad and made copious notes over her lunch of sandwiches and coffee. Iris had written off the village folk as 'deadly dull, most of them'. Well, that was all a matter of opinion. The ones she had met so far, including Iris herself, made a fascinating study.

FIVE

ON SATURDAY AFTERNOON, MELISSA PREPARED A casserole for her evening meal. While it was cooking, she sat down and wrote to Simon.

At last I'm beginning to get straight. The chaos has been unbelievable—yesterday it came to a head, with the carpet fitters crawling all over the place and Charlie the carpenter getting in their way, trying to fix things that should have been fixed before I moved in. It became quite fraught at one stage and I had to make cups of tea in relays to keep them apart.

I'm thrilled with the cottage and its situation and can't wait to show it to you. Do try and make a trip to the UK this summer. Your room has a lovely view over a valley whose sides are dotted with sheep and gambolling lambs. I think they're enchanting but my next-door neighbour tells me, 'wait till they start shearing'; it seems that the lambs have trouble recognizing their shorn mothers and it can take twelve hours or more for them to sort themselves out. Meanwhile they're bleating like a non-stop chorus from *Animal Farm* and sleep becomes difficult!

My next-door neighbour is an arty lady called Iris . . .

Melissa devoted a couple of pages to Iris, Gloria, the Rector and the Rector's wife, a humorless lady with an expression of permanent disapproval who had called on her that morning to try and recruit her for the Woman's Institute and the church flower-arranging rota. She smiled as she pictured Simon's reaction to his mother's new environment. Her smile faded as she referred once more to his letter.

You ask about Aubrey. Please don't. I'm trying to get him out of my system. Yes, I know he's reliable and kind and supportive and has always been a very present help in time of trouble but he was getting such a BORE! He would insist on treating me as utterly helpless and in need of protection, which I'm fast discovering I'm not, and it was getting very wearing. I did battle very successfully with the builder over getting some remedial jobs done and I've already discovered that I can use a hammer and a screwdriver. I've put up hooks for my pictures (a nice man in the DIY shop showed me how) and I'm sure there are lots of other jobs I can learn to do. Iris will help, she's amazing. She can do carpentry, paint gates and mend fences when she's not designing fabrics. She's going to help me plan my garden. I suspect she'll make me grow organic vegetables and cultivate stinging nettles for the butterflies.

Do write again soon. I love to have your news.

Having signed and sealed her letter, Melissa decided to walk into the village straight away to post it, even though the next collection was not until Monday morning. The spell of fine, dry weather was threatening to break. A layer of thin cloud veiled a fretful sun and a cool wind ran along the valley, ruffling the surface of the brook. Melissa buttoned up her jacket and strode briskly along the track to the main road. Iris, toiling in her garden, waved a gloved hand in greeting as she passed.

The village lay at the head of the valley. The stone houses clung to the hillside in irregular tiers and clusters, looking as if they had been washed up by a tidal wave that had receded, leaving them stranded. They huddled shoulder-to-shoulder, some tall and narrow, some squat and sprawling along the irregular streets. Now and again a slit of a side road, climbing at a daunting angle, gave glimpses of a second rank of similarly assorted dwellings, separated from the front row by a double bank of steeply sloping gardens. Ice-cream-coloured blossom danced in the breeze, mats of purple aubretia lay scattered over rockeries and cottage walls were bright with the young foliage of climbing roses and Virginia creeper.

The first spots of rain fell on Melissa's hand as she dropped her letter in the box. She glanced uneasily at the sky. The cloud was rapidly thickening and the breeze had strengthened. There had been mention of showers on the radio; she should have dressed more sensibly.

'Good afternoon, Mrs Craig!' The Rector skidded to a halt and jumped off his bicycle. 'Looks as if we're in for a squall.'

'I was just thinking the same thing. I'm going to get caught if I don't hurry.'

'Take the short cut,' he suggested. 'I'll show you where it is. It'll save you seven or eight minutes.' He walked with her as far as the entrance to the churchyard, pointed out the lichen-covered gate half-hidden behind some mouldering tombstones and parted from her with a cheery: 'See you in church tomorrow!'

The path ran downhill through woodland. It was stony in places, criss-crossed with brambles and, as the Rector had warned her, inclined to be muddy even though the weather had been dry for a week. After a wet spell it would be a quagmire.

The rain began in earnest, pattering down through the trees. She walked as fast as she dared, afraid of wrenching an ankle on a stone and wondering whether it would after all have been better to take the road. When she reached the bottom of the path and emerged into the open, it was raining quite hard.

She was standing at the top of a tall bank, looking down at the valley bottom at a point where a bridge with a metal handrail spanned the little brook. The grassy slope fell away steeply at her feet, treacherous and slippery in the wet. In her haste she almost slid down it but checked herself just in time. Start to run down there, she thought, and you'd have a job to stop. You'd be lucky to reach the bottom without breaking a leg.

Melissa turned for home, breaking into a run. The rain came down harder than ever; by the time she reached the old shepherd's hut it was pouring. Without a second thought she took shelter inside.

It was unexpectedly dark. On the one previous occasion when she had come here, the sun was shining and she had merely poked her head round the door, a detached and curious observer. Now, she felt herself enshrouded in its atmosphere of damp and decay. A gust of wind whistled round her shoulders and set the door creaking.

Her heart was thumping and she was panting slightly. She really ought to take more exercise. She took out a handkerchief and dried her face, squinting at the sky through a gap in the stone wall, trying to assess the direction of the wind and whether there was a break in the clouds.

'Quite a downpour!' said a man's voice behind her.

Melissa spun round. Deep in the shadows behind the door stood a tall figure. She backed away in alarm as he took a step towards her. As he moved into the half-light she could see that he was young and well-built, fresh-faced and with fiercely penetrating blue eyes. He was bare-headed with short dark hair and his hands were thrust into the pocket of his waxed jacket.

'Don't be afeared,' he said in a soothing voice. 'He won't hurt you.'

It was all Melissa could do to contain a scream. She remembered hearing that psychopaths sometimes thought and spoke of themselves in the third person in order to absolve themselves from responsibility for their violent acts. She felt cold in the pit of her stomach and her heart pounded more violently than ever. She shot a despairing glance beyond the man. Perhaps, if she was quick enough, she could get through the door before he grabbed her. Then a slight movement near the floor caught her attention. A black dog, its body almost entirely concealed behind its master, was peering round his legs with a curious, not unfriendly eye.

The dog's presence was reassuring. Psychopaths who lay in wait in deserted places in order to attack defenceless women did not normally take their dogs with them. Melissa managed a shaky smile. 'I'm . . . not really used to dogs,' she said, glad now of the excuse for her display of nerves.

'You'll be the writing lady from Hawthorn Cottage.' He spoke with the broad Gloucester vowels that were becoming familiar to Melissa and somehow reminded her of the fat woolly sheep grazing the slopes opposite her cottage. She relaxed still further.

'That's right,' she admitted. 'How did you know?'

He laughed. 'Things get around pretty quick in these parts.'

The fact that he had identified her so easily suggested that he knew Gloria. Perhaps he was Mr Parkin? He seemed about the right age but he did not quite fit in with her notion of a second-hand car dealer. She thought of asking him but changed her mind. If she were mistaken it could be embarrassing. She tried the indirect approach.

'Do you live in the village?'

He shook his head. 'Rookery Farm . . . the other end of the valley. Nearly into Lower Benbury.'

'But you must know the people in Upper Benbury?'

He grinned. 'Of course. We got no pub, so we all come over to the Woolpack on a Friday. Stan Parkin was in there last night with Gloria. She was telling everyone about you!'

'Oh dear!' It was exactly what Iris had advised her to avoid. She should have extracted a promise of silence from Gloria in exchange for an unlimited supply of Mills and Boon. She felt a momentary nostalgia for the anonymity of London.

Her companion went outside and stood looking up at the sky. 'Nearly stopped!' he called back. 'I'll be off now.'

'Oh, good!' said Melissa. 'It's been nice meeting you, Mr . . . ?'

'Woodman,' he said. 'Dick Woodman.' He raised a hand and strode off, his dog at his heels.

Melissa watched him for a few seconds as he made his way confidently down the steeply sloping bank, planting his feet sideways among the tussocks while the dog bounded surefootedly ahead. A fresh idea for the new novel germinated in her mind as she made her way home and she settled down to eat her casserole and jacket potato with a notebook at her elbow.

At eight o'clock her agent rang.

'Mel?'

'Joe! How nice to hear from you!'

'Thought I'd see how you were getting on.'

'That's very kind of you. I'm fine, thanks. There's still a lot to do but I'm gradually getting straight.'

'Did the move go smoothly?'

'Yes and no. The removal men were super but there were quite a few unfinished jobs on the cottage. I've had one or two battles with the builder.'

'I hope you didn't let him bully you!'

'You mean, like you do?'

'Touché. But my bullying is always done with your best interests at heart.'

'So you say. Anyway, I handled this merchant so firmly that he ended up offering me a job, strictly on the strength of my being such a tough customer!'

'Good for you! Time you learned to stand up for yourself!'

'I shall bear that in mind in our future dealings. Incidentally, you'll be interested to hear I'm already working on a new book.' She hadn't meant to say anything just yet but she knew he'd be pleased.

'Really? Thought you were taking a couple of months' break.'

'So did I but . . . you remember that shepherd's hut I mentioned in my last letter?'

'Mm-hm.'

'It has rather a gruesome history.' She recounted Gloria's version of Daniel's demise which, as she expected, appealed to his sense of humour.

'You seem to be in fruitful territory,' he chuckled.

'Oh, I am. I've already met the model for my first corpse. He nearly frightened me to death when I took shelter in Daniel's hut.'

'Then he deserves to be bumped off. Tell me more.'

'It's only just beginning to gel but I'm getting the outline of the plot. A ring of antique dealers and art thieves. Local farmers and landowners . . . pillars of the establishment . . . maybe a JP . . . all putting up a great show of collaborating with the law and fooling everyone nicely until one of them gets greedy and goes into drugs and becomes a danger to the others . . .'

'Sounds promising. Listen, Mel, I've got to be in your neck of the woods on Tuesday. Any chance of calling by?'

'But of course! Come to lunch.'

'Not lunch, I shan't be finished soon enough. Say some time after three o'clock?'

'Fine. I'll look forward to it.'

It would be nice to see Joe. He'd be her first visitor, not counting the disapproving Mrs Calloway. She'd try and get a synopsis roughed out for him to look at. He'd been unusually patient, knowing how busy she was with the move, but he was always keen to know what she was working on next. She washed up her supper things and got down to work.

Six

'I LIKE IT,' SAID JOE WHEN MELISSA HAD SHOWN him round the cottage. 'Especially this room.' He stood with his hands in his pockets, looking out of the sitting-room window. 'You've got a superb view. Of course,' he added cheerfully, 'you'll probably be snowed up for weeks in winter, with no electricity and no way of getting out to the shops . . . but I expect you've thought of that.'

Melissa laughed. 'I could hardly help but think of it when Aubrey harped on the same theme almost non-stop. He went further than you, he had me lying outside my own back door with a broken leg, my piteous cries for help borne away on the unheeding wind, undiscovered until the melting snow revealed my frozen corpse!'

Joe laughed with her but at the mention of Aubrey's name he gave her a keen look.

'What does Aubrey think of the cottage?' he asked.

'He hasn't seen it.' Joe's deep-set eyes held a question which she could have ignored but did not. 'Aubrey's wife is pressuring him to go back to her,' she said.

Joe's eyebrows went up and the skin over his cheekbones seemed to tighten. He looked away, rattling the change in his pockets. 'Do you suppose he will?' he asked.

It occurred to Melissa that she had never before mentioned to Joe that Aubrey was married and that she had no particular reason for doing so now. Not that it mattered; it was merely that it was unlike her to have blurted it out like that. The other night, over supper with Iris, she had attributed her lack of reserve to the elderflower champagne. She had no such excuse now. Perhaps

there was something in the Cotswold air, or the atmosphere of
the cottage itself, that inspired openness.

'I don't know,' she replied. 'I told him he should think seriously
about it and he got very emotional and said I was trying to get rid
of him.'

'And were you?'

The question came swiftly and she could tell by his expression
that he had spoken without thinking. He looked like someone at a
dinner party who had a too-hot morsel of food in his mouth and
was doing his best, out of politeness, to conceal his discomfort.
The notion both amused and puzzled her. She knew him well
enough to be certain that he was unlikely to be shocked at the
notion of one of his authors having an affair with someone else's
partner.

'Not consciously,' she said, after a moment's thought. 'He's
been very good to me and I'm very fond of him, but he really is
a bit of an old fuss-pot . . .' She broke off, thinking that this just
wouldn't do. It would be an act of gross disloyalty to Aubrey to
begin cataloguing his short-comings to someone with whom she
had nothing but a professional relationship.

'I expect it's because he cares for you,' said Joe. He had moved
back to the window and was staring out, drumming with two
fingers on one of the small glass panes.

'I'm sure he does.' She had uneasy memories of her last
meeting with Aubrey. It had ended with her screaming at him
in a way of which she hardly knew herself capable, telling him to
stop treating her as if she were a half-wit, that she had managed
perfectly well before meeting him, that she'd had enough of being
cossetted and pampered and plied with roses and chocolates as
if she were a simpering starlet in a television commercial. He
had taken it all without reproaching her, a patient, long-suffering
expression on his rather pudgy, formless features, murmuring that
he quite understood that she was feeling overwrought with all
the hassle of the move, and generally making her feel guilty at
hurting him.

'And . . . do you care for him?' asked Joe, still gently probing.
This time he touched a raw nerve.

'I think, if you don't mind, I'd rather not talk about Aubrey
any more,' she said.

'Of course . . . I'm sorry, I'm afraid I've been much too inquisi-
tive.'

'There's no need to apologise. We've known one another long enough to exchange a few confidences now and again. Let me get you some tea. Have a look at this while I put the kettle on.' She handed him a folder containing the synopsis of the new novel and pointed to an armchair. 'Sit down . . . relax . . . tell me what you think.'

The phone rang while she was making tea.

'Get that, will you?' she called from the kitchen. 'I'll be with you in a minute. It's probably the builder.'

When she carried the tea-tray into the sitting-room, she found Joe holding the receiver and staring at it with a puzzled expression.

'Who is it?'

'Some nutter or other.' He put the receiver down. 'Wanted to speak to someone called Babs . . . wants to see her . . . wouldn't listen when I said he'd got the wrong number.'

'Oh Lord, not him again!' Melissa put down the tray and began pouring the tea. 'I hoped I'd heard the last of him. He's becoming a bit of a pest.'

'You mean he's phoned before?'

'Twice. Did he say he'd be at their usual place tonight?'

'That's right. No, not quite. Say it again.'

'Say what again?'

'Where did he say he'd be?'

'At their usual place. He didn't say where it was.'

'Just a minute. Did he say "our usual place" or "the *usual* place"?'

'Good heavens, I've no idea. Does it make a difference?'

'It might. I'm sure when I spoke to him he said, "the *usual* place" with the stress on "usual".'

Melissa shook her head in bafflement. 'I haven't the least idea what you're driving at. Have a piece of cake and help yourself to sugar.'

'Thanks. Listen, if you want to meet a friend at someone else's house or flat, you say "see you at *Ken*'s place", or "*Lulu*'s place", don't you?'

'Ye . . . es.'

'But if you've got a regular rendezvous, you just say "our usual place", with equal stress on both words.'

'You might . . . yes, I suppose so. But I don't see what . . . ?'

'Come on now, as the creator of Nathan Latimer the brilliant and resourceful detective, tell me what "The Usual Place" might be.'

Melissa shut her eyes and began mouthing the words under her breath.

'You look like a nervous drama student rehearsing for an audition,' Joe teased. 'Well?'

'Got it!' she said, ignoring the taunt. 'A night-club, or maybe a wine-bar or something like that.'

'Take a Brownie point!'

'So where does that get us?' Melissa wrinkled her brows. 'Ah, brainwave! I can make The Usual Place the name of some sleazy dive used by the crooks in my novel.'

'There you are, your cranky caller has been of some use after all.'

'Now why didn't I spot that for myself? I must be slipping.'

'Not you. Your mind was full of other things like plumbing and getting carpets laid.'

'Too right. I didn't pay any attention to the way he was speaking; I was irritated because he totally ignored what I was saying. It's queer, the way he takes no notice when he's told it's a wrong number.'

'Maybe something wrong with the line—you hear him but he can't hear you . . .'

'Or a taped message . . . ?'

'Why on earth would anyone tape a message like that?'

'I've no idea, I was just brainstorming. Anyway, I seem to remember the words varied slightly. Was there a pause before he began speaking?'

'Yes, I think there was. Perhaps he's ill . . . or has a speech impediment . . .'

'Or he's not quite right in the head.'

'It's very odd.'

'Anyway, let's get back to how I can use it in *The Shepherd's Hut*.' Melissa nodded towards the folder lying on the arm of Joe's chair.

'Is that what you plan to call it?' He sounded unimpressed.

'It'll do for a working title. Something better will occur to me later on. What's your reaction?'

Joe sank his teeth into a slice of cake and spoke between mouthfuls. 'Looks quite promising. How do you think you can work in your mystery caller?'

'Isn't it obvious? One of the gang will run a café or a restaurant, or maybe a club, called The Usual Place, as a front . . .'

'Just a moment,' said Joe, 'you did say you're setting this yarn locally, didn't you?'

'That's right.'

'Then it might be as well to make certain there isn't a genuine Usual Place. You don't want to get sued for defamation!'

'That's a thought. I'll try the Yellow Pages.' She fetched the directory and opened it at the section headed 'Restaurants.' 'Well, would you believe it, look at this!'

He peered over her shoulder and read aloud where she was pointing. ' "Meet your friends at The Usual Place. Fully licensed, first-class food, local produce delivered fresh daily. Rooms available for private functions." That's a pity. You'll have to think of something else.'

'Damn! No, wait . . . they can't claim sole rights to the name, can they?'

Joe frowned. He was always inclined to take such questions seriously and to err on the side of caution. 'Perhaps not, so long as there's nothing in your book that they could claim was defamatory. You'll have to make sure there's no resemblance to your fictitious Usual Place. Go and suss it out, and then create something with an entirely different image. You see . . .' He showed every sign of preparing to deliver one of his lectures.

Melissa slapped the book shut and pretended to threaten him with it. 'Really, Joe, you're as bad as Aubrey! He thinks I'm incapable of figuring out the obvious.'

'Sorry! Just pointing out the pitfalls. Do go on with your plot, please, please!' His exaggerated air of contrition was almost embarrassing in its boyishness. He had never shown her this side of himself before.

She picked up the folder and made a show of riffling through the sheets of her synopsis to avoid looking at him. 'When the gang want to pass on the word about a shipment, one of them will make a coded phone call pretending to be someone trying to make a date with a girlfriend.'

Joe nodded. 'In case someone overhears, or the line is bugged?'

'Something like that. And I can bring in that business of stress that we were talking about just now. Nathan Latimer will overhear a call and pick it up the way you did . . .'

'Of course, I always knew that you based your brilliant sleuth on me!' Joe assumed an expression of fatuous conceit and Melissa laughed in spite of herself.

'Perhaps,' she said after a moment's thought, 'he didn't say "The *Usual* Place" when I answered him. Perhaps he'd been told always to say "our usual place", so that no one would guess he was referring to the pub, and he happened to slip up when you answered . . . but then, if he was pretending to call a girlfriend, he'd be expecting a prearranged response and . . .'

'Hang on!' said Joe. 'Aren't you getting fact and fiction tangled up? You aren't seriously suggesting that your man really is a member of the local Mafia?'

'No, of course I'm not.' The absurdity of what she had been saying dawned on her. For the last few minutes, fantasy had indeed become interwoven with reality in her mind. It was a disturbing sensation. Joe was looking amused but she did not return his smile.

'Don't look so worried,' he said. 'If it happens again, I suggest you report it to the telephone people. You could request a change of number. That would put a stop to it.'

'I could do that, I suppose.'

Joe stood up, looking at his watch.

'I really must be going,' he said.

'It's been lovely seeing you,' said Melissa. 'I wasn't planning to start on a new book for at least a couple of months, but what with the history of the shepherd's hut and Dick Woodman lurking in the shadows, and now this coded telephone call we've dreamed up, I can't wait to get down to work.'

'Good girl!' There was an unaccustomed undertone of warmth in his voice. He moved a little closer so that she caught the tweedy smell of his jacket and the clean tang of his breath. 'Keep me posted won't you?'

'I will.'

'Fine.' He slid a hand through her right arm and gave it a little squeeze as they walked towards the car. The pressure was vaguely disturbing.

'I may have to come down again in a couple of months or so,' he said as he settled into the driving seat of his dark blue Audi. 'I've just taken on a fearsome old agony aunt who's retired to Cheltenham to write a novel based on some of her juicier correspondence. She's a semi-invalid who doesn't travel and she doesn't trust the post, which is ironic when you think she spent most of her professional life receiving and answering letters!'

'Let me know when you're coming and drop in to see me again.'

'I hoped you'd say that.'

'How's Georgina, by the way?'

'She's well.' He was fumbling with his seat-belt, his head half-turned away.

'And Paul? Is he enjoying life at Oxford?'

'He's fine, thank you, and loving every minute!'

'I'm so glad.'

Melissa had met Joe's wife once, at a book-launching party. Thin, with restless eyes and a drooping mouth, she had given the impression of being utterly bored. She seemed an unlikely mother to the eager-looking youngster whom Melissa, through a succession of portraits on Joe's desk, had watched develop from a freckled thirteen-year-old into a handsome undergraduate with clean-cut features and an engaging smile. Whenever she visited Joe in his office there had been a new photograph of Paul for her to admire while his father looked on with quiet pride. There was never a picture of Georgina but it had not occurred to Melissa that there might be anything wrong with the marriage. Now, as she stood and watched the Audi turn into the lane, she remembered the flatness of Joe's tone as he answered her inquiry about his wife and contrasted it with the warmth in his face and voice as he spoke of his son.

'That Aubrey?' Iris, in shapeless slacks, a baggy sweater and gardening gloves, came out of her garden through the side gate, her hoe balanced on her shoulder like a rifle.

'Hello, Iris! No, that's Joe Martin, my agent.'

'Thought not. Looks too interesting. Heard from Aubrey lately?'

'He rang the day I moved in, after I got home from your place. Haven't heard a peep since.'

'Must be sulking,' said Iris with gleeful malice. She began jabbing with her hoe at the weeds growing alongside her fence.

'Your garden's a picture!' Melissa commented.

Iris surveyed her neat rows of seedling vegetables and purred with satisfaction before casting her eyes at her neighbour's neglected plot. 'Time you got started. Get a few spuds in. Main crop. Too late for earlies.'

'Do I have to get special potatoes to plant?'

'Of course!' Iris leaned on her hoe and smiled the patient smile of a teacher with a backward but willing pupil. 'Garden centre might have some left. Need some tools as well. Fork, spade, rake, hoe . . .'

'I don't suppose you could spare the time to come with me to the garden centre?' said Melissa impulsively. 'I'd really appreciate your advice.'

Iris rubbed her nose with the back of her glove. 'Don't see why not.' Her voice was gruff but she seemed pleased at the request. 'Tomorrow morning do?'

'Fine—oh, not tomorrow. Gloria's coming in the morning, and I've invited Mr and Mrs Calloway to tea in the afternoon. How about Thursday?'

Iris frowned and then shrugged. 'Thursday morning, then,' she grunted, renewing her attack on the weeds. 'Want to start on the digging in the meantime? Borrow a fork.'

'Thanks. Maybe I will. By the way, do you know of a restaurant called The Usual Place?'

The hoe delivered an extra vicious jab and a clump of grass flew into the air. 'Yes, I know it.' Iris's voice was thickly laced with disapproval. 'Our Gloria works there some evenings . . . if you can call what she does work!'

Unable to think of a suitable comment, Melissa left Iris to her weeding and went indoors. She cut some sandwiches and made herself a flask of tea, retrieved the folder containing her synopsis and went to her study to spend the rest of the day working on *The Shepherd's Hut*.

SEVEN

'I HEAR YOU WORK AT THE USUAL PLACE,' MELISSA remarked as she and Gloria shared a coffee-break. She had worked far into the evening on *The Shepherd's Hut* and the coded telephone call that was to play a significant part in the plot was still on her mind when she awoke on Wednesday morning.

Gloria showed only mild surprise at the question.

' 's right. I helps in the bar two evenings a week. Did Miss Ash tell you?'

'Yes, as a matter of fact she did.'

Gloria giggled. 'Thought so! She don't approve. Says she's heard about things that go on there!' By intonation she put 'things' in quotes.

'Oh? What things?' asked Melissa, who had a shrewd idea but was curious to hear Gloria's version of them.

One of the big brown eyes closed in a wink that was like a nudge in the ribs. 'Naughty things! They has private rooms, you see, for clubs to meet, and they has entertainers, like!' Another wink and more quotation marks.

'Really? What sort of entertainers?'

'You know!' Gloria's eyes glowed with mischief. 'Strippers for one thing.'

Melissa shook her head and tried to sound shocked. 'I can't understand how any woman can bring herself to do that!'

Gloria nearly choked over her coffee. 'Men does it too!' she chortled. 'Tuesday afternoons there's a show for the girls. They turns up in droves for a sight of Gorgeous George and his Crazy Cucumber! Course, they tells their husbands it's for the bingo . . . !'

'Good gracious!' murmured Melissa. 'I can't imagine any of

45

the ladies of Upper Benbury going to anything like that!'

A second explosion of mirth all but toppled Gloria from her stool. 'You never know!' she wheezed as soon as she regained her breath.

This time, Melissa was genuinely shocked. 'You aren't suggesting . . . ?'

Gloria shook her head and mopped her eyes with a crumpled tissue. 'Ain't heard of any,' she admitted with evident regret. 'But I wouldn't put it past one or two of them!' Her rolling eyes made it plain that a detailed cross-examination would not be unwelcome but Melissa decided not to pursue the point.

She returned to her original motive for bringing up the subject of The Usual Place. 'Do you know a girl there called Babs?' she asked.

Gloria cocked her yellow head on one side like a reflective canary. 'There was a Babs working at The Usual Place a while back,' she said after a moment's thought.

'Do you know where she lives?'

'No . . . she left just before I started. Seems there was quite a to-do over some feller who was chasing her.' She raised her thickly pencilled eyebrows at Melissa. 'She a friend of yours?'

'No, I don't actually know her. Someone rang my number the other day, thinking I was Babs and wanting to meet at The Usual Place.'

'Well, it couldn't have been the same feller. That one got smashed up in a car accident. Went there asking for Babs and they told him she'd walked out. He wouldn't believe it and started getting stroppy. The manager told him to naff off and not come back. Next thing they hear, he's gone off and wrapped his car round a tree on the way home.'

'How awful! Was he badly hurt?'

'Killed, so I heard,' said Gloria in a tone suggesting that he had got no more than he deserved. She slid off her stool and prepared to start work again. Evidently her attention span was short; she had already lost interest in Babs and her ill-starred admirer but she was full of concern for Melissa.

'You feeling all right?' she asked. 'You looks pale.'

Melissa shook her head. Her stomach felt full of ice cubes but she managed to pull herself together and forced a shaky smile. 'I'm quite all right, thank you,' she said. 'I'm tired, that's all. I was working until very late last night.'

Gloria's eyes widened. 'You writing another book?' she asked. 'Ooh my, it must be wonderful to be so clever. Is there any romance in this one?'

'I'm afraid not, it's another thriller.' Gloria's face fell. 'Tell me,' Melissa went on, 'how long have you been working at The Usual Place?'

Gloria pursed her lips and began counting on her fingers. 'Let's see now, my Charlene's six in June and she'd just had her fifth birthday so it'll be . . .'

'About ten months,' said Melissa.

Gloria's mouth opened at this display of rapid mental arithmetic. '' 's right,' she said.

'And you say the accident to Babs's boyfriend happened just before you started.'

'' 'bout a couple of weeks before, I'd say.' Gloria glanced at the clock. 'Is that the time? I'd best get on and do the bathroom!'

Left alone in the kitchen, Melissa pursued her line of thought. She was still feeling the effects of shock at the story of the accident but common sense came to the rescue. If her mysterious caller and the man whose pursuit of Babs had ended so disastrously were one and the same, then obviously he had survived the accident. Dead men do not make telephone calls. But it must have been a pretty serious crash and would have been reported in the local paper. A visit to their office, or possibly the reference library, was indicated. But how was it that nearly a year later the man was still pestering Babs to meet him at The Usual Place? And where had he got hold of Melissa's telephone number?

It could, of course, have at some time been Babs's number. Perhaps she'd moved away; in that case her old number would, after an interval, have been allocated to another subscriber. Or the man was confused after the accident and had simply got the number wrong. There could be several perfectly simple explanations.

The first question presented more of a problem. The more she thought about it, the more it seemed that there was something far from normal in the man's behaviour. She smelled a story and knew she would not rest until she had got to the bottom of it. After Gloria's departure she ate a hasty snack and spent a couple of hours weeding her garden with the elderly fork that Iris had thoughtfully produced the previous evening. The mechanical exercise left her mind free to pursue the problem and by the time she went indoors she had settled on a line of enquiry.

*   *   *

At four o'clock, the Rector and his lady arrived to take tea with their new parishioner. Mrs Calloway was considerably shorter than her husband. She had straight grey hair cropped close to a round head on a long thin neck, narrow shoulders, very small breasts and heavy hips—like a cello with an extra leg, thought Melissa as she helped her off with her coat. She smelled of lavender water and there were uneven dabs of face-powder on her cheeks and on the end of her nose, which was small and sharp and acted as a ski-slope for the heavy spectacles which she was constantly pushing back into place.

Melissa gave her guests a conducted tour of the ground floor and would have shown them upstairs as well but the offer was firmly declined by Mrs Calloway who managed to convey, by intonation and disapproving stare, that there was impropriety, if not downright immorality, in the prospect of her husband's being afforded so much as a glimpse of Melissa's bedroom. Disappointment flickered across the Rector's chubby features; he would, Melissa sensed, have liked to see where another woman slept. As a young girl, Mrs Calloway might once have had a certain gamine attraction but in middle age she had neither charm nor femininity. Melissa wondered if her husband ever fantasised.

'It's delightful, quite delightful!' declared Mr Calloway at intervals, admiring living-rooms, kitchen broom-cupboard and downstairs loo with equal effusiveness. When they returned to the sitting-room he settled in Melissa's favourite armchair and sat beaming and expressing approval of everything he saw while his wife perched on the edge of the settee, clutching her handbag and muttering that they couldn't stay long. Having failed to lure Melissa into either flower-arranging or the Women's Institute, in both cases on the plea of pressure of work, she obviously considered the visit a complete waste of time.

His wife's disapproval did nothing to inhibit the Rector's appetite. He ate and drank heartily and was lavish in his praise of the scones and fruit-cake.

'All home-made, I'm sure!' he said, holding out his cup for the second refill.

'I don't know how you manage it,' his wife remarked sourly, 'with all the calls on your time!'

'Yes, indeed!' agreed Mr Calloway, either oblivious to or deliberately ignoring the sarcasm. 'Getting settled into a new house, 'on top of all your writing . . . and I see you've been busy in the garden too. You must find your days very full!'

'Miss Ash has kindly offered to help me with the garden, or at any rate to advise me about it,' said Melissa, 'and I'm very lucky to have found Mrs Parkin to help in the house.'

'Ah, yes, dear Miss Ash, so very kind,' beamed Mr Calloway. 'You are indeed fortunate in your neighbour . . . and Mrs Parkin is a real treasure, isn't she, my dear?'

Mrs Calloway glared into her cup, her mouth screwed up as if her tea had turned into vinegar. 'She's a vulgar little slut!' she hissed. 'I only put up with her because there's no one else in the village prepared to do housework!'

Her husband's smile wavered, like a sun struggling to penetrate hazy cloud. 'Come, my dear, we mustn't be uncharitable,' he wheedled. 'I know the gossips say unkind things against Glor . . . Mrs Parkin but you know my views on repeating unsubstantiated rumours. She's a devoted mother, and you yourself must admit that she's a first-class worker.'

The argument had no visible effect on his wife, who merely sniffed, declined Melissa's offer of more tea and announced that it was time to go.

As she stood up, her sharp, darting eyes fell on a group of photographs on a corner cupboard. There was one of Simon's father, eternally radiating the boyish charm that Melissa had once found irresistible, which she kept on display more out of loyalty to his parents than out of sentiment. The rest were of Simon: with his grandparents; in the school cricket team; at Oxford, self-conscious in gown and mortar-board. Mrs Calloway scanned them all with little mews of rapture, finally homing in on a portrait of Melissa and her son as a toddler at her knee, a toy train clutched in a chubby fist.

'Aaah!' she exclaimed, sounding like Iris addressing Binkie. 'Bless his little heart, isn't he lovely!'

For the first time, Melissa felt a spark of sympathy between herself and the Rector's charmless spouse. 'Yes,' she responded with pride, 'he was a beautiful baby.'

'What's his name?'

'Simon.'

'Simon.' Mrs Calloway repeated the name in a crooning whisper, as though she were tiptoeing round the crib of a sleeping infant. 'How old is he now?'

'Twenty-five.' Melissa indicated the main photograph. 'That was taken three years ago, when he graduated.'

'What does he do?'

'He's an engineer, he works in the States.'

'Aah!' The expression of sour disapproval had given way to a gentle, maternal tenderness. 'I've got two boys, you know. Such a shame they have to grow up!' She shot an accusing glance at her husband as if he had some responsibility for the passage of time. He spread his hands and gave a helpless little smile. 'I didn't know you had any children, Mrs Craig.' For the first time Melissa felt that she had done something meritorious.

'Just the one. His father died before he was born.'

'What a pity! It would have been nice for Simon to have a brother or sister.' She made clucking noises, implying that the procreation of children was the sole reason for a husband's existence.

'Did you come by the footpath?' asked Melissa as she escorted her guests to the door.

'We did not!' declared Mrs Calloway. 'I'—she laid heavy stress on the pronoun—"am not prepared to soil my shoes and stockings tramping through mud and dead leaves!' She glared at her husband's feet and legs as if they bore evidence of previous short cuts.

He gave a sheepish, choirboy's grin. 'It brushes off!' he protested.

His wife ignored him. 'Thank you for the tea,' she said to Melissa, and her smile was almost friendly.

'Yes indeed!' said Mr Calloway. '*Most* kind . . . quite delightful . . . delicious cakes . . . thank you so much!' He made scooping gestures as if doffing an invisible hat.

Iris was working in her garden as they left. She passed the time of day with them before strolling over for a chat with Melissa.

'Miserable bitch!' she muttered as soon as the visitors were out of earshot. 'Can't think why he married her!'

'They do seem an oddly assorted couple,' agreed Melissa. 'How old are their sons?'

'Grown up. Take after their father. Lovely boys. Army, both of them. See you've made a start,' she went on, indicating the garden.

'Yes, I did a bit this morning. It's hard work though—when you're not used to it,' she added defensively as Iris gave a slightly superior smile and marched across to inspect her efforts at close quarters.

'Should really double dig,' she commented. 'Soil's a bit heavy. Put in some leaf-mould. No chemical fertilisers, stick to organics. Make a compost heap!' she continued, striding over to a corner behind the garage. 'Do fine here, out of sight, gets the sun, rot down a treat!'

'I'll do that,' murmured Melissa.

'Want a hand for an hour?' Iris offered. To do any more gardening that day was the last thing Melissa wanted but it was so plain that Iris wanted to help that she felt unable to refuse.

'That's kind of you. I'll just run in and change.'

Iris nodded, heading back to her own cottage. 'Getting another fork. Shan't be a tick,' she called over her shoulder.

By the time the potato patch had been prepared and Melissa had cooked and eaten her supper, she was too tired to do anything but flop into a chair and read for an hour before going to bed.

The next morning was spent with Iris, first at the garden centre and subsequently in the garden planting potatoes. Feeling that a return of hospitality was long overdue, Melissa invited her neighbour to supper the following evening and spent part of the afternoon hunting through her cookery books for vegetarian recipes and making up a list of ingredients missing from her store-cupboard.

After supper she went to her study to work on *The Shepherd's Hut* but the more she tried to enter into the minds of her characters and manipulate the threads of her plot, the more her thoughts kept switching back to the actual people and events that had set her ideas in motion. It was all too ridiculous. Every day, writers were drawing on their own experiences, embroidering them with imaginary and sometimes bizarre or sinister detail. That was the very essence of fiction. She herself had been doing it quite successfully for years. So why should reality, instead of fading into the background as it normally did, now insist on taking the centre of the stage? She had a sense of unease, almost of foreboding. In the end she gave up and went to bed.

EIGHT

IN THE MORNING SHE DROVE INTO GLOUCESTER. IT was her first visit to the city and she would have liked to explore it at leisure but just now there were other things to do. She found a health food shop and a greengrocer, took her purchases back to the car and then, in accordance with the plan she had worked out the previous day, asked a passerby the way to the office of the local paper.

Her informant, a harassed-looking woman with a shopping-bag, gabbled something, pointed in the direction of the cathedral and hurried on her way. Attempting to follow the imprecise directions, Melissa took a wrong turning and found herself in a narrow passage. On one side was a second-hand bookshop, on the other a bar and restaurant with a modern frontage that only just escaped being vulgarly ostentatious. The name was emblazoned in gilt letters on its plate-glass window. The Usual Place.

The door stood open to the warm spring sunshine and Melissa went inside. It was not yet twelve o'clock but already a few customers were taking an early lunch. At the far end was a bar where two or three men and one woman were perched on stools, chatting and joking with a genial, balding man in shirtsleeves who was serving them with drinks.

Melissa climbed on to a stool and ordered a dry sherry from a plump, cheerful-looking barmaid.

'Glass or schooner?'

'Glass, please.'

The woman poured the drink, took the money and handed over the change with a pleasant smile.

'Nice day,' she commented.

'Lovely.'

Melissa sipped her sherry, helped herself from a dish of nuts and glanced around.

The bar was separated from the restaurant by an elaborate structure incorporating an aquarium and a display of flowering and foliage plants which on closer inspection proved to be plastic. There was a buffet with an assortment of cold meats and salads while a menu of predictable hot dishes suggested rapid transfer from freezer to customer via the microwave. The bar and tables were scattered with cork mats imprinted with an exhortation to meet one's friends at The Usual Place; pseudo-classical music issued from inescapable loudspeakers. Everything was clean, wholesome-looking and totally undistinguished. It seemed an unlikely setting for strippers and the 'private functions' Gloria had giggled over but no doubt the evening clientèle would be of a different breed from the lunchtime trade.

It would not, Melissa felt, be difficult to create a fictitious Usual Place that bore no resemblance whatever to this. She began playing with some ideas, absently twirling the stem of her empty glass. The barmaid sauntered across.

'Same again?'

'No, better not, make it an orange juice, please.'

The woman smiled as she poured. 'Don't drink and drive, eh?'

There was something about her that reminded Melissa of Gloria. She had the same open, friendly expression, the same warm West Country burr.

'Tell me,' she said as she paid for her orange juice, 'have you been here long?'

The woman looked faintly surprised but replied without hesitation. 'About two years . . . why?'

'I was wondering if you remember a girl called Babs who used to work here?'

'Babs Carter? Yes, I remember her. Little madam, she was— oh, I beg your pardon, is she a friend of yours?'

'No, I don't actually know her. It's just that I keep getting odd telephone calls from a man who thinks I'm Babs and wants to meet me here. I don't suppose you've any idea who he might be?'

'Doesn't he give his name?'

'No. He sounds kind of strange and when I tell him he's got the wrong number he just hangs up.'

The woman frowned thoughtfully, shaking her head. More customers came up to the bar and with a murmured excuse she moved away to serve them. Presently, Melissa noticed her speaking to the barman and nodding in her direction; after a moment he came sauntering across. He was a big, sensual-looking man; instinct told Melissa that he fancied himself as something of a lady-killer.

'Ruby tells me you were asking about Babs Carter,' he said, leaning a forearm on the bar and treating her to an admiring glance and a whiff of expensive body-lotion.

'That's right. You don't happen to know where she lives, do you?'

'Sorry love, no idea. She left us . . . oh, must be nearly a year ago.'

'And you don't know where she's working now?'

'I seem to remember hearing she'd left town but I haven't a clue where she went.'

'Do you think any of your other employees might know? Has she kept in touch with any of them?'

'Shouldn't think so. These girls come and go . . . I've got better things to do than run around after them.' His large, well-manicured hands indicated a certain frustration at the unpredictability of young females and Melissa nodded in sympathy.

'I heard her boyfriend had a bad car accident.'

The man was helping himself to nuts, popping them into his full-lipped mouth with one hand and nudging the dish towards Melissa with the other.

'Ah, that one,' he ruminated. 'Nasty business that. His own fault, of course. Got so worked up he didn't know what he was doing. Came round here making a nuisance of himself and we had to chuck him out. Next thing we heard they had to cut him out of his car on the Golden Valley by-pass.'

Melissa shuddered. 'Poor chap. I suppose he was lucky not to have been killed. Could it be him making the phone calls, do you think?'

The man considered while disposing of another handful of nuts. 'Might be,' he said with a shrug. 'He used to meet Babs here sometimes. Couldn't think what she saw in him . . . not her type at all.'

'You don't happen to know his name, or where he lives?'

'Sorry, love, can't help you.' He straightened up and signalled a response to an impatient customer. 'I'd get your number changed if you get any more of those calls,' he advised as he moved away. 'That guy was a bit of a weirdo even before the accident.'

Melissa finished her orange juice, slid from her stool and went outside. Someone touched her on the arm and she turned to see a fresh-faced young man in a bomber jacket and jeans. He had fair hair and an engaging smile.

'Excuse me!' he said. 'Can you spare a moment?'

'What is it?' From his clothes, he might have been a student but a closer look told her that he was older than he at first appeared.

'My name's Bruce Ingram.' He fumbled in an inside pocket and brought out a card. 'I'm a reporter on the *Gazette*.'

'I see.' Melissa hesitated for a moment, fingering the card. 'Well, Mr Ingram, my agent usually arranges interviews for me. Would you like me to . . .'

'Your agent?' His jaw dropped and his blue-green eyes rounded in consternation. 'Are you . . . I mean . . . should I . . . ?' He was floundering like a schoolboy who has forgotten his homework.

Melissa restrained a smile. 'Recognize me? Not necessarily . . . unless you read crime fiction, that is.'

'You're a crime writer?'

'My name's Melissa Craig but my pen-name is Mel . . .'

'Mel Craig! Of course I should have recognised you, please forgive me! I've read your books and seen your picture on them . . .' He looked so abashed that Melissa was tempted to pat him on the head.

'Don't apologise. It's a very old picture anyway. Now, if it isn't an interview, what can I do for you?'

'I was in there just now, while you were talking to Pete Crane.' He jerked his head in the direction of The Usual Place. 'I hope you don't think I was eavesdropping, but I pricked up my ears when I heard Babs Carter's name mentioned. And I thought I heard you say you'd been in touch with Clive Shepherd?'

'Who?'

'Clive Shepherd. The fellow who had the accident.'

'You mean Babs's boyfriend. Is that his name?'

'Yes. Didn't you know?'

'No. Is he a friend of yours?'

'I've only set eyes on him a couple of times but I know quite a lot about him.'

'Then perhaps you can explain why he keeps ringing my number?'

'I can't account for that, I'm afraid . . . but I'm amazed to hear that he's capable of ringing any number.'

'Because of his accident?'

'Yes. He was pretty badly smashed up and they didn't think he'd live. Last report I had, he was making a very slow physical recovery but suffering almost total amnesia.'

'I think his memory must be coming back. He remembers Babs even if he does get her number wrong . . . and he sounds terribly confused and emotional. But . . . if he's not a friend of yours, do you mind telling me why you're so interested in him?'

'Willingly, but let's not talk here. Will you let me buy you some lunch?'

'That's kind of you but I don't normally eat much at midday.'

'A sandwich, then . . . or a pizza? There's a very decent trattoria just over the road.'

'All right, a pizza then.'

Bruce led her across Westgate and into a small restaurant with marble-topped tables and a Roman frieze on the walls. He found a table for two tucked behind a reproduction urn with a spider-plant straggling over the sides. The place was half-full and buzzing with conversation.

'It's a good place to talk,' said Bruce as they sat down. 'Plenty of background noise and not much chance of being overheard.'

'Sounds intriguing!' said Melissa. There was the usual interval while the menu was consulted and the order given. 'Now, what's all this about?'

Bruce cleared his throat and hesitated. 'I'd like to ask you a question but I'm afraid you'll think I'm being impertinent.'

'Don't worry, I don't eat reporters when there's an R in the month.'

'Well then, I was wondering about your interest in Babs Carter . . . I mean, she can't be a friend of yours? I do have a very good reason for asking,' he hurried on as Melissa's eyebrows lifted.

'Why shouldn't she be a friend of mine?' she asked curiously.

Bruce shuffled his feet and played with the reproduction Roman lamp that held sugar. 'Look, I've met her and I'm pretty sure you don't move in the same circles.'

'You'd be surprised at the people I get to know in my researches!'

'Of course, I was forgetting . . .' He ran his hands through his short curly hair and then clapped them over his eyes. 'Ingram's put his foot in it . . . again!'

Melissa burst out laughing, to the evident delight of the waitress who brought their order.

'No, you're quite right,' she said when the girl had gone and Bruce had emerged from behind his sheltering fingers. 'I've never set eyes on Babs or any of her friends. You obviously didn't hear what I was saying to Ruby about the telephone calls.' Quickly, she ran over the details, including the process of deduction that led her to discover the existence of The Usual Place.

Bruce's eyes sparkled in admiration. 'That was jolly clever of you!' he said. Melissa accepted the compliment without a qualm; Joe would never find out. Bruce leaned forward and dropped his voice. 'You know, this is the most super bit of luck, meeting you like this. Would you care to help solve a real-life mystery?'

'If you mean the phone calls, I thought . . .'

'No, not that. I mean the mystery of Babs's disappearance, and Clive's accident.'

Melissa stared at him. 'The people at The Usual Place didn't seem to think that there was anything particularly mysterious about them.'

Bruce shrugged. 'Why should they? If you ask me, Pete wasn't sorry to see the back of Babs . . . or rather, he was glad to see the back of Clive. It used to get up his nose, seeing him hunched on the corner of the bar all evening when Babs was working, glowering over his tomato juice. By all accounts he—Clive, that is—was trying all he knew to get her to leave The Usual Place . . .' He broke off as the waitress brought their order.

'What sort of a girl was Babs?' asked Melissa, picking up her knife and fork.

Bruce considered while chewing a mouthful of pizza. 'Pretty, lovely figure, loads of sex-appeal. Liked to give the impression of being a tough little cookie but I thought she was a nice kid at heart. Not exactly the innocent virgin though; in fact she used to take the odd favoured client home after the show on Friday and Saturday nights. Did you know they have strip shows at The Usual Place, by the way?' he added, rather self-consciously Melissa thought.

She grinned. 'Yes, I know. Boys and girls, so I hear.'

'Huh?'

She told him about Gorgeous George and he flushed to the ears.
It must be her presence that he found inhibiting, she thought; it
was unusual, and rather refreshing, to meet a man who found that
sort of thing embarrassing.

'Yes, do go on,' she urged.

'Where was I? Oh, yes, Babs . . . well, apart from her work in
the bar and the night-club, she did a few modelling jobs. One
way and the other she must have picked up quite a tidy little
income.'

'The barman said Clive wasn't really her sort.'

'I'd have said that too, but after I'd ferreted around a bit
I began to wonder.' For a while, Bruce concentrated on his
food.

Melissa felt the adrenalin beginning to flow. She smelled a
story and knew from experience that she must allow him to tell
it in his own time and in his own way. Too many questions could
be a distraction. So she waited patiently while he organised his
thoughts.

'The official version is that Babs packed up and left her digs
and her job without notice,' he said after a minute or two. 'When
Clive called for her one evening and got no answer, he tackled
the landlady and was told she'd gone, leaving her key with a
note to say it was time she was moving on. He made a bit of a
scene, called the old woman a liar and her son ordered him out.
Then he went tearing round to The Usual Place and got a similar
story—Babs hadn't shown up for a couple of days. I happened to
be there and it was not a pretty sight. He was almost hysterical,
banging on the bar and shouting that someone must know where
she was, she wouldn't go off without a word to him and they
needn't think they'd get away with it. He wouldn't quieten down
so Pete—he's the manager, by the way, not just the barman—
threw him out.'

'Pete said he was a bit of a weirdo,' observed Melissa, as the
waitress removed their empty plates. 'That was delicious, thank
you very much.'

'Would you like anything else? I can recommend the Neapolitan
ice-cream.'

'Sounds lovely.'

'And coffee?'

'Please—cappuccino.' He gave the order, planted his elbows
on the table and leaned forward.

'I wouldn't have called Clive a weirdo,' he said emphatically. 'Eccentric maybe, a bit strait-laced, but perfectly sane . . . at least, he was before the accident.'

He was looking directly at Melissa and she became aware of the intensity of his gaze, the square set of his chin and the fine lines at the corners of his eyes and mouth. Beneath the boyish-looking exterior was a serious and very attractive man . . . but this wouldn't do. She forced her mind to concentrate on what he was saying.

'It was later on that night that he had his accident. On a clear stretch of road. He'd had no more than a pint of beer, there was nothing wrong with his car, it was dark but it wasn't raining, no other vehicle involved. The only explanation the police could offer was that he was in such a state over not being able to contact Babs that he was driving recklessly and simply lost it.'

'And you don't believe that?'

'I did at first.' He waited while the waitress brought the ices and coffee. 'Then I started thinking. Babs must have mixed with some pretty dubious characters . . . she could have been at risk in any number of ways. Suppose she said something to Clive that worried him . . . made him concerned for her safety. Then, without saying a word, she vanishes. That would account for him being so frantic and kicking up such a fuss. It wasn't like him, you see . . . by all accounts he was normally a very quiet sort of chap.'

'So you think that there's a real chance that something has happened to Babs?'

Bruce nodded. 'Yes . . . and the more I think about it, the more certain I am that Clive's accident was . . . no accident.'

Melissa stared at him in horror. 'You can't be serious!'

'It wouldn't be the first time someone's been run off the road to keep them quiet.'

'But it's fantastic . . . you've no evidence.'

'I know,' he admitted. 'But I do have a very strong hunch . . . no, don't laugh!' he pleaded at the sight of her smile. 'It just doesn't add up. Why should Babs walk out on Clive? I talked to some of the girls she worked with and they told me she led him a hell of a dance but she said more than once that Jesus freaks were a pain in the ass but they could still be a good prospect.'

'Why should she call Clive a Jesus freak?'

'He was rather religious, a bit puritanical by all accounts, although his colleagues quite liked him . . . without ever really getting to know him.'

'What was his job, by the way?'

'Insurance agent, making a modest but unspectacular living selling endowment policies. That's how he met Babs, seems she wanted to provide for her old age. He fell for her in a big way. I had a chat with his manager and he told me Clive was a conscientious employee but very reserved. He never spoke about his family but they all knew of his obsession with Babs.'

'If he had such an ordinary sort of job, why should Babs think he was a good prospect?'

'That's something I haven't been able to find out yet.'

'I can understand why he hated her working at The Usual Place.'

'I suspect he was hoping to reform her.'

'Let me get this straight,' said Melissa. 'You think that Babs has been abducted, or perhaps killed, that Clive knew something that made him suspicious and that his accident was staged to make sure he didn't start snooping around or go to the police.'

Bruce nodded eagerly, like a terrier that had scented a rabbit. 'That's it in a nutshell.'

'I suppose this is an obvious question, but have you been to the police?'

'Oh yes.'

'And?'

'Considering I gave them virtually nothing to go on, they did a pretty good job of checking. They enquired at her digs and interviewed Pete and the rest of the staff at The Usual Place. They also checked out the Up Front Modelling Agency where she was registered. I believe they even went to the DHSS to find out if she'd got a job elsewhere.'

'Any luck?'

'Zilch. DHSS had never heard of her so she'd obviously been working at her various jobs on a casual basis. She wasn't registered with any local doctor or dentist.'

'What about the note she's supposed to have left—did they see that?'

'No, that had been destroyed, but there was no reason to suspect the old landlady of lying.' Bruce heaved a deep sigh. 'Everywhere they drew a blank. It seems Babs had always been a bit of a loner.

as far as girl friends were concerned, and she never really confided in any of them. They weren't even sure where she came from. Some thought she was a local girl but there was some talk of her having spent some time in London.'

'What about men, besides Clive, of course?'

'As I said, she had her favourite weekend customers but she was pretty discreet and there was never any trouble.'

'So the conclusion seems to be that she's a natural drifter who just decided to up and go. Is that what the police think?'

'With nothing concrete to go on, what else can they think? No one has officially reported her missing and she was certainly over eighteen so she was free to move on if she wanted to.'

'And the accident?'

'Nothing whatever to suggest that another car was involved.'

'Well,' said Melissa, 'unless you can turn up some new facts, it doesn't look as if you're going to get anywhere.' She was disappointed. Nothing Bruce had told her seemed worth following up; he had a bee in his bonnet, that was all. She glanced at her watch. 'I'm afraid I have to be getting home. I've got someone coming to supper tonight and I'm planning to do some writing this afternoon.'

'New novel?'

'That's right.'

He helped her on with her coat and paid the bill. Outside, he said, 'Before you go, can I ask you one last question?'

'Of course.'

'As a crime writer used to devising mysteries, what are your feelings about this one?'

'To be honest, I don't think there's much mystery about it. One way or the other, Babs had had enough of Clive and chose that way of getting shot of him.'

'She could have just told him to naff off.'

'And he could have refused to go. Doing a bunk might have been the only way of getting him off her back. You said he was obsessed with her, she described him as a pain in the ass. Maybe she decided she couldn't take him any more, prospects or no prospects. He might have been a bit unstable. Oh dear, I'm talking about him as if he were dead, aren't I?' The thought gave her goose-pimples.

'The way he is, he might just as well be,' said Bruce sombrely. 'Do you know how he's getting on?'

'I check the hospital from time to time. I'm hoping that eventually he'll be well enough for me to ask him some questions.'

'Do you think that's wise? After all he's been through I'd be inclined to let well alone.'

'Really? I was hoping you might . . .' His downcast expression reminded her of a dog deprived of its bone. Then a mischievous twinkle appeared in his eyes as he added, 'I'll bet Nathan Latimer wouldn't let well alone!'

Melissa laughed. 'Point taken! All right, I'll make a bargain with you. If you come up with anything fresh, let me know and I'll consider reopening the case.' She took out one of her cards and handed it to him with a gesture of mock formality.

'Thanks.' He put it carefully away in his wallet. 'Well, goodbye for now, Ms Craig.'

'Call me Melissa,' she said with a smile. She could almost hear his tail thumping as she turned away.

NINE

IT WAS HALF PAST ONE WHEN MELISSA GOT BACK TO her car. The drive home would take about twenty minutes, say another ten to unpack her shopping and stow it away. Iris was invited for seven o'clock, which meant she would have to start cooking at about half past five. Allowing for a short tea-break, she could fit in over three hours' work on her novel.

As she left the outskirts of the city and began the uphill climb towards the Cotswold escarpment, she was struck by an odd string of coincidences. A real corpse had once been discovered in the shepherd's hut where she was planning to plant her fictitious one. A character called Clive Shepherd had crossed her path. And now it was seriously suggested that a former employee of The Usual Place, which she intended to transform and make into a centre for some illicit operations that were not as yet quite clear in her head, was possibly a murder victim. It was curious how her imaginings kept finding echoes in fact.

It was at least a relief that the originator of the bizarre telephone calls had been identified, even if the reason for her being on the receiving end was still a mystery. She felt sympathy for Clive, by all accounts a worthwhile young man whose life had been shattered by his obsession with a girl who plainly cared nothing for him. At least he was beginning to show some improvement. If he should phone again she would address him by name, try to establish a relationship with him and explain, very gently, that Babs had moved away and he must try and forget her. Or perhaps it would be better if she went to the hospital and saw him. She could have a chat with his doctor or the matron and ask their advice. She might in some way be able to help his recovery.

As for the scenario Bruce had painted, she dismissed it as being utterly fantastic. On his own admission, he had nothing to go on—merely a gut feeling, his so-called hunch. Convinced that he was barking up the wrong tree, Melissa put the whole thing out of her mind and switched her thoughts to her new novel.

The sun was warm after the previous night's rain. Gardens, meadows, hedgerows and trees sparkled with a vibrant freshness. Soon, the woodlands would become a collage of almost uniform green but now, for these few magical weeks of spring, they were a tapestry of a dozen tender shades, delicately embroidered, embellishing but not yet completely veiling the perfect symmetry of their branches.

She wound the window down and a soft breeze ruffled her hair and flowed over her face. She felt alert and eager, her head tingled as if an electric current was passing through it. She recognised the symptoms. After many hours of painstaking preparation—sketching out the framework of a plot, shaping her characters, creating their background and identifying some areas of research—she was ready to go. Even before she turned off the main road and began the gentle, winding, two-mile descent that led, paradoxically, into Upper Benbury, the opening paragraphs were taking shape in her head:

The cloud came hurtling out of the west like some monstrous bird of prey, dragging a curtain of rain in its talons. Nathan Latimer stopped halfway up the field to watch it. The sight of its onward rush exhilarated him; his pulses took their beat from the elemental forces around him. Not until the valley bottom disappeared in the squall did it dawn on him that he stood directly in its path.

On the other side of the field, under some trees, was an old shepherd's hut. Nathan legged it across the rough grass as fast as he could, pursued by the wind and rain that had suddenly changed from performers in a spectacle into hunters seeking to devour him. A cloud of leaves, torn loose by the gale, whirled round his head and flew into his face before tumbling like dying birds into the stubble.

'Dying birds . . . I rather like that!' Melissa changed gear as the hill grew steeper. 'Builds up a nice creepy atmosphere before

Nathan trips over the body.' She hummed a tune as her thoughts flowed on, conjuring up a picture of the shepherd's hut.

The dilapidated stone structure, half its roof missing, had long been abandoned. The last incumbent had secured it with a padlock which was still intact but the top hinge had rusted away and the door swung crazily inward like a drunkard struggling to remain upright. With difficulty, Nathan scrambled through the opening, cursing as he struck his head on the low stone lintel. Baulked of its prey, the squall lashed at the hut as if in frustration, flinging water through the broken roof and shrieking in and out of cracks in the crumbling walls.

An approaching vehicle interrupted the flow. Melissa pulled into the hedge to make way for a brown van with 'Benbury Estate Farms' painted on its side. 'Now, where was I? Must get this bit right.' She let in the clutch and rolled slowly down the lane, her thoughts still on Nathan and his predicament. Any minute now . . .

It was a dismal place, the air dank and foul-smelling, the ground yielding soggily under his feet. The rain discovered yet another weak point in the roof and began dripping steadily down the back of his neck. He shifted his position and nearly fell over something lying against the wall, something firm but not hard, nor yet soft and yielding as a heap of hay or sacking might have been. His eyes had not adjusted to the gloom but he could just make out a dark shape. A dead animal, perhaps a sheep, that had somehow blundered into the hut but been unable to clamber out again the past the inward swinging door. Rotten luck on a poor beast, trapped there and starving to death. No wonder the place stank. He backed uneasily away. Accustomed and hardened as he was to the violence of the city, he had yet to come to terms with nature red in tooth and claw.

The rain was still pouring down. Nathan squinted through a gap in the wall and saw the edge of the cloud and beyond it, on the horizon, a brilliant band of blue and gold. In a few minutes the squall would pass. Just time for a cigarette. The flame of the match joined with the grey light filtering through the roof and enabled him to see clearly the object in the corner. It was not, after all, the body of an animal. Animals do not wear boots and trousers.

It would need editing, of course, but it was a start. She was nearly home, eager to get indoors and put it down on paper. She reached the point a short distance outside the village where the track swung away to the right. She always enjoyed the moment when, rounding a curve, she saw the valley open out ahead with the cottages, hers and Iris's, snuggling cosily at the foot of the bank.

There was nothing cosy about the setting on this occasion. Two police cars were parked outside Iris's cottage.

A small knot of people had gathered round the stile. Most of them were strangers to Melissa but one or two she remembered seeing around the village. Some of them were looking northwards along the valley to where, in the distance, groups of uniformed figures moved about, apparently searching the ground. Others were gaping at Iris, who was standing by her garden gate where a woman police officer seemed to be trying to reason with her. There was something unnatural and disturbing about Iris's appearance. She was rigid, her thin hands were locked together against her mouth and her eyes were wild, as if some hideous image was trapped inside them. She seemed to be taking no notice of the policewoman but was staring past her in the same direction as the onlookers. Her face was the colour of clay. Melissa hurried over to her.

'What in the world's going on?' she exclaimed.

At the sound of her voice, Iris unfroze as if a switch had been pressed. She reached out with both hands, her mouth twitching and her words coming in staccato jerks.

'Melissa! Oh, Melissa, I found it . . . I dug it up . . . oh, my God!' She doubled up and retched, noisily and uselessly. 'Nothing left to throw up!' she moaned, clawing at her stomach.

'Are you a friend of hers, madam?' asked the policewoman.

'I'm her next-door neighbour.'

'Could you see if you can calm her down? I've been trying to persuade her to let me take her indoors but I can't get her to move. Inspector Grieves will want to have a word with her presently.'

'I'll do what I can. Whatever's happened?'

'She's had a rather nasty shock,' said the policewoman. 'It seems she came across the remains of a body in the woods.'

'Good heavens, how horrible! Come on, Iris, what you need is a stiff drink.' Gently Melissa took her by the arm. 'We'll be in my house,' she called over her shoulder.

'Ghouls!' Iris muttered, glaring furiously at the bystanders as she allowed herself to be led away.

'Never mind them.' Melissa sat her down in the kitchen, fetched a shawl to wrap around her shoulders and poured out a good measure of brandy.

Iris surveyed the glass with suspicion. 'Don't normally touch that stuff,' she declared.

'This doesn't seem to be a normal day, so drink it up.' Melissa commanded. She put a box of cream crackers on the table. 'You'd better have one or two of these, your stomach must be pretty empty.'

After a momentary hesitation, Iris took several sips of the spirit and reached for a biscuit. It was an unexpected reversal of roles. So far during their short acquaintance she had been the dominant one yet here she was, doing what she was told like a frightened child.

There was an interval while Iris sipped and hiccupped and nibbled. After a few minutes her breathing settled down and colour returned to her face. She swallowed the last of her brandy and put down the glass. She had stopped trembling but her hands moved restlessly, clenching and unclenching as they lay on the table, then clawing at her face and tugging at the hair that stood out in springy disorder round her face.

'Oh, Jesus!' Her voice was a tremulous squeaky whisper. 'It was so awful, an arm, fingers, bits of bone with something beastly clinging to them . . . and the smell!'

Melissa slid an arm round her and patted her shoulder. Her own stomach stirred queasily as she pictured Iris disinterring a partly decomposed corpse. It was enough to make anyone throw up. The recollection that not ten minutes before she had blithely arranged for Nathan Latimer to make a similar discovery began sending shockwaves through her own system.

'I think I could do with a snort as well!' she declared. 'Do you want another?'

'Leaf-mould for the garden!' Iris wailed, holding out her glass. Tears ran down her cheeks and dribbled from her chin. 'That's all I wanted. Went out early. Got two bags . . . decided to have just one more . . . and I dug my shovel in deep . . .' Her face was awash, smeary with dirt and tears. Melissa tore a sheet from her kitchen roll and handed it over.

'Come on now, try and pull yourself together. The inspector will be here in a minute.'

Iris looked aghast. 'Have I got to talk to the police?' Mechanically, she wiped her eyes, scrubbed at her cheeks and blew her nose. She examined her hands, still grimy with leaf-mould.

'I'm afraid so,' said Melissa, 'but don't worry, it'll only be a formality. He'll simply want to know what you were doing there and what time it was and so on. The policewoman will be there too.'

As she spoke, there was a knock at the door.

Iris clutched at Melissa's arm. 'You'll stay with me?' she begged.

'If I'm allowed to.'

'Shan't tell him anything unless he lets you stay,' Iris insisted. 'Haven't done anything wrong. Want a witness.' At least she was beginning to sound more like herself.

'Don't worry. You go and wash your face,' ordered Melissa as she went to open the door.

Before the inspector had a chance to put his first question to a nervous-looking Iris, the telephone rang.

'I'll take it upstairs,' said Melissa, avoiding her neighbour's imploring eye.

'Melissa? Bruce Ingram,' said the voice at the other end. 'I hear there's been a bit of excitement in Upper Benbury!'

Melissa was taken aback. She had, of course, expected the press to be on to it before long but not quite so soon as this. 'You're quick off the mark,' she said, trying not to sound hostile. 'Surely it wasn't mentioned at today's police briefing . . . there hasn't been time.'

'Aha, you know your procedure!' He sounded impressed. 'No, I just happened to be at the police station checking on something else when the call came through.'

'Well, it's no use talking to me. You'll have to get your story somewhere else.'

'I'm not after a story.'

'Oh, pull the other one! A journalist is always after a story.'

'No kidding. Upper Benbury isn't on my patch.'

'Then what do you want?'

'Can anyone overhear us?'

'Shouldn't think so. I'm upstairs and a police inspector is in the room below talking to her-who-found-the-body. I gather she dug it up along with leaf-mould for her garden.'

'You know what I'm thinking, don't you?'

'No . . . what?'

'Bet you money that's Babs's body your friend just dug up!' His excitement sizzled along the wire. 'It may take a while to identify, of course . . .'

'Oh, no!' Melissa remembered her rash promise, given only an hour or so ago, and her heart sank. 'Whatever makes you think that?'

'I've got a very strong hunch . . .'

'You seem to get rather a lot of hunches.'

'And they're usually right. This'll give us a start on the Bill. When can we meet to plan our strategy?'

'Our . . . now wait a minute . . .' It was one thing to solve the puzzle of some freak telephone calls. Getting involved in murder was something Melissa preferred to confine to the pages of her novels. 'You're not going to drag me into this,' she insisted.

'You did say, if I came up with anything fresh . . .' he reminded her.

'There's absolutely nothing whatever to connect this body with Babs. We don't know yet if it's a man or a woman, and even if it is a woman . . .'

'It is Babs!' he insisted, 'I told you, I have . . .'

'I know . . . a hunch,' Melissa finished for him. 'Well you follow your hunch and leave me to get on with my novel.' It was all getting too involved, there were too many real coincidences without Bruce inventing any more. 'Please, leave me out of it!' she begged.

But Bruce was relentless, his tenacity wrapped in persuasive charm. 'Oh, come on, think of the edge it'll give you on the competition to do a bit of real-life sleuthing. Many crime novelists would give their right arms for an opportunity like this!'

Melissa gave a resigned sigh. 'I'd be glad if you'd keep the bit about crime novelists to yourself,' she pleaded. 'It's gone round the village as it is and I'd rather it didn't go any further.'

Bruce chuckled. 'No interviews given, I take the point. Besides, the last thing we want at the moment is media attention. When we've cracked the case you'll be glad of the publicity. Think of the boost to your sales!'

Melissa rolled her eyes to the ceiling. All this talk of cracking the case was too absurd. She was an author, not a private eye.

Still, he had a point about the publicity. She could picture the gleam in Joe's eye when he heard about it. It would probably be a wild-goose chase but it might just lead to something.

'Exactly what do you have in mind?' she asked cautiously.

'My plan's a bit vague at the moment, but I'm working on it. I'll get back to you as soon as I've figured out the details. I just wanted to be sure I could count on your cooperation.'

Melissa became alarmed, 'Look,' she said nervously, 'I'm not promising anything . . .'

'Okay, understood, I'll be in touch. Bye!'

The Rector arrived just as the police were leaving. He came by the footpath, scrambling over the stile and breaking into a shambling trot towards the cottages. It was plain from his demeanour that the news had reached him and Melissa greeted him with relief, certain that Iris would find his presence reassuring.

'Miss Ash is with me, do come in!' she said.

'Thank you!' he puffed.

She guessed he had run much of the way. His pale hair hung in wisps, his shoes were muddy and the bottoms of his trousers were damp and stained. His normally pink cheeks were the colour of clotted cream, his eyes were dilated and the crevices beneath them glistened with sweat.

'I've just had the news from Mrs Foster at the shop. This is terrible, terrible!' His hand shook as he mopped his face with a handkerchief. 'What a dreadful thing to happen in our village!' he moaned. 'Who would have dreamed . . .'

His demeanour was not, Melissa felt, very impressive. She was disappointed in him; it was almost as if he was looking for strength and support from her instead of bringing it to an afflicted member of his flock.

'Miss Ash found the body and she is very distressed,' she told him, a trifle severely. 'I hope you will do your best to comfort her. I've done what I could but as a comparative stranger . . .'

'Yes, yes, of course.' He put away the handkerchief and followed Melissa into the sitting-room. Iris had not moved since the police had finished taking her statement. Binkie, who had adopted Hawthorn Cottage as his second home and slipped in through the open door when they left, lay asleep on her lap. She sat with her head bent over him, cradling him with her arms like a child clinging for solace to a favourite doll. When Mr Calloway entered she managed, for the first time, the ghost of a smile.

'Oh, Rector! Good of you to come!' she faltered.

Melissa withdrew, murmuring something about tea. There was yet another knock before she reached the kitchen. It was Mrs Calloway, also in search of Iris.

'She's here,' said Melissa for what seemed the hundredth time that day. 'Your husband's with her. I'm just going to make tea; would you care for a cup?'

Ignoring the question, Mrs Calloway brushed past her and rushed into the sitting-room. 'My dear Miss Ash!' Compassion softened the edges of the normally shrill and strident voice. 'What a dreadful shock you must have had! Oh, you poor, poor dear!' She crouched down, her glasses skating perilously close to the tip of her nose, and slid an arm round Iris's shoulders. 'I've been in town shopping . . . I had no idea . . . Mrs Foster told me when I went in to pick up the bread. I came at once . . . there, there, it's all right, here's a clean hanky if you need it . . .'

'Got one, thanks,' snapped Iris, displaying the sodden piece of kitchen paper that Melissa had supplied.

Mrs Calloway returned her handkerchief to the pocket of her shapeless woollen car coat, showing no sign of offence at this ungracious rebuff. She gave the unresponsive Iris a motherly squeeze.

'You must come and stay with us tonight, mustn't she, Henry?' She looked to her husband for an endorsement of the invitation. He jumped as if he had been miles away.

'Eh? Oh, yes . . . yes, of course, if she'd like to,' he agreed.

'We've got plenty of room and you simply mustn't be alone after that dreadful experience,' insisted Mrs Calloway.

Iris wriggled free of the encircling arm, dislodging an indignant Binkie in the process. 'Quite all right in my own place,' she muttered with an obstinate lift of her chin. 'Having supper with Melissa, thanks all the same.' The last words came with a certain amount of effort. She might be the Rector's devoted slave but even in her affliction she was not prepared to accept favours from his wife.

'But you can't possibly sleep alone in the house!'

Iris gave a disdainful sniff. All this solicitude from a woman she disliked seemed to be doing more to restore her to normal than the Rector's inadequate efforts at consolation. Melissa found herself feeling sorry for Mrs Calloway, in whose unpromising bosom

there obviously lay a rich vein of Christian charity. She wished
Iris would show some appreciation of the woman's genuine wish
to be kind. But Iris would have none of it.

'Not scared. Got Binkie. Not afraid of ghosts if that's what you
mean,' she asserted.

'I really do think . . .' Mrs Calloway put a hand on Iris's arm,
making one last appeal in the face of defeat. 'You'd be much
better at the Rectory, just for tonight.' She turned her large brown
eyes, which were easily her best feature, on her husband. 'You
talk to her, Henry!'

The Rector put a finger inside his dog-collar and waggled it.
'Ermm . . . well, my dear, Miss Ash knows her own feelings
best,' he said feebly.

The brown eyes, which had been shining with sympathy, glazed
over. It was plain that Mrs Calloway did not enjoy being thwarted.
She had come to the house to do a kindness and had got neither
thanks from the ungrateful recipient nor support from her husband. She glared up at him for a moment and then rose to her feet.
As she did so, her gaze fell on his stained shoes and trousers.

'What on earth possessed you to go trampling through the
woods after all that rain?' she scolded him. 'We'd better go
home at once so that I can clean the mud off your clothes. It's
plain we're not wanted here!'

'It was very good of you to call,' said Melissa as she let
them out. 'I'll keep an eye on her. I'm sure she doesn't mean
to be ungrateful but she's still a bit shocked, you know,' she
added, aware that it must seem a little presumptuous for her
to be apologising for Iris, whom she met only ten days ago, to
people who had known her for years.

Mrs Calloway was quick to put her in her place. 'Of course,
she's *always* been difficult!' she snapped, with a jerk of the head
towards the sitting-room.

Thankfully, Melissa closed the door behind them and went to
make the tea. Her next task would be to prepare Iris for the arrival
of the press.

TEN

NEXT MORNING, MELISSA WOKE EARLY, BREWED A pot of tea and went straight to her study to work on *The Shepherd's Hut*. She had the capacity to draft chunks of text in her head and to recall them without difficulty up to twenty-four hours later, sometimes longer. All she had to do was to sit at her machine and give her whole attention to what she was writing.

It began well. In half an hour the opening to the first chapter, the few paragraphs that she had composed on the drive home from Gloucester, were on paper. Now the story had to move on. She closed her eyes and projected her imagination into the darkened hut, breathing the foetid air and peering down at the shape in the corner. She conjured up the howl of the wind and the creak and grown of the overhanging trees as her hero became aware of what was lying on the ground.

Normally, she had no difficulty when working in shutting her mind to reality but this morning it was to reality that she turned for inspiration. Yesterday she had listened to Iris, still shaken but rational and coherent, repeating the story she had told the police. Now, hunched over her desk with her hands covering her eyes, she created moving images of Iris in her head: marching off down the valley, light of heart with her plastic sacks and her shovel; plunging into the wood where she had recently spotted a deep hollow beneath an uprooted tree, full of rich, crumbling compost; contentedly filling her sacks, humming to herself as she worked, the way Melissa had heard her while pottering in her garden; pausing for a rest while she listened to the peaceful woodland noises, then making one final thrust and finding *that* dangling obscenely in front of her. She had stood petrified as the nature of her discovery blasted her mind, then flung away her shovel and fled for home.

Melissa asked herself if a man of the calibre of her detective, Nathan Latimer, would experience a similar reaction. He would certainly not run away but he might, in those chilling circumstances and if her writing was vivid enough, feel a sense of revulsion and possibly shock. She bent over her typewriter, totally absorbed in her task. The milkman and the postman came and went unheeded; now and again the telephone rang but the sound merely bounced off the edges of her awareness.

After a couple of hours of intensive effort she sat back, exhausted but with a sense of achievement. She got up and moved about, flexing her arms, her fingers, her spine. She became aware of the sounds of car engines and banging doors and went to the window. The reporters had begun to arrive. She stood for a while watching the straggling group of men and women picking their way along the footpath, floundering at times on the uneven turf, cameras and notebooks at the ready.

The police would still be at the scene; there had probably been an overnight guard on the spot where the body was found. No doubt they were still hunting for clues, possibly digging for remains missed in the previous day's search. Meanwhile, in some cold laboratory smelling of disinfectant and decay, the pathologist would be continuing the work of trying to establish the identity of the victim and the cause and time of death so that the police could begin tracking down the killer.

Melissa began playing with Bruce's theory and considering its implications. If, as he maintained, the body was Babs's, how had it come to this place? Had she been brought here dead or alive? Why had the killer chosen Benbury Woods to hide the body? Was he—it must surely be a he—someone local? A cold hand seemed to brush her spine as she imagined the girl's remains lying for ten long months under layer upon layer of woodland detritus, part of the long, slow process of disintegration, decomposition and absorption into the soil. Earth returning to earth, leaving only a few bones and sickening shreds of what had once been warm living flesh.

It being Saturday morning, some local children came to watch the excitement. Such a thing had never happened in the village since the death of old Daniel, who was to them no more than a legend from a time long past. This was real, it was going to be in the papers and on the radio, perhaps even on the telly. They stood around in little knots, staring and giggling. A herd of cows wandered down the hill and hung their heads over a stone wall to see what was going on.

Melissa wondered how Iris was feeling this morning. The previous evening she had demonstrated an astonishing resilience. Oddly enough, she had shown more concern for her beloved Rector than for herself. 'Sensitive man,' she said more than once. 'Dreadfully upset by all this. And *she*'s no comfort to him.' The prospect of being interviewed by reporters had intrigued rather than alarmed her. She had eaten with relish the supper that Melissa had eventually found time to prepare, sunk a good two-thirds of a bottle of red wine and tottered home around midnight, insisting that she was perfectly all right, thank you, in response to the offer of a bed at Hawthorn Cottage.

As Melissa watched, Iris appeared in her garden. She had abandoned her tent-like pinafore dress and skinny jersey for a quite reasonable looking shirt and a well pressed pair of slacks. Her short, straight hair was smoothly brushed and carefully parted. She began poking a hoe at non-existent weeds in her onion-bed, from where she could keep an eye on the comings and goings down the valley. Presently the reporters began trickling back; they pounced on Iris and plied her with questions. Melissa, keeping well out of sight, watched in amusement as the photographers took their pictures: Iris standing at her front door, Iris leaning on her hoe, Iris pointing down the valley to show where she had made what would no doubt be described in the rubrics as her gruesome discovery. A TV crew appeared with video camera and microphone and she went through it all over again. She appeared to be thoroughly enjoying it.

At about six o'clock, Joe rang.

'I've just been watching the news on the box,' he said. 'How come you've let your neighbour hog all the limelight?'

'Joe, you are disgusting,' she retorted. 'Anyone would think it was entertainment.'

'That's how the media treat it, and that's how the Great Unwashed like to think of it. Shock-horror-gloat, they go. And if you'd been there getting in on the act, think of the effect on sales!'

'Think of the effect on my privacy!' retorted Melissa. 'I'm trying to write a novel, or had you forgotten?'

'But of course not. That's one of the things I'm phoning about. How soon can you let me have it?'

'Good heavens, I've only done a first draft of chapter one. Christmas at the earliest.'

'Oh, come on, you can do better than that. Let's say the end of September. We'll dream up a good blurb for the jacket: 'This novel was conceived and written while a real-life murder hunt was taking place on the author's doorstep.' With any luck identification will take a while and the killer won't be tracked down for ages. Your publishers will be happy to slot your book in ahead of schedule on the grounds of topicality. What do you say?'

'I say you are a heartless, hard-nosed, slave-driving opportunist!'

'I love it when you talk dirty!' Joe growled. 'Let's see now. Five months and a bit at a thousand words a day leaves you plenty of time for editing and research. Piece of cake for a writer of your competence and experience.'

'Stop flanneling,' said Melissa. 'I'll do it in my own time, thank you very much, and if you lean on me too hard I'll give up crime and start writing for the parish magazine. Ten per cent of my share of twenty-five pence a copy a month will just about buy a lemon for your gin and tonic. So there!' She banged down the receiver, imaging with glee Joe's frustration at not having the last word. She had let him set the pace for far too long.

Bruce rang a few minutes later.

'Is the coast clear?' he asked.

'Clear of what?'

'My fellow newshounds. I'm anxious not to be associated with the "Grisly Find in Picturesque Woodland" story.'

'Is that what they're calling it?'

'Haven't you seen this evening's *Gazette*?'

'I have not. I've spent the entire day working. What does it say?'

'The police have issued a brief statement. Preliminary examination of the remains indicate that they are of a young woman and that she has been dead for some considerable time. What did I tell you?'

'It'll be some time before there's any positive ID. There may have been other girls gone missing in the last few months . . .' She knew that her voice lacked conviction even before Bruce pounced.

'You don't really believe that . . . and you did agree to help.'

'I never promised,' she said feebly.

'Please! Think of it as research.' Bruce was beginning to reveal considerable powers of persuasion.

Melissa heaved a sigh. 'Tell me what you have in mind, then.'

'You really want to know?'

'You'll give me no peace until I let you tell me. Do you want to come round for a drink?'

'Be with you in twenty minutes.'

He was at the door in eighteen. Seeing his sharp outfit of dark blue shirt and light blue designer slacks with a matching jacket slung over one shoulder, Melissa was glad that she had put on some make-up and changed out of the elderly tracksuit that was her normal working garb into something more flattering.

'You know,' he said as he followed her into the sitting-room, 'you are not at all like the usual run of women crimewriters.'

'No? How many have you met?'

He grinned. 'Actually, you're the first. I think I've based my conception on portraits of Dame Agatha. She always seemed to look forbidding and faintly sinister.'

'I've always thought she was a fine-looking woman.'

'I think you are,' he said softly. 'But much more feminine.'

'Thank you,' she replied drily. It would not do to encourage this line of approach. 'What can I get you to drink? I've got the usual things.'

'Perhaps we could leave the drink for later. What I'd like to do before it gets dark is visit the scene of the crime.'

'I'm not exactly sure where it is. I've never been to that part of the wood.'

'You mean you didn't join the merry throng of sightseers? I pictured you up front, notebook in hand, soaking up the atmosphere and recording everything for a future bestseller!'

Melissa poked out her tongue at him and the laughter lines at the corners of his eyes deepened in response. It was good to relax after a day of intensive effort and Bruce's combination of youthful enthusiasm and mature assurance was both stimulating and restful.

'I've been keeping out of the way while the press were swarming about,' she told him. 'Anyway, what are you expecting to see? The police will have been over every inch of the ground with a toothcomb so there won't be so much as a trouser-button left lying about.'

'I know that, I'm not looking for clues. I just want to figure out the lie of the land. Presumably it's some way from the road?'

'I told you, I've really no idea.'

'Then let's go and see for ourselves. A walk in the fresh air'll do you good after a day at your desk.'

'That's true. Well, if you insist, I know the way roughly from what Iris told me and there should be plenty of tracks to follow. It's probably muddy,' she added, eyeing his spotless clothes. 'You'll get your trousers stained if you're not careful.'

'Don't worry, I'll tuck 'em into my socks,' said Bruce cheerfully and did so. 'There! What about asking Iris to come along and show us the way?'

'I doubt if she'd agree. She's had a nasty jolt and I think she'll be avoiding that part of the wood for quite a while. The Rector could tell us though. I suspect he went to look even before coming to see Iris.' Involuntarily, she smiled at the memory of Mr Calloway's sheepish expression as his wife scolded him for getting his clothes muddy. 'He might even enjoy the chance to do a bit of sleuthing. He's one of my most faithful readers!'

'Let's invite him, then! As long as he can keep a secret. We don't want it to get around that we're poking our noses in.'

'He can keep a secret all right. Even his wife doesn't know of his addiction to crime fiction, or so he thinks. She's quite a battle-axe . . . she'd never allow him to come yomping through the woods with us on a Saturday evening.'

'Oh, well, it was just a thought. Shall we go?'

Melissa put on old shoes and an anorak and they set off down the well-trodden path. There was no sign of Iris; she was probably eating her supper. Thoughts of food reminded Melissa that she had existed all day on tea, fruit and sandwiches. Mentally, she ran through the contents of her freezer and decided she could easily rustle up a meal for two when they got back. If Bruce hadn't already eaten, of course. If he had, he could sit and watch while she had hers, or go home.

They trudged along in single file until they reached Daniel's hut. Here the path divided, one track swinging off to the right and climbing into the woods behind the church.

'It looks as if we go straight on,' said Melissa. The damp grass ahead had been trampled and muddy patches churned up by scores of feet. They walked on in silence. A short distance ahead the trees, which had so far been confined to the upper slopes of the valley, suddenly closed in on them. A wide track, waterlogged in places and deeply rutted, ran down the hill from the right, crossed their path and plunged into dense woodland a few yards further on. A mist of bluebells drifted among the undergrowth; birds darted to and fro.

'Lovely spot,' commented Bruce. 'Now, which way do we go?'

'Left, I think.'

They picked their way along the edge of the track, trying to avoid the worst of the mud. There was a mossy dampness in the air and the sound of their voices echoed softly among the trees.

'Who owns the land round here?' asked Bruce.

'There's an outfit called Benbury Estates that owns thousands of acres and several farms. I believe these woods are part of Rookery Farm. I'm told that one of their sidelines is raising pheasants and letting out their land to shooting parties in the season.'

As she spoke, they came to a junction with a second track.

'We must be nearly there.' Melissa pointed to where the ground was criss-crossed with heavy tyre-marks. 'Those were made by a tractor but it looks as if a four-wheeler was parked here, probably a police Land Rover.'

Bruce's mouth crimped and he gave a nod of approval. 'Nathan Latimer, ace detective, swings into action!'

'Shut up!' She gave his arm a thump. They stood still for a moment, following with their eyes the line of trampled undergrowth running in among the trees. The sky had become overcast and the light filtering through the leaves was a cheerless grey. Bruce put on his jacket against the chilly breeze and Melissa huddled into her anorak. Then she saw it.

'There!' she whispered, pointing to where a fallen tree lay in a tangle of brambles. The mighty root system reared and yawned before them like the mouth of a cavern. All around were signs of massive disturbance; the police search had been thorough. Melissa moved forward but Bruce put a hand on her arm.

'There's someone there—look!' he whispered, pointing at a man in dark clothes near the uprooted tree. He was hatless, standing with his head bent and his hands clasped in front of him.

'It's the Rector!' said Melissa in surprise. 'Whatever is he doing?'

'Saying a prayer for the soul of the departed, by the looks of it,' murmured Bruce. 'A nice thought.'

Melissa gave him a keen glance, suspecting him of facetiousness, but he appeared genuinely moved.

'The poor man's been dreadfully upset by all this,' she said. 'Almost as shocked as if he'd found the body himself.'

'It's a nasty thing to happen in one's back yard,' Bruce murmured reflectively.

Melissa nodded. 'He loves to walk in these woods. This affair will haunt him every time he comes this way.'

They had been speaking in low voices and the man ahead gave no sign of having heard. For a moment or two they hesitated. Overhead, the trees rustled and birds fluttered and chirped among the branches. The call of a cuckoo sounded, foolish and faintly irreverent. Then Mr Calloway looked up and saw the two watchers.

He appeared startled for a moment, then picked his way towards them. In the subdued light his face had a sickly pallor and the corners of his mouth were turned down as if under the weight of the sagging cheeks. He looked utterly miserable.

'Ah, Mrs Craig,' he said in a husky voice. 'A dreadful business, quite dreadful!'

'Terrible!' agreed Melissa. 'This is Mr Ingram,' she added in response to an enquiring glance. 'Our Rector, Mr Calloway.'

The men shook hands.

'I think we've met before, haven't we, sir?' said Bruce.

The Rector looked at him with mournful eyes, shaking his head. 'Not that I remember but I'm a little confused at the moment. The shock, you know. That poor creature!' he went on, half-turning towards the spot where earth and decaying leaves lay in heaps. 'Lying there all that time, all alone!'

'At least she'll have a decent burial once the autopsy is over,' said Bruce. He spoke diffidently, as if it was presumption on his part to offer comfort to one whose job it was to minister to others. His words seemed to have the opposite effect for the Rector's distress deepened visibly.

'So it was a woman? Oh dear, oh dear!' For some reason this seemed to make matters so much worse. 'Have they . . . do they know who it . . . she . . . was?'

'Not so far as I know,' said Bruce. 'But according to this evening's *Gazette*, it was definitely a woman's body.'

'Poor soul!' The Rector took out a handkerchief and wiped his nose. The wind began to blow more strongly, tossing aside the treetops and revealing hurrying masses of dark cloud.

'Better not hang around, sir, it's going to chuck it down in a minute,' said Bruce.

The Rector gave a faint smile as if the younger man's deference pleased him. 'That's all right, my boy. Don't worry about me.'

After a moment's hesitation, Bruce tucked a hand under Melissa's arm and led her back the way they had come.

ELEVEN

THE WIND WAS AGAINST THEM AS THEY HURRIED back, casting anxious glances at the sky. The rain began just as they were scrambling over the stile and a few seconds after they got indoors it was falling in sheets.

'What about that drink you offered me?' said Bruce, helping Melissa off with her jacket.

She led the way into the kitchen and showed him where the bottles were kept. 'Help yourself. There's ice and lemon in the fridge. I'm going to get some food, I'm absolutely ravenous. Have you eaten this evening?'

'Yes, but I can always find room for more. My mother says I'm a bottomless pit!'

'You live at home?'

'No, I share a house in Barnwood with a couple of friends. My parents live in Upton so I see them quite often. What shall I pour for you?'

'Gin and tonic, please.' She was rummaging in the freezer. 'Do you fancy spaghetti bolognese?'

'Try me!' He poured the drinks, passed one to her and perched on a stool while she put the sauce to thaw in the microwave and boiled water for the spaghetti. 'I see you're into wholewheat pasta!' he said with evident approval.

'That's Iris's influence.'

'Your neighbour, the one who found Babs's body?'

Melissa nodded, pushing spaghetti into the saucepan and eyeing him through the steam. 'You're still sticking to your theory that it is Babs?'

He nodded emphatically over the rim of his glass.

'But why take her body to Benbury Woods? It's a long way from her usual haunts, from what you've told me.'

'As a crime novelist, surely you'll agree that dumping a body miles from the scene of the crime is par for the course nowadays. Confuses the fuzz, keeps the reader guessing, et cetera et cetera. Isn't it the same in real life?'

'True. Perhaps the killer is familiar with the area and knew of that particular spot, knew that there was that really deep hollow where it was unlikely that anyone would find the body if it was properly covered up.'

'Familiar with the area, or actually living nearby. By the way, have you got an Ordnance map?'

'I've got a footpath map, if that's any good.'

'Even better.'

She fetched it from the sitting-room. 'I haven't put it to much use yet, I'm afraid.'

Bruce spread the map on the kitchen table and Melissa pointed with the handle of her wooden spoon. 'Here are our cottages, here's the path leading to the church past Daniel's hut, and here . . .' the spoon traced a hesitant line towards a patch of green speckled with minuscule toytown trees '. . . here is where we met that muddy track. We went this way.'

Bruce jabbed at the map with a forefinger. 'That's where the body was found, just by this junction with the second track. It must have been taken there in some sort of vehicle. Let's see where the tracks lead.' There was a brief silence while a finger moved in one direction and a wooden spoon-handle in the other. They converged on Rookery Farm. Neither track gave access to a public road, but a third led from the farm to a lane leading into Lower Benbury.

'Aha!' said Bruce. 'That's interesting.'

'It explains one thing,' said Melissa. 'I wondered why there were no police vehicles outside this place today, but of course they must have been given permission to use the private roads and tracks. The hoi polloi had to park here and make their way to the scene of the crime on foot.'

Bruce pretended to take offence. ' "Hoi polloi" is no way to refer to the honourable members of the Fourth Estate!'

Melissa pulled a face at him and went to test the spaghetti.

'It also explains how easy it would have been to transport the body to where it was found,' he went on. 'Tractor or Land Rover

as far as this junction and then it's only a matter of a few yards
to the burial spot. And no one would have taken any notice of
the tyre-marks because vehicles would be passing that way all the
time on estate business.'

'But wouldn't there be a risk that the people at the farm would
spot them?'

'Suppose it *was* the people at the farm? How much do you
know about these Benbury Estates people?'

'Not much. Remember, I've only lived here a couple of weeks.
I believe the owners live in a big house called Benbury Park. Iris
has been my main source of information so far and I gather from
her that they keep their distance from the village folk. I did
meet someone from Rookery Farm a few days ago,' she added,
remembering her unnerving encounter with Dick Woodman. 'As
a matter of fact, I've just killed him off!' She made a menacing
pass with her wooden spoon.

'Another case for Nathan Latimer?' Bruce grinned, then grew
serious again. 'Who was this chap?'

'A young man, quite pleasant-looking once I'd got over the
shock.' She gave a brief account of the episode in Daniel's hut.

Bruce listened with close attention. 'Would you say he was of
the landed gentry class?'

'He spoke with a local accent . . . he could have been the farm
owner, or possibly the manager.'

'Barbour jacket and green wellies with straps?'

Melissa thought for a moment. 'He was wearing a waxie,
yes, but it was a working garment, not the kind the yuppies
go for. And heavy boots, the sort you'd wear round a farm.
He had a dog with him. Now I come to think of it, he'd probably been checking the sheep. The wholesome, outdoor type—
I can't somehow picture him consorting with the likes of Babs
Carter.'

'We can't eliminate anyone at this stage. Suppose he'd been
sneaking off to The Usual Place on a Friday night and going back
to her flat? Suppose she found out he was married and started
blackmailing him? Suppose . . .'

'He spends Friday evenings at the Woolpack playing skittles
along with practically the whole village,' Melissa pointed out.
'And he didn't strike me as being a very lucrative prospect for
a blackmailer. I think we can safely eliminate him from our list
of suspects.'

Bruce shook his head reproachfully. 'I'm surprised at you,' he said. 'I thought it was often the least likely suspect who turns out to be the villain.'

'In detective novels, yes,' agreed Melissa. 'Not so often in real life.' She had been studying the map as she spoke. 'Look, there's another track branching off the one where the body was found.'

Bruce looked over her shoulder as she traced it. It led directly to Benbury Park. 'Hmm . . .' he murmured. 'I wonder . . .'

Melissa began serving the spaghetti. 'I can't think any more until I've eaten,' she said. 'There's a bottle of Chianti in the cupboard and you'll find a corkscrew in that drawer.'

They ate and drank for a time in silence before Melissa asked, 'So what's this devious plan you have up your sleeve?'

Bruce looked pained. 'Devious? Me?'

'You as good as admitted on the phone that you were hatching some scheme and unless I'm mistaken, you've got a part lined up for me, so let's have it!'

Bruce laid down his fork and picked up his glass. His eyes twinkled with mischief.

'I thought,' he said, after swallowing a mouthful of wine, 'you might like to have a facial and get your hair done. Oh, and maybe a manicure and a body massage. And then you could go and sign on at the Up Front Model Agency!'

A forkful of spaghetti fell on to Melissa's plate.

'You've got a nerve!' she spluttered. 'Why would I want to do that?'

'Second career!' Bruce grinned, then grew serious. 'Let me explain. I've been racking my brains as to a possible motive for killing Babs. There's the straightforward sex angle—she picks up a pervert or some other nasty character by mistake—but from what I know so far it doesn't seem very likely. The police spoke to one or two of the girls at the club and they said she had a few regular favourites among the audience at the strip shows and if anyone she didn't fancy made a pass at her they soon got put down.'

'You mean she did it for love as well as the money?'

'More or less.'

'Did the police interview any of her regulars?'

'Not that I know of. It wasn't a full-scale enquiry, remember . . . no crime had been reported and such evidence as there was suggested her disappearance was voluntary.'

'Which you don't accept?'

'Right.'

'Go on, then.'

'I've already mentioned blackmail. Suppose she got to know her regulars well enough to be able to threaten to tell their wives?'

'Suppose she did? I can't see how it would help for me to get my picture in an advertisement for frozen food.'

'I'm coming to that . . . but I'm sure they'd find something more glamorous than fish fingers for you to promote.'

'You're too kind.'

'Not at all. I can see you looking sultry and seductive over a bottle of exotic liqueur at the very least . . . or wallowing in a bubble bath!'

'Do stop playing the fool and get to the point.'

'Right. My third possibility is altogether more serious. Suppose Babs had somehow stumbled on some kind of racket, either at the agency or at the beauty salon?'

'What beauty salon?'

'Oh, didn't I tell you? She had a flat—or rather, a bed-sitter—over a beauty salon in Gloucester.'

'No, you didn't but . . . what sort of a racket are you thinking of?'

'One of my contacts was telling me a couple of days ago that the Drugs Squad are convinced there's a big organisation somewhere in the county, bringing in everything from hash to heroin. Now and again they pick up small fry but so far the big boys have kept their tracks covered. The problem's particularly bad in the city.'

'It's a big problem everywhere,' Melissa agreed thoughtfully, remembering one of Simon's friends at Oxford, a brilliant scholar who had died of an accidental overdose. Any contribution, however small, towards controlling the menace would be worthwhile.

'Just suppose, for example,' Bruce went on, 'that either the agency or the beauty salon was being used as a centre for drug distribution—both, even—and that Babs somehow tumbled to it. Suppose she'd threatened to blow the whistle or demanded a cut . . . and someone decided she was too dangerous to stay alive . . . does that sound feasible?' He scanned her face with what she had come to think of as his eager terrier expression.

'It's feasible, of course, but . . .'

'So will you do it?'

'Do what?'

'Suss out the salon and . . .'

'Now, wait a minute.' It suddenly dawned on Melissa that his earlier suggestion, which she had dismissed as a flippant irrelevance, had been made in earnest. 'Do you seriously expect me to go snooping round some scruffy little back-street hairdresser and then make a fool of myself trying to con a blasé young photographer into using me as a model? I've got better things to do with my time.'

'Then you won't help?'

Melissa got up and began clearing away the dishes. 'You haven't given me one concrete reason for believing that anything sinister is going on. All you can offer is hunches.' She came to her decision. 'No, nothing doing.'

Bruce put down his glass and stood up. 'Forgive me for having wasted your time. Just forget the whole thing. Thank you for a delicious supper,' he added stiffly. He looked snubbed, young and vulnerable.

'I didn't mean to sound ratty,' she said more gently. 'Things have been quite fraught lately. I came down here hoping for a quiet life where I can work in peace and the minute I arrive all hell's let loose—weird phone calls, bodies being dug up, reporters and police swarming all over the place . . . and now you're trying to get me to join in a wild-goose chase after a drugs gang. It's all a bit much!'

His smile of apology was disarming but behind it was a hint of sadness.

'I'm sorry. I do get carried away, I know. But suddenly it seemed to hit me . . . what could lie behind Babs's disappearance. She was no angel, God knows, but she was a pretty little thing and she didn't deserve to die . . .'

'You don't know for certain that she did die,' Melissa pointed out wearily.

'All right, you win.' Dejectedly, he began putting on his jacket. He was no longer an eager terrier; almost, she thought, she could see his ears droop. She felt herself relenting.

'Give me a day or two to think about it,' she said. 'I've been up since the crack of dawn . . . and I'm too tired to think straight.'

Bruce glanced at his watch and whistled. 'And now it's ten o'clock! You must be shattered. I'm so sorry, I'll go at once. I'll give you a call tomorrow or the day after . . . and thanks once more for the supper, it was really delicious.' His spirits had risen visibly. With his swift changes of mood, he reminded her of Simon.

'You're welcome,' she said, meaning it.

At the door she held out her hand and to her surprise he raised it to his lips.

'It's been a privilege to spend the evening with you,' he said.

'I've enjoyed it,' she replied sincerely.

He got into his car and she switched on the outside light so that he could see to turn round. As he drove slowly away, one hand waving from the rolled-down driver's window, another car appeared, bumping hesitantly along the track. It pulled up at her door, the engine and the headlights were switched off, and Aubrey got out.

He rushed at her, enfolding her in a huge and clumsy embrace.

'Oh, my darling girl, thank God you're all right!' He was breathing heavily and his mouth was not at its freshest.

'Whatever do you mean? Of course I'm all right.' She did her best not to sound cross. 'Why didn't you phone?'

Aubrey waved his large hands in agitation. 'But I did . . . several times. There was no reply and I was nearly out of my mind with worry.'

'Ah, yes, I did hear it once or twice but I was working and I couldn't be bothered to answer. You'd better come in.' Once inside he grabbed her and kissed her again, greedily. His chin was bristly. Melissa disengaged and led the way into the kitchen.

'I can't think why you had to get in such a state. People don't sit by their phones all day, you know.' She filled the kettle and switched it on. 'I was just going to get ready for bed. Do you want some tea?' The mention of bed was a mistake. She knew from experience that the gleam in Aubrey's eye was not inspired by the prospect of tea. Oh no! she thought, not tonight.

'I thought of you, caught up in all this dreadful business with no one to look after you,' he said, with genuine concern. 'As soon as I heard "Upper Benbury" on the news I thought to myself, my darling girl needs me, I must go to her!'

'That was very nice and thoughtful of you,' said Melissa, telling herself that she was extremely fortunate to be the object of so much consideration. 'But I'm really quite all right. It was my next-door neighbour who found the body, not me.'

'Your next-door . . . I never realised it was as close as that! They just mentioned the name of the village on the news. Oh, my poor darling!' He leapt to his feet, protective arms outstretched.

She dodged him and made a grab for the teapot. 'Careful, you'll get scalded!'

Reluctantly, he sat down again. 'I suppose that fellow who just left was a reporter? Have they been pestering you? If any of them come round tomorrow I'll send them packing.'

'Bruce hasn't been pestering me,' said Melissa quickly, then remembered that in a way he had been doing just that although the word had never entered her head at the time. Aubrey's pale brown eyes and full, slightly loose mouth registered suspicion.

'You mean it was a social visit? Bit late to come calling, isn't it?'

'He's just gone home. You're the one making the late call,' she said pointedly.

'That's different,' he protested.

'Is it?' She turned away to get cups and saucers from the cupboard. I mustn't get angry with him, she told herself, it isn't fair. He really cares, he's come tearing down here at half past ten at night just to make sure I'm all right. I haven't seen him for three weeks and I was pretty rotten to him last time we met and I snubbed him on the phone . . .

A sulky expression had settled on Aubrey's pudgy face and she had to make a conscious effort to push aside the memory of Bruce's clean-cut features and alert humorous eyes.

'Look, Aubrey,' she said, handing him a cup of tea and pushing the sugar-bowl across the table. 'It's very sweet of you to be so concerned for me and I do appreciate it, but I'm really quite capable of looking after myself. I've tried to make you understand and I just wish you'd accept . . .'

'Ah!' He took the tea and grabbed her hand. 'My darling girl, I know exactly why you're doing this and I love you all the more for it.' His thumb massaged her palm, lust glowed in his eye.

Melissa drew her hand away. 'Why I'm doing what?'

'Pretending you don't care! It's because of Denise, isn't it?'

'She is your wife,' murmured Melissa. She was being a coward, hiding behind the fact that Denise wanted to patch up the marriage after a long estrangement.

'She doesn't love me, not the way you do.'

Melissa felt her jaw tightening. She drank her tea and got up, rinsing her cup at the sink. Her hands were trembling. Any minute now she'd explode and there'd be a scene. And she was so very, very tired.

'Aubrey,' she said quietly. 'I am very fond of you'—that at least was true—'and you have been extremely good to me, but I'm not going to let you break up your marriage on my account.' Chicken, her brain screamed at her, miserable bloody chicken! Why can't you just tell him the truth? You don't love him, you've never really loved him; any man with an ounce of perception would have sensed it without being told.

He was behind her, his arms around her, turning her to face him. She felt his hard tumescence pressing against her body and his hand moving purposefully down her spine. Then the telephone rang.

'Oh, shit!' Aubrey's hand stopped in mid-grope but he kept Melissa firmly clamped against him. 'Who the hell's that?'

She gripped his shoulders and pushed him away, thankful for the respite. 'I'll go and find out.' She hurried into the sitting-room and picked up the phone.

'Babs?' The voice was weak and hesitant but the note of hysteria had gone and he sounded rational. Her heart began to thump.

'Hello, Clive.' She concentrated on sounding calm and receptive, anxious to say nothing to upset him.

'Is Babs there? I must speak to Babs!'

'She's not here at the moment.'

'When . . . when will she be back?'

Melissa sensed that he was on a knife-edge between amnesia and a return to normality. She would have to play this very carefully, not hustle him.

'Can you ring again tomorrow?' she asked.

There was no answer, but a movement behind her made her turn around. Aubrey was standing in the doorway, unashamedly listening. He had taken off his jacket and was in the act of removing his tie. Aubrey believed in making good use of every minute of his time. She turned her back on him.

'Clive? Are you still there?'

'I have to talk to Babs! It's important . . .' The words came in jerks; he was beginning to get agitated.

Aubrey had moved round in front of her and was mouthing enquiries and instructions. If only he wasn't there she could think more clearly how to handle this. She flapped a hand at him in exasperation.

'Listen, Clive, I can't talk now. Ring again tomorrow . . . please. Will you do that?'

There was a pause. Faint, inarticulate sounds came over the wire. Sounds of distress, quickly controlled.

'Tomorrow? Will Babs be there tomorrow?'

'I hope so.'

There was a sigh at the end of the wire and the phone was put down. Melissa sat for a moment staring at the receiver in her hand and muttering 'Damn! Damn!' under her breath before she too hung up. If she'd been on her own she might have found out something useful. There was no guarantee that Clive would remember to ring tomorrow and it might be days before she heard from him again. Then she remembered that Bruce had been monitoring his progress. He must know which hospital Clive was in. She would talk to Bruce tomorrow and perhaps together they would go to see him.

'Who is Clive and why the hell is he ringing you at this ungodly hour?' demanded Aubrey.

Melissa gave him a savage glare. 'It's only just gone eleven.' She pushed past him and went back to the kitchen. She had had enough of Aubrey. She wanted to think. Above all, she wanted to sleep. 'What's it got to do with you anyway?'

She could have told him the truth, of course, but why should she? He'd only fuss and interfere, and it was none of his business. He switched off the light as he followed her from the room. Even in moments of agitation he never forgot life's little economies.

'You haven't done badly in a couple of weeks, have you?' he jeered at her. 'One just leaving as I arrive, another phoning an hour later. Not bad going at all!' His voice was harsh with frustration and jealousy.

Melissa felt herself reaching flash-point. She drew a deep breath and began counting to ten. When she turned to face him she thought how stupid he looked with his flushed face, his narrowed eyes and his half-open mouth. For a moment, she hated him.

'You dirty-minded sod!' Her voice shook with rage and weariness. "Either apologise for that insinuation or get out of my house!' Her knees began to buckle; she grabbed a stool and sat down.

Aubrey's expression of righteous wrath collapsed. 'Darling girl, I didn't mean it! Please forgive me!' He was abject, squatting before her, holding her hands, love and devotion swimming in his pale eyes. He was a kind, good man and she wished she could love him but knew she never could. Gently, she freed her hands and got up.

'All right, let's forget it. Aubrey, I've had a gruelling day and I need sleep. Did you bring an overnight bag?'

'In the car,' he said eagerly. 'I'll run and fetch it.'

'I'll go and make up the spare bed for you.'

For a second, she thought he was going to protest but he thought better of it and went to get his bag. A few minutes later, as they stood on the landing after she had locked up, shown him where he was to sleep and pointed out the bathroom, he attempted to kiss her. She offered him her cheek and he turned sullenly away.

'Goodnight,' he mumbled.

The builder had not considered it necessary to provide locks on the bedroom doors. A pity, thought Melissa, propping a chair under the handle and hoping it would hold. It was a wise precaution. A little while later she heard scraping sounds as the handle was turned from outside. Later still—she could not be certain whether she had slept or not—the stairs creaked. A car started and drove quietly away. After that she slept soundly and peacefully.

TWELVE

MELISSA SLEPT SOUNDLY UNTIL EIGHT O'CLOCK. Except during periods of extreme anxiety she tended to wake with an uncluttered mind that enabled her to make a slow, unhurried transition from slumber into full consciousness. Only then did she begin to run over events past and map out the day ahead. This morning was no exception. It was several minutes before she remembered what had happened the previous evening. She got up and drew back the curtains.

Aubrey's car had gone. The sky was still overcast but the clouds were gossamer-thin with hints of blue behind them. She pushed the window open and leaned out, taking deep draughts of the early-morning freshness, savouring it as if it were champagne. The air had a heightened clarity after the rain and as she watched, the sun burst through, sparkling on the wet grass and casting a sheet of pale gold across the valley.

She put on a dressing-gown and went to the bathroom. The clean towel she had given Aubrey lay neatly folded over the edge of the wash-basin. She checked his room; his bed had not been slept in. She went downstairs. On the kitchen table was a sheet of paper torn from a notebook. 'I shall not trouble you again,' he had written.

Her eyes began to sting. Poor Aubrey. She pictured him, lonely and rejected as he drove home through the night, and felt guilty. Then she felt angry. It wasn't her fault if she didn't love him. She had tried, knowing how much he cared for her, but it simply hadn't happened. And whenever she sought to explain this to him he hadn't wanted to know, preferring to believe—because it was what he wanted and because it was in his nature to hide from disagreeable realities by pretending they didn't exist—that she was nobly denying her own feelings to give him a chance to mend his marriage. Well, he had accepted defeat at last and she was free. It was a good sensation. She went back upstairs and spent a blissful half-hour soaking in the bath and planning her day.

By nine o'clock the sky was clear and wonderfully blue. The saturated earth lay steaming contentedly in the sun. In the garden, blackbirds tugged at reluctant worms and sparrows squabbled over tit-bits. The cuckoo's monotonous call echoed and re-echoed up the valley, reminding Melissa of the scene by the woodland grave, of her half-promise to Bruce and thence to Clive's latest phone call. They represented problems that would have to be faced but for the moment she put them out of her mind. She had a good hour and a half before it was time to leave for church and she put it to good use by going over yesterday's output of *The Shepherd's Hut*.

When she came out of her front door at a quarter to eleven, Iris was waiting for her, clad in the tweed coat and skirt that seemed to be her regular church-going attire. She looked cheerful and alert.

'Got rid of Aubrey, then!'

'How did you know it was Aubrey?' It was odd, she thought, that what she would have found an intolerable impertinence from someone like Mrs Calloway was perfectly acceptable from Iris.

'Saw your face when he arrived. Heard him leave, too. Tell him to push off, did you?' There was a trace of malevolent glee in Iris's chuckle.

'Not in so many words, but he got the message. By the way, in all the excitement I don't think I told you I've cracked the mystery of the weird phone calls.' As they turned into the lane and began the climb into the village, she ran briefly through her visit to The Usual Place, her meeting with Bruce and his account of Clive's accident.

'Bruce is convinced that the body in the woods is Babs's,' she finished. 'He called round yesterday evening to talk about it. He was just leaving as Aubrey arrived. I expect you saw him. He's got some theory . . .' She gave her friend an anxious sideways glance, afraid that all this might be a distressing reminder of her ordeal, but Iris took it in her stride. Moreover, she had a theory of her own.

'Sex-killing!' she said flatly, as if there could be no doubt. 'All tarts, those girls! Get their come-uppance sooner or later. He sees to that!' she added with a solemn glance at the sky.

They had reached the centre of the village where they soon fell in with a group of fellow-worshippers. The subject of Babs and the possibility of divine retribution was allowed to drop.

During the service the Rector, pale and with a slightly exaggerated air of solemnity but otherwise perfectly composed, delivered a sermon on the twin themes of forgiveness and salvation, reminding his flock that none was without sin. Listening to his voice booming confidently round the little church, Melissa recalled his agitation as he stood by the grave. There had been something strange about him, she thought. Something he had said, perhaps? Whatever it was, it eluded her.

After the service, the congregation stood outside in groups to exchange views on the sermon. A tweedy man with a brick-red face and a white moustache challenged the Rector in a parade-ground voice to consider how the victim's family might feel about such damned wishy-washy attitudes towards violent crime.

'Major Ford!' Iris whispered to Melissa. 'Leads the local hangers and floggers brigade!'

While the Rector was doing his best to placate the irate major, a detachment of gloved and hatted ladies with handbags dangling from their arms buttonholed Melissa.

'Fancy a thing like that in Benbury!' said Mrs Foster, the dumpy little party who kept the village shop. She had a round, pink, rather childish face with matching voice, wispy hair and fluttery eyelids. 'I expect you'll be writing it into a story before long?' There were excited and admiring murmurs from other members of the group.

'I hope you'll do no such thing!' Mrs Calloway, who had been talking to an adjacent group, swung round to butt in before Melissa could open her mouth. 'And I also hope,' she added, giving her spectacles a vicious upward shove, 'that your books don't contain any *nastiness*!'

Melissa pointed out that it was difficult to conceive a murder without nastiness but Mrs Calloway, a crimson tide riding up her neck, declared that wasn't what she had in mind.

Iris nudged Melissa in the ribs. 'She means sex!' she hissed in a gloating stage-whisper that was obviously meant to be heard.

The edge of the blush travelled up Mrs Calloway's face and disappeared under the brim of her hat. She shot a glance of pure hatred at Iris and turned away.

'Poor old Henry,' said Melissa as she and Iris set off for home. 'I wonder he hasn't wrung her neck long ago!'

Iris's face assumed the familiar expression of adoring imbecility. 'Mr Calloway,' she said, and her tone carried an implied reproof at Melissa's use of his Christian name, 'is a saint. He wouldn't harm a fly.' Preferring not to become embroiled in a discussion of the Rector's sanctity, Melissa changed the subject.

'You were talking the other day about the people at Benbury Park,' she said. 'Have you ever met them?'

Iris shook her head. 'Stuck-up lot, don't mix with peasants. Ask the Rector.'

'Does he know them, then?'

'Calls now and again. Pastoral duty and all that. Never gets any joy but perseveres. Why?'

'I was just wondering how they reacted to a body being dug up in their woodland.'

Iris sniffed. 'Probably more bothered at their precious pheasants being disturbed than about the victim.'

'I suppose, technically, you were trespassing on their land?'

Iris shrugged. 'So what? Lived here years before they came. Former owners didn't mind.' She marched on in silence for a few minutes. 'Perhaps one of them did it.'

'Committed the murder, you mean?'

'Could be. Filthy rich, might be international crooks.'

Melissa concealed a smile. Anyone who refused admittance to Henry Calloway was damned in Iris's eyes.

They had reached home. Iris stopped with her hand on the latch of her gate. 'Come for a drink?'

'Er . . . better not, thanks all the same. I've left something in the oven.'

Iris gave a sardonic grin. 'Meat, I suppose. You're welcome. See you later, then.'

When she got indoors Melissa dialed Bruce's number but there was no reply. Not surprising really. Young men living independently were unlikely to spend Sundays quietly at home. He was probably out with a girlfriend, or spending the day with his parents. She rather hoped it was the latter.

The joint she had left in the automatic oven was sizzling merrily and smelled delicious. It was a pity Iris was vegetarian; it would have been nice to have her company. No point in asking her round for a sherry either. Even the smell of meat, she had once declared, made her puke.

Melissa drank her sherry, dished up her meal and ate it in the kitchen with her notes for *The Shepherd's Hut* at her elbow. From time to time she jotted down details that occurred to her for fleshing out the characters or tidying up the plot. Then she took a fresh sheet of paper and began making separate notes about the actual events of the past two weeks. There was a lot of material here that she could use, if not in this novel then in the future. She should have done it before but there hadn't been time. She made a second set of notes about the people she had met since coming to Benbury. One or two points struck her as possibly significant and she highlighted them with a coloured pen.

In the evening she tried Bruce's number again. This time he was there.

'I've just come in,' he said. 'Been helping my father mend his garage roof. I suppose you've been at your desk all day, devising fiendishly clever red herrings to baffle your readers!'

'Not quite all day. Believe it or not I've been gardening this afternoon. It was too nice to stop indoors and Iris nobbled me the minute I put my nose outside, telling me it was time I sowed my carrots.'

'That lady sounds quite a character,' said Bruce. 'I'd like to meet her.'

'Maybe you will. But listen, I didn't ring you to talk about horticulture.' She told him about Clive's latest call. 'He does seem to be getting better, although I don't think he's back to normal by a long way. What do you think I should say if he does phone again?'

'Tell him you'll come and see him. I'll come with you; it'll be easier talking to him face to face. We might really be getting somewhere!'

'You know where he is?'

'He's been moved from Gloucester Royal Hospital to a private clinic in Clifton. I'll check to find out if it's okay for us to visit.' He sounded excited, like a hound on the scent. 'It looks as if there's been a breakthrough, doesn't it?'

'Has it ever occurred to you that some other people might be interested in him?' asked Melissa.

'How do you mean?'

'If your hunch is right, and there is a link between Clive's accident and Babs's murder—if she *was* murdered, that is—then it might be very inconvenient if he were to recover his memory.'

'Hell's teeth! Yes, I see what you mean. We'd better get down there as soon as possible. Could you make it one evening this week, if I fix it with Matron?'

'Sure.'

'I'll be in touch. Anything else?'

'Only that, according to Iris, the Rector makes pastoral calls at Benbury Park from time to time and gets the elbow. On the basis of this affront to her beloved Rector she's prepared to write the owners off as international crooks!' If she expected appreciation of the jest, she was disappointed.

Bruce pounced. 'My God, she could be right!'

'Oh, leave off, will you? They're probably perfectly harmless people who simply don't want to be bothered.'

'Still, it wouldn't hurt to find out a bit more about them. The Rector would at least know who they are.'

Melissa heaved a sigh. 'If I have an opportunity, I'll ask him,' she said. Anything to shut you up, she added mentally. 'And you'll contact me again when you've arranged for us to visit Clive?'

'Will do. Have you . . . er . . . decided yet?'

'About what?'

'What we were discussing last night.'

'Oh, that. No, not yet. I'm still thinking it over.'

'I see.' He had obviously hoped for a firm commitment but realised he wasn't going to get it just yet. 'Well, I'd better get off the line in case Clive is trying to get through. Ciao!'

'Goodbye, Bruce!'

She waited up until after eleven o'clock but there was no call from Clive that evening.

THIRTEEN

MONDAY MORNING WAS GREY AND COOL WITH A blustery wind and intermittent rain making a slanting Morse Code pattern on the windows. Melissa, still in her dressing-gown, nibbled toast and drank coffee while watching a blackbird foraging on the patch of weed-ridden grass that, with the aid of her new mower and shears, she had hacked into what might some day become a lawn. There was plenty to do out there, and still a few things to see to in the cottage once Mr Allenby's dilatory workers had finished the odd jobs. Today, however, she had earmarked for writing.

She finished her breakfast, took a shower and put on one of the loose-fitting leisure suits that she preferred to wear about the house. It was a warm golden brown and it occurred to her as she glanced in the mirror that it accentuated the colour of her eyes. She seldom bothered with make-up when she was at home on her own but as she tied her long dark hair back with a velvet ribbon she remembered the hint of admiration in Bruce's voice as he jokingly remarked on the appearance of women crime writers in general and herself in particular. 'A fine figure of a woman' and 'feminine', he had called her. Well, she thought, peering a little closer, she had quite good bone structure, her skin was clear and considering she'd be forty-five next birthday her figure was pretty good. Still, Bruce couldn't be much over thirty, the gap was far too wide. Forget it, she told her reflection, strangling the notion at birth. She threw down her hairbrush and went to her study.

Bruce rang at six o'clock, while she was cooking her supper. He sounded excited.

'They've released a report from the pathologist. The deceased was a woman, probably in her twenties. There was a fracture of the hyoid bone, indicating manual strangulation, but they're being cagey about how long the body had been there. A lot of scientific waffle about soil conditions affecting the rate of decomposition but they think between eight and twelve months. Babs went missing ten months ago. It all fits so far!' His voice rose a couple of tones and he was almost panting with excitement.

'Did they find any clues to identity?' asked Melissa cautiously.

'A pair of hoop earrings and some slave bangles. Babs used to go in for that type of cheap jewelry.'

'So do dozens of girls,' Melissa pointed out, reluctant to pour cold water but determined to be realistic. 'What about clothing?'

'Black high-heeled shoes. Mass-produced, nothing distinctive. Some shreds of cloth, still undergoing tests. No indications to date of sexual assault but after all this time you'd hardly expect it. It all fits!' he repeated excitedly.

'Anything else?'

'They're hoping to identify her from dental records. They'll be circulating all the local dentists, asking them to check. That could take some time, of course.'

'But we already know that Babs wasn't registered with a local dentist.'

'That's right, but of course the police aren't looking for Babs at the moment so they've got to go through all the hoops. It's going to take time but I'm positive we're on the right track.'

'Mm . . . it's all circumstantial. Doesn't take us very far forward, does it?'

'It certainly doesn't take us backwards.' She could tell he was disappointed by her lack of enthusiasm.

'No, that's true. Sorry, I didn't mean to sound off-putting.'

'So long as the body remains unidentified, the killers aren't under any immediate threat so they'll carry on with their operations as usual. Now tell me what you've found out.'

'I told you yesterday.'

'I mean since then.'

'Since then, I've been working on my book. I can't be a full-time amateur sleuth and a full-time writer, you know.'

'Sorry!' She could picture his rueful grin. 'I just wondered if you'd had a word with the Rector or anyone . . . ?'

'You're the first person I've spoken to all day.'

'Hell's teeth, don't you find it lonely?'

'On the contrary, I've been in the company of some fascinating people . . . crooked art dealers and unscrupulous collectors with a murderer chucked in for good measure . . . riveting company!'

'What . . . oh, I see!' He sounded sheepish. 'Well, I'll keep you posted. I'm off home now. I'll be ringing the clinic later this evening.'

'Oh, yes, about Clive. Good. Let me know.'

'You're still game to come down there with me? We could have a meal afterwards and compare notes.'

'That sounds like a nice idea.'

'Fine. I'll be in touch.'

Melissa ate her supper and afterwards went for a stroll round her garden. The sky had cleared and the sun was warm. She scanned her newly created vegetable bed and felt a surge of excitement at the sight of tiny green tufts where she had planted potatoes. She hurried next door to break the news to Iris.

The back door of Elder Cottage stood ajar but there was no sign of her neighbour. She pressed the bell and a muffled voice called: 'Who is it?'

'It's Melissa. Are you busy?'

'Come through. Sitting-room.'

Melissa found herself staring at a headless, inverted trunk clad entirely in black. 'Good heavens!' she exclaimed. 'Whatever are you doing?'

'With you in a minute.' After a short interlude the torso developed arms and legs and unrolled itself on to the floor. 'The Plough,' Iris explained, lifting her head. 'Marvellous for the circulation. Strengthens the back. The Fish next, to balance up.' She lay back, breathing deeply and noisily. Then she arched her spine, tilted her chin to the ceiling until she was resting on the top of her head and folded her hands on her chest like a knight on a tombstone. Binkie, who had been watching the proceedings from an armchair, slid to the floor and climbed on to her stomach, purring in delight.

'Push off, Binkie!' said Iris good-humouredly, without moving a muscle. Ignoring the command, Binkie showed every sign of settling down. Melissa scooped him up and returned him to his chair.

'Shall I come back later?' she asked as Iris gently subsided, relaxed and closed her eyes.

'No, wait. Shan't be long.'

Melissa sat down and tickled Binkie's ears. Presently Iris opened her eyes, sat up, crossed her legs and rose to her feet in one lithe movement. Her thin body in its skintight black leotard was a supple, elongated shadow.

'I wish I could do that,' said Melissa. 'I've never practised yoga. Maybe I should start.'

'Nothing like it. Strengthens the body, calms the mind. Want a cuppa?'

'Not just now, thanks. I think my potatoes are through.'

Iris shook her head. 'Can't be!'

'Why not?'

'Much too early. Must be weeds!' The grey eyes sparkled with good-humoured mockery at Melissa's disappointment. 'Care to see my studio? Got a new design I'd like you to see.'

'I'd love to.'

Iris led the way upstairs and opened a door into a room that seemed to vibrate with light. The ceiling had been entirely removed to reveal the rafters and the roof was lined with plasterboard which was, like the walls, painted a brilliant white. There was a window at one end and a second window let into the slope of the roof.

In addition to the usual litter of artist's materials there was a shelf containing bolts of plain cloth in a variety of shades. An old-fashioned easel supporting a large rectangle of white board stood at an angle in one corner. Fastened to it was a sheet of paper on which a design had been executed in bold black strokes. Iris waved a hand at it.

'Tell me what you think. No polite noises. Tell the truth.'

Melissa stood in front of the easel and stared at the design. It was an abstract, of course—or was it? Didn't those spiky, criss-crossed strokes suggest a forest? It had strength and vigour but there was a subtle, underlying hint of menace. Here and there, hardly noticeable at first but gradually becoming more apparent, almost as if they were increasing in size, were tiny patches of brilliant red. Some were half-hidden in crevices between two branching lines; some hinted at a slowly spreading stain on a tree-trunk; others, elongated, like scarlet drops about to fall, clung to the tapering ends of what could have been twigs. It was plain that although Iris had quickly recovered from the initial shock of her discovery, deep down she had been very disturbed indeed.

'Well?' Iris was impatient for a reaction.

'It's . . . it's very dramatic,' Melissa said slowly. 'And, in a way, frightening.' Iris was watching her with an anxious, almost a hungry expression in her eyes. 'I think I can see why you did it,' she said gently.

Iris released a deep, quiet breath. 'Thought you'd understand. Not commercial, of course. Who'd want to live with that?' She covered the design with a sheet of plain paper. 'Feel better now. Got it out of my system.'

'Could I see some of your other designs?'

'Some other time. Care for a walk?'

'Yes, if you like. I'll have to change, though.'

'Me too. See you in a minute.'

For a while they strolled in silence along the edge of the brook. Iris led the way along the narrow path, straight-backed, swinging her arms in her toy-soldier walk. She was bare-headed and the setting sun picked out gleams of coppery gold in her hair. With her fine features she must have been attractive once, even beautiful.

The air was still and bright, the sky almost cloudless. A tiny plane buzzed overhead and Iris stopped to watch it, hands cupped over her eyes.

'Think they'll find out who did it?' she asked abruptly.

'The murder, you mean? First they have to identify the victim.' Melissa repeated the details of the police report that Bruce had passed on to her. 'It could take several weeks.'

'That young man of yours, you said he had a theory?'

Melissa hesitated. She wasn't sure how much she wanted to confide in Iris, who had shown an unexpected readiness to talk to the press.

'It's all very vague at present,' she prevaricated. 'He doesn't want to say much in case he's mistaken.'

'Can understand that,' Iris grunted. 'Nobody wants to appear a fool. Oh look,' she went on, her voice squeaky with delight. 'Here comes the Rector!'

He had apparently emerged from the woods. He was wearing an old tweed jacket over his clerical vest and collar and his grey flannel trousers were tucked into gum-boots. His greeting was determinedly cheery but there was a hint of sadness about his eyes. He, too, was still feeling the effects of the tragedy.

'Good evening, ladies! Out for a breath of air? Lovely evening!'

They agreed that it was indeed a most beautiful evening and spent a minute or two enlarging on this theme. It was Iris who broke the chain of cliché.

'Mrs Craig was asking yesterday about the Benbury Park people, Rector,' she said. 'Told her you could help.'

'Really?' Mr Calloway walked along beside them, his face alight with interest and anticipation. 'Is this in the cause of research for the new novel?'

'That's right,' said Melissa, hoping she might be forgiven the white lie. In a way it was true. An historic Cotswold manor-house might do very well as the nerve-centre for her gang of art thieves. Perhaps, with the Rector's assistance, she might even wangle a visit.

Mr Calloway was beaming and rubbing his hands together. 'Ah, I can tell it's going to be one of those nice old-fashioned murder mysteries! They're the best kind, I always think! Weekend house-party . . . body in the library and a bloodstained knife in the butler's pantry . . . ?' he looked eagerly at Melissa for confirmation.

'Something like that!' she agreed, smiling. 'The problem is, I've never been inside a privately owned mansion. Houses that are open to the public don't have quite the same atmosphere as someone's home.'

'True . . . true . . . and atmosphere is so important, isn't it?' He spoke with the air of a connoisseur. 'I'm not at all sure whether the present owners would be willing . . . they don't actually live in the place . . . it's run by the staff.'

'Estate manager, farm manager, gamekeeper,' recited Iris. 'Swan about as if they owned the place. Owners never show their faces except for the shooting and polo parties. Not Colonel Brent-Smith's way . . . supervised everything himself.'

'Yes, they are away a great deal,' sighed the Rector. 'And even when they're there, they don't take an interest in the life of the village the way the Brent-Smiths used to.' He turned a woebegone gaze on Melissa. 'You know, Mrs Craig, they used to open the gardens for charity year after year . . . and they were always most generous to the church. Five hundred pounds they contributed to the roof restoration fund . . . but when I wrote to ask Mr Francis for some help in repairing the central heating, he never even acknowledged my letter.'

'Is he the owner or the estate manager?'

'He's one of the owners. It's a kind of consortium . . . they bought the property as an investment. I understand some of the partners live in London. Gregory Francis is a local businessman, quite a well-known antiques dealer, but even he doesn't actually live in the house.'

'So it isn't really a family home?' Melissa felt surprisingly disappointed. Talk of the Brent-Smiths and their commitment to the estate and to the village had conjured up a scenario that she would have enjoyed building into her novel.

'I'm afraid not,' said the Rector, 'but I tell you what I could do . . . I could introduce you to the Vowdens over at Rillingford. They have a lovely old Queen Anne house . . . much smaller than Benbury Park, of course . . . no butler's pantry or anything like that, haha, but I'm sure they'd be delighted to help you.'

'Thank you, that's very kind,' said Melissa gratefully. 'I do appreciate your interest.'

'Any time, any time! And if you want to know anything about shooting parties, I suggest you have a word with Dick Woodman. He knows the gamekeeper and he helps out. I believe he tells some good yarns in the Woolpack on a Saturday night during the season. It sounds as if some of these wealthy gentlemen hardly know one end of a gun from the other!'

'Tough on the beaters!' commented Iris with a sniff.

'Yes, indeed,' chuckled Mr Calloway. The encounter seemed to have cheered him enormously. He glanced at his watch. 'I must be getting back,' he declared. 'Anthea will be wondering what has become of me. Please excuse me, ladies.' With a wave, he strode off towards the village, leaving Iris and Melissa to follow more slowly.

Bruce rang again shortly after Melissa returned home.

'I spoke to Matron,' he said. 'A neurologist is coming to see Clive tomorrow. I'm to check again and if he gives the okay we can go along on Wednesday evening.'

'How much have you told her?' asked Melissa.

'Nothing about the murder. Just about the phone calls. She already knew, of course, about his obsession with Babs and The Usual Place but hadn't realized he'd been trying to contact her. She seems to think it might help him to talk to someone who knows Babs.'

'Well, you've met her, I haven't.'

'True, but you're the one who's been getting the calls.'

'Well, we'll just have to play it by ear, won't we?'

'Right. Nothing to report your end?'

'Not really. I've just been speaking to the Rector about Benbury Park.' She passed on the little information the Rector had been able to give her. 'It sounds as if the house becomes a sort of leisure centre for Hooray Henrys at weekends. Shooting parties, polo meetings . . . that sort of thing.'

'That could provide useful cover for a drugs operation, couldn't it?' said Bruce eagerly. Melissa burst out laughing. 'What's so funny?' he demanded.

'You are. Every kind of business from a North Sea oil rig to an ice-cream cart could be useful cover for something crooked according to you!'

'I'll make you take me seriously one of these days,' he declared.

'Good. Keep trying!'

'I'll phone you tomorrow then . . . ciao!'

By a lucky chance she had an opportunity to speak to Dick Woodman the very next day. She had taken a break from her writing to work for a while in the garden when he passed Hawthorn Cottage with his dog at his heels. He was only too pleased to stop for a chat and when he realized that the writing lady from London was actually seeking his help for one of her story-books, his chest swelled with pride.

'I've been hearing from the Rector about the shooting parties,' Melissa said.

This was sufficient to launch Dick into an enthusiastic account of the organisation of a shoot, which Melissa found vaguely repellent. Raising large numbers of living creatures merely to give the well-heeled something to shoot at was bad enough; to employ men to drive them out into the open so that they provided easy targets outraged her sense of fair play. Suspecting that Dick would find her views eccentric and possibly ludicrous, she kept them to herself and switched the conversation to the people who made up the shooting parties.

'It's mostly the local landowners and gentry, and sometimes people down from London,' he explained. 'The polo now, that brings in a different class of folk altogether.'

'How do you mean . . . different?'

'Richer,' said Dick with a grin. 'Loaded they are. Some of them come in their private choppers and aeroplanes.'

Melissa was impressed.

'Is there an airfield at Benbury Park?'

'There's a landing strip . . . just for little planes.'

'And a polo ground?'

'No, that's in Cirencester. There's polo there most Sundays during the season. Some of the visitors stay at the Park . . . some of them, the ones who're actually playing, keep their ponies there.'

'It sounds like a sort of hotel.'

Dick seemed to find this immensely amusing. 'It's not open to the likes of you and me, if you get my meaning,' he chuckled. 'More like a posh sort of club for Mr Francis and his friends.'

'I'm told that the village people aren't made welcome at Benbury Park,' said Melissa.

Dick shrugged. 'Ah well, you know how it is with rich folk. They like to keep themselves to themselves.'

'Do you help the gamekeeper with the pheasants? I'd love to see the chicks some time.'

Dick shook his head with evident regret. 'Ah, now that might be a problem. Mr Hepple doesn't care for strangers round the place . . . it disturbs the birds, you see. I could ask him, though.' He hesitated for a moment, then asked, 'What's your story about, then? Spies? The IRA?'

Melissa shook her head, smiling. 'Nothing like that . . . just a gang of art thieves.'

'Ah!' Dick nodded approval. 'Well then, there's the perfect set-up. The crooks come in pretending they're here for the sport and bring the loot hidden under their tackle. You could hide a lot of pictures in a Range Rover, couldn't you?'

'What a clever idea!' said Melissa. 'Thank you very much!'

'Tell you what!' said Dick, whose imagination had obviously been set alight. 'I'll keep my eyes open, like. If I spot anything that might help . . . with ideas, I mean . . . I'll drop in when I pass this way.'

Melissa was taken aback by this show of enthusiasm. 'That's very kind of you,' was all she could think of to say.

He turned as if to go, then thought of something else.

'We won't say anything about this, eh?'

'Of course not,' she agreed. 'It's our secret.'

He winked and set off down the valley with the dog trotting at his heels. Melissa went indoors to devise more clues to put Nathan Latimer on the trail of her fictitious band of crooked antiques dealers and some means for them to airlift their loot out of the country.

Bruce rang after supper to confirm that Matron had agreed that they should visit Clive the following evening.

'I'll pick you up at five o'clock,' he said. 'We're only going to be allowed a short visit so we can compare notes over a drink before dinner.'

'Fine.'

'How's the book coming on?'

'It's going through a rather turgid patch and I'm trying to think of a way to liven things up. My detective has just had a phone call from an informer and I thought of having a bizarre, off-beat sort of rendezvous for them to meet.'

'Mmm . . . instead of the usual sleazy pub or bench in the park?'

'That's right. Any ideas?'

There was a pause before Bruce said cautiously, 'Your Chief Inspector . . . Latimer, isn't it?'

'Nathan Latimer.' She felt absurdly gratified that he really was familiar with her books.

'Hasn't he got a female side-kick?'

'Yes . . . Sergeant Dilys Morgan.'

'Yes indeed, boyo.' He assumed a stage Welsh accent. 'How about making the informer a male stripper, a sort of Gorgeous George? Nathan Latimer could send Dilys along to the strip club, and . . .' The last word was spoken with rising emphasis that indicated the most brilliant part was yet to come '. . . you could go along to Gorgeous George's show one afternoon, just to make sure you get the atmosphere right.'

'Well, of all the . . . !' It was no good trying to sound offended when she could hardly contain her laughter.

'Come now, don't pretend to be shocked. You hinted when we first met that you'd encountered some pretty dubious characters in the interests of research. I'll bet those afternoon affairs at The Usual Place are pretty tame in comparison with . . . er . . .'

'In comparison with what? I hope you weren't about to suggest that I'm in the habit of frequenting dens of vice?'

'No, of course not . . . I meant the evening ones for the boys,' he said hastily. 'Well, do I get a Brownie point?'

'It's worth thinking about . . . but I wouldn't want to be recognised.'

'No problem. Give a false name, wear a wig and a pair of dark glasses . . . no, I've got a better idea!' His voice rose in renewed excitement.

Ears up, nose twitching, tail thumping, she thought with amusement. What was coming now?

'Go and get yourself a new hairdo and make-up at Petronella's in the morning . . . that way you can kill two birds with one stone.'

'Sorry, I don't follow you. Who or what is Petronella's?'

'The beauty shop I was telling you about . . . where Babs used to live.'

'Oh, there.' Accidentally or deliberately, Melissa had allowed his earlier proposition to slip her memory. 'So what second stone do you have in mind?'

'Sussing the place out for possible drugs dealing, of course.'

'Of course . . . how stupid of me not to think of it! When the girl asks me what shampoo I'd like I'll say "grass", or "smack" maybe, or "today I feel like chasing the Dragon".'

'There's no need to be sarcastic,' he said, sounding offended. "I should naturally expect someone of your intelligence to be more subtle than that. A hairdo, a make-up and a manicure, say, would keep you there for . . . how long, a couple of hours? You'd have plenty of time to look around, get chatting to the staff and so on. What do you say? I did come up with a useful idea for your book . . .' Persuasive syrup began to trickle down the wires.

'I didn't say I was going to use it,' she said, rather feebly.

'You said it was worth thinking about. How about a quid pro quo? Please?'

'Oh, very well,' she sighed. 'I'll see what I can do. I'll have to find out from Gloria how one sets about getting into this dive . . . there may be some kind of membership scheme.'

'Well, she works in the bar there, doesn't she? She ought to be able to fix it for you.'

'She may tell half the village about it, that's what's bothering me.'

'Buy her silence with autographed copies of all your books.'

'She doesn't read crime novels . . . she only likes a nice love story.'

'I'm sure you'll be able to persuade her to be discreet.' There was a brisk finality in his tone that indicated the affair was settled. 'See you tomorrow, then . . . five o'clock?'

'All right. Goodbye.'

Wondering what she had let herself in for, Melissa went back to her study to consider the possibility of arranging a rendez-vous with a male stripper for her rather prudish Sergeant Dilys Morgan.

Fourteen

On Wednesday morning Gloria turned up even more exuberant, colourful and exotically perfumed than usual. She was in high spirits, having the previous day attended the final of a children's beauty contest at which her youngest had been declared the winner. She produced photographs of a pretty little moppet with her mother's enormous eyes and radiant smile and treated Melissa to a detailed account of the brilliance of the occasion and the impeccable performance of her offspring. 'Just like a real model,' declared the proud mother, limpid brown eyes aglow. All through their coffee-break she held forth about the charm of the judge (an actor from a popular soap opera, 'ever so dishy, he was,'), the shortcomings of the other contestants, none of whom could hold a candle to her Charlene, and the latter's prospects in the glittering world of television commercials.

When at last she paused for breath, Melissa put in her request for an entrée into the Tuesday afternoon diversions at The Usual Place. Despite her careful insistence that this was purely in the cause of research, the request caused astonishment and much hilarity on Gloria's part.

'Ooh my, fancy a lady like you wanting to see Gorgeous George!' she hooted, clutching her plump stomach. 'Wait till I tells my Stanley, he'll wet his knickers!'

'I'd be obliged if you didn't tell anyone, not even your husband,' said Melissa severely. Mentally, she was cursing Bruce for putting this ridiculous enterprise into her head. 'If anyone at The Usual Place were to find out that I'm going there in order to write about it, I'd be thrown out. This is just between you and me. Promise!'

Grudgingly Gloria promised. 'All right, I won't say nothing to no one.' After a moment's thought her regret at not being allowed to tell her Stanley changed to excitement at the notion of a secret shared with the author of a mystery novel. 'It'll be like one of they spy stories on the telly!' she gloated. 'I'll fix it for you to join the U.P. Club. You has to pay a membership fee, five pound I think it is, okay?'

'That's all right,' said Melissa, wondering if it would be tax deductible and trying to visualise her accountant's reaction. 'I'd like to go along next Tuesday if it can be arranged.'

Gloria nodded. She had her facial muscles more or less under control but her eyes were rolling with mirth. 'I'll see what I can do,' she said. 'Tell you what, when your book's finished, can I tell folks I helped you with it?'

'You can indeed, and you shall have a free autographed copy,' Melissa promised.

Gloria sighed with happiness. Her cup was full and she tackled the bathroom with even more gusto than usual.

Cedar Lawns, an exclusive private clinic, occupied a large Victorian stone house with an additional modern wing, standing in extensive grounds on the outskirts of Bristol with a commanding view of the Downs. It was approached through iron gates mounted on stone pillars and along a drive flanked on either side by the graceful, spreading trees that had inspired the name.

'It's like a country hotel,' Bruce remarked as he and Melissa walked from the car park to the front door. 'I'll bet it costs an arm and a leg to be treated here!'

She nodded. 'Looks as if there's money in Clive's family. Is that what Babs meant when she said he was a "good prospect", I wonder?'

The entrance hall was bright, cheerful and smelled of wax polish and pot pourri. At a small reception desk a girl with smooth fair hair and sea-blue eyes sat at a typewriter, a telephone at her elbow. Bruce strolled over, gave his name and asked to see the matron. The girl flashed him an admiring smile as she picked up the phone and pressed a button; she continued to smile while waiting for a reply. Bruce's personality had that effect.

Matron received them in her office, a comfortably furnished room overlooking a garden bright with daffodils and early tulips. She had a fresh, wholesome appearance with the clear eyes and tranquil expression of a nun. She was small and slight but her voice was strong and authoritative. Her staff, Melissa knew instinctively, would jump to do her bidding. She spoke of Clive Shepherd with affection and admiration.

'He had enough serious injuries to kill him several times over,' she informed her visitors. 'The surgeons were amazed at the way he pulled through; he simply refused to give up. He was in intensive care for several weeks, you know, just hanging on by a thread.'

'So I understand,' said Bruce. 'Is he up and about yet?'

'His right leg is in a cast and it is still a great effort for him to walk but otherwise his recovery has been nothing short of miraculous. Of course, he has good and bad days but on the whole he is progressing extraordinarily well. I understand that you know the young woman he calls Babs?' she went on, her placid gaze settling on Bruce.

'I've met her, but I haven't seen her recently.'

'And you,' she turned to Melissa, 'have been getting telephone calls from him?'

'We've been assuming it's him, although he's never given a name,' Melissa explained. 'But I talked it over with Mr Ingram and it seems fairly certain. At first he sounded terribly confused but the last time he rang he spoke much more rationally and when I addressed him by name he accepted it quite naturally.'

Matron nodded. 'We're hoping that contact with someone who actually knows this girl will help his memory to return,' she said. 'It seems to be coming back slowly although he has absolutely no recollection of events leading up to the accident, or of the accident itself.' She pressed a bell-push on her desk. 'I can only allow a short visit because he does get agitated rather easily. Still, the neurologist was pleased with his progress when he examined him yesterday.'

'Incidentally,' said Bruce, 'do you, or Clive's parents, know anything about his relationship with Babs?'

Matron drew a sharp little breath through pursed lips. 'Clive has no mother. I have never met his father although I have spoken to him on the telephone.'

'You mean, he doesn't come to see Clive?' asked Melissa in astonishment.

Matron shook her head. 'I'm afraid not, and I do not think he would be welcomed if he did.' She hesitated, looking down at her blotter and tracing its outline with one finger. 'I should not really discuss a patient's private affairs with strangers, but it seems that the two are totally estranged. Even a mention of his father seems to upset Clive.'

'Would it have anything to do with his affair with Babs, do you think?' asked Melissa.

'That would not have helped at all, I'm sure, but I have reason to think the trouble goes much deeper than that.' Matron looked from one to the other, a mixture of doubt and compassion in her eyes. 'I . . . I do not think, as you are not members of his family, I can tell you any more.'

'We quite understand and we'll be very careful not to upset him,' said Melissa. 'Thank you for allowing us to see him.'

'Not at all. I'm sure if this obsession with Babs could be resolved, it would be a help to him.' There was a knock at the door and a young woman in a blue overall entered the room. 'Nurse will show you to Clive's room. Only a few minutes, remember. I'll send her along when your time is up . . . and please, if he shows any signs of agitation, ring the bell by the bed and she will come at once.'

Clive Shepherd, clad in pajamas and dressing-gown, was seated in an armchair with a rug over his knees when Melissa and Bruce entered his room but despite their protests he struggled to his feet with the aid of a crutch. He was tall and thin, with hollow cheeks and dark, deep-set eyes. Apart from the cast on his right leg and a scar that ran up his right temple and vanished under a fold of straight dark hair, he showed no outward signs of his injuries.

The hand he offered them was cold but its grip was firm and strong and Melissa sensed something of the implacable will that had kept him alive. When he spoke, there was animation in his voice. Evidently he was having a good day.

'I understand you're a friend of Babs?' The dark eyes probed hers, searching.

'Er . . . not exactly,' said Melissa, feeling as if she were picking her way among broken glass. 'Bruce knows her. You and I have spoken once or twice on the telephone.'

'Ah, yes!' A flame of recollection spurted in his eyes, like the wick of a lamp suddenly turned up. 'You asked me to ring again . . . tomorrow?' The flame flickered uncertainly; the intervening days had become blurred.

'I thought it would be nice to come and see you instead,' said Melissa with a friendly smile which he returned, rather hesitantly. It transformed his face, giving him an almost saintly appearance.

'And you?' he turned back to Bruce. 'You know her? You've seen her?'

It was Bruce's turn to improvise. 'Not this week,' he said. 'I think she must be away. I work quite close to The Usual Place and I see her there now and again when I drop in for a drink.'

Clive sighed deeply and his smile faded. Something like anger smouldered in his eyes. 'I keep telling her, I don't like her working at that place. I asked her to meet me there but they said she'd gone. I don't believe them. Why wouldn't they let me talk to her?' His skeletal fingers gripped the arms of his chair.

The first signs of agitation, thought Melissa. Bruce had noticed it too and replied in a calm, soothing voice.

'She's taken a few days off, by the looks of things. Gone to see her family, perhaps.'

Clive shook his head and his knuckles began to whiten. 'She hasn't any family. She was brought up in homes. I'm the only one who's ever cared about her.' His eyes became moist and his mouth worked.

'Oh well, I shouldn't worry,' said Bruce. He was calm and reassuring with a touch of authority in his voice, like a doctor with a good bedside manner, thought Melissa. It worked, too. Clive's grip on the chair relaxed and he sat back and closed his eyes.

'Shall I give her a message if I see her?' Bruce went on.

The effect of this offer was alarming. Clive sat bolt upright and clutched at Bruce, gripping his arms with both hands.

'Tell her not to do it!' he said fiercely. 'It's a fool's game . . . dangerous . . . and wicked!' His colour had risen and he was breathing hard. The visitors exchanged nervous glances.

'Calm down, mate,' said Bruce. 'No need to get uptight.'

'She mustn't . . . do it!' The voice was getting weaker. "Dangerous game . . . black . . .' He released his grip and a blankness settled over his face. He sank back with closed eyes.

Bruce, rubbing his arms, half-rose from the chair in alarm. 'We'd better ring for Nurse,' he muttered.

Melissa was already on her feet, reaching for the bell, but at that moment there was a gentle knock and the nurse who had escorted them reappeared. She hurried over to Clive, pulled out a watch and began checking his pulse.

'Is he all right?' asked Melissa anxiously. 'We were talking quite quietly when he suddenly got very uptight . . .' She stared at the thin face with its sunken cheeks and livid scar and felt her throat contract. If Babs was dead, sooner or later he would be sure to find out, and the knowledge would bring unspeakable hurt.

As she watched, Clive opened his eyes and smiled. Melissa was reminded of pictures of medieval saints.

'It's been nice talking to you,' he said in a tired but rational voice. He held out his hand. 'Please come again.' With a flick of her eyes and a brief nod the nurse dismissed them.

'We'll see you again soon,' promised Bruce. Clive made no effort to get up this time, but his handclasp was as firm as ever.

When they got back to the entrance hall, Bruce went over to the reception desk. The same girl was sitting there and he gave her a paralysing smile of which Melissa felt the ricochet effect.

'Would you do something for me?' he asked in a voice rich with unimaginable promise.

The girl looked up at him with adoration in the sea-blue eyes. Yes, yes! they said. For you I will walk barefoot over hot coals!

'What do you want me to do?' she murmured.

'When anyone rings or calls to enquire about Mr Shepherd, just make a note of their name and ask where they can be reached. I'm organising a fund-raising event for the Intensive Therapy Unit in Gloucester.' he went on, his manner dripping with the milk of human kindness. 'I'm trying to contact friends of former patients, to invite them to contribute. I believe Mr Shepherd was in there before coming here, wasn't he?'

Melissa could barely control her amazement at this outrageous story. Convinced that no one could possibly fall for it, she braced herself for a flood of awkward questions but there were none. The girl appeared to take the bait without hesitation.

'What a simply lovely idea!' she cooed.

'I'll give you my number. Have you got something I can write on?' No prizes for guessing why he doesn't give her his card, thought Melissa.

The hand that passed him the memo pad trembled with excitement.

'Shall I ask people to ring you direct?'

'No, just tell them I'll be in touch. You ring me with the details, okay?'

Of course! proclaimed the shining eyes. Any excuse to talk to you is more than okay by me! I'll bet if you tilted her up she'd say 'Mama', thought Melissa bitchily.

'What's your name?' asked Bruce.

'It's Rowena.'

'Pretty name for a pretty girl!' She simpered with delight. 'Oh, by the way!' He tilted his face a little closer to hers, 'Don't go telling the rest of the staff here. It might get back to someone at the hospital and I want it to be a surprise.'

She looked doubtful. 'What about when my colleague's on duty?'

Bruce looked non-plussed for a moment. 'Ah . . . well, I'll have to rely on you both to be discreet.'

'You can rely on me,' she assured him earnestly.

'Thanks so much, Rowena. I'll wait to hear from you. Bye!' He blew her a kiss as he turned away, bringing a blush to her cheeks and setting her eyelashes fluttering.

'You are quite preposterous!' said Melissa as they returned to the car. She tried to sound severe but laughter escaped. 'May you be forgiven all those lies, and for arousing false hopes in that poor girl's quivering bosom.'

'Her bosom did quiver rather nicely, now you come to mention it,' said Bruce with a sidelong glance which Melissa ignored.

'I can't really see what you hope to gain by that exercise anyway,' she persisted. 'I mean, if someone with evil intent does enquire after Clive, he or she isn't likely to give a phone number.'

'Of course not, but at least we'll know that someone who doesn't wish to be identified is showing an interest. And in that case,' he started the engine and began driving slowly back towards the gate, 'Clive could be in deadly danger.'

'Then we'd have to tell the police.'

'Yes, of course.' He sounded reluctant.

'Where to now?' she asked, noticing that he was taking a different road to the way they had come.

'To a pub for a drink, and then we'll think about dinner.'

'That sounds like a good idea.'

The evening was mild and they found a pub with a garden overlooking the river. Bruce fetched the drinks and they sat on rustic seats and watched the antics of a blackbird splashing around in the bird-bath. Other customers sat quietly chatting and laughing, enjoying the late sunshine that settled over the countryside in a velvety golden haze. It was tempting to forget such sordid matters as crime and its attendant miseries. They were, however, uppermost in Bruce's mind.

'Well,' he said after a long pull at his pint of real ale. 'Now we know that Babs was contemplating blackmail.'

'We don't know for certain,' objected Melissa. 'She does seem to have been contemplating something that Clive disapproved of and thought was dangerous, but we don't really know what it was.'

'Oh come on, he distinctly said . . .'

'He said something that sounded like "black" but it could have meant something quite different.'

'Such as?'

'Oh, I don't know. He's supposed to be religious, he might have been talking about the blackness of her soul if she didn't turn from her sinful ways.'

Bruce looked down his nose. 'You don't really believe that!'

'I suppose you may be right, but . . .'

'I know I am.'

Privately, she too was sure of it but the consequences of admitting it alarmed her. She felt herself being drawn into a shadowy, sinister web. She concentrated on mutilating the lemon in her gin and tonic, aware that Bruce was watching her closely.

'How would Nathan Latimer tackle this?' he said suddenly.

She frowned. 'Are you taking the mickey?'

'Not a bit. Your Nathan is a stickler for the old logical deductive process, so unleash him!'

She could see that beneath the teasing manner he was perfectly serious. He wanted her help. She took a mouthful from her glass and set it down.

'All right, let's start with what we know for certain. Clive is infatuated with Babs but disapproves of her lifestyle and would like her to leave The Usual Place. Eventually she does that but she doesn't say a word to Clive. She also leaves her flat without leaving an address. No one has seen her since and most people, including the police, seem to accept that she's gone off of her own accord, except Clive. He is last seen at The Usual Place with his knickers in a fearful twist, hinting that someone is keeping something from him. At least, I'm assuming that was the last time he was seen. Was he traced anywhere else?'

'Yes, after he was chucked out of The Usual Place he went to at least two pubs in the city but he didn't drink very much according to witnesses . . . just sat in a corner with half a pint, looking miserable. At the last sighting, he was definitely on his own.'

'And the next thing we know, he's had a near-fatal accident. By the way, you were there while he was making that scene . . . did you hear him say anything about this "dangerous game" Babs was supposed to be playing?'

Bruce thought for a moment. 'It's getting on for a year ago, so I can't be sure of every word. My impression was that he wasn't prepared to accept that Babs would take off without a word, that he was convinced someone knew where she was and he was determined to get to the bottom of her disappearance. "They needn't think they can get away with it" sticks in my head. But no,' he concluded after some further thought, 'I'm sure that if he'd said anything that suggested blackmail, I'd have remembered.'

'So according to what he's been saying to us this evening, he knew—or thought he knew—more than he was prepared to say at the time?'

'Why do you say "thought he knew"?' asked Bruce.

'Babs and Clive come from very different backgrounds. He said she was brought up in homes whereas he's obviously well-educated. Streetwise kids use a lot of slang expressions . . . maybe he didn't really understand some of the things she came out with . . .'

'Are you saying you don't believe Babs was planning to black-mail anyone?'

'No,' Melissa said slowly, 'I'm simply saying that we can't list that under the things we know for certain, just on Clive's say-so. For the moment, we have to file it under a "possible/probable" heading.'

Bruce gave her a searching look. 'Which do you think—pos-sible or probable?' he asked.

Melissa took another sip from her drink. In spite of her reluc-tance to become involved, that part of her brain that enjoyed devising puzzles for Nathan Latimer to solve was ticking over fast.

'I haven't quite decided. Tell me, how many people would you say were in the bar that night?'

'It was pretty busy, but not packed to capacity.'

'Could it be that someone there who knew what had happened to Babs quietly slipped out and followed him when he left?'

'That's exactly what I've been saying,' Bruce was quick to point out. 'That's why I'm convinced his so-called accident was contrived . . . you're beginning to believe that too, aren't you?'

'Not necessarily, although I'm not saying for sure that it wasn't. We can't discount the possibility that Babs did tell someone— perhaps one of her regulars—that she was planning to leave town, that that person was in the bar and out of the kindness of his heart went after Clive to tell him he was wasting his time looking for her.'

Bruce looked disappointed. 'That still doesn't account for the accident.'

'It could do. If this person didn't put the message across very tactfully, and it came out inadvertently that Babs was a hooker as well as a stripper . . . that would really have upset Clive . . . it might have sent him right over the edge for the time being.'

'So you're going back to what you said at the start . . . that Babs deliberately dropped out of Clive's life because she'd got bored with him and he wouldn't stop pestering her?' Bruce's expression made Melissa think of a wounded basset-hound.

'I didn't say that,' she said, unable to restrain a smile. 'I was merely saying that on the basis of what we know for certain, that could be the case.'

Bruce put down his empty glass with an impatient gesture. 'I don't believe it. Babs believed that Clive had prospects . . . people heard her say so. We know now that she was right; someone in his family, probably his father, is wealthy enough to keep him indefinitely at Cedar Lawns. So why drop him?'

'Ah, but suppose Clive mentioned that his father was well off but made it clear that they were estranged. Babs could have hung on for a while in the hope that there'd be a reconciliation, realised after all that it wasn't going to happen and tried to put an end to the association. Clive, believing she was in love with him, and being crazy about her, wouldn't let her go.'

'You think that's how it was?'

'You asked me how Nathan Latimer would reason the thing through, and that's what I've been trying to do.'

'You haven't answered the question. Do you believe there are absolutely no suspicious circumstances in either Babs's disappearance or Clive's accident?'

'No,' Melissa said quietly. 'To be honest, that's what I'd like to believe . . . but no. I'm not sure about Clive's smash-up—that could have been a genuine accident—but I do think Babs was up to something dangerous, and it could well have been connected with drugs. But how we go about proving it, or even turning up some piece of evidence to get the police to start an investigation . . . that's something else. Is there something wrong?' she added.

Bruce had been massaging his forearm for several seconds and was now staring down at it as if he had made an unpleasant discovery. He began rolling up his shirt-sleeve.

'Remember when Clive got so excited and grabbed me by the arms?' he said. 'I thought at the time, this bloke's got hands like rat-traps. Look.'

The two of them stared in astonishment at the purple marks where fingers had dug into the flesh.

'I'm sure that the girl whose body was found in the woods was Babs,' Bruce went on, slowly, as if thinking aloud. 'It's been established that she died from manual strangulation. We suspect that after he left The Usual Place that night Clive may have learned things about her that he didn't know before.' He lifted his head and looked directly at Melissa, his eyes troubled. 'What do you suppose his reaction might have been?'

'Good Lord!' said Melissa. There was a long silence while they considered the implications.

'Maybe he found her after leaving The Usual Place . . .'

'. . . and killed her in a fit of jealous rage . . .'

'. . . after a few drinks . . .'

'. . . buried her body . . .'

'. . . drove off like a madman . . .'

'. . . maybe hoping to kill himself . . .'

'. . . and then fought like hell to live? Not logical,' Melissa finished. 'No, I can't believe it, not Clive. There was a sort of saintliness about him, he's no killer.'

'Then we come back to my original theory,' said Bruce with a certain satisfaction. 'She knew something and was trying to use what she knew to extort money. Clive tried, unsuccessfully, to talk her out of it. Her intended victim killed her to shut her up. But how did her body come to be in Benbury Woods?'

'We don't know that it was,' she pointed out. 'Even if we assume that Babs is dead—and I'm beginning to think she is—we certainly don't know that the body that Iris found is hers. There's nothing except your famous hunch to connect the two.'

Bruce grinned. His faith in his hunch was obviously intact.

'You crime writers are all the same! Every little loose end has to be tied up!'

'Our readers would give us a hard time if they weren't! Anyway, everyone knows journalists invent what they don't know. There's the difference between us.'

'I prefer to think about the things we have in common,' Bruce said softly.

'Did you say something about dinner?' retorted Melissa, avoiding his eye. 'I'm starving.'

'So am I. Let's go.'

They drove for several miles to a country restaurant where Bruce had reserved a table. From their seat in a window alcove they had a rolling view of pasture and woodland rising to the distant ridge of the Cotswolds. The slanting sun picked out a stone farmstead or two and painted long shadows at the feet of grazing cattle and horses.

'Lovely part of the world, isn't it?' remarked Bruce as they tucked into roast duckling. 'Aren't you glad you came to live here?'

'In some ways,' said Melissa pointedly.

He grinned, but did not bite. 'Have you decided yet to make an assignation with Gorgeous George?'

'If Gloria can stop giggling for long enough to arrange it, I shall shortly be a member of the U.P. Club, whatever that may be. I've made her promise to keep it a secret but if it gets out, every eyebrow in the village will go up and Mrs Calloway will draw aside her skirts every time I pass her. It's going to cost me a fiver,' she added.

'Only a fiver! That's a spit in the ocean out of your royalties!' he retorted cheekily. She gave him an icy stare. 'All right, only kidding. When's the performance?'

'Every Tuesday afternoon, so Gloria says. I haven't quite made up my mind to go.'

'Of course you'll go, you're burning with curiosity,' he taunted her. 'How else can you make your background authentic? You will go to Petronella's first, won't you?' he added, turning on a smile similar in quality to that which had turned Rowena to jelly.

Melissa determined to show that she was made of sterner stuff. 'I'll let you know in due course,' she parried.

Bruce reached out and took her hand. 'Melissa, let's be serious. We know for sure that huge quantities of drugs are coming in, and I honestly believe there's a connection with Babs's murder . . . all right, her disappearance,' he corrected himself as she opened her mouth to contradict him. 'Petronella's is ideally set up to provide cover for a dealer. All I'm asking you to do is have a very discreet look around. There's no risk to you . . . there's a perfectly genuine business being run there, with plenty of genuine, ordinary clients . . . and it's quite a decent, clean-looking place, not at all scruffy or down-at-heel . . .'

Melissa put her hands to her forehead and groaned. 'Oh Lord, what am I letting myself in for?'

'You could be doing something really fine,' he persisted. 'There are a lot of nice kids out there, destroying themselves, and their families, so that a few ruthless, greedy bastards can live off the fat of the land.'

Melissa felt the last rags of her resistance falling away. 'Oh, very well!' she said. 'I'll go to Petronella's . . . but I draw the line at the model agency.'

Bruce raised his glass. 'I'll bear that in mind,' he promised. 'Here's to good hunting . . . and another bestseller from Mel Craig! Now, what sweet would you like?'

Melissa drank, and was committed. It was such a pleasant evening and the good food and wine lay comfortably in her stomach. She felt relaxed, uninhibited and a little reckless. But later on, when she was once more alone in the quiet, isolated cottage that had still not quite accepted her, she became aware of something else, something that quickened her pulse-beat and sent a frisson across her nerve-ends.

It was excitement, spiked with fear.

FIFTEEN

DESPITE BRUCE'S ASSURANCES ABOUT THE STAND-
ards of cleanliness at Petronella's Vanity Box, Melissa preferred to
make up her own mind. On her next shopping trip into Gloucester
she went along there to reconnoitre.

The salon occupied the ground floor of a house in a gaunt
Victorian terrace a short distance from the Cross. A similar row
on the opposite side was still awaiting renovation but a board
outside indicated that the site had been acquired by developers
and would in due course be converted to shops and flats. It was
an area which, after years of going downhill, appeared to be on
its way back.

Petronella's, sandwiched between a driving school and a
launderette, had a bright modern shopfront. A huge basket of
artificial flowers in varying shades of pink occupied the centre
of the window, looking rather like a galleon in full rig on a sea
of billowing carmine gauze. Glimpses of girls in pink overalls
flitting to and fro in the interior emphasised, in a subdued but
decided fashion, the essential femininity of the clientèle. Melissa
studied the price list placed discreetly to one side: the range of
services was extensive, the charges seemed reasonable and the
place certainly looked wholesome enough. She decided to take the
plunge and pushed open the door, setting off a dainty musical-box
tinkle.

Inside, the pinkness extended remorselessly to every detail.
Walls, ceiling and paintwork were pale rose; in varying shades,
the theme was echoed in lampshades, chairs, towels and wash-
basins. Piano music from concealed speakers floated in the scented
atmosphere like trails of candy floss.

The slender young man at the reception desk, who appeared to be the manager, had evidently chosen his candy-striped shirt to blend with his surroundings.

'A facial treatment and make-up, followed by a restyle and manicure . . . certainly, madam! Next Tuesday morning? Shall we say half past ten?' The faint lisp and effusive manner were wholly in character. 'What name is it?'

'Mrs Collins.'

He wrote the time of her appointment on a pink card and bowed from the waist as he handed it to her. 'Thank you, Mrs Collins. We look forward to seeing you next Tuesday. My name's Justin.' He scuttled round the desk to open the door for her.

The question of a name had arisen in discussions with Gloria, who had expressed no surprise at Melissa's desire to join the U.P. Club incognito.

'They all does it . . . just so's their husbands never finds out!' she explained, shaking with laughter. 'Some of the names they thinks up is ever so fancy. Why don't you call yourself Meryl . . . that's a lovely name . . . the surname don't matter really . . . so long as it's not real!' she added with an explosive giggle. In the end they had settled on Meryl Collins and the very act of giving the assumed name lent to Melissa's appointment at Petronella's a tinge of excitement. At the same time it seemed rather ridiculous, like wearing a cocktail dress at a children's party.

When she got home she wrote the appointment on her kitchen calendar and copied Petronella's telephone number into her diary. To her surprise, she found that she was writing down her own number. She looked more closely and realised that she had inadvertently transposed the first two figures.

Was this how Clive had come to dial her number . . . by retaining the correct digits but recalling them in the wrong order? Was it Petronella's number that he had been trying to call? Since Babs had once lived above the salon, it seemed likely. If she had no phone of her own, she might have had an arrangement with someone there to take messages for her. In that case, if that person was still there, Melissa might be able to glean something about Babs's relationship with Clive.

It crossed her mind to phone Bruce and tell him of her discovery but she decided against it. He would read all kinds of sinister possibilities into what was probably no more than a bizarre coincidence. One of many that had dogged her recently, she reflected.

When she presented herself for her appointment the following Tuesday morning she found Justin arranging bottles of shampoo on a stand. He treated her to one of his brilliant smiles and summoned a girl in a white overall with 'Petronella's' embroidered in pink on the collar.

'Debbie, Mrs Collins is here.'

'Thank you, Mr Justin. Will you come this way please?'

Debbie had red hair, a pale skin dusted with freckles and a wooden expression. In a tiny room at the back of the salon, Melissa was helped off with her dress, swaddled in a soft blanket, installed on a couch and had her make-up removed with cool, fragrant lotions. It was a long time since she had been pampered in this way and she decided to make the most of it. She relaxed and closed her eyes, then reminded herself that one of her reasons for being here was to do a little gentle sleuthing and that she could begin by questioning the young beautician who was doing such blissful things to her face.

'Have you worked here long, Debbie?' she asked.

'Since last October,' the girl replied. 'Your skin's inclined to be dry.'

'Yes, I know. Do you like it here?'

'It's all right. What cleanser do you use?'

'Cold cream. Are you kept busy?'

'It varies. Cold cream's too greasy, it clogs the pores.'

'I'll get you to recommend a cleanser, then. Is Justin a good boss?'

'He's all right. You can have a free sample.'

There was no hint in the girl's flat monotone that she had seen the funny side of this exchange and Melissa suppressed her inclination to giggle. It was plain that Debbie was not going to be a mine of information; in any case she had not been here while Babs was living above the shop so there was a limit to what she might know. Moreover, the warmth, the soothing creams being expertly massaged into her skin and the soporific, all-pervading music were having their effect. A face-mask was applied, pads laid over her eyes; Melissa drifted away on fluffy pink clouds.

She awoke while the mask was being sponged off with warm water. She was allowed to get dressed, wrapped in a pink gown and given coffee in a mug with pink roses on it while Debbie laid out her range of make-up colours for inspection. When, after a brief consultation, she set to work, Melissa watched in astonishment as her face was transformed.

'I don't think my own son would recognise me!' she exclaimed when it was finished.

'Don't you like it?' asked Debbie tonelessly. If she was disappointed at Melissa's reaction, one would never have guessed.

'I like it very much . . . it's just the effect I was hoping for,' Melissa assured her and a barely perceptible smile fluttered over the pale, sharp features.

'That's good. You're ready for Dawn now.'

'Is Dawn going to do my hair?'

'That's right.'

Dawn had a pert, pretty face, an impish smile and a hairstyle like a sweep's brush. She took handfuls of Melissa's shoulder-length locks, manipulated them this way and that, and asked her what style she wanted.

'Of course, you could have it cut short,' she said hopefully.

'I prefer it long,' said Melissa firmly. 'Normally I tie it back with a ribbon or else let it hang loose. What else can I do that's easy to manage?'

'You could try wearing it up.' Dawn coiled the hair around her fingers and held it in a tapering mound.

'It looks rather like a walnut whip,' said Melissa.

Dawn tittered. 'It suits you,' she said. 'Don't you like it?'

'Yes, I think I do. Can I do it myself, though?'

'Dead easy, I'll show you. You need a trim. I'll do that after your shampoo.'

Dawn was only too ready to chat as she wielded her scissors. She had done her apprenticeship at Petronella's and stayed on after qualifying. It wasn't always as smart as it was now, she said; quite scruffy in fact when she first went there but it was the only place she could get at the time. The new shop front and all the new decorations and fittings had been done about two years ago. Yes, she liked working there, Justin was a good boss, never pestered the girls and always shared the tips out fairly. Dawn wound Melissa's hair up in huge rollers, encased them in shrimp-coloured net, sat her under the dryer and summoned Julie, the manicurist.

Julie was equally communicative. From her, Melissa learned that business had been so bad before the renovations that everyone was expecting it to close down. Instead, the proprietress had spent 'loadsamoney' on a complete refit and taken on extra staff.

'Dunno where she got the cash,' Julie whispered, tucking Melissa's hand into what looked like a sandwich toaster to dry the first coat of varnish. 'There was a time when you'd think she bought her clothes at a jumble sale. Now she swans around in a fur coat like Lady Muck!'

The salon seemed to be doing a brisk trade. Justin was kept busy answering the telephone, receiving customers and supervising his staff. Several times he received deliveries of parcels which he handed over to an apprentice to unpack and check, except for one, delivered by a motorcyclist in black leather, which he stowed carefully under the desk.

A stout, heavily made-up woman in a simulated leopard-skin jacket came in. Julie bent her head over Melissa's hand and whispered, 'That's Mrs Farrell, the owner!' as Justin personally installed the newcomer at a wash-basin and began shampooing her pale yellow hair.

'You pay extra for Justin,' Julie explained, massaging cream into Melissa's hands. 'Except for her . . . she gets hers done for free. That's your manicure done.' She checked the timer on the drier. 'Another ten minutes and you should be ready.'

While Dawn was removing the rollers, Melissa asked casually, 'Did you ever know a girl called Babs who lived over this shop?'

'Babs Carter? I used to do her hair.'

'Have you seen her lately?'

Dawn shook her head, setting the sweep's brush aquiver. 'Did a bunk, didn't she? Never said a word to anyone.'

'Did you know her well?'

'We used to chat a bit. She did modelling so she had to have her hair done regular.'

'Did anyone here ever take phone messages for her?'

'Now and again. It was usually one of her boyfriends.'

'Would that have been Clive Shepherd?'

'His name was Clive, yes . . . I didn't know his other name. Is he a friend of yours?'

'I've met him,' said Melissa cautiously.

'He was nice,' said Dawn with a rush of warmth. 'He talked a bit posh but he was ever so friendly. Babs treated him rotten.' Her mouth formed an angry little pout.

'Oh?'

'Sometimes, when he called round for her, she wouldn't answer her bell. We knew she was in, and we knew he'd arranged to come round because we'd taken the message, but if she didn't feel like seeing him she just didn't open the door. You'd see him out there, looking up at her window, and then he'd go away looking miserable. When he found out she'd gone away for good without telling him, he was shattered . . . it was ever so sad. I liked him a lot.' The last words were hardly necessary.

'Do you think Babs tried to pack him up before she left?' Melissa asked.

'Don't know really. She'd say one thing one day, another thing the next. She went out with him quite a few times . . . went round to his flat once.' Dawn winked into the mirror. 'Nothing happened though. She told me afterwards, she didn't think he knew how!'

'She liked him, then?'

'I think she really preferred older men . . . but she liked the idea of his father's money.'

'His father's rich?'

'So she said . . . but he told her they'd quarrelled so he probably wouldn't have got any money out of him. You've seen Clive lately?'

'I went to visit him in hospital . . . he's very worried about Babs. That's why I asked if you'd seen her.'

'Clive in hospital? Is he ill?' Dawn's mobile face registered acute concern.

'Hadn't you heard? He had a bad car accident two days after Babs dis . . . went away.'

'Oh, no!' The voice was a breathless squeak of shock and distress. 'I didn't know. He's been in hospital all this time? He must have been hurt pretty bad.'

'He nearly died. He lost his memory but it's coming back slowly.' In the mirror, Melissa saw the girl's eyes fill. 'He's out of danger,' she added gently.

'That's good.' Dawn sniffed and dabbed her eyes with the back of her hand. 'I wonder if that's why that copper came round . . . trying to find Babs to tell her.'

'A policeman? Did you speak to him?'

'No, he didn't come in here. We saw him at the side door . . . the one that leads into the house. I expect he saw Mrs Farrell.'

Dawn dropped her voice. 'That's her . . . Justin's doing her hair. She owns the shop and lives upstairs . . . we thought perhaps her son had been in trouble again.' She finished brushing out Melissa's hair and began building it into a glossy whorl on her crown. 'You'd better watch this so's you can do it yourself,' she advised as her fingers twisted and manipulated and pushed hairpins into place. 'How does that look?'

'Smashing!' The transformation was complete. Melissa hardly recognised herself. 'Thanks very much.'

'Pleasure!' said Dawn but her eyes were still full of anxiety. 'When did you see Clive?'

'Last week.'

The girl hesitated before saying, 'Do you think I could go and see him?'

'I don't see why not,' said Melissa, thinking that this might be a very good idea and a possible way of taking Clive's mind off Babs. 'I don't think he gets many visitors. He's still quite poorly . . . you'd better ring first. It's a private clinic. I can give you the address but you'll have to look up the number.' She tore a sheet from her notebook and wrote down the details.

'Thanks ever so.' There was a light in Dawn's eyes that gave Melissa hope.

The door chimes tinkled and a slim girl in a grey coat and skirt entered, shot a quick glance at Justin, who was laughing prettily at some witticism from his influential client, and scurried across to speak to Dawn. Melissa took off the pink gown and brushed out her skirt while the two discussed plans for the evening in hasty undertones. Then the girl, whom Dawn addressed as Tracy, hurried out. Almost immediately a door slammed close by and the sound of footsteps running up a flight of stairs echoed from the other side of the salon wall.

'Tracy lives in Babs's old room,' Dawn explained, helping Melissa on with her coat. 'She only works round the corner so she comes home for lunch.'

Melissa settled her bill, put a generous tip in the staff box and was bowed out of the premises by Justin, who had handed over a rollered and netted Mrs Farrell to an apprentice who was escorting her to a dryer. It was just twelve o'clock and the proceedings at the U.P. Club did not begin until half past two. Melissa wandered up to the door adjacent to Petronella's and examined the two bell-pushes; one was labelled 'Farrell' and the other 'T. Simpson.'

After a moment's hesitation she pressed the second.

The footsteps came running down again and Tracy opened the door. She had taken off her jacket, revealing a blouse patterned with the emblem of a leading building society. In one hand she held a half-eaten sandwich.

'Tracy Simpson?'

'That's right.'

'My name's . . . Meryl Collins.' Almost, Melissa had forgotten her alias. 'I'm told Babs Carter used to live here.'

'She left nearly a year ago.'

'Yes, I know. Dawn told me.'

'Oh, yes?' Tracy took another bite of her sandwich. Melissa began to wonder what on earth she was doing here. An inexplicable impulse had prompted her to ring Tracy's bell and already she was regretting it. Still, the thing was done and she might as well try to sound convincing.

'Do you think I could come in for a moment? I'm trying to get in touch with Babs, you see . . . her boyfriend is in hospital and he's very worried about her.'

Tracy made no attempt to move aside. 'I don't know where she went. Try asking Mrs Farrell. She lives on the first floor . . . but she's next door having her hair done at the moment.'

'Yes, I know . . . I've just come from there.' Suddenly, Melissa had an intense desire to see the room where Babs had lived, a feeling that it might hold a clue that had been overlooked. 'I don't suppose Babs left anything behind? You haven't found . . . ?'

Tracy gave Melissa a strange look, then held the door open wider and motioned her inside.

'You'd better come up.' She led the way to a room on the top floor that occupied the entire width of the house. It had been furnished, apparently from junk-shops, as a bed-sitting room. In one corner was a kitchenette with a small sink and a miniature electric cooker. On the stained dining table was a tin tray with a mug of coffee and a packet of sandwiches.

'I'm sorry, I've interrupted your lunch,' said Melissa.

'Not to worry,' said Tracy. She took a swig from the mug, helped herself to another sandwich and went across to a rickety-looking chest that stood under the window and evidently doubled as a dressing-table. From a drawer, she took out a large plain manila envelope and handed it to Melissa. She looked acutely embarrassed.

'I dropped my comb behind the chest of drawers the other day and found these,' she said. 'I think they must have been hers. They're nasty,' she added as Melissa turned over the unsealed envelope and prepared to examine the contents.

One glance was sufficient to confirm that they were very nasty indeed. As Melissa had been at pains to point out to Bruce, she had on occasions encountered some fairly dubious characters and situations but this was the first time she had come across hard porn. Sickened, she pushed the photographs back into the envelope.

'I haven't shown them to anyone else,' said Tracy. 'Are they . . . is it Babs?'

'I imagine so . . . I've never actually met her,' said Melissa. She thought of Clive and wondered if he had any inkling.

'I don't know what to do with them.' Tracy finished her last sandwich and screwed up the plastic wrapper. 'If I put them in the dustbin, someone might find them. I've got nowhere to burn them. I thought of putting them through the office shredder but there's always someone about.' She picked up her mug, then put it down. 'Care for a coffee?'

'No, thanks all the same,' said Melissa. 'I'm going to have some lunch in a minute. Had you thought of handing these over to your landlady?'

Tracy looked appalled at the suggestion. 'And let her lecherous son get his grubby paws on them? Not likely!'

'Do you have trouble with him?'

Tracy grinned. She had well-cut features, a firm mouth and a determined set to her chin; her figure was slim but sturdy.

'I've been to classes in self-defence. I know how to handle his sort,' she said. The gleam in her eye suggested that she might welcome a chance to prove it.

'What about the police?'

'If old Ma Farrell found out I'd brought the fuzz round here, she'd kick me out.'

'Would you like me to take charge of them?' offered Melissa. 'I know someone who might be able to find out where they came from.'

'Would you?' Tracy appeared relieved. 'I hate the thought of that stuff in my room. The people who deal in it ought to be shot . . . and the girls who pose for the pictures . . . makes you sick!'

'You're absolutely right,' agreed Melissa. She found a plastic supermarket carrier in her shopping bag and put the envelope inside. 'I'll be going now. Don't bother to come down.'

As she closed the street door behind her, Mrs Farrell emerged from Petronella's. Her hair had been sculpted into a sphere that sat on top of her flushed face like a scoop of vanilla ice-cream on a dish of strawberries. She stared suspiciously as Melissa walked past her.

It was not until she had walked several yards, and heard the street door slam for the second time, that Melissa realised that Mrs Farrell, who had entered the salon with nothing but her handbag, had emerged carrying a parcel that looked exactly like the one Justin had stowed so carefully under his desk.

SIXTEEN

BEFORE LOOKING FOR SOMEWHERE TO HAVE LUNCH, Melissa went to the Photo-Me booth in the Post Office. The card admitting her to membership of the U.P. Club, which Gloria had handed over with much giggling and eye-rolling, had a space for a photograph without which, the holder was advised, there would be no admission. As she sat on the stool, posing and waiting for lights to flash, Melissa told herself for the umpteenth time that what she was doing was idiotic. Authentic backgrounds were all very well but she should have drawn the line at this. Supposing one of her readers, or worse, someone from the village, were to spot her? When at length the photographs clattered out of the machine, she was reassured; it would have taken a very sharp eye indeed to identify them as her own likeness.

She had lunch in the cafeteria of a large store, browsed for a while among the fashions and eventually made her way along Westgate and turned into the alley leading to The Usual Place. It had begun to drizzle with rain. Mindful of her new hair-style, which she felt was rather becoming, she put up the folding umbrella that she carried in her handbag.

The Usual Place had not yet closed after the lunchtime session and the last few customers were drifting out. She strolled past, glancing casually inside. It was a relief to see Pete Crane busily tidying up behind the bar. Presumably someone else would be in charge of admission to the U.P. Club, which meant that her disguise would not be subject to his scrutiny. It was quite absurd, but she felt even more excited, nervous even, over this escapade than she had over the visit to Petronella's.

Gloria had directed her to a side entrance and as she approach-ed, two women coming from the opposite direction turned in ahead of her, chatting to one another beneath their umbrellas. At least she would not be the first to arrive. She followed them to the door. Inside, in a vestibule like the reception area of a small hotel, a plump blonde woman with glass-green eyes sat behind a desk, checking the cards of new arrivals. In nasal, metallic tones generously sprinkled with glottal stops she was exchanging boisterous and highly suggestive comments with the women ahead of Melissa, who were evidently well-known to her. They addressed her familiarly as Annie and she barely glanced at the cards that they waved under her rather prominent nose.

'New member?' The eyes flicked from Melissa's proffered card to her face. They rested there for barely half a second, but she could almost hear the click of an internal camera. Annie would certainly know her again. 'Meryl Collins!' She pronounced the name with a knowing twitch of her scarlet lips as if she knew perfectly well it was assumed. 'You can leave your things in the cloakroom,' she said, jerking her head in the direction taken by the other women, who were just emerging from an alcove on the right of the passage, minus their umbrellas, coats and shopping-bags. 'Enjoy the show!'

'Thank you,' said Melissa politely but Annie was already busy with the next arrivals.

Melissa made her way to the cloakroom, which turned out to be a deep alcove fitted with hooks and shelves. The building was old and she guessed that the alcove had once been a china closet. A number of coats were already hanging up, there were wet umbrellas in a stand, packages on the shelves and several bulging supermarket carriers on the floor. Four canvas shopping trolleys were parked neatly side by side at the back of the alcove, with space for one more.

While Melissa was removing her coat and arranging her own belongings, two more women came in, one dragging a trolley which she lined up beside the others while expressing surprise that there was room for it just there and wondering volubly where Tara had got to. The second woman had no shopping, merely a large dripping umbrella which she thrust into the stand. They greeted Melissa with friendly smiles and introduced themselves as Sharon and Sue. Just in time, she remembered her name was Meryl. New arrivals were pressing in rapidly and Melissa and her new friends squeezed past and made their way upstairs.

'Did you hear Annie saying they've got a new boy today?' said Sharon, a small, scrawny woman well into middle age with a pallid complexion and curly dark hair that Melissa suspected was not her own.

'You mean, Georgie-boy isn't performing?' Sue's painted mouth formed an 'O' of disappointment. She was about the same age as her friend but her heavy make-up, pale blue trouser suit and high-heeled sandals were a gallant if unsuccessful attempt to disguise the fact. She turned to Melissa with a woeful expression. 'Now that is a shame! Gorgeous George is really smashing; the show won't be the same without him!'

'So I've heard!' Melissa did her best to register acute disappointment and felt she was doing it rather well. There was something warm and friendly about the two women, enlivening the monotony of their daily lives with a bit of harmless but risqué fun. She began to feel more at ease.

'So who've we got then?' demanded Sue.

'Sultry Sam, the Sizzling Sex-Pot!' said Sharon with disdain. 'He'd better be good, that's all!'

At the top of the stairs they drifted into a large room smelling of stale tobacco-smoke and dotted with small tables and chairs, a number of which were already occupied. At the far end was a small stage with curtains, spotlights and an upright piano to one side. As Melissa had half-expected, most of the audience were middle-aged and had obviously dressed themselves up for the occasion. There was a buzz of chatter and an air of expectation.

Sharon and Sue exchanged effusive greetings with a pair of stout, homely creatures standing just inside the door who looked as if they would be more at home at a meeting of the Mothers' Union. Cordially urging Melissa to join them, they all sat down together and proceeded for her benefit to identify everyone present, reeling off a string of names, all of which were highly improbable and most of which she promptly forgot.

At one of the tables close to the stage was a small group dominated by a woman with magenta hair, a loud voice and an awesomely sculpted bosom. She was expressing indignation at the change of programme and relied on a single adjective, frequently repeated, to record her disappointment. Sharon and Sue, sitting one on either side of Melissa, twittered in disapproval.

'Her name's Lorraine but we calls her Effie . . .'

'On account of she keeps saying eff.'

'Effing this and effing that . . .'

'So vulgar . . .'

'Can't think why Annie lets her in . . .'

'She's a friend of Annie's . . .'

'Annie's not vulgar . . .'

'She doesn't use that word . . .'

The room was filling rapidly. While the others at her table gossiped Melissa sat back and looked around. There was a bar along one wall but towels were draped over the pump handles and only the coffee and tea-making equipment appeared to be operating. She wondered if the reason had anything to do with not wishing the audience to become over-excited during the performance and had to put her hand over her mouth to suppress a giggle.

It was almost half past two. Melissa suddenly remembered the envelope that Tracy had given her, which she had left in her shopping-bag. She had no idea of the level of security at the U.P. Club but if any light-fingered person should have access to the cloakroom during the performance and make off with the photographs, all chance of tracking down their source would vanish.

'I've just remembered, I left something very important downstairs,' she whispered in Sharon's ear. 'I think I'll pop down and get it.'

'Oh, I wouldn't worry,' said Sharon. 'Annie's down there all the time during the performance . . . she keeps an eye on our things.'

'It'll be quite all right,' Sue chipped in. 'A fly couldn't get in there without Annie spotting it!'

'Remember that time when Jackie went down for her hankie . . . ?'

'In such a hurry, she felt in someone else's pocket . . .'

'Annie was on to her in a second . . .'

'And it was Jackie's first time here . . .'

'So embarrassing . . .'

'Genuine mistake of course . . .'

Their chorus was interrupted by Pete Crane appearing on the little stage to a generous round of applause. He beamed on the assembly and addressed them in a jovial bellow.

'Good afternoon, girls!'

'Good afternoon, Pete!' they responded, Effie's voice rising fortissimo above the others.

At their first meeting over the bar at The Usual Place, Melissa had suspected Pete of being a womaniser. His attitude towards this entirely female gathering now confirmed the impression. He exuded a sensuous bonhomie; his smile had a raffish brilliance and his voice a lubricity that she found slightly off-putting. She wondered if he was Annie's husband. They both spoke with a south-east London accent.

'Lovely to see all of you,' he declared, rubbing his hands. 'And we can see nearly all of Marlene, can't we?' There were sniggers as attention was briefly focussed on a gipsyish woman of statuesque proportions. 'I love that blouse you're nearly wearing, darling!' This evoked uproarious laughter, with Marlene's bosom threatening to wobble clean out of her scanty corsage. Plainly, Pete considered himself to be the warm-up act and there was no doubt that he had an enthusiastic following.

'Welcome to our two new members as well!' he continued. 'I hope you realise your good fortune, Meryl and Annabel!' His round eyes, the colour of aniseed balls, singled out first Melissa and then a tiny, fragile-looking woman wearing dark glasses. Curious but friendly glances homed in on the two newcomers. 'It just so happened a couple of our members moved house or you'd never have got in. We don't often get vacancies, do we, girls?'

A chorus of 'No's rippled obediently round the room.

'Right then!' said Pete. 'I know you don't want to listen to me rabbiting on. You can't wait for the bingo to start, can you?' A huge wink and an exaggerated emphasis on 'bingo' raised another round of titters. 'So have your fifty pees ready, girls, Johnnie's coming round with the cards. Fifty pees, eh?' His eyes rolled suggestively. 'Must be all the lager you drank last night, Marlene!' More squeals of appreciation.

Johnnie, a white-faced lad in jeans and a sleeveless denim jacket was well ahead with the distribution, having started before Pete began speaking. Some people bought several cards, Sharon and Sue took two apiece and Melissa one.

'Course, this is just a cover-up,' explained Sue unnecessarily, nudging Melissa in the ribs. 'It doesn't go on for too long before the real show starts.'

'The prizes aren't bad, though,' said Sharon. 'It comes in handy to take something home now and again. Stops the old man getting suspicious. You married?'

Melissa shook her head.

'Lucky old you!'

The games proceeded at a brisk pace. The winners collected their prizes from Pete along with a smacking kiss, a slap on the bottom and an assurance that the wrappings concealed nothing they couldn't show their husbands. An interval was declared for refreshments, during which Melissa, directed by Sharon, slipped out to the toilet on the landing. Glancing down the stairs she saw Annie, still mounting guard in the hall. The green eyes flicked upwards as she passed to and fro, missing nothing. Her vigilance was reassuring.

Back in the hall, the curtains were closed and a single spotlight switched on. Conversation quickly died away as Pete remounted the stage.

'Right, girls, this is the big moment! Fags out, fasten your seat-belts, prepare for take-off!' He paused to savour the gleeful response to the innuendo. 'Now, as you know, the bad news is that your old mate Gorgeous George can't be with us today.' A sigh ran round the room. 'But the good news is we have with us a lad who'll drive you just as crazy. A big welcome then for Sultry Sam, the Sizzling Sex-Pot!'

Above the applause Effie was heard to shout, 'C'me on, Sammy my love, show us yer knackers!' Sue and Sharon tutted in shocked distress.

To a background of throbbing, sensual music the curtains slid apart and the spotlight picked up a stocky figure in black jacket and trousers standing in a gorilla-like posture near the back of the stage. A hank of dark hair fell over the forehead and the full, red mouth was bunched in a pout. Sultry Sam slithered towards the front of the stage in a series of undulating jerks and with much suggestive twitching of the hips. Then, ignoring his audience, he began to pose before an imaginary mirror, offering first his left and then his right profile, tilting back his head to display his muscular neck, then lowering it like a bull about to charge, scowling upwards from beneath his heavy black brows. He turned his back and glared over one shoulder into space, then leaned forward and dug his hands into the back pockets of his trousers. The spotlight glistened on the soft black leather as, to a swelling murmur of approval, it tightened over his well-shaped buttocks.

The music increased in intensity. Nonchalantly wandering about the stage, Sultry Sam began to unfasten his jacket. A glimpse of bronze, hairless chest embellished with a silver medallion drew sighs of admiration. Having discarded his jacket he slowly peeled off his shirt, expanded his rib-cage, pulled in his stomach and flexed his biceps to a mounting chorus of anticipation. Then, with a languid yawn, he dropped on to a stool and began, very slowly, unzipping his high-heeled boots. The sounds of approval changed to impatient mutterings.

Melissa was fascinated, as much by the audience as by the performance. There must have been forty women in the room and the attention of every one was riveted on the stage. Some were leaning on their elbows, some had their hands to their mouths, others gripped the edge of their table. Quite a few seemed to be breathing heavily and one or two had covered their faces as if in embarrassment but missed nothing through their spread-out fingers.

The music grew louder and the tempo quickened. Sultry Sam shed his tight black trousers to reveal a pair of smooth brown muscular legs topped by shiny red boxer shorts which he pulled down a few inches and then pulled up again. With variations, he continued this tantalising performance until someone—Effie, of course—screamed 'Get 'em off!' With a smouldering look in her direction he removed the shorts, only to reveal another, much scantier garment whose sole means of support seemed to be a dangling piece of scarlet ribbon.

By this time the women were squealing and chanting hysterically, waving their arms and bouncing in their seats like a crowd of children at a Punch and Judy show. Sultry Sam left the stage and began prancing among the tables, which had been cunningly arranged so that he could remain just out of reach of outstretched hands making grabs at him as he wiggled past. As the music reached a crescendo he turned, raced back on to the stage and tweaked at the ribbon. His final, flimsy covering fell away; to delighted, awestruck gasps he executed a pirouette worthy of a ballet dancer before scurrying into the wings.

Above the cheering and clapping came Effie's full-throated call to battle: 'After him, girls!' Like a herd of cattle stampeding, a section of the audience left their tables and rushed on to the stage. Sharon and Sue remained firmly seated, shaking their heads.

'I do wish she wouldn't,' sighed Sharon.

'She does get carried away,' agreed Sue.

From somewhere out of sight came a masculine shout of mock protest and the sounds of a scuffle before a door slammed. Still shrieking with laughter, the pursuers began returning to their seats.

'Seems as if Sultry Sam won by a short head!' whispered Melissa.

It was clear, however, from Effie's lewd comments and gestures, that the margin was not short and had nothing to do with a head.

'She's such a bad influence,' said Sharon sadly.

'Lowers the tone,' agreed Sue.

'See you next week, then?' said Sharon as they put on their coats and retrieved their belongings, closely supervised by Annie.

'You must see Gorgeous George,' insisted Sue. 'He'll be back soon, won't he, Annie?'

'Should be,' said Annie. 'Pulled a muscle in the gym, that's all . . . nothing serious.'

'No bits missing, eh?' cackled Effie. Sharon was searching for her shopping, which someone appeared to have moved.

'That Tara!' she said crossly. 'Anyone would think she owned that corner at the back.'

'Cheek!' said Sue.

Promising to come to next week's show if she could manage it, Melissa said goodbye to her new friends and headed for the car park. She was grateful for the fact that it was now raining steadily, which meant that she was unlikely to be spotted by any of her neighbours while driving through the village in her flamboyant make-up. She put the car away, scurried indoors and made a beeline for the bathroom to remove the worst of Debbie's excesses. After some consideration she decided to keep her hair the way it was for the rest of the day. She must try to remember how Dawn did it.

She went into her study to record the day's activities. Her impressions of the U.P. Club she put to one side in preparation for next day's work on her novel. Her observations at Petronella's and her meeting with Tracy were more factual. The events of the afternoon had driven the matter of the photographs to the back of her mind but now, as she wrote, an awareness of their probable implications began taking shape. They seemed to confirm Bruce's conviction that something sinister was behind Babs's disappearance.

Bruce telephoned at half past six.

'How did you get on?' he wanted to know.

'I think we may be on to something,' she said, 'but I don't think it's quite what you were expecting.'

'Yes?' The line fairly throbbed with excitement.

'I'd rather not talk about it over the telephone. Can you come round for a drink?'

'Of course . . . when?'

'Give me time to get a bite to eat . . . say in about forty-five minutes?'

'I haven't eaten either. Why don't I pick up something at the take-away for both of us?'

'What a good idea . . . I don't feel a bit like cooking.'

'Chinese or Indian?'

'Indian, I think.' Something hot and spicy would seem appropriate this evening, she thought, and immediately felt guilty. Things had become too serious for flippancy.

By the time Bruce arrived, the rain had stopped. He picked his way to the front door, carefully dodging the puddles that had changed from muddy grey to a glossy blue dappled with flecks of gold. He handed over a bag of plastic containers and opened cans of lager while Melissa transferred the food to the dishes she had put to warm in the oven.

'It smells good.' She sniffed appreciatively as she closed the oven door. 'I didn't realise until you phoned just how hungry I am . . . I've had nothing since lunch.'

'Perhaps you'd like to eat first and tell me your adventures afterwards?'

'I'll tell while we eat but perhaps the exhibits had better wait or you might lose your appetite.'

His grin vanished as he realized that she was not joking. 'Exhibits?'

'Some rather nasty pictures.'

Bruce's eyes saucered and he seemed for the moment lost for words.

Melissa put plates and cutlery on the table. 'Do you mind eating in the kitchen?'

He brushed aside the question with an impatient gesture. 'You mean porno pictures? Who of? How did you get hold of them?'

Briefly, she told him while they helped themselves to the food. 'You can see them afterwards . . . and if you don't mind I'd rather not be in the room while you're looking. I assume they're of Babs . . .' Melissa picked up her fork and regarded her plate with distaste.

'Something wrong with it?'

'No . . . no, it looks delicious. It's just . . . I didn't look at all the pictures but the ones I did see were pretty revolting.'

'Let's talk about something else for a bit. What about your visit to Petronella's? Your hair looks great, by the way.' The admiration in his eyes was pleasantly disturbing.

'Thank you,' she said. 'You should have seen me when I got home. The make-up Debbie gave me . . . it was more a disguise.'

'Isn't that what you wanted for your assignation with Gorgeous George? How did that go, by the way?'

'I thought the performance was rather tame but the audience reaction was fascinating. Imagine forty grown women shrieking like a bunch of kids on a Sunday School treat . . . and then squabbling over parking places for their shopping trolleys!'

'Nothing to shock your strait-laced detective sergeant, then?'

'Oh, I'm sure I can make it shocking enough for Dilys . . .'

He shouted with laughter as she described the antics of Effie and Sultry Sam. 'And did you learn anything interesting at Petronella's?'

'Not really . . . at least, nothing that couldn't have a perfectly innocent explanation.' She ran through her conversations with Julie and Dawn, not forgetting the package that Mrs Farrell collected from the salon. As she expected, Bruce pounced on this with joyful barks.

'It could well have been a parcel of drugs!' he exclaimed. "That would account for the sudden show of wealth . . . the new salon, the fancy fur coat and all the rest . . . and you say the son's been in trouble . . . it all fits!'

'Don't get carried away,' said Melissa. 'Mrs Farrell could have inherited some money, or won the pools, or raised a bank loan. The district is up-and-coming and plenty of finance houses would regard it as a good investment. And you can't assume that the parcel contained drugs just because it came by special delivery.'

'No, I suppose not,' admitted Bruce with some reluctance. 'But you say the son's got a criminal record?'

'Dawn hinted at some trouble with the police but it could have been nothing more sinister than a breach of the peace on a Saturday night. You could check on that, couldn't you? You must have a police contact, all reporters do.'

'Yes, of course.' He put down his fork and finished his lager. Melissa began clearing the table. 'What about these photographs?'

'Here.' She fetched the envelope and handed it to him. 'If you don't mind, I'll go upstairs while you look at them.'

When she returned a few minutes later, Bruce was staring out of the window, plainly shaken by what he had seen. His mouth was set and his eyes were hard as flint.

'Are they Babs?' she asked.

'Some of them could be almost anyone . . . but two or three are unmistakably Babs.' He began prowling jerkily round the room. 'She was a stripper, she was a hooker, she was on to the main chance, but still there was something . . . childlike . . . appealing about her. I'd never have dreamed she'd do . . . that!'

'Money, of course. Maybe she was saving up for her old age,' said Melissa acidly, then stopped short, the coffee jar in her hand. 'I've just remembered something you told me the first time I met you . . . didn't she meet Clive because she wanted to take out an endowment policy? If he was prepared to marry her, he'd represent security. He said she'd been brought up in homes . . . maybe she was scared stiff of being left destitute.' She filled the coffee machine and switched it on.

'I'd forgotten that endowment policy,' said Bruce. 'That's something we could check on. The premiums would have stopped when she disappeared.'

'If she's still alive, she could be paying them to another branch of the company,' Melissa pointed out.

Bruce nodded absently. 'What would a girl get for that kind of session?' he mused, gesturing at the envelope, his mouth twisted in disgust. 'Fifty quid? A hundred?'

Melissa shook her head. 'I've no idea but it would have to be a lot more than the normal modelling fee and if she wasn't spending it, she'd want somewhere safe to keep it. A building society perhaps . . . there's one just round the corner from Petronella's. Tracy works there.'

'Something else to check on,' said Bruce. 'We could enquire if they've got an account in Babs's name . . . and if it's been used lately . . . and whether . . .'

'Now just a minute.' Melissa filled mugs with coffee and put milk and sugar on the table. 'No building society is going to give that sort of information about one of their customers without authority.' She sipped coffee, knowing that he was not going to like what she was going to say. 'I think,' she said, looking him in the eye, 'you should hand those photographs over to the police.

They may be able to trace where they came from.'

'But I know where they came from!' Bruce leapt to his feet, like a dog about to chase a stick. 'The Up Front Model Agency . . . of course! I knew they were into some kind of racket . . . but it isn't drugs, it's porn!' He bounded excitedly round the room, then grabbed at the envelope, pulled out the photographs and examined their backs. 'There's a code number on these . . . it should be traceable. Suppose we got hold of some of their pictures and compared them?'

Melissa eyed him warily. 'The police . . .' she began.

'The hell with the police . . . this is our show!'

'Now wait a minute . . . leave me out of it . . .'

'But it's a doddle!' he insisted. 'You're a knock-out with that hairdo . . . you'd need a bit more make-up; go back and see Debbie . . . they'd jump at you. There are bound to be other pictures you could . . .'

'Oh, I'm sure they keep a few spicy examples lying around to amuse the clients while they're waiting!' said Melissa. 'No, Bruce, forget it. There's no way I'm going to poke around in that agency.'

'But why? There's no risk . . .'

'No risk, he says! I don't think you've really grasped what we've stumbled against. People who deal in porn can be just as dangerous as drugs dealers . . . in fact the two often go together. You've got one hard bit of evidence . . . take it to the police and tell them everything you know.' She looked away from him to avoid the smile that she found so hard to resist. Hard, but not impossible. 'Leave me out of it,' she begged. 'I've got work to do. Deadlines. An agent breathing down my neck. *Go away!*'

'Oh, very well.' He was disappointed, he was conceding for the moment but she suspected she had not heard the last of it. 'I'm going . . . I've got some hard thinking to do.'

Melissa thrust the envelope into his hands and propelled him towards the door. 'Police,' she said firmly as she opened it.

It was after nine o'clock but there was still plenty of light. The spring was well advanced and the valley was awash with hawthorn blossom. Even the ash trees, always late-comers to the scene, wore wisps of green lace.

'Lovely evening,' said Bruce, taking a deep breath. 'I quite envy you, living in this peaceful rural paradise.'

'It hasn't been very peaceful, or paradisical lately,' said Melissa drily.

Bruce grinned, walked towards his car and then turned back.

'By the way, I nearly forgot to tell you, I've remembered where I met your padre!'

'Mr Calloway? Where was that?'

'You aren't going to believe this!'

'Well?'

'I only remembered the other evening because I saw him there again.' His sly, almost furtive expression suggested a schoolboy about to tell a smutty joke.

'For goodness' sake, where?' Melissa asked impatiently.

'The Usual Place.'

'Well, what's so strange about that? People go to restaurants for perfectly innocent reasons. It isn't all strippers and bingo.'

'It is for the dirty old men who sneak through that side door on a Friday night!' Bruce gave a malicious chuckle as he added, 'They haven't got the nerve of the hussies who pile in bold as brass for their afternoon sessions of bingo-in-inverted-commas!'

Melissa was not impressed. 'So I'm a brazen hussy now, am I? And what were you doing, skulking round that side door—or shouldn't I ask?'

Bruce assumed an air of injured innocence. 'I was taking a short cut to the car park, if you must know. But your reverend was there for the bum-and-tit show all right, and very sheepish he looked in his soft hat and dark glasses!'

Melissa was on the point of protesting that he must be mistaken but Iris, weeding behind her hedge unobserved by either of them, got there first. She shot up like a furious jack-in-the-box, her face scarlet and her eyes glittering with rage.

'How dare you spread such . . . such filth!' she hissed. She made a stabbing gesture towards Bruce with a weeding fork and then rounded on Melissa. 'This your young man with all the clever theories?'

'Oh . . . er . . . Bruce Ingram of the *Gazette*—Miss Ash,' murmured Melissa in embarrassment.

'The *Gazette*!' spluttered Iris, brandishing the fork under Bruce's nose. 'You planning to print your lies in that rag?'

'Here, hang on!' Bruce protested, keeping a wary eye on the fork. 'The *Gazette* is a family paper. We shan't be running a feature on vicars and tarts if that's what you're worried about!'

He gave a sickly grin which seemed to enrage Iris even further.

'Don't you dare publish a word of this garbage . . . !' she began, but Bruce, recovering his poise, managed one of his most charming smiles.

'Miss Ash,' he said earnestly, 'I promise you I'm not looking for a story and I won't mention what you have just overheard to anyone else. I only told Mel—Mrs Craig—because when I met your Rector the other day I was sure I'd seen him before but couldn't remember where.'

Iris lowered her arm but she did not take her eyes off him. 'Swear it?' she said sharply. He nodded. 'Ruin a man's life, that sort of scandal can. All lies, but mud sticks.'

'You're quite right.' He sounded sincere. He turned back to Melissa. 'I'll be in touch.'

'You meant that?' she whispered urgently as he got into his car and reached for the ignition. 'Promise you won't let that get splashed around?'

'I promise.'

Feeling faintly sick, Melissa turned away and went indoors, ignoring Bruce's farewell wave. A few minutes later there was a knock. Iris stood in the porch with Binkie clutched in her arms.

'Got to talk to you,' she muttered, her eyes on the ground.

'Of course . . . come in. Would you like some coffee?'

'Thanks.' In the kitchen, Iris prowled restlessly to and fro with her cheek pressed against Binkie's head while Melissa loaded the supper things into the dish-washer and brewed more coffee.

'Rather stay out here,' she said when Melissa suggested going to the sitting-room. She sat down with the cat on her lap, staring at the mug on the table in front of her.

'Can you trust him?' she asked suddenly.

'You mean Bruce?'

'Hate reporters. Love a bit of dirt. One of them asked me . . . after I found *it* . . . if I lived alone. Know what he was thinking, dirty beast. Told him to mind his own business!'

'I'm pretty sure Bruce meant what he said,' replied Melissa. 'The *Gazette* isn't a scandal-sheet.'

Iris continued her contemplation of the steaming coffee-mug.

'It's true, you know,' she blurted out after a long silence.

'What is?' Melissa asked the question mechanically but already she knew the answer and felt immensely sad.

'What he said about . . .' Iris seemed unable to finish.

'About Mr Calloway, you mean?' Melissa prompted in a low voice.

Iris nodded. Her hands were cupped round Binkie's head, her thin shoulders sagged, her head was bent and her eyes were closed. It *was* almost as if she were praying. Melissa's mind went back to the evening when she and Bruce had come upon the Rector standing with bowed head beside that woodland grave. Did he know, or at least suspect, whose body had lain there? She remembered now what it was that had struck her as strange. It was the way he had said, 'So it *was* a woman', as if he had half-expected it.

'How do you know it's true?' she asked.

'Saw him once. Long time ago. Me and a friend had supper in . . . that place. We'd just come out. Saw him dive up that alley, through a side door. He didn't see me. Found out later what went on there.' She lifted her head and turned a ravaged face to Melissa. 'He could have come to me!' she moaned. Her eyes were streaming, her mouth worked, her arms encircled the cat in a despairing embrace. Words jerked out of her in gasps as she fought for control. 'She . . . wouldn't let him touch her . . . once she had the boys . . . needn't have gone for tarts . . . could have had me!' Her voice rose to a wail in which Binkie joined as her grip on him tightened.

'Oh, Iris!' Melissa felt her own eyes fill. 'Who told you this . . . about Mrs Calloway, I mean?'

Iris's mouth twisted in contempt. 'She did! Boasted about it. Thinks herself so pure and virtuous. Thought I was the same. Not married, ergo think sex is dirty. She's the dirty one, the frigid miserable bitch. She drove him to . . . that!'

'Here, drink this.' Melissa put a glass of brandy beside the untouched mug of coffee. Oh my God, she thought, where is all this going to end?

SEVENTEEN

NEXT MORNING, GLORIA WAS BURSTING WITH CURIosity about the proceedings at the U.P. Club. Melissa, still depressed by the revelations of the previous evening, tried to play the whole thing down. Gloria attributed her lack of enthusiasm to disappointment.

'What a pity you missed Gorgeous George!' she sighed. 'I was dying to know if what they says about him is really true!'

'You haven't seen him, then?'

'Can't, can I? I has to fetch the kids from school. Besides, my Stanley's place is only just around the corner. He'd half-kill me if he spotted me going in there!' She wriggled with delight at the thought and a pair of earrings that Melissa had not seen before swung wildly to and fro.

'They're nice!' Melissa remarked, hoping to divert attention from the antics of Gorgeous George and his public.

'Like them?' Gloria tilted her head to invite closer inspection. 'Solid gold. My Stan says I deserve the best!' Her brown eyes glowed with love and pride.

'I think your Stan's quite right,' said Melissa gently.

'Ooh, thanks!' Gloria gave the earrings an affectionate pat before beginning to assemble her cleaning materials. 'Mustn't waste any more time, must I?' She bustled off with the vacuum cleaner and Melissa went upstairs to write letters.

Later, just as they were finishing their coffee-break, there was a knock at the door. It was the Rector. In the fresh morning light his appearance was more wholesome and cherubic than ever. It was difficult to associate him with grubby little adventures at The Usual Place.

'Good morning, Mr Calloway,' said Melissa. 'Do come in!'

'Thank you.' He wiped his feet carefully before stepping inside. 'I see Gloria—Mrs Parkin—is here.' He nodded towards the red Escort, beaming.

'That's right. She comes to me every Wednesday morning. We've just been having coffee; would you like a cup?'

'Now that is most kind.' He followed her eagerly into the kitchen where Gloria was rinsing her mug at the sink. She greeted him with a cheery smile as she reached forward to pick up a teacloth, treating him to a glimpse of cleavage which brought a sparkle to his eyes.

'Morning, Rector. Bit chilly this morning, innit?'

'Just a little, but at least the rain has stopped.' He rubbed his hands and cleared his throat.

'Right then, Mrs Craig, I'll be getting on with upstairs.' Gloria collected her paraphernalia, contriving as she did so to drop a duster. Melissa, spooning out instant coffee, noticed Mr Calloway's appreciative eye on her well-rounded rear as she bent to retrieve it. Yesterday, she might have felt indulgent amusement, but not now.

'I've brought this month's parish magazine,' he said, extracting it from his carrier bag with one hand and accepting the proffered cup with the other. 'I was wondering . . . would it be an impertinence to ask if you would take out an annual subscription? Only three pounds, you know, and it would help to reduce the paperwork.'

'But of course.' Melissa took her handbag from a drawer.

'That is most kind of you.' He put the three pounds in a little purse and made a note in his pocket-book. 'And . . . hrmm . . . I wonder if I could possibly prevail on you to contribute the occasional article?'

Melissa concealed a smile, remembering Iris's warning. 'What sort of article . . . not about crime, surely?'

'Oh no, no, of course not. Just a little piece . . . I leave the topic to you, as a professional writer . . .' He made a vague gesture as if trying to conjure inspiration out of the air. 'Just now and again, you know . . . it's so difficult to get fresh ideas from our limited list of contributors . . . of course, they all do a splendid job,' he hurried on, glancing around as if afraid that some of them might be listening and take offence.

'Well, I'll think about it,' Melissa promised. 'Excuse me,' she added as the telephone rang. She went into the sitting-room to answer it. Bruce was on the line.

'Hot news!' he told her. 'A dentist in Worcester has identified the body in Benbury Woods as a former patient. He treated her about six years ago when she was living in a children's home. Her name was on the records as Barbara Cartwright.'

'Which you think she changed to Babs Carter?'

'Exactly. The police are trying to trace what became of her after she left the home. We know where she fetched up, don't we?' Waves of excitement flowed along the wire.

'Are you going to tell them?'

'No need. They'll find out soon enough.'

'Have you handed those pictures over to them?'

'Not yet. Haven't had time.'

'I think you should make time. Any news of Clive?'

'Rowena's reported two calls. That girl is a jewel.'

'And?' Melissa suppressed a twinge of something she refused to recognise as jealousy.

'His manager rang to enquire about his chances of coming back to work. He's okay . . . he's been to see Clive several times.'

'And the other call?'

'A man called Preston, on behalf of Clive's father.'

'Genuine?'

'Oh, yes, it's routine. The old man never contacts the hospital personally.'

'Not exactly a loving relationship, is it? Well, nothing sinister so far.'

'Rowena's going to keep on monitoring. I must go now. I have to do a stint in the Magistrate's Court. I'll keep you posted.'

When Melissa returned to the kitchen, the Rector was standing at the window.

'I've been admiring your garden,' he said. 'You've made splendid progress.'

'Yes, it's coming on. Iris gives me plenty of advice and encouragement.'

'Ah, yes, Miss Ash is a dedicated gardener!' He turned to Melissa, concern in his eyes. 'I trust she has recovered from her terrible experience?'

'Oh yes, I think so. She's pretty resilient.' There was a short silence before Melissa came to her decision. 'That was a friend of mine who works on the *Gazette*,' she said. 'He told me that the body Iris discovered in the woods has been identified.'

'Really?' Mr Calloway's face lengthened. 'Was it someone local?'

'A former inmate of a children's home near Worcester called Barbara Cartwright.'

Apprehension flickered in the grey-green eyes. 'Worcester?' he whispered.

'My friend believes that she came to Gloucester, changed her name to Babs Carter and worked as a bar attendant and stripper at The Usual Place.'

The moment she had spoken, she wished she hadn't. The Rector's face puckered like a shrunken toy balloon and his healthy pink colour faded to an ashy grey. His mouth worked but no sound came.

'You knew her?' Melissa asked.

He gave a great sigh that was almost a sob. 'I knew a girl called Babs who . . . worked there.'

'I thought perhaps you did.'

'She . . . told me she came from Worcester.'

There was a clattering overhead and the sound of the toilet being flushed. They both looked up in alarm. They had completely forgotten Gloria's presence.

'Don't worry, she can't possibly have heard,' Melissa said quickly.

'How did you find out?'

'I'm afraid you were seen at least twice at The Usual Place, going in by the side way.'

He closed his eyes and swallowed. 'Who by?'

'As far as I know, by people who are unlikely to give you away . . . unless of course it was you who . . .' The notion seemed so monstrous that she could not finish.

'Killed her? Oh no, no! I . . . loved her!' The words were barely audible. Upstairs, Gloria's voice rose in song above the hum of the vacuum cleaner.

'You'd better come into the sitting-room and have a drop of brandy,' Melissa suggested, but he made an emphatic gesture of refusal.

'No, no, that would never do. Anthea would notice. I must go, I have to think. Poor little Babs!'

'The identification isn't absolutely certain . . . I mean, the police haven't yet connected Barbara Cartwright with Babs Carter, but I don't expect it will take them long.'

'You think they will find out I knew her, and ask questions?'

'It's possible.'

He got to his feet. He seemed to have aged ten years in a few minutes.

'Thank you for warning me,' he said quietly. 'You won't . . . ?'

'I shall forget all about this conversation.' Melissa handed him the carrier bag containing the rest of the parish magazines. 'Don't go without this . . . and I'll give some thought to a few articles for you!' She raised her voice to a hearty brightness as Gloria began clumping down the stairs. Mr Calloway took his cue like a professional actor.

'That's really most kind of you!' He even managed a smile on his way out. 'Good morning, ladies!'

'He don't look too good, do he?' commented Gloria, rummaging in the cupboard for furniture polish. 'Must be his indigestion. Always drinks his coffee too fast, he do!'

When Gloria had gone, Melissa ate a hasty lunch and went to her study. Recent events were fermenting in her mind along with the plot of her book. It was like having two casseroles in the oven at the same time, with one boiling over into the other. She had started to keep two sets of notes, one of actual happenings and the other with ideas for the story. Several times she had found herself making entries in the wrong file.

After recording the events and conversations of that morning, she sat for a long time staring at her typewriter, unable to forget the misery in Mr Calloway's eyes. She did not for one moment believe he was a killer, but others might. If he were traced and questioned by the police there was a strong possibility that the press would get hold of it. Reporters would descend on him like crows on the carcase of a rabbit. His life and that of his wife and his sons would be devastated.

Then there was Iris. She had found the body. If her discovery should lead, after the slow but inexorable processes it had set in train, to the exposure of Mr Calloway's weakness, the secret of which she had—unbeknown to him—guarded for so long, she would almost feel responsible for bringing about the ruin of the man she worshipped.

Melissa got up from her desk and moved restlessly about the room, trying to switch her mind back to her work. She had reached a point in her novel where a second murder was about to take place. Thinking back to the first chapter and the discovery of a corpse in the shepherd's hut, she recalled that, even while she was absorbed in planning the opening paragraphs, Iris had been recoiling in horror from the realisation of what she had exhumed. Just a coincidence of course, but there had been others, less sinister but nonetheless bringing a sense of edginess to events that were in themselves commonplace.

Melissa had never believed in the supernatural yet now she found herself fancying that some mischievous spirit with a warped sense of humour was at work, using the creative powers of her mind to reveal past crimes or, worse still, to lead her into predictions of future violence and terror. There were moments, especially on chilly sunless evenings or on windy nights when she awoke to the moan of the wind through the broken walls of Daniel's hut, when she had an uneasy sensation that Hawthorn Cottage had not yet accepted her as its rightful owner. Could it be possible that the shade of old Jacko, who had lived there in solitude for so many years, was hostile to her presence and had hit on a bizarre and horrifying form of revenge? It was a chilling, if wholly irrational, thought.

Exhorting herself not to be ridiculous, she jerked back her chair and went downstairs, feeling a need to be out of doors. She thought of asking Iris to come for a walk but decided against it. Sooner or later, she would learn about the identification of Babs's body, but that could wait. The last thing Melissa wanted was to talk about it now.

The weather was cool and cloudy with a fresh breeze blowing from the west. Melissa put on her anorak and thick shoes and set off, following the path down to the brook. At this time of day there was seldom anyone about although presently, when the schools were out and if the rain held off, there would be children playing by the brook and in the evening a few people would bring their dogs to let off steam chasing rabbits up and down the banks. Once, this had been a well-trodden path for Benbury folk trudging to their labour on the outlying farms. Now, such as still worked on the land went by car.

Soon, Melissa found herself alone on the edge of Benbury Wood. The strengthening breeze made a rushing sound through the treetops. Branches creaked overhead. Small, invisible feet scurried among the undergrowth. Without admitting to herself that she felt in any way nervous, she avoided the dim paths and followed one she had not taken before, skirting the woods and climbing away to the left. It was steep, overgrown with brambles and evidently little used, but after a couple of hundred yards it gave without warning on to a farm track. She crossed over, picking her way round a heap of loose stones, and found herself on the crest of a broad, flat ridge looking out over the Severn Vale.

Away to her right, the ridge curved westwards; to her left it ran almost due south. In front of her, a little below the skyline and nestling in the curve like a baby in the crook of its mother's elbow, was a handsome stone house set in landscaped grounds, partly hidden by trees and surrounded by a high stone wall. Through gaps in the trees, Melissa caught glimpses of a broad grassy track running in a straight line past the back of the property and along the ridge into the distance.

There was the sound of an approaching tractor. Presently it appeared, dragging a trailer-load of straw with a black dog sitting on top. The driver lifted a hand in casual greeting as he passed, then gave a broad grin of recognition. It was Dick Woodman. He pulled over to the edge of the track and leaned out of his cab.

'Out for a walk, then?' he called.

'That's right,' she shouted back. 'I haven't been this way before.'

He jumped down, leaving the tractor engine belching diesel fumes into the undergrowth.

'That's Benbury Park down there,' he told her.

'I wondered if it was.'

'See that? That strip of grass that looks like a race-track?'

'Yes, what is it?'

'That's their private airstrip!' He looked as proud as if he owned the property and she obliged him by looking impressed. She looked down again at the house, thinking what a perfect setting it would make for her novel. There was a pair of heavy iron gates let into the wall with a short drive on to the strip where no doubt cars would come to collect the airborne guests and drive them to the house with their luggage, their equipment and whatever else they might bring with them. It was frustrating not to be able to visit the house. It crossed her mind that the Rector had said nothing further about introducing her to the Vowdens. Well, he had other things on his mind now, poor man.

'There's to be a big party coming in at the weekend for the

polo,' Dick went on. 'They come every weekend during the season. You want to see what they get through! Champagne by the bucketful and food from one of the fancy restaurants where they sell their fruit and veg from Hanger Hill.'

'What's Hanger Hill?'

'Another of the estate farms. Got a pick-your-own over by the old turnpike. Soon be strawberry time . . . my Jennie makes lovely jam and strawberry tarts!' He smacked his lips. 'Well, I must be on my way. I'm still keeping my eyes open for tit-bits for your story-book!' He climbed back into the cab of his tractor.

'What sort of tit-bits?' she called after him.

He looked down and winked. 'Never know, do you, with all those rich foreign folks!'

'Don't let anyone see you snooping around or you'll be in trouble!' advised Melissa with a laugh as she returned his wave.

She retraced her steps, feeling a great deal better than when she set out. Meeting Dick, with his cheerful grin and warm Cotswold accent, had helped her to clear her brain of foolish, disturbing fancies. He was in a sense the living contradiction of them since he had, as she had jokingly told Joe Martin, been the model for her first murder victim. And there he was, solidly alive, going about his daily tasks with his tractor and his dog, making everything sane and normal again.

The encounter had also reminded her of a problem she had been wrestling with for her book. Some research was called for.

After tea she sat down to answer Simon's latest letter. He was having a wonderful time, the heat was a bit of a problem but only when moving from air-conditioned premises to an air-conditioned car. With any luck he'd be able to get over to England later this summer. Fancy a real-life corpse—if that wasn't a contradiction in terms, ho ho!—being dug up almost on his mother's doorstep. How was the new novel coming along? A carefully casual reference to Aubrey told her that, while not wanting to pry, he was disappointed by the break and would like to think it was temporary.

She had a loyal, considerate son. She was fondly convinced that he would never have taken the job in the States if it had meant leaving her on her own. Aubrey had come on the scene at what had seemed to be exactly the right moment and had been at great pains to win the younger man's confidence and reassure him that his mother was loved and cared for. Still, he would have to accept that the relationship was definitely at an end.

Of course, I know you think of my welfare and don't like me to be alone and all that, but you mustn't worry. I admit that when you started growing up and making your own life I went through a spell of something like panic, especially with Grandpa retiring and he and Grandma moving so far away from London. Looking back, I'm sure that was what attracted me to Aubrey in the first place. I thought I needed looking after but he overdid the protective male and I had to break away. I really am much happier now, truly, and have been learning some quite surprising things about myself. So please, no more worrying, okay?

'Oh, hell!' Melissa ripped the letter across and took a fresh sheet of paper. 'Why this orgy of self-justification?' She began again.

I've finally broken with Aubrey and it was a great relief. I should have done it ages ago.
    The book is coming on slowly. You'd be surprised how life keeps getting in the way. Death too. Our murder victim has been identified but local interest in her has waned recently. Everyone's far more exercised about an elderly widow who's been left with a tiny pension and is trying to raise some money by selling part of her enormous garden as a building plot. From the way Major Ford is rallying opposition, anyone would think this would mean our being threatened by space invaders!
    Gloria's Stanley has bought her a pair of earrings that no honest car dealer could afford. I suspect that Iris is right and I know one shouldn't side with crooks but I'd hate for him to be caught. It would break Gloria's heart and she's such a dear . . .

Melissa finished her letter, sealed it and went downstairs. It was a little after five; if she took the short cut she could just catch the evening post.
    There was no one about as she skirted Daniel's hut, took the path through the woods and made her way across the churchyard. The west door of the church stood ajar and the Rector's bicycle

was propped against the wall alongside. On her way back from the letter-box she saw that the door was closed and the bicycle leaning just inside the gate. No doubt its owner had gone back for something he had forgotten. She crossed the churchyard and began picking her way down the path towards home.

She was almost at the bottom when a figure stepped out from among the trees. For a moment she was startled; then she recognised Henry Calloway. He stood awkwardly, directing darting glances here and there as if trying to give the impression that he had come upon her by chance while out walking instead of hurrying down to waylay her. His face was pale and his expression troubled.

'Mrs Craig, I wonder if you could possibly spare me a few moments? I know your time is precious but . . .'

'Of course!' She was at pains to project warmth into her voice. He was plainly in desperate need of someone to talk to. Had he been almost anyone else she would have invited him to her cottage for a sherry but if they were seen, tongues might wag and things were complicated enough already. So she stood still, shading her eyes from the late afternoon sunlight that slanted through the young leaves overhead, and waited. It took a little time; for several moments he fidgeted with a twig ripped from a beech sapling, caressing the young shoots with plump, gentle but powerful fingers.

'She was so small, so vulnerable, under that hard little shell,' he began at last. 'Life had not been kind to her.'

'You mean Babs?'

He nodded. 'She had been terribly . . . damaged in her early life.'

'In what way?' prompted Melissa when it seemed he could not go on.

'I believe the modern expression is "abused",' he said uncomfortably.

'Who by?'

'Her father. Her mother died when she was a baby and a very close relationship with him developed . . . too close, it seems. Somehow the welfare workers learned of it and she was taken into care. She loved her father very deeply and the separation broke her heart. Soon after, he was killed in a car accident and she never saw him again.'

'Poor kid,' said Melissa softly. It explained a lot.

'I think that was what drew her to me . . . she saw me as a father figure as well as a lover.' His fingers became still for the moment and he cradled the twig in the palm of his hand. 'After we had made love, she would lie in the crook of my arm like a tired child.' His face worked and tears streamed down his face.

Melissa felt her own eyes burn in sympathy. 'Did she know you were a priest?'

'She may have suspected but I never confessed. I was too ashamed.' He bit his lip and the beech twig became more engrossing than ever.

'When she disappeared what did you think?'

'I . . .' For a moment he could not go on but he swallowed hard and continued. 'I was told she had left. I was concerned that something might have happened to her. Girls like her are exposed to all kinds of danger.'

'Did you make any enquiries?'

'How could I? Someone might have found out who I was . . . it would have meant ruin for me . . . and my family. The other girls didn't seem to think there was anything unusual . . . people in that milieu are so casual about these matters.'

Melissa felt her sympathy evaporate. 'So why should you worry?' she said scornfully.

He bowed his head. 'I deserved that.'

'At least Clive cared enough to go looking for her.'

For the first time since the conversation started, he raised his head and looked directly at her.

'You know about Clive?'

'Yes.' She did not offer to explain. 'Did Babs ever speak about him?'

'From time to time, in a very strange way. She insisted he was not her lover. I gather he was quite strait-laced and I'm afraid she rather despised him for it. She called him . . . some kind of a freak.'

'A Jesus freak, would it have been?'

The Rector winced and nodded, tearing viciously at the sapling twig. 'I think she intended to use him to her advantage. She was obsessed with the fear of poverty in her old age.'

'Do you think she planned to marry him?'

'She used to drop odd hints, although half the time she used such peculiar expressions that I was never sure what she meant. But I had the impression that she felt she had something to gain from the relationship although I believe he had quite an ordinary job.'

'I understand his father is quite well-to-do. Perhaps she knew that?'

'She may have done. I think she was a little afraid of him, though.'

'Of Clive? Why do you say that?'

There was a long silence while Henry Calloway contemplated the mangled remains of the twig.

'She told me once that they had quarrelled, quite violently. It seems he had a quick temper. For him, it was bad enough that she worked in a bar. She was terrified that if he found out she . . .'

'Was a stripper and a prostitute as well?' It was obvious that he could not finish the sentence. 'Didn't it strike you as odd that if she hoped to settle down with Clive, she didn't do as he evidently wanted and give up her job? There can't have been much money in that, and in the long run . . .'

'It wasn't just a job to her,' muttered the Rector. 'She enjoyed . . . making love.' The admission brought a sheet of flame to his face.

'Did she take you to her lodgings?'

He nodded.

'Did you ever see anyone there, or notice anything strange going on?'

He looked at her in some surprise. 'Strange? No, nothing. Her room was at the top of the house and I understand the owner lived on the first floor, above a women's hairdresser. The shop was always closed when I went there and I never actually saw anyone else.' The round face puckered in distress. 'What shall I do?' he quavered. 'I don't know how to face people . . . Anthea will surely know something is wrong. I managed to keep my indiscretions from her but this . . . thank God, she is away at present . . . her sister has had a mild stroke. One shouldn't rejoice at the misfortunes of others but at least it has saved me from telling yet more lies.' His cheeks sagged and his mouth hung open. He reminded Melissa of Aubrey at his most abject and it sickened her. 'Mrs Craig, please help me, advise me.'

'You know very well what you should do.' She was startled by the harshness in her own voice. 'You have information which could be of great help to the police in their enquiries. Sooner or later those enquiries will almost certainly lead to you. If they find out that you have withheld information, you can't expect much sympathy. If you go to them now, and can convince them that you had nothing to do with Babs's death, they may be able to keep your name out of it.'

'You really think so?' For the first time, a glimmer of hope shone in the pale eyes. 'But then again, you see, we aren't absolutely sure that the . . . the victim . . . really is Babs, are we?' He was clutching at straws. Melissa wondered what Iris would feel if she could see him now.

'You don't really believe that.' It was ironic, she thought, that she should be saying this after putting that very point to Bruce. But now she was as certain as he was. Babs was dead, she had been strangled and her body buried in the woods, and the murder might well be tied up with some dangerous racket using the Up Front Model Agency and possibly also Petronella's Vanity Box as cover.

On the other hand it might simply be, as Iris had declared, a sordid sex-killing. Then Clive would be a suspect, and Henry Calloway, and any one of an unknown number of Babs's regulars. It was the kind of case that the press would go to town on and the public lick its chops over. For the Rector of Benbury, it would mean disgrace and ruin.

Henry Calloway flung away the broken twig and squared his shoulders.

'I shall do as you say, Mrs Craig,' he said in a firm voice. 'Thank you for listening to me.'

EIGHTEEN

THE NEWS OF THE IDENTIFICATION OF THE BODY DIS-
covered nearly two weeks previously in the woods near Upper
Benbury rated only the briefest report in the local papers, being
totally overshadowed by an horrific rape and murder case in Kent.
Only one or two of the national dailies considered it worth a
mention. The police would of course proceed, painstakingly and
methodically, to trace the tortuous, overgrown paths that had
led Barbara Cartwright from the dubious shelter of a children's
home to a grave in a Gloucestershire woodland. At some stage
they might invite the public to help. But for the moment, the
murder-loving public had other things on its collective mind.

For several days Melissa was able to concentrate on her book
with few interruptions that were not of her own choosing. Iris,
too, was hard at work on an entry for a design competition
sponsored by a prestigious national magazine. In between stints
at typewriter and easel the two women tended their gardens,
compared notes on the progress of their crops, called into the
village for necessary shopping or stretched their legs along the
valley footpaths. Their neighbourly relationship was developing
into a satisfying and comfortable friendship. By mutual consent
they avoided any reference to the tragedy.

In church on Sunday the Rector was pale but outwardly cheerful, having evidently made superhuman efforts to conceal his grief
and shock. His wife was still away, caring for her temporarily
disabled sister. Melissa pictured him, urging her to stay as long as
she was needed, terrified that her searching eye would penetrate
the thin veneer of composure.

On Sunday afternoon, Iris loaded a battered holdall and an

enormous portfolio into her car and departed on a business trip to London.

'See you on Friday!' she called out of the window. 'Remember to feed Binkie!' Melissa felt a sense of desolation as she drove away.

Bruce telephoned on Monday afternoon.

'I checked on young Farrell's record.'

'Yes?'

'Several convictions for receiving, but only small stuff.'

'That doesn't tell us much, does it?'

'No, not really. By the way, be sure to get a copy of today's *Gazette*!'

'Why, what's happened?'

'You'll see. Can't stop now . . . I'll call again this evening.'

Mrs Foster, engrossed in the paper when Melissa went to collect her copy, was full of the news that was splashed across the front page.

'Woodland Corpse Sensation', ran the headline. 'As a result of information received,' the story continued, 'the police are examining the theory that the remains recently discovered in Benbury Woods are those of a young woman who worked in a local night-club.'

'Wonder what she was doing here?' Mrs Foster speculated in her squeaky little voice, eyelids fluttering with excitement. 'No better than she should be, I don't doubt!' She leaned across the counter, thrusting her round pink face towards Melissa. 'D'you think someone in this village did it?' she asked fearfully.

'I hardly think so,' said Melissa, willing it to be true. She paid for her paper and hurried away, sensing Mrs Foster's disappointment that she did not stay to rake over the details. Not that there was much to rake over as yet. There had not been time to uncover much about the victim's short life—just a few sketchy details and a photograph of a girl with china-doll eyes and a shy, childlike smile. Mr Peter Crane, the manager of The Usual Place, had expressed his distress at the news. 'A quiet girl who didn't mix much with the others at the club,' he was quoted as saying. 'She left quite suddenly without saying where she was going but this was not unknown for casual workers. We're all very shocked.'

'Have you given those photographs to the police?' Melissa demanded when Bruce telephoned that evening.

'I have.' He sounded smug and virtuous.

'Did you say how you came by them?' She had forgotten, in her anxiety to avoid further active involvement in his schemes, to ask him to keep her name out of it.

He chuckled, having obviously read her thoughts. 'Don't worry . . . journalists are careful to protect the anonymity of their sources. I told them I recognised the model as Babs and pointed them in the direction of the Up Front Agency. I can't wait to hear what they turn up there.'

'So you're not still miffed because I wouldn't . . .'

'Oh, no!' He seemed anxious to reassure her. 'I did think it would have been exciting to suss out the agency ourselves, but . . .'

'*Our*selves? What was your part in the operation going to be?'

'Er . . . well, figuratively speaking!' She pictured his disarming grin. 'Anyway, I thought it over and I saw your point of view . . . and I'm very grateful for your help. We might be hearing something in a day or two. By the way, who d'you suppose tipped the fuzz off about Babs?'

'I've no idea.' If anyone was going to drag Henry Calloway's name into the affair, it would not be Melissa Craig.

'How's the book going?'

'A bit iffy at the moment. All this real-life sleuthing seems to have blunted my creativity.'

'Can I help? You know what brilliant ideas I have! Who was it suggested the U.P. Club for a rendezvous with your supergrass?'

'Yes . . . well, I don't think I'm going to be able to use that after all.'

'You mean you're abandoning my brilliant suggestion? Now I really am hurt!'

'Well, you come up with a plausible method of distributing supplies of drugs via a strip club patronised by a load of giggling housewives.'

'Dish 'em out with the bingo cards?' Bruce suggested hopefully.

'Much too slap-happy. You can't have all the women involved . . . that would be ridiculous . . . so sooner or later, some dope would be handed to a respectable mum by mistake. No, it's got to be something really slick and foolproof.'

'How about popping it into selected handbags during the performance? They'd all have their eyes glued to Gorgeous George, waiting for him to drop his fig-leaf!'

'Hmm . . .' Melissa considered for a moment, then rejected. 'That would mean someone moving around in the dark. Sooner or later an innocent member of the audience would notice and start asking questions . . . no, this is a professional operation I'm writing about, not a bunch of bungling amateurs.'

'Ah, I've got it!' He assumed the voice of a ham actor playing Dracula. 'A secret panel in the cloakroom that opens to reveal a bony hand dropping parcels of smack into the shopping bags!'

'You are absurd!' Melissa laughed aloud and immediately felt more relaxed. She had been working much too hard these last few days. 'Anyway, take a Brownie point for trying. I'll give it a bit more thought.'

'Do. I'm looking forward to reading about Sergeant Dilys Morgan complaining to Nathan Latimer about having to sit through "that sort of thing"! I'll keep you posted on developments my end.'

'So long then . . . no, wait a minute!'

'What is it?'

'That last suggestion of yours . . .'

'What about it?'

'The cloakroom at the U.P. Club . . . it's like a huge cupboard with a door in the back wall. I noticed it because it's got one of those old-fashioned porcelain door-handles with some fancy design on it . . . but I didn't think anything of it at the time.'

'Well, there you are then . . . that's more likely than a secret panel.'

'No, forget the book . . . you remember I told you how there was a lot of hoo-ha about who parked her shopping trolley where, and whose got moved because it was in someone else's place?'

'Yes, but what . . .'

'Don't you see? The same five women normally arrive before everyone else and park their trolleys along the end, in front of that door. Something went wrong last week and one of them was late, but when Sharon parked her trolley by the door, it was moved and the regular one was put there. She . . . I . . . everyone just assumed the owner was being childish.'

'And you're suggesting . . . hell's teeth! It's feasible, isn't it?'

'I'll say it's feasible. From its position, that door leads into the restaurant, which is closed during the afternoon. When the fun and games upstairs are at their height, someone could easily whip open the door, deliver the goods and shut it again . . . it'd take less than half a minute to deal with all five trolleys, and Annie's constantly on guard to make sure nothing goes wrong.'

'These trolley things . . . are they the sort with a canvas bag that fastens with a zip at the top?'

'That's right . . . they sit on little wheeled frames.'

'I believe you're on to something!' She could picture him, eyes alight with excitement. 'I've known all along that Babs was tangling with something dangerous but I never thought of The Usual Place . . . I was so sure it was tied up with the model agency or . . .'

'I think,' Melissa interrupted, 'that I'll pay a second visit to the U.P. Club tomorrow.'

'Am I really hearing right? Is this the lady who didn't want to know about any more really-life sleuthing?'

'Be quiet and let me think.' Melissa's brain was in overdrive. 'Can you arrange to be near The Usual Place about four tomorrow afternoon?'

'As far as I know . . . what have you got in mind?'

'We could really do with some help . . . someone reliable who'll keep their mouth shut.'

'I'll speak to Sophie . . . my colleague . . . it's her patch. Now would you mind telling me . . . ?'

Early the following afternoon Melissa, her hair carefully wound into a top-knot secured with Spanish combs, drove out of the village and parked in a quiet lay-by. With the aid of plenty of lipstick, mascara, eye-shadow and blusher she transformed herself into Meryl Collins before driving on into Gloucester, thankful that none of her neighbours had happened to pass by and wonder what she was up to. Her hands were trembling, making her aware of the tension building up, the adrenalin pumping round her body.

At Bruce's suggestion, she left her car in a street-level park close to the cathedral. If any of their quarry should be making a delivery by car, he said, that was the most likely place for them to be parked. Following his directions, she found herself approaching The Usual Place from the rear along a narrow and very congested service road. A brewer's lorry was unloading barrels through a trap-door in the pavement; in the cellar below she caught a glimpse of Pete Crane directing operations. Behind the lorry, a lad in a white apron was throwing empty vegetable crates into a brown delivery van. One of its rear doors was folded back and the other bore the words 'Hill Farm Produce Daily' one above the other in white letters. Melissa edged past and turned into the passage leading to the entrance to the U.P. Club. It was almost half past two. Already, it seemed, she was an established member, for Annie nodded her through with barely a glance at her card.

'Thought you weren't coming!' she remarked. 'I was just going to lock up.' She moved out from behind the desk and dropped the catch on the street door.

'Got held up at the check-out, didn't I?' Melissa had been practising a touch of the local accent and felt rather pleased with the result. Annie responded with a flick of her furry eye-lashes.

It was a fine spring afternoon and only a few light jackets hung above the assortment of shopping-bags and baskets in the little vestibule. Five trolleys were lined up against the door and on the pretext of rummaging for her purse, Melissa managed a quick study of them. If last week was anything to go by, they belonged to the regulars. All had a zip fastener across the top and in each case the fastener was only partially closed.

Sharon and Sue, seated at their usual table, greeted her with delight.

'There you are!'

'We wondered if you were coming!'

'We've saved you a place . . .'

'Ever so glad to see you . . .'

'We were just saying, weren't we . . . ?'

'What a pity if Meryl doesn't come . . .'

'And Gorgeous George is back . . .'

They chirruped away like sparrows in a hedge until Pete entered, delayed a few minutes by the arrival of the beer lorry. His innuendo-laden announcement that their favourite performer had returned was greeted with squeals of delight and a round of applause. Effie's strident voice was heard to utter some expressions of approval which evoked ribald laughter in some quarters but sorrowful head-shaking on the part of Sharon and Sue.

'She doesn't improve.'

'Always the same.'

'So vulgar.'

Melissa observed Pete as he postured and gestured. At first acquaintance she had simply accepted him at his face value: a big man with a touch of coarseness and a hint of the lady-killer who was pleasant and good-humoured with the customers in the bar and acted the genial, risqué master of ceremonies at the less-well-publicised activities upstairs. A man with the right sort of personality for the job.

Now she saw him from a very different standpoint. She sensed an underlying hardness in his voice, a lack of sincerity in his too-ready smile and a hint of cruelty about his full-lipped mouth. There was a sleekness about him; his clothes and wristwatch were expensive. She was ready to believe he could be involved in some lucrative but questionable dealings.

She watched the gesticulating hands, large and powerful, and with a growing sense of apprehension imagined them locked round the neck of a helpless girl. Was she really on the right trail? Was this strutting, wise-cracking showman not only a dealer in a filthy traffic but also Babs's killer? Throughout the statutory bingo session her mind was working furiously.

Five minutes into Gorgeous George's performance, she decided that she infinitely preferred Sultry Sam. He might be less well-endowed in certain respects but his act had a certain subtlety lacking in his rival, whose appeal was more of the caveman variety. Still, there were plenty in the audience who appeared only too willing to be clubbed. Even the restrained Sharon and Sue were bouncing up and down in their seats. Melissa suddenly thought of Aubrey, pictured his look of horrified disgust if he knew where she was and clapped both hands over her mouth to stifle her laughter. As the performance came to an end, her neighbours mistook her mirth for a different emotion.

'Smashing, isn't he!'

'Thought he'd get you going!'

'Young Sam was only an amateur . . .'

'Our Georgie knows his stuff . . .'

It was some while before the excitement began to die down and chairs were scraped back. If things went the same as last time, there would be an interlude of chatter before anyone made a move to the door. Melissa got to her feet.

'I must be getting along,' she murmured. 'Got some more shopping to do.'

'Nice to see you again,' said Sharon.

'See you next time!' added Sue.

Expecting to find Annie on guard, Melissa had formulated a plan to engage her in conversation until the others arrived to collect their belongings but, to her astonishment, Annie was nowhere to be seen. She felt a stab of dismay, thinking that this must surely mean that there was nothing there to guard, that the whole idea was nothing but a product of her own over-fertile imagination.

Apparently not. Melissa's heart began thumping as she ran her eye along the line of trolleys and saw that every zip was now tightly closed. It was what she had hoped and expected to see and must surely mean that during the performance, someone had slipped a package inside each canvas bag and fastened it. The drop had apparently been made—probably through the door from the restaurant—but something must have gone wrong with the security system for the place to be left unguarded.

There was as yet no sign of an exodus from upstairs. Melissa peered out into the corridor. It was still deserted; the sound of a flushing cistern overhead indicated Annie's probable whereabouts. On an impulse, Melissa dived back, unfastened the bag on the nearest trolley and peered inside. Moving aside a copy of the *Gazette* that lay on top, she saw nothing but perfectly innocent-looking groceries. She closed the zip, her heart hammering like a drum-roll, and once more checked the corridor. Still no one. She went to the next trolley, and then the next. She had just finished with the fourth when a chorus of feminine chatter exploded at the head of the stairs. Evidently it coincided with Annie's emergence from the ladies' room.

'Super show today, Annie!'

'Georgie-boy was in great form!'

'Here, you feeling all right?'

'You look a bit green!'

'Got an upset stomach, then?'

Annie, it seemed, was suffering from the effects of some suspect shellfish which had forced her to desert her post. The tread of feet down the stairs proceeded slowly while she supplied details and received sympathy. Melissa, elated with her success so far and taking a calculated risk, managed a quick peep into the last trolley. Her sense of triumph, as she saw what she expected to see, was at boiling point. She tugged at the zip to close it. It refused to budge. She tugged again, harder. Still it wouldn't move and her sweating fingers lost their grip. Her face grew hot, a tight knot formed in her stomach and her hands trembled as she wrestled with the slippery scrap of metal.

Her fellow-members of the U.P. Club were almost at the bottom of the stairs. In a few seconds the first one would reach the cloakroom. Melissa jerked the zip further open and plucked frantically at a thread caught in the teeth. In the nick of time she managed to free it; the wretched thing yielded at last and slid home. She kicked off one shoe and when the chattering group swept in she had assumed an expression of pain and was rubbing solicitously at her ankle.

'Meryl! You all right?' asked Sharon anxiously.

'Slipped on the stairs and gave my foot a wrench,' Melissa explained.

'That's what you get for hurrying,' reproved Sue.

'All in the wars today!' commented someone else. 'Poor Annie's got the trots!'

Amid the chorus of concern, Melissa was aware that Annie, looking pale and shaken, was staring at her string shopping bag, which contained nothing but a packet of biscuits and half a dozen apples, all clearly visible. There was alarm in the green eyes that appraised the contents.

Amid laughter and chat, everyone gathered up their belongings and began to leave. Lost in the mêlée, Melissa contrived to remain until she had identified the owners of the suspect trolleys. It came as a slight surprise that Effie was one of them.

Outside, she sauntered across to where Bruce was browsing among some dilapidated volumes outside the second-hand bookshop. Feeling like a professional private eye, she bent down to study some ancient maps in the window. 'The brunette in the green tights is one, and the dumpy lady with frizzy hair is another,' she murmured out of the corner of her mouth. 'Look out for copies of the *Gazette*.'

'Roger.' She saw him gesture to someone inside the shop as she moved away in pursuit of Effie.

It was exciting, doing something in real life that she had so often described in her novels. It was also surprisingly simple.

Effie had a distinctive walk, taking short, quick steps but moving comparatively slowly. Melissa, with her long stride, found no difficulty in keeping up with her. The pavements were fairly congested with home-going shoppers but Effie was on the tall side and her magenta head was easy to spot, bouncing up and down among the crowds along Westgate.

She appeared to be heading for the bus station and Melissa began to fear that she might find herself travelling to some unfamiliar neighbourhood, become hopelessly disoriented and lose her quarry into the bargain. Effie, however, was not yet ready to take a bus. Instead she entered a café. On the pretext of studying the menu displayed outside, Melissa peered through the window.

Effie had parked her trolley under the flap at the end of the counter. She bent down, evidently fumbling with the zip, and produced a purse and the copy of the *Gazette* which she placed on the counter in front of her. A gaunt-faced assistant with thinning hair and a gold ring in one ear shambled forward to serve her. He filled a glass with milk from a cooler, pushed it across the counter, took her money and put it in the till. His eyes flickered as if asking a question and as she picked up the glass, Effie's magenta head moved in a barely perceptible nod. She took her milk and the newspaper to a table a few feet away, sat down with her back to the door, lit a cigarette and began scanning the headlines.

Melissa decided to take a chance. She entered the café, bought a cup of tea and retreated with it to a corner. Effie, deep in her newspaper as she sipped her milk, appeared totally oblivious to her surroundings.

There were no other customers waiting to be served and the assistant was standing close to the point where Effie had left her trolley, giving every appearance of being bored and unoccupied. He fiddled with the rows of cups lined up beside the steaming urn and polished a few spoons. Then he dropped one and bent down to retrieve it. The wheels of the trolley were just visible from where Melissa was sitting and she was certain they moved slightly.

The man straightened up, raised the flap and came out from behind the counter carrying a tray. He began gathering up used crockery and glasses, emptying ashtrays and flipping a grubby cloth across the tables. When he came to Effie's table he picked up first her empty glass and then the newspaper, which lay apparently discarded in front of her.

'Finished with this, love?'

'Yes, thanks.' Effie stubbed out her half-finished cigarette, reclaimed her shopping trolley and left.

'We're getting somewhere at last!' said Bruce when he rang that evening. He was almost panting with eagerness. 'Frizzy Lizzy was a doddle, she only went just round the corner to a used car lot at the back of Shire Hall.'

Melissa felt a small prick of apprehension. She had a feeling he was about to tell her something she did not want to hear.

'She hung around for a bit,' Bruce went on, 'pretending to be looking at cars while a flashy-looking character was giving a spiel to a prospective customer. It was a classic performance . . . like something out of a TV sit-com.' He chuckled at the remembrance.

'Well?' prompted Melissa.

'The customer was asking a lot of questions, Lizzy was wandering up and down with her trolley and Flash Harry was watching her out of the corner of his eye and looking distinctly fidgety. Then a patrol car came cruising by and I could swear he turned several shades paler.' Bruce paused for dramatic effect.

Melissa became impatient. 'There's no need to flog the suspense factor, just tell me what happened! Did Lizzy hand anything over?'

'I'm coming to that. Lizzy started looking at her watch as if she had a train to catch. The customer was still asking questions and he must have wanted to look at the engine because matey upped the bonnet and started her up. Then he left the bloke peering at it and sprinted over to a sort of hut they use as an office. Lizzy followed him, they both went inside, she came out a few moments later and trollied off towards Southgate.'

'And Flash Harry?'

'He came out of the office almost immediately, but here's the interesting thing. He locked it behind him before going back to talk to the customer. It wasn't locked when they went in.'

'Are you sure?'

'Quite sure. The door was actually standing open.'

'Mm,' Melissa murmured. 'It certainly looks as if Lizzie handed over something valuable.'

'You said something about the *Gazette* when you came out of the U.P. Club.'

'There was a copy of the *Gazette* in every one of the suspect trolleys, right on the top.' She described her search and he whistled in admiration.

'That was cool!'

'I didn't feel very cool at the time. It was a stroke of luck that the coast was clear. By the way, did you get the name of Flash Harry's outfit?'

'It's called—just a moment, I pinched a leaflet off the bonnet of one of the cars. Here we are: "Cathedral Cars", proprietor Stanley J. Parkin.'

Melissa closed her eyes. Exactly what she had feared. Her heart ached for Gloria.

'How did you get on?' Bruce wanted to know.

For a moment, she could not answer. She wanted to pull out then and there, to have nothing more to do with this wretched game of detectives. Turn over stones and you find something nasty. Let someone else do it.

'Melissa? Are you still there?'

It was no good trying to wriggle out now. The Drugs Squad would be brought in and she'd have to tell them all she knew. It was her duty as a citizen. She pulled herself together.

'Yes, I'm here—how did your colleague get on?'

'Sophie? Not quite so well as we did, I'm afraid. She trailed Green Tights as far as the car park and as it happened her own car was parked not far away but by the time she got back to it, Green Tights was just disappearing through the exit. Sophie drove around for a while, hoping to pick her up, but no luck. She did make a note of the car though. She's mad keen to get an exclusive . . . she wants us to try again next week.'

'Us?' Alarm bells rang in Melissa's brain.

'Yes . . . you're game, aren't you? And listen, take a trolley of your own this time and . . .'

'Just a minute,' Melissa cut in. 'You're not suggesting I try and switch . . . ?' There was a pause. 'You are suggesting I switch trolleys . . . oh, my God, haven't I done enough? And supposing some of this leaks out . . . the villians might get wind of it and . . .' All manner of lurid possibilities, many of them from her own books, presented themselves. Once again, she was seized by a fierce desire to be free of the entire enterprise, to wipe the slate of reality clean and retreat into her safe little world where the crimes were make-believe, the complications of her own devising and the villians cozily brought to book by the relentless, hawk-eyed Nathan Latimer.

'Don't worry,' Bruce was assuring her. 'Sophie'll be like a clam. No one's going to rob her of her scoop!' He sounded almost contemptuous.

'And you're doing it out of pure altruism, I suppose!' She knew it sounded waspish but she was beginning to feel over-wrought.

'Some of us have motives other than sensationalism,' he protested.

'Oh, yes, of course, exposing the ills in society . . . the Public Has a Right to Know!'

'Now you're being cynical.'

'Realistic. Everyone knows reporters are totally ruthless in pursuit of a story.'

'Not this one. I didn't follow up the indiscretions of your precious reverend, did I? Revealing that a man has a weakness for gawping at strippers would hardly further the cause of social justice and it'd probably destroy his family.'

'What about Flash Harry's family?' Gloria's face took shape in front of her, a smiling sunflower with love and pride glowing in warm brown eyes. The strain of the day was beginning to tell. Melissa felt close to tears.

'The kids who're being ruined by drugs have got families as well,' Bruce said quietly.

'You're quite the little boy-scout, aren't you? Just out of interest, how long have you been doing this job?'

There was a pause.

'Not very long,' he admitted at last. 'I did a few other things before I thought of taking a crack at journalism. It seemed quite a promising way to help put right a few wrongs in society.'

'What else have you done?'

'Oh, various things. I did VSO when I came down from university, and taught English in the Middle East for a while, and then I started to train as a social worker . . .'

Somehow it came as no surprise. He had never shown the killer instinct of a hard-nosed newshound, rather the persistent dogged-ness of a man with a mission. The sophisticated and sometimes flippant charm concealed a dedicated idealist. Melissa, calm again after her outburst, found herself increasingly warm towards him.

'So,' Bruce was saying. 'Are we going to plan our next step?'

'Why not tell the police what we've found out?'

'What do we tell them? It's all circumstantial; we didn't actually see anything suspicious handed over. We could wait till next week and tail the other three couriers . . . just to consolidate. Hey, I've just had a brainwave! We're agreed that the drugs were concealed in the newspapers, aren't we?'

'I'd say it was odds-on, but as you've just said, it's purely circumstantial.'

'That's what I mean—we must get proof. You always take a shopping-bag of your own along, don't you?'

Melissa tightened her grip on the receiver. She could guess what was coming and it scared her. 'I don't want to know about this,' she said faintly.

'But it's a cinch! All you do is swap your copy of the *Gazette* for one of theirs. Much easier than switching trolleys . . . someone might spot that. I'll give you a free copy, you won't have to buy one!'

'Big deal. How d'you think I'm going to get away with that?'

'You managed to snoop into all five trolleys today. Next time you'd only need to open one. Don't you see, we could actually get our hands on a consignment of drugs! Can't you picture us down at the nick, unfolding a copy of our worthy family newspaper and revealing the little plastic sachet taped inside? It'd be like a scene straight out of one of your novels!'

'That's where I'd rather keep it. Look, it was pure chance that Annie had the trots this afternoon and left the coast clear. I'd never get away with that performance twice.'

'Yes, you could, you'll think of something . . .'

'You are so naïve it isn't true. I'll bet Annie had the fright of her life this afternoon when she came down and found me there on my own. You should have seen her eyes on my shopping-bag. If she hadn't been able to see everything in it, it's caviar to fish fingers she'd have found some excuse to detain me and have me searched. From now on there'll be some kind of back-up in case there's another emergency.'

'With your inventive brain . . .'

'Oh, my God, why do I listen to you? Go away and leave me in peace!' Angrily, Melissa banged down the receiver. It was a crazy, hare-brained and potentially dangerous thing he was asking her to do. The trouble was, he was so damnably persuasive, she was afraid that she might find herself, against her better judgment, agreeing to it.

But as it happened, things turned out rather differently.

Nineteen

THE NEXT TWO DAYS WERE FAIRLY UNEVENTFUL.
The calm before the storm, as Melissa remembered afterwards.
Wednesday brought a letter from Aubrey. Since she had left
him no option, he wrote, he had returned to Denise. Using a
distorted reasoning and specious arguments that made her grind
her teeth with fury, he attempted to lay at Melissa's door the
entire responsibility for the failure of their relationship and what
he described as his 'miserable existence from now on'. It was a
whining, self-pitying letter and she took considerable satisfaction
in using it that afternoon to light a bonfire.

On Thursday she had a call from Bruce.

'I've just been talking to the matron of Cedar Lawns,' he said.
'She's a bit anxious about Clive and wonders if we were thinking
of paying him another visit.'

'We did promise to go again, didn't we? How's he getting
on?'

'Physically, fine, and he's less confused than he was but he's
in what Matron calls a rather strange state of mind.'

'What does she mean by that?'

'She didn't really explain.'

'Does he know Babs's body has been found?'

'I don't think so, and I don't think Matron does either. Anyway,
she didn't mention it and I didn't tell her. I thought it better to wait
until one of us went over there. I'm tied up all day tomorrow and
I'm away at the weekend. Is there any chance of your going?'

'Where are we now—tomorrow's Friday, isn't it?'

'That's right, Friday the thirteenth. Are you superstitious?'

'Not a bit.' Melissa was riffling through her diary. 'Let's see.
I've got an appointment tomorrow morning. I could go to Cedar

Lawns in the afternoon. Shall I ring Matron and arrange it?'

'Would you? That'd be great. I'll give you a bell on Sunday evening.'

Melissa smiled to herself as she put the phone down, wondering what his reaction would have been if she had told him where she was going on Friday morning.

The girl who answered the phone at the flying school had sounded intrigued when she found she was talking to a crime writer, said she was sure they could help her with her research and told her to ask for Wally Morgan. Melissa, half-expecting to meet a gimlet-eyed, square-jawed and possibly bearded individual in greasy overalls, was surprised to find herself shaking hands with a chic, slim, vivacious woman of about thirty-five with softly waving chestnut hair and a puckish smile.

'I'm Wally Morgan,' she introduced herself, adding with a grimace, as if accustomed to raised eyebrows and puzzled glances, 'it's actually Wallis—my mother was a great admirer of the Duchess of Windsor. I suppose I should be thankful she wasn't a fan of Tallulah Bankhead! Do sit down.'

She waved Melissa to a chair in front of a table on which was spread a map of the British Isles. It was covered with solid blue lines, which Wally told her were designated air routes, and dotted lines enclosing areas of restricted flying space.

'Outside these areas, which are mostly the major airports and military bases,' she explained, 'the air space is uncontrolled up to eight and a half thousand feet.'

'You mean, anyone can fly around quite freely, without any kind of restrictions?' asked Melissa in surprise.

Wally nodded. 'So long as they keep outside the controlled zones and observe the rules about minimum heights and so on— yes.'

'What about overseas trips—to and from France, for example?'

'Ah, that's different. You'd have to leave from and land at a customs-designated airfield. Would that be a problem?'

'It would rather. My crooks wouldn't welcome a customs examination!'

Wally chuckled. 'What are they going to be carrying, or shouldn't I ask?'

'You'll have to read the book!' said Melissa. 'I'll send you an autographed copy.'

'Thanks. Now, let's see how we can help. Of course, if your man comes in and out regularly, he could build up a rapport with the customs people both sides of the Channel. He'd need a valid reason for his trips and he'd have to fly a clean aircraft the first few times. After that he'd probably be okay and they'd nod him through, but it would be a calculated risk. There might be some eager-beaver new boy on duty, or the Special Branch might be on the look-out for terrorists and request a close check on everyone entering or leaving.'

'Suppose he just sneaked in and landed quietly on his own airstrip without going through the formalities?'

Wally grinned. 'He wouldn't get far. He'd be picked up on the radar and tracked home. Then he'd really be in trouble. Of course,' she added thoughtfully, 'he could take a chance and come in below radar level, but in a way that would make him more conspicuous. The chances are still strong that he'd be spotted and reported.'

'How about coming in low at night?'

'Uh-huh. Too dangerous. He could easily hit a pylon or fly into a hill in the dark.'

'Oh, dear!' Melissa felt her plot crumbling. 'I've got this scenario, you see, of wealthy types coming in from various parts of the UK and the Continent to play polo and join shooting parties and so on. Most of them are on the level but every so often there's an illegal cargo brought in or ferried out via this private airstrip belonging to the owner of a Cotswold mansion.'

Wally's eyes sparkled. 'What fun! I was just thinking—I flew from here to Daventry the other day and I counted over twenty private strips. I wonder if any of them are used for smuggling?'

'If they are, they must have figured out how to dodge the customs. Can't you think of any way it might be done?'

'Let's see.' Wally lit a cigarette and drew on it in silence for a moment, deep in thought. Then she got up and went over to a map of Europe pinned to the wall.

'Whereabouts is your man coming from?' she asked.

'Oh . . . let's say somewhere along the coast of Northern France. Le Touquet or somewhere round there.'

'If he takes off from a strip directly in the path of a mail plane or a regular air-express delivery, he could come in piggy-back. Under the tail of the other plane,' she went on, seeing Melissa's blank expression. 'That way, there'd only be one blip on the radar screen, that of the authorised plane.'

'Could he do this without being spotted?'

'He'd have to take off without lights, of course, and then tail the other plane across the Channel. Once he was about fifty miles beyond the coast, he could just drop off and land on his own strip. He'd need landing lights, of course, but you can arrange for him to have those, can't you?'

'Of course!' Melissa scribbled furiously in her notebook. 'Is it usual for private strips to be lit?'

'Oh yes, quite a few of them are. Some of the lights can be pilot-operated by remote control. Your crooks would have to be careful to establish some legitimate use of the strip at night and make sure the local controllers knew about it.' Wally rubbed her hands together. 'Have we devised a way to commit the perfect crime? Are your crooks going to get away with it?'

'Certainly not!' Melissa assured her. 'They'll all get their come-uppance and right will triumph. My readers will expect it.'

'Well, be sure and come back to me if you need any more help.'

'I will, and thanks very much.'

Melissa went back to her car and headed towards Bristol. At a set of traffic lights on the outskirts of Gloucester she pulled up behind a van similar to the one she had seen parked behind The Usual Place. With both rear doors closed, the complete legend read: 'Hanger Hill Farm, Fresh Produce Delivered Daily'. Recalling Dick Woodman's comment about the fancy restaurants that catered for the jet-set weekenders at Benbury Park, she wondered whether The Usual Place was one of them. She decided it was unlikely. Owners of private planes and helicopters would demand something a little more soigné than scampi and chips or microwaved lasagne.

A short distance from her destination she stopped for a ploughman's lunch at a country pub. The weather was fine, the sky the colour of harebells and the mid-May sunshine softly warm on her skin. When she had finished eating she followed a footpath along the banks of a stream and watched enthralled as a kingfisher, a tiny dart of dazzling colour, plunged from a willow branch into the bright, clear water. She was so absorbed that she forgot the time and it was after three o'clock when she arrived at Cedar Lawns.

'You'll find Clive considerably better in himself,' said Matron, seated nun-like with folded hands behind her big desk. 'His memory started to come back quite suddenly about a week ago. He remembers driving his car just before the accident but nothing about the crash itself. He became rather disturbed and excited and we had to put him under sedation. Then he seemed to go into a kind of . . . not a depression, exactly, but a mood almost of resignation, as though something sad but inevitable was about to happen. It's a state of mind I've seen in terminally ill patients who've come to terms with death.'

Melissa looked at her in horror. 'Are you saying Clive thinks he's going to die?'

'I know of no reason why he should.' Matron's tone was reassuring. 'Physically, he's making excellent progress. The plaster has been removed from his leg and the physiotherapist is very pleased with him. You'll notice a big improvement.'

'Does he have any friends who come to visit him?'

'Not many. His manager has been once or twice, and one or two people from his church come occasionally. Last Sunday afternoon a girl came to see him . . . now, what was her name? It began with a "D".'

'Dawn?' Melissa suggested.

'That's it . . . Dawn. Do you know her?'

'She's my hairdresser . . . she knew Babs. She told me Babs treated Clive badly and I had the impression that she was rather keen on him herself. I knew she was planning to come and see him.'

'I hope she'll come again . . . the nurses said he seemed more cheerful afterwards. I'm glad you're here . . . he seemed to take a fancy to you and Mr Ingram and he remembers your visit.'

'I'm sorry we haven't been before. I'm working on a book, and I know Bruce has been very busy. Tell me, does Clive still talk about Babs?'

'Now, that's a strange thing. There was a time when he seemed to speak of nothing else. Now he hardly mentions her. Has there been any news?'

'You haven't read about it in the papers?'

'No? What do they say?'

'Babs is dead. She was murdered.'

Matron's hands flew to her mouth and her eyes dilated; she listened to the story in shocked silence.

'So that's why she disappeared so suddenly!' she said when Melissa had finished. 'How absolutely terrible!'

'Could Clive have seen the reports, do you think? Would that account for his sudden change of mood?'

'I don't think so.' Matron passed a hand across her forehead. Despite her years of professional experience of sorrow and death, she appeared genuinely moved. 'That poor boy has suffered so much already! When did this story appear?'

'It was in the Gloucester *Gazette* on Monday. I'm surprised no one here spotted it.'

Matron shook her head, frowning. 'We don't have the Gloucester papers. I suppose our local paper might have carried the story, but no one has mentioned it to me.'

'If Clive asks about Babs, what should I tell him? I don't want to distress him but he's sure to find out sooner or later.'

'I . . . don't know what to say.' Matron sat very still for a few moments with her head bent and her eyes closed as if she was seeking guidance. When she opened them she had regained her composure. 'I think, if he asks, you should tell him what you know. I'm sure you will break the news gently.'

'I will,' Melissa promised. 'May I go and see him now?'

'Yes, of course. You remember the way?'

When Melissa entered his room, Clive was leaning on the sill of the open window. He was fully dressed in shirt, pullover and slacks, with only the walking-stick propped against his armchair to show that he was not fully recovered from his injuries. He turned and his face lit up. Once more, she was struck by the charm of his smile.

'How nice of you to come! Isn't it a lovely day! Are we going to have a good summer, do you think?' The conventional phrases reminded Melissa of a hostess welcoming a guest to a formal luncheon party, polite but impersonal. Perhaps he was not quite at ease with her.

'You're looking loads better,' she told him, as indeed he was. He had filled out, there was colour in his cheeks and the livid scar on his face had begun to fade. 'Are you able to get out and enjoy the sunshine?'

'I've been out in the garden this morning.'

'It's a beautiful garden, isn't it? How far can you walk?'

'Not very far. A little further each day.' He sounded neither enthusiastic nor downhearted, merely detached, as if his progress or lack of it was of no consequence to him. 'Won't you sit down? Perhaps you'd like to bring that chair and sit here in the sunshine—I'm sorry I can't offer to move it for you.'

'I expect you're looking forward to going home?' said Melissa breezily as she settled herself opposite Clive.

'Home? Where is home?' He smiled again, a sad, slow smile of martyrdom. It was a depressing start.

'But surely . . .' Melissa fumbled for words. 'I mean, where did you live before your accident? Haven't you any family?'

The smile faded and his deep-set eyes seemed to turn almost black.

'My mother is dead. I have no brothers or sisters, no aunts or uncles and no cousins. I am alone in the world.'

Melissa felt the force of his hatred of the father whom he would not even mention, and shivered. She tried again.

'Will you go back to your old job, do you think?'

'I suppose so. Does it matter?'

'But of course it matters.' Melissa became brisk, practical, the way she used to be with Simon in his fits of adolescent depression. 'You are young and strong. You've made a marvellous recovery from some terrible injuries. Now you must begin to plan for your future!'

'I have no future,' he said in a calm, flat voice.

'Of course you have . . .' she began, but her voice trailed off as she recognised the look of resignation that Matron had described, the look of a man who has withdrawn from the business of living. His next words came as a shock.

'Not any more, not now Babs is dead.' He dropped his voice and glanced round as if afraid of being overheard. 'I haven't told them here. They didn't know her, you see. But you knew her, didn't you?'

'Who told you she was dead?' asked Melissa quietly, hoping he wouldn't press her on this point. So long as he believed she had known Babs, he might talk more freely and possibly reveal something that would lead to her murderer.

'No one told me. I know it . . . here!' He tapped his forehead. Still he spoke in the same flat tone, looking towards Melissa but somehow through her and wearing an expression of weary patience.

Keeping her own voice cool and casual and choosing her words with care, she began probing.

'When did you last see her?'

'Two days before my accident. We had an argument.'

'Was she very upset?'

The question seemed almost to amuse him. 'Babs? No . . . I was the one who was upset. I was distraught. She laughed at me and I wanted to shake her. That frightened me . . . I didn't know I was capable of feeling so angry.' He gave one of his swift, illuminating smiles. It was easy to see why Dawn found him so attractive. 'We're taught that anger is a deadly sin, aren't we?' he said with a strange blend of sadness and humour.

'What was the argument about?' Melissa asked.

He spread his hands in a pathetic gesture. Like his face, they had fleshed out since her last visit although even then, as she remembered with an uneasy twinge, they had been strong enough to leave marks on Bruce's arm that had lasted for several hours.

'She thought only of money,' he told her. 'She reminded me for a moment of . . . my father.' He seemed reluctant to speak the word. 'I told her that love was more important. She said love was all right but only when there was money to go with it. She said she knew how to get some.'

'Did she say how?'

'Blackmail.' There was a haunted look in his eyes, as though he was reliving a painful memory. 'She was planning to blackmail someone.'

'She told you that?' Excitement made it difficult for Melissa to remain calm. 'Did she say who?'

'No. She didn't use the word blackmail but I'm certain that was what she had in mind. I told her it was dangerous and stupid . . . and wicked. I said that people get hurt when they try that sort of game. I told her God would punish her . . . but she only laughed. And I was right, wasn't I? She's dead . . . dead!' The last words came in a jerky gasp. His fingers clenched and his mouth worked as he struggled to control himself.

'What makes you so sure she's dead?' Melissa asked when he became calmer.

He did not seem to have heard the question but sat staring at her with blank, unfocused eyes. Her hopes began to ebb.

'You said Babs ran away after a quarrel,' she prompted in a slow, clear voice, praying that his scarred mind had not already clouded over again in an effort to shield itself from memories too painful to face. 'Do you know where she went? Did something happen to her?'

He looked down at his hands, lying relaxed now in his lap. His lips moved silently as if he was repeating the questions and trying to make some sense from them.

She held her breath. When he looked up, her hopes rushed ahead. He had become keen and alert, outwardly normal, almost animated.

'I phoned Petronella's the next day, or the day after—I'm not sure which,' he said. 'I worried, desperate to see her and beg her not to go through with her wicked plan.'

'Did you speak to her?'

'No. They said she had gone. I couldn't believe it. We'd quarrelled before and made it up. Why should she just leave without a word? I went round to see that old woman and her son . . . they showed me a note but I still couldn't accept it.' His face was bleak. 'She didn't tell you she was going away, did she?'

It was a dangerous moment. Melissa knew instinctively that if she said the wrong thing, the fragile link with reality might snap.

'She never said a word to me about it,' she said, after a second's hesitation. He gave a deep sigh and dropped his eyes again. 'What did you do then?' she asked gently.

'I went to The Usual Place. It's a restaurant with a night-club attached to it. She . . . worked there. I wanted her to leave but she wouldn't. I wanted to marry her, take care of her. We wouldn't have been rich but I could have given her a real home. She used to jeer at me, called me names . . . she could be very cruel sometimes.' He put a hand to his head, overcome by despair.

Tears blurred Melissa's eyes. He was so young, barely Simon's age, and so alone. In a spontaneous wish to give him some comfort, she reached out to him. He snatched at her hand as if it were a lifeline, gripped it so tightly that she gave a little gasp of pain, then released her with a murmur of apology.

'What happened at The Usual Place?' she prompted.

'The manager—I think his name's Pete—told me the same story, that she'd left without notice. I was sure he was lying. He was sneering, implying she'd gone off with another man. I lost my temper and banged on the counter. I could have smashed his stupid face in but it wouldn't have done any good.' His breath quickened and his face flushed.

Melissa took his hand again. 'Don't upset yourself,' she said soothingly. 'Just tell me what you did.'

'What could I do? I left . . . I went and had a glass of beer in a pub somewhere. I'm not used to drink and it made me feel peculiar. I was frantic, worrying about what had become of Babs. I went back to my car. I think I sat there for a while, wondering what to do. I remember driving out towards the by-pass . . .'

'Was there much traffic about?' Melissa was thinking of Bruce's assertion that the accident had been deliberately contrived. 'Was anyone driving dangerously or trying to cut you up?'

He half-closed his eyes, trying to remember.

'It was very late. The road was almost empty. At some point there was a car behind me . . . I saw its lights in my mirror. Then they weren't there any more. I suppose I was going too fast . . . that's all I remember.'

It neither confirmed nor contradicted Bruce's theory. Clive's accident could have been of his own making. According to Rowena, there had been no suspicious enquiries to suggest that there might be a threat to his safety but if the police knew of his quarrel with Babs he would be in danger just the same, of a very different kind. The afternoon sun streamed in, casting the shadow of a branch on the wall behind his chair. It hung and swayed above his head like an outstretched, menacing hand.

'Forgive me for saying this,' said Melissa. 'You and Babs . . . you came from such different backgrounds . . . what did you have in common?'

'We had one outstanding thing in common,' he said quietly.

'You mean, you were in love?'

He gave a half-smile and a slight shake of the head. 'I loved her, yes . . . and she might have grown to love me one day, if only she had trusted me. She'd been so badly hurt, you see. No, what we had in common was that we had both lost our fathers.' So she had told her story to Clive, as well as to Henry Calloway.

'That isn't quite true in your case, is it?' said Melissa. 'I know Babs was an orphan but your father is still alive and he . . .' She was about to say, 'cares enough about you to shell out a fortune for your treatment even though you refuse to see him', but he gave her no chance.

'Worships Mammon!' he burst out. 'The only kind of love he can feel is love of money and he's not too fussy how he makes it!' He clenched his fists, his nostrils flaring.

'Please don't upset yourself,' Melissa urged. 'I only wanted to say that . . . everyone has some feelings, some good qualities. You believe in God . . . you must believe that!'

He shrugged. 'I doubt it in his case. He's got a heart of stone. That's why I left after Mother died.' A sudden bitterness twisted his mouth, anger hardened his eyes. 'He killed her with his selfish greed . . . broke her heart. I couldn't live under his roof after that.' He moved restlessly in his chair.

Melissa began to get alarmed. 'Please, let's talk about something else,' she begged. 'It's bad for you to get excited. Shall I ring for some tea?'

'What a good idea! You must think me a shocking host.' He reached for the telephone. For no apparent reason his agitation vanished and the peaceful, resigned look returned, settling almost visibly, like a shroud, around his head and shoulders. The sun went in and the temperature fell sharply. Melissa suppressed a shiver.

'You're cold. Shall I close the window?' Once again the considerate host, he struggled out of his chair and limped across the room, leaning on his stick.

A maid brought tea and Melissa poured it out. Clive's hand was steady as he took his cup and saucer.

'They seem to look after you pretty well,' she remarked.

'Oh yes, they're very good.' He scrutinised a slice of fruit-cake before eating it. 'The food's quite good too.'

'I believe Dawn came to see you,' said Melissa.

'Yes, wasn't it kind!' His tone was bright and conversational, his smile spontaneous and natural. A seed of hope began to germinate in Melissa's mind. She must see Dawn again, tell her that her visit had done some good. No doubt she would need little encouragement to repeat it.

When they had finished their tea, Melissa got up to go. He insisted on walking with her along the corridor as far as the staircase. He moved slowly, leaning heavily on his stick.

'It was very kind of you to call,' he said.

'Shall I come again?'

He gave a faint, sad smile. 'I may not be here much longer.'

'I'll check on the telephone beforehand. If you've left, they can tell me where to find you.'

'Yes, that would be best.' He propped himself against the wall, released his stick and held out his right hand. 'Goodbye, and thank you. Oh, by the way, did I tell you? Babs is dead.' It was as if a shutter had come down. His voice was as matter-of-fact as if he were commenting on the weather but his eyes looked through Melissa into somewhere beyond her reach. She watched him limp back to his room and then went slowly downstairs.

In the hall, Rowena glanced up from her desk and beckoned.

'Matron says, could you spare her five minutes before you leave?'

'Of course.'

Matron looked up eagerly when Melissa entered her office.

'How did you find him?' she asked.

'Much improved, as you said,' Melissa replied. 'Part of the time he speaks quite normally but every so often he sort of switches off . . . it's as if he moves into another world.'

Matron nodded. 'It's not unusual for the memory to be erratic at this stage. We hope the lapses will become less and less frequent. Did you tell him the news about Babs?'

'I didn't have to.' Melissa gave a brief account of her visit.

'He knew, or strongly suspected, that she was planning to extort money from someone. He says he warned her that she was playing a dangerous game. When she disappeared, he must have been afraid that something had happened to her. Now he seems certain, and it will take time for him to come to terms with it.'

'Have the police any idea who killed her?'

'I believe they have one or two leads, but nothing definite.'

'I'm surprised Clive didn't go to the police himself if he was so sure something had happened to the girl.' Matron passed a hand over her forehead and shook her head as if she too was having difficulty in accepting the sordid truth.

'I guess he knew that Babs associated with some pretty dubious characters,' said Melissa. 'He'd been trying to protect her and was probably afraid of getting her into worse trouble. It must have been a terrible predicament for him.'

'Why a decent young man like Clive should get mixed up with that sort of girl is beyond me!' sighed Matron. 'At least, this could help to account for his odd changes of mood. I shall have to report to the neurologist.'

'Will he recover completely, do you think?' asked Melissa.

'I don't think I'm competent to answer that question,' said Matron. 'We must hope for the best . . . but it may take a long time. A lot will depend on how supportive his friends are when he leaves here . . .'

'Bruce Ingram and I will certainly keep in close touch with him,' said Melissa, responding swiftly to the appeal in the blue eyes that had temporarily lost some of their serenity. 'And if my guess is right, Dawn will as well.'

'That's very encouraging . . . thank you.'

Melissa stood up. 'I'll come again soon,' she promised. 'Goodbye.'

Back in reception, she stopped for a word with Rowena.

'Clive seems to be making progress,' she said.

'Yes, isn't it good news!' The girl's manner was bright and intelligent. So her apparently guileless acceptance of Bruce's absurd subterfuge *had* been an excuse to further their acquaintance. Again she felt a stab of jealousy. Bruce was a good-looking man with a winsome personality, Rowena was young and pretty . . . and she, Melissa, was 'a fine-looking woman', but one well past her prime.

'I suppose he'll be leaving soon,' Rowena observed. 'He's been costing his dad a fortune.'

'But he never comes to see him?'

Rowena shook her head. 'I believe they had a row. They daren't mention him to Clive, he gets so screwed up. If he realised who was paying the bills he'd probably hit the ceiling.'

'I can imagine. I . . . don't suppose you could give me his father's phone number?'

'I shouldn't really . . .'

'Please . . . I only want to help Clive.'

'All right. Don't tell Matron, will you?'

'Of course not.'

The girl reached for her notebook just as the phone on her desk began ringing. She was evidently accustomed to doing several things at once, for she quickly ran her thumb along the index and jotted down a number with one hand while taking the call with the other. Someone was evidently asking after a patient and Rowena, a model of brisk efficiency, simultaneously balanced the instrument under her chin, began referring to a register and held out a scrap of paper. Melissa took it, nodded her thanks and mimed a farewell.

Instead of taking the motorway, Melissa drove homewards along the A38. There was very little traffic and with any luck she would be round Gloucester before the evening rush got under way. Her thoughts were tumbling round in her head like milk in a churn, every so often congealing into what seemed like a lead, then dissolving into a formless mass of vague possibilities. There were so few hard facts, so much pure conjecture.

'Come on, girl,' she muttered to herself. 'Think . . . imagine Nathan Latimer confronted with all this. Begin at the beginning.'

Clive knew Babs was planning to blackmail someone . . . ah, but did he? What exactly had she said to give that impression? Could she just have been pretending, knowing how strait-laced he was and taking a perverse pleasure in upsetting him? Worse, could he have invented the story as cover after a quarrel had got out of hand? Loath as she was to believe him capable of violence, least of all against the girl he loved, he had admitted to almost uncontrollable feelings of anger, and his hands were very strong . . .

'Oh, come on!' she said again as she slowed down to pass through a village. 'You don't really believe Clive did it.' No, replied a small voice in her brain, but others might if they heard what he was saying this afternoon.

All right, what are the alternatives? The Up Front Agency has an unsavoury sideline and no one knew that better than Babs. Wait a minute, though, there was nothing on those pictures to show where they were taken. It was Bruce who had jumped to conclusions. Maybe they came from a different source altogether . . . one of Babs's weekend regulars for example?

Thoughts of the regulars brought Henry Calloway to mind. But he had been to the police and told them what he knew. That was hardly the action of a murderer. Still, he might have reasoned that if, as Melissa had pointed out, the police would have traced him eventually, it would deflect suspicion if he had volunteered his information in advance. Suppose Babs had discovered his identity and threatened to tell his wife . . . or even the Church authorities? It seemed unlikely; from what the Rector had said, there was love and tenderness on both sides in their relationship.

What about the Farrells? The son was known to the police as a receiver . . . did he have other rackets as yet undiscovered, like peddling pornography? Perhaps his supplies were delivered by special messenger to Petronella's, to be picked up casually by his mother. Babs could have found out and decided that she could make even more money—a lot of money, perhaps; the disgusting trade was lucrative if you found the right customers—from blackmail.

Then there was the fact—no, not yet a fact but a strong probability—that drugs were being distributed from The Usual Place via certain members of the U.P. Club. Babs could have tumbled to that as well. Maybe the two rackets were interconnected; drugs and porn were often to be found in unholy partnership. A rootless girl, however streetwise she might be in some respects, would be no match for dealers in that sort of trade. The decision to eliminate her might have been a collective one. And if the partners feared that she had confided in Clive, then Bruce could well be right and they had tried to silence him as well.

'So where does that leave us?' murmured Melissa as, thankfully, she escaped from the city and began the familiar climb up the Cotswold escarpment. 'If Clive didn't kill Babs, and I don't want to believe he did, then two strong possibilities are: someone at The Usual Place or the Up Front Agency. My money's on Pete Crane . . . scratch the surface of that spurious bonhomie and you'll find a thoroughly nasty piece of work.'

She was nearly home. Iris was expected this evening. It might help to talk it over with her. Bruce, she knew, was otherwise engaged—with Rowena? Forget about that.

'One final question,' she reminded herself as she turned into the lane. 'If drugs are involved, and if Pete is the mastermind, where is he getting his supplies? Petronella's?'

TWENTY

MELISSA WAS JUST CLOSING HER GARAGE DOOR WHEN Iris's elderly Morris Minor came bumping along the track. Her spirits lifted at the sight.

'Am I glad to see you!' she called as her friend got out of the car.

Iris gave her a penetrating glance. 'You look tuckered!' she commented. 'Been working too hard?'

'I wish that was the only reason. I've had a harrowing afternoon.'

'Sorry to hear that.' Iris lugged her ancient holdall from the boot. 'Got supper organised?'

'I hadn't thought . . . I'm not really hungry.'

'Must eat. Plenty in the freezer. Fresh fruit here.' She held up a bulging string bag. 'Come and share.' The prospect of company was even more inviting than the thought of food.

'I'd like to, if it's not too much trouble.'

'No trouble. Half past six all right?'

'That'll be lovely!'

Iris slammed down the boot and went indoors. Binkie, appearing from nowhere, rushed after her and was greeted with little cries of rapture. Melissa, glancing in the hall mirror as she returned to her own cottage, gave herself a watery smile. It was true, she did look exhausted. It was good to have Iris back, a relief to think there would be someone to talk to in the evenings. She flopped into an armchair, put her feet up and closed her eyes. She felt herself nodding off when the telephone rang. Wearily, she picked up the receiver.

'Hello?'

'This is Dick Woodman.' His speech was slow and stilted, as

if he was unused to using the phone. 'Can I speak to you?'

'Of course.'

'Something funny's going on.' His voice dropped to a hoarse whisper. 'You want to hear about it?'

'What sort of thing?'

'Can't figure it out. I heard someone talking to Mr Hepple, the keeper.'

'What were they saying?'

'Something about a sow farrowing tonight and he must be on the alert. We've got no sow farrowing here, and if we had it'd be no concern of Mr Hepple. And I saw . . .' He broke off. 'Can't talk now. Can I come and see you?'

Melissa suppressed a yawn. She was still half-asleep and had not the faintest idea what he was talking about but could think of no reason to refuse.

'Yes, if you like. When?'

'This evening be all right? I always come over to the Woolpack on a Friday. If I leave a bit early and drop in on my way home about ten, would that be okay?' His speech had quickened; over the wire she could hear approaching footsteps and the sound of men's voices.

'Yes, fine, I'll be here.'

He put down the receiver and Melissa sat back and closed her eyes again. Someone hammered on the door and she went to open it, yawning and blinking. Iris was standing in the porch, grinning like a witch.

'Thought so. You fell asleep.'

'Oh, God, I suppose I must have. What time is it?'

'Quarter to seven. Supper's ready.'

'Give me a few minutes to freshen up and I'll be round.'

An hour later, Melissa was relaxing in an armchair in Iris's sitting-room with a mug of coffee beside her and a loudly purring Binkie on her lap.

'That was a super meal!' she said. 'You should open a vegetarian restaurant.'

Iris's lip curled. 'No, thanks. Hate people en masse.' She sank into her customary position on the floor and reached out to tickle the cat's ears. 'Want to sit with Muvver or stay wiv oo's Auntie?' Binkie remained where he was. Melissa listened patiently to the futile coaxing until Iris gave up, reverted to her normal voice and asked if she was feeling better.

'Oh, I don't know!' She put her hands to her face. 'I've got myself involved in something that I don't fully understand and I have a feeling that any minute, something horrible is going to come crawling out of the woodwork.'

Iris said nothing. She reminded Melissa of a garden gnome as she sat there, straight-backed and cross-legged, her head cocked on one side and her eyes as sharp as needles.

'It's a very complicated story,' Melissa began. 'I'd like to tell you . . . it would help me organise my own thoughts.'

It took a surprisingly long time. As she talked, Melissa saw disapproval dawning in her friend's eyes and a hint of blue in their greyness that gave them the quality of bright steel. When she described the way they had trailed the couriers from the U.P. Club and Bruce's plans for a second attempt, disapproval turned to anger.

'Got you on a string, this toy-boy of yours!' she burst out.

Melissa flushed. 'Don't call him that!' she said uneasily. 'He does tend to go over the top a bit but he really is a serious investigative journalist. I know I've let him talk me into things I wouldn't have done on my own but it's been quite exciting . . . and very useful background for a novel at the same time. There's absolutely nothing between us.'

Iris sniffed. 'Should hope not. Hate to see you make an ass of yourself.'

Melissa, stroking Binkie's head, thought wryly of Iris's own hopeless passion for poor Mr Calloway. Did it ever occur to her that she too could easily have made an ass of herself?

'Well, go on!' Iris commanded. 'Must be more than that.'

'Yes, there is.' Without mentioning the Rector's possible involvement, Melissa went over the implications of what she had learned from Clive that afternoon.

Iris's mouth crimped in disgust. 'Dirty little whore! Deserved all she got!'

'That's not quite fair . . . she had a traumatic childhood,' Melissa reminded her. 'What worries me, though, is that Clive could well be a prime suspect.'

'You think he might have done it?'

'I don't know what to think. The first time we saw him, he was so quiet and . . . sort of saintly . . . he obviously cared deeply for Babs and I couldn't believe he'd hurt her. Now I'm not so sure. He's capable of intense anger—I saw it in his eyes—and he admitted to feelings of violence. He's strong, too . . . his fingers are like steel clamps.' Again she recalled the marks on Bruce's forearms.

'Well, if he did it, they'll get him. Not your problem.'

'He should at least have a good lawyer. I'm thinking of ringing his father to warn him what's likely to happen. I've got his number.'

Iris shrugged. 'Could do. Then wash your hands of the other business.'

'What other business?'

'This drugs business your . . . this cub reporter keeps on about. If Clive killed Babs, that blows his theory out of the window.' Iris's lips curved in a cat-like smirk. Plainly, she considered Bruce bad for Melissa and was anxious to see him removed from her life. Perversely, Melissa found herself siding with him.

'It merely gives another possible motive for the murder. Clive himself believes Babs was planning blackmail.'

'So he says. Could have been a red herring. He could have killed Babs, buried her body and had the blackmail story all ready in case things went wrong.'

'But he didn't know where she was.'

'Could have found her, between The Usual Place and the accident. Plenty of time. Or he could already have killed her and then been pretending to rush around looking for her. An even redder herring, so to speak!' Iris, enlarging on her theory, was growing animated.

It was Melissa's turn to pour cold water. 'You'll be saying next he planned the accident. He was badly smashed up, remember? And you can't tell me he could remember his story after suffering brain-damage and amnesia!'

'Might have done. Strange thing, the human mind.'

Melissa gave a resigned sigh. What difference, in the end, would it make to Clive? Whether he was guilty of murder or not, he was scarred for life. There were other casualties, too, in this wretched business. Henry Calloway, Gloria . . . yes, and all the victims of the drugs racket that Bruce kept reminding her about.

'I can't wash my hands of it now,' she said, half to herself. 'They *are* pushing drugs from the U.P. Club and I want to help prove it.'

Iris banged her mug down on the floor in a fury. 'By swapping copies of that beastly little rag?'

'If I can figure out how.'

'You're mad! End up a corpse yourself! Go to the police!'

'We intend to, but we want to have something concrete to show them. Bruce says . . .'

'Damn Bruce! Little boy playing cops and robbers while you take the risks! Don't be a bloody fool!'

Melissa had to admit that similar thoughts, less forcefully expressed, had occurred to her from time to time but in the end she had always yielded to Bruce's powers of persuasion. She gave a sigh of exasperation.

'There are times,' she said, 'when I think I'd have done better to have stayed in London. At least the people there who kept trying to organise me were family or old friends!'

Iris stared stiff-backed into the empty grate. 'Sorry!' she muttered. 'Didn't mean to interfere.'

Remorsefully, Melissa put a hand on her friend's thin shoulder. 'I wasn't getting at you, honestly!' she said. 'It's . . . oh, I don't know! Ever since I came here I've had someone on my back . . . first Bruce with his crusade . . . and Joe breathing down my neck . . . and then there's old Mother Foster; every time I go into the shop she's got some trivial bit of gossip she wants me to write into a book. And the Rector keeps suggesting the most hackneyed ideas for plots. Even Dick Woodman plays a game called "looking out for tit-bits for my story-books". Oh, Lord, that reminds me, he's coming round presently. I'd better get back.'

'Dick Woodman? Coming to see you? What about?'

Melissa stood up and Binkie slid from her lap with a resentful squawk.

'He sounded quite mysterious . . . said he couldn't talk on the phone but something funny was going on and could he come and see me after leaving the Woolpack this evening.'

'Remember what I said. Stay out of trouble!'

Melissa was touched by the concern in her friend's face. Her voice, too, had a softer edge than usual. 'I'll try!' she promised.

'Tell me what Dick says?'

'You think it's likely to be important?'

'Might be. Very down-to-earth chap is Dick. Plenty of common sense.'

'Why don't you join us and hear for yourself? Come round for a nightcap.'

'Thanks, I will. Be round in a little while. Sooner if I hear a knock on your door.'

It was nearly nine o'clock and the embers of the sunset flamed blood-red behind the swaying black tree-shapes on the skyline. Clouds were piling up from the north-west with a promise of rain. As Melissa let herself into Hawthorn Cottage, a faint, sorrowful sigh was borne along the valley by the rising wind. Hastily she closed the door and switched on the porch light. She was curious to know what Dick had to say but wished he'd left it until some other time. It had been quite a day and she doubted if her tired brain could cope with any more that night.

'He said he was going to leave the Woolpack early,' said Melissa, yawning as the clock chimed half past ten. 'What time does it close?'

'Not till half past.' Iris, sitting as usual on the floor with folds of plaid worsted heaped round her knees, took a swig from her glass. 'They play skittles on a Friday night. Expect he stayed to the finish after all. Shouldn't worry.'

Eleven o'clock sounded, then eleven fifteen. At half past eleven Melissa went to the door and peered out. The wind was blowing more strongly but there was no rain in the fresh, sweet air. Out of the blackness came faint squeakings, rustlings, the hoot of an owl. There was no sign of any human life.

'Expect he had a few too many and forgot all about it,' observed Iris, looking over Melissa's shoulder. 'Didn't he give you any idea of what it was about?'

Melissa frowned. 'I really can't remember. I was half-asleep at the time but I got the impression that he'd heard something and seen something unusual and thought I'd be interested. Someone was coming and he didn't want to be overheard.'

'Not coming now, that's for sure.' Iris threw her jacket over her shoulders and stepped outside. The two of them stood for a moment looking up at the sky. The gaps in the hurrying clouds were peppered with stars. Iris took a deep, satisfied breath. 'Aah, that's better! Get London out of my lungs. Well, goodnight, sleep well!'

'Goodnight!'

Melissa locked and bolted the door and went round checking that windows were fastened and the back entrance secure. She switched off the downstairs lights and went upstairs. She was very, very tired. Normally she read for a while before settling down for sleep but tonight she put out her lamp as soon as she was in bed and flopped on to her pillow with a deep sigh of utter weariness. It had been an exhausting and, in many ways, a disturbing day. The interview with Wally had been stimulating, promising an original dénouement to her novel, but uppermost in her mind was her visit to Clive.

It was all so depressing. If, as seemed likely, he were to be questioned about Babs's death, who would advise him? He was in such a strange state of mind that he might easily say something to incriminate himself. He was in desperate need of help and yet he was steadfastly turning his face from the one person who cared for him. It was inconsistent with his undoubtedly strong religious feelings; she remembered Henry Calloway's sermon on forgiveness after the discovery of Babs's body and wondered if he would be willing to talk to Clive, then reflected that in the circumstances it would hardly be tactful to suggest it.

She had Clive's father's telephone number. Perhaps it was up to her. Tomorrow she would call him, make an appointment to go and see him and let him know of his son's plight. She seemed to have won Clive's confidence; there might be something she could do to heal the breach between father and son.

Sleep was very near. As she felt herself drifting away, she wondered why Dick had changed his mind about coming to see her. Iris's diagnosis was probably correct. He'd be along tomorrow. She tried to remember his precise words on the telephone. Something funny was going on . . . he'd seen something . . . and there was a sow . . . what was the word? Harrowing? No, farrowing. She had never come across it and although she had picked up quite a lot of information about rural life since moving to Upper Benbury she knew little about the habits of livestock. Visions of the Empress of Blandings floated before her and she wondered drowsily if Dick had overheard plans for a commando-style raid of the type constantly feared by Lord Emsworth. The notion brought with it a welcome note of light relief and she fell asleep with a smile on her lips.

She was awakened by the sound of the wind and a flurry of rain on the windows. The luminous hands of her bedside clock stood at half past two. She closed her eyes again but although her body was ready for more sleep, her mind had clicked awake. It was a familiar sensation and she knew it might be an hour or more before she could hope to drop off again. Hot milk sometimes helped. Grumbling to herself, she got up, huddled into a dressing-gown and went downstairs.

As she sat sipping her hot milk and nibbling a digestive biscuit, she found her mind harking back to Dick's telephone call. It was odd that he hadn't shown up after the eager, almost urgent way he had spoken. With an effort, she recalled his exact words. 'We've got no sow farrowing here, and if we had, it'd be no concern of Mr Hepple's.' What, precisely, did that word mean? She put down her mug, fetched a dictionary and studied the definition. 'Farrow: give birth to pigs; litter of pigs.' Pigs! The solution roared into her head like an express train. Piggyback!

She leapt to her feet, shooting an anxious glance at the clock. A quarter to three. Already it might be all over but it was worth a try. She'd need warm clothes, something waterproof. She rushed up to her bedroom and dragged on a pair of thick, dark-coloured slacks, warm socks and a heavy jersey, then tore back downstairs, threw on her hooded anorak, thrust her feet into wellingtons and grabbed a torch, gloves and keys. At five minutes to three she let herself quietly out of the cottage.

The rain had eased and was little but a sprinkling in the wind that brushed her hands and face as she stood waiting for her eyes to adjust to the darkness. At first it seemed total but the clouds were thin enough for the moonlight to penetrate in places and after a few moments she found she could manage without a torch. From habit, she made for the stile, then changed her mind and decided to use the road. Taking the valley route would have meant scrambling up a steep, overgrown path that she had walked only once. Impossible without using the torch and there might be someone on the look-out. The thought of being spotted made her stomach turn over. Just for a moment, her courage wavered. Wouldn't it make more sense to call the police and tell them of her suspicions? But time was precious; even if they took her seriously it might be all over before they arrived. Resolutely, she set off along the lane that led out of the village.

It sloped downhill for a quarter of a mile or so before crossing a culvert and starting its narrow and twisting climb towards the crest of the ridge. At the top, wooden gates on either side led into fields. Melissa went to the one on the right and fumbled with the catch. It was padlocked. A little awkwardly, her rubber soles slithering on the damp wood, she clambered over.

At first, she made her way easily along the edge of a field of young corn bounded by a low hedgerow. The clouds were thinning rapidly and she could see her way quite clearly. In the far corner of the field a second gate, open this time, gave on to a track leading into woodland. Instinctively, she walked more slowly, moving stealthily along the rutted ground, looking over her shoulder at every movement of branches in the wind, every rustle in the undergrowth. She ducked nervously as an owl swooped silently out of the trees towards her; the lumbering shape of a badger, crossing her path a few yards ahead, made her gasp with momentary alarm. Her knees shook and she stumbled over a stone and nearly fell, her outstretched hand grabbing uselessly at empty darkness.

She peered round, searching for a landmark. Nothing looked familiar. In that world of strange sounds, shadows and mysterious light, she had a sense of losing touch with reality. She imagined a watcher behind every tree; the moon was a beacon to reveal her presence to unseen, hostile forces. It was the onset of panic; she stood stock-still in the middle of the track and the hammering of her heart in her throat nearly choked her. She longed to switch on the torch but dared not.

'Where is that heap of stones?' she mouthed in despair. 'There was a heap of stones, a heap of stones.' She repeated the words as if they were a magic formula, a defence against the invisible menace around her. Then it was there, a pale shape, glimmering white like a ghostly animal at the side of the track.

She began picking her way towards the edge of the wood. A twig snapped under her foot with the noise of a firecracker. For the second time, panic threatened to take hold of her. It wasn't too late to go back. She could abandon this hare-brained adventure and be safely indoors in less than half an hour. She would phone the police, tell them the whole story and let the forces of law and order take command. If her suspicions were correct she was tackling, unaided and defenceless, ruthless criminals playing for high stakes. If she was spotted, her chances of survival were virtually nil.

She had almost talked herself into returning home when she heard the plane, droning faintly in the distance. She wasn't too late. No question now of going back. As silently as possible, she crept forward. The land began to fall away in front of her, a gap in the trees opened and she saw the house lying below, a block of stone split by the moon into geometric sections of light and shade. There was no sign of life; every window was dark. It seemed for the moment unreal, a mirage floating in the moonlight, liable to vanish at any moment in a swirl of mist. But there was no mist and the sound of the plane grew steadily stronger.

She found a shallow depression with gently sloping sides that might have been constructed as an observation post. Lying flat on her stomach, she wriggled forward until by lifting her head above the rim she could see the entire house with its surrounding wall.

The plane was getting closer. She craned her neck, searching the sky. A pinhead of light appeared to the left, a shooting star in slow motion. The sound grew louder, the light lower. Without warning, the ground beneath her seemed to burst into flames. Instinctively, she ducked her head, pressing her face to the ground. Landing lights, of course; Wally had said they could be activated by remote control from the aircraft. She raised her head again to watch.

The plane was almost down, a black shape against the milky backdrop of the sky. For a few moments she lost sight of it behind the trees; then it was rolling along the strip towards her. It slid past and came to a halt alongside the wall. Before the noise of the engines had died away, the gates opened and a Land Rover drove out, swung in a wide arc and reversed towards the plane until it vanished behind the fuselage. There were sounds of activity and of men's voices, and although for several minutes Melissa could see nothing of what was going on, she guessed that the plane was being unloaded. Then a man holding a Doberman on a leash came into view. He lit a cigarette and began strolling up and down. Once he looked straight towards Melissa's hiding-place and she ducked her head again, terrified of being spotted and caught, although her reason told her she must be totally invisible from such a distance. Just the same, she kept rigidly still.

Melissa had no idea how long it was before there was a slight rumble and a sharp metallic sound, indicating that the plane door had been slammed shut. The dog-handler finished his cigarette, stamped it out and moved towards the gate. Melissa held her breath as she waited for the Land Rover to start up and disappear. Another couple of minutes and it would be safe for her to steal away.

The silence was shattered by a furious squawking, the sound

of madly fluttering wings and something or someone thrashing in the bushes not far from where Melissa lay hidden. The dog began barking and the effect on the scene below was for a split second almost comic, like a film sequence suddenly speeded up. Two figures leapt out to join the man with the dog while the Land Rover started up, shot forward and disappeared through the entrance. The gates shut with a clang behind it and simultaneously the landing lights went out—but not before Melissa saw that two of the men were carrying guns. The dog-handler switched on a powerful torch and began sweeping the steep, wooded bank to her right. This was no comedy. The beam travelled remorselessly in her direction, like the eye of a rapacious animal tracking its quarry. Thankful at least that her clothes were dark-coloured, Melissa pulled her hood over her head, buried her face in her arms, and froze.

So this was how it felt to be afraid. So often she had tried to describe the sensation without ever having experienced the sheer, stark, numbing terror she was trying to convey. Now she knew. This fear was tangible, its smell was in her nostrils and the sharp, sour taste of it tainted her mouth. It crept down her throat like some foul parasite, worming its way into every corner of her body and sucking up her strength so that even had she wanted to move she would have been powerless.

The men were climbing the bank towards her. She could hear heavy boots dragging through the grass and the whimpering and snuffling of the dog as it strained on the leash. Through half-open eyes she saw the torchlight probing among the trees, getting nearer. One of the men spoke and it sounded as if he was almost on top of her.

'Must have been a fox picking off a pheasant,' he said. 'Nobody there.'

'Can't afford to take chances,' said another. 'We'll let Dingo have a sniff around.'

Melissa could smell her own sweat. It seemed to engulf her like a miasma. The dog would get wind of it and she would be lost. The footsteps circled round, approaching, retreating, returning. She felt sure the men knew where she was; they must know, they were playing a hideous, sadistic game of cat and mouse. At any moment they would burst in on her with their guns and their dog and shoot her where she lay like a mesmerised rabbit. She began to pray, silently, despairingly: 'Please, let it be quick!'

Then came a cacophony of baying, snarling and snapping followed by a yelp. The men swore and shouted and crashed about in the undergrowth.

'What the hell's going on?' one of them shouted.

'Found an earth, didn't he? Vixen gave him a bloody nose!'

'Serve him right. What does he think he is, a bleeding fox-hound?'

'Come here, Dingo, you useless stupid bastard!' There was a tirade of abuse and another yelp of pain as the unfortunate Dingo collected a further penalty for his mistake. 'There's no one there, let's get back.' The men moved away and their voices grew fainter.

At last came the faint clang of metal as the gates opened and closed for the second time that night.

It was a long time before Melissa, lying prone in her burrow, dared to breathe normally or relax muscles that had been stretched as taut as wires. Eventually, she raised her head and crawled forward. Except for the plane standing innocently on the grass, everything was the same as when she arrived.

Not quite everything. Dawn was breaking and it was getting lighter every minute. Anyone keeping watch with binoculars would soon be able to detect movement among the trees. Better get back. Holding her breath, she began to crawl away. Not until she was out of sight of the house did she dare to stand upright and flex her cramped limbs.

The sky to the east glowed in a harmony of soft pink and gold. In the trees and bushes, birds had begun their first sleepy whistling. It was light enough now to take the shorter way home through the valley. She scrambled down the steep path; at the bottom she broke into a run, stumbling now and then on the uneven, tussocky grass, coming at last to the track leading towards the village.

The brook chattered softly alongside her. It was the first time she had seen the valley at this hour and the countryside had the appearance of a stage set, gradually illuminated. She could make out the village houses dotted among the trees, the stone roofs changing imperceptibly from grey to pink, and below, huddled beneath their bank as if they too had experienced something of the terror of that night, her own and Iris's cottages. She stopped for a moment to recover her breath and to experience a wave of thankfulness that she was alive, and free, and nearly home.

She had almost reached the bridge when she saw the body.

TWENTY-ONE

AT FIRST, SHE THOUGHT IT WAS A SACK OR A BUN-
dle of old clothing that someone had dumped in the water. Then
she saw the outstretched arms and the back of the half-submerged
head.

'Oh, no! Please, God, no!' She ran forward, jumped down the
bank into the shallow water and grasped the motionless form at
hip and shoulder. It took all her strength to roll the man on to
his back.

In one of her books, she had described a recently drowned
corpse using a book on forensic medicine in the reference library.
There had been a coloured picture that had haunted her dreams
for several nights and the details came back now with hideous
clarity: the patchy, livid discoloration of the skin; the glazed,
half-open eyes, expressionless yet somehow conveying a sense of
hurt bewilderment; the froth of bubbles creeping from the mouth:
all were there on the dead face of Dick Woodman. Mechanically,
she lifted one of the hands. The flesh was clammy, the arm already
stiffening with the onset of rigor mortis, the fingers clenched in
their last despairing attempt to hold on to life. Traces of green
waterweed clung slimily to the wrist.

Melissa knew that in a little while she would experience all the
symptoms of shock but for the moment she was ice-cool. By some
trick of the mind, a kind of psychological osmosis, her identity had
been suspended and that of Nathan Latimer, the detective she had
created and whose thought processes she had so often directed,
had taken her over. Almost in a dream, she allowed her eyes to
move round, absorbing every detail of what she saw.

The police would want to know the exact position of the body
when she found it and she spent several moments committing it

to memory. She studied the dead man more closely. There was a mark on the forehead that looked different from the others. She put a finger on it and felt the swelling while her brain clicked away like a machine.

She glanced up to the point where the path from the village emerged below the church. If Dick had intended to call on her after leaving the Woolpack he would have used that path and turned left at Daniel's hut, walking along the top of the steep, uneven bank towards Hawthorn Cottage. Could it be that in the darkness he had gone off the path? She remembered thinking once before that anyone losing their footing on that slope might not be able to stop. If Dick had been coming home in the dark, perhaps with a few pints of Old Peculier inside him, he could easily have come charging down out of control like the crowds of exuberant youngsters who risked broken limbs at the annual cheese-rolling at Coopers Hill. He could have stumbled and hit his head on the handrail and there would have been no one around to drag him, unconscious, from the water. Such accidents had been known to happen.

Yet there was something wrong. She could sense it. Dick had grown up in the neighbourhood, had tramped this valley hundreds of times. She remembered watching him as he nimbly picked his way down the slope with the assured tread of one who had been doing it all his life. And he wasn't a hard drinker—several times she had heard people say so.

Again, she examined the body. There was no tie and the collar of the soaked shirt lay open. She noticed something else and hesitated for a moment, frowning, before the full realisation of what had happened hit her like a blow in the stomach and the world dipped and spun around her as if she were on some crazy fairground switchback. No longer was she playing the part of Nathan Latimer, ace detective; she was not even Mel Craig, crime writer, but simply a badly frightened woman who had stumbled on a corpse. Her gorge rose, she turned her back on the sprawling figure and fled. Sobbing and gasping, she reached her front door and fumbled for her key, making futile stabs at the lock with a shaking hand until at last she managed to let herself in. She staggered into the kitchen and doubled up over the sink, retching and shivering.

She must pull herself together and call the police. She dashed cold water over her face, dried it with a towel and filled the kettle.

A cup of strong coffee would help to steady her but more than anything she felt an overwhelming need for familiar company. Iris would come. Iris had been through a similar experience and would know how she felt. She rushed to the phone and dialled the number with stiff, chilled fingers. The reaction to her incoherent gabbling was swift and typical.

'Be round right away!'

In three minutes, Iris was at the door. She had dragged on her gardening clothes and her tousled hair stood away from her face as if drawn by a cartoonist trying to convey fright.

'Are you sure he's dead?' she asked. 'Shouldn't we try the kiss of life or something?'

'He's been dead a long time.' Melissa closed the door. Back in the kitchen she stood in a helpless trance watching the steam belching from the kettle. Iris took charge, spooning out instant coffee and pouring boiling water.

'Where d'you keep the brandy?'

Melissa pointed to a cupboard and Iris dragged out the bottle, slopped some of the spirit into a mug of coffee and handed it over.

'Drink that and tell me what happened.'

'Oh, Iris, he was murdered!' Melissa felt her mouth twist and pucker as the tears began to flow. She covered her face with her hands.

'Murdered?' The grey eyes dilated in disbelief. 'Not possible. Who'd murder Dick?'

'It's true.' Melissa could hear her own sobs reverberating in her head. 'Someone . . . held his face . . . under the water . . . until he was dead.'

Iris gasped in horror. 'How can you be sure?'

'I . . . it happened in one of my books . . . a doctor helped me describe the marks . . . they were just like the ones on Dick's neck.' Melissa wrung her hands in her anguish. She was out of control, she could hear her sobs getting higher and wilder and could do nothing to contain them. Words pumped out of her mouth like blood from a wound. 'It's my fault!' she screamed. 'My . . . fault, my . . . my fault, my . . .'

'*Shut up!*'

Iris had her by the shoulders; she saw the raised hand and felt the sharp sting on her cheek. She put her own palm to her face and then held it in front of her eyes, staring in bewilderment.

'No blood. Didn't hit you that hard!' said Iris. 'Get that drink own you!'

'He was looking out for tit-bits for my story-books!' Melissa crubbed at her eyes and took deep, dragging breaths in a fight o bring her voice under control. 'It was like a game . . . we were oking about it the other day . . . I warned him not to be caught nooping around but it never dawned on me that there was any eal danger. He must have stumbled on something and been killed o stop him talking.' The tears flowed again. 'I feel so guilty!' she vhispered.

The skin over Iris's high cheekbones and pointed chin tight-ned, making her face a triangular mask.

'Mustn't blame yourself . . . couldn't possibly have known. Iave you called the police?'

Melissa shook her head. 'N . . . not yet. I was in such a state . . . called you first.'

'Must do it right away. Want me to?'

'Would you?'

'Sit tight. Shan't be long.'

Melissa sat miserably hunched at the table, gripping her mug. Mechanically, she sipped at the coffee but it was too hot and ourned her mouth. She could hear Iris on the telephone, giving lirections. A moment later she came back to the kitchen.

'On their way. Like me to come with you?'

'Come where?'

'You have to show them where it is.'

'Oh, don't call him it!' The neutral, impersonal pronoun at once educed the man to a cipher, robbing him of all human dignity. It vas his life, not his identity, that had drained away in the waters ne had fished as a boy and crossed a thousand times in the course of his daily toil. Only a few hours before, he had been a strong young man, full of good-humour and kindliness, someone she had net on her walks, stopping to exchange comments on the sheep or the weather, to pat his dog and enquire after his family. Now ne was nothing but an inanimate thing, soon to be the subject of letached examination and dissection in some cheerless laboratory smelling of antiseptics and death. Melissa put a hand to her throb-bing head.

'First Babs, now Dick!' she moaned. 'I feel as if I've put a jinx on this place. You must wish I'd never come to live here.'

'Fiddlesticks!' said Iris.

The uniformed officer who knocked on the door a short time later greeted them courteously and asked what seemed to be the trouble, 'rather like a doctor called out to a case of stomach-ache' Melissa reflected later. Sergeant Cook was a middle-aged, kindly faced man who exuded an impression of all-round capability and who would, she felt, deal with drunks, delinquent children and violent criminals with the same unflappable competence. He introduced his colleague, a young constable who seemed a little on edge.

'Think it's junior's first stiff!' Iris whispered in Melissa's ear as they waited by the stile for the two policemen to vault across.

'It's mine too!' Melissa whispered back.

Iris squeezed her arm. 'Stick by me—I'm an old hand!'

The grim little jest and the physical contact helped to steady her. The hysteria had passed, the paralysis was clearing from her brain.

The four of them made their way down to the brook. Melissa felt a tightening of her stomach muscles as they approached the bridge and she saw once again the still form on the ground beside it, but her voice was firm as she said, 'There he is.'

'Wait here please, ladies,' said Sergeant Cook. 'You watch where you're putting your feet, young Matthews,' he admonished the constable as they moved ahead. 'May be clues on the ground.'

Matthews nodded apprehensively. Iris and Melissa watched, shivering, as the two men briefly examined the body. A radio hissed and crackled, metallic voices echoing in the stillness.

To Melissa it seemed both predictable and unreal, a macabre example of déjà vu, like watching a video of a scenario that she had described, without having ever actually witnessed it, in a dozen novels. Her mind ran ahead to the sequence of arrivals and events to come: the car-loads of detectives and the van bringing equipment; the pathologist, trying to assess the time of death; the photographer, stepping gingerly around the victim, shooting from every angle. They would cordon off the area and go over it with a toothcomb for clues; they would empty Dick's pockets into plastic bag before the final, grisly ritual of securing the hands and parcelling up the remains for conveyance to the mortuary slab. Would she be in trouble for moving the body? Surely not, she had only been acting on the frail, outside chance that there was still a life to be saved.

Sergeant Cook came back to them, leaving Matthews on guard. He trod the path as if walking barefoot on broken glass.

'Shall we go back to your house, ladies? A senior CID officer is on his way and he'll want to get statements from you.'

'Yes, of course.'

Chief Inspector Harris was a thickset man whose features appeared to have been roughly moulded in reddish clay and left to dry in the sun. He had an unsmiling manner, small but penetrating eyes and a voice that suggested oily sandpaper. He chose an upright instead of an easy chair and waved the detective sergeant who accompanied him to a window-seat. Melissa sank into her usual armchair and Iris slid to the floor beside her and was promptly forgotten.

'I understand it was you who found the body, Mrs Craig?' said Harris. His tone was almost conversational.

Melissa nodded.

'And according to Sergeant Cook, you recognised it as being that of a Mr Woodman of Rookery Farm.'

'That's right.'

'What did you do when you came on the body?'

'I pulled the man on to his back to get his face out of the water.'

'Did you make any attempt at resuscitation?'

'No.'

'Why not?' Melissa hesitated and after a second or two Harris prompted, 'You were, perhaps, too shocked by your discovery?'

'It wasn't that. I just knew there was no point . . . he was dead.'

'You're a doctor?'

Melissa shifted uneasily. 'No but I . . .' She hesitated.

The keen eyes never left her face. 'Yes, Mrs Craig?'

'I've seen pictures of drowning victims. I'm a crime writer, you see and . . .' The stumbling explanation sounded novelettish and far-fetched, almost an excuse for having lost her head and run from the scene in terror. The fear assailed her that she might after all have made a dreadful mistake, that Dick Woodman had still been alive when she found him and that had she stayed to give practical help he might have been saved. If that were true, and she had to carry that responsibility through the rest of her life . . . the prospect was too hideous to contemplate. But it wasn't true;

the livid marks on Dick's neck and the wisps of green on his wrists were the proof.

'So you thought you recognised the symptoms of drowning,' said Harris.

She sensed rather than heard the sarcasm in his voice. He was making her look a fool. Worse. A fool who had been guilty of criminal neglect. The injustice of it made her face burn.

'I recognised the symptoms of murder,' she retorted.

She was aware of the detective sergeant's head jerking up from his notebook and heard him gasp in surprise but Harris merely lifted an eyebrow and said, 'You think this man was murdered?'

'It seemed at first that it must have been an accident, that he'd come too fast down the bank, missed his footing and knocked himself out in falling. Then I saw the marks on his neck and I was sure they'd been made by someone holding him under the water. And I believe,' she added as Harris appeared to be about to speak, 'that he was killed somewhere else and brought to that spot to make it look like an accident. I also think I know why he was killed.'

The eyebrow rose a little further and the eyes almost disappeared. 'Perhaps you'd care to explain, Mrs Craig.'

'I'm sure you noticed the pondweed clinging to one wrist. The only place you'll find that kind of weed is in still water. The brook is fed by several springs and runs quite fast through the valley.'

'Indeed?' If he was impressed, he gave no sign. He sat motionless in his chair, his legs planted apart and his thick, reddish hands spread over his knees. It was easy to imagine how even a hardened criminal might be unnerved by the deceptive simplicity of his questions and the piercing quality of his eyes. But she wasn't afraid of him any more; despite his inscrutable exterior she sensed that she had won his respect, however grudging. His next question, however, threw her into complete confusion.

'Are you in the habit of taking walks so early in the morning?'

'I . . .' she put a hand to her head. 'Oh, my God, I'd forgotten! The drugs . . . the plane . . . that's why they killed him, you see!' The events of the night swirled round in her head and she put her hands up to her eyes.

'I think perhaps you had better start at the beginning,' said Harris patiently. 'What time did you leave the house, and why?'

'Dick Woodman telephoned early yesterday evening and asked to come and see me, but I'll have to go back much further than

.hat. It's a very long and complicated story.'

'Take your time, Mrs Craig.' He listened impassively while Melissa recounted her visit to the flying school, Wally's description of a piggy-back rider, her subsequent deduction that the reference to a sow farrowing that had puzzled Dick was in fact a coded reference to an expected illicit arrival of a plane-load of drugs. She described how she had seen the plane land, her narrow escape from detection and finally her discovery of Dick's body as she made her way home. When she had finished, Harris sat silent for a while as if mentally digesting her story.

'Perhaps,' he said at last, 'you can explain why you are so sure this plane contained drugs?'

'I'll try.' She began with Clive's phone calls and her first meeting with Bruce Ingram. As the story proceeded, Harris at last betrayed some reaction. His lower jaw moved a fraction and his eyes became marginally wider; when she described her initial visit to the U.P. Club, he and the sergeant exchanged meaning glances that brought a self-conscious flush to her cheeks. He did not, however, interrupt again until she came to her second visit and the way she and Bruce had trailed the couriers.

'Just a minute,' he interposed. 'You told me that your friend on the *Gazette* handed over to us some pornographic photographs of a woman believed to be the victim of the Benbury Woods killing. Did he mention to the officer that he believed drugs were also involved?'

'No, I don't think so. At first he was convinced that the Up Front Agency was mixed up in a drugs ring. Then when I found the photographs, he decided it was a porn racket Babs had stumbled on. He ... wanted me to sign on at the model agency to "suss it out", he said ... but I refused. I told him he should hand the photos to the police at once.'

'Quite right too!' A ghost of a smile lurking on Harris's face made Melissa conscious of her bedraggled state. She probably looked tired and haggard, hardly a potential model. No doubt the young sergeant was laughing up his sleeve at her as well. She wanted to crawl into a corner and hide but Harris hadn't finished with her yet.

'So what gave you the idea that The Usual Place might be part of a drugs network?' he asked patiently.

'It arose out of a problem I was having with my current novel. It began with a bit of wild guesswork but the more we talked about it, the more it seemed an actual possibility.'

'So you decided to do a little more private sleuthing?'

'We really only meant to spy out the land and see where the women went with the trolleys, but when the opportunity presented itself to look inside them, it seemed too good to pass up.' Melissa quailed at the sudden anger flaring in the detective's eyes.

'Did you have any idea of the risks you were running?' he demanded. 'Suppose you had been caught! Your duty was to come straight to us and tell us what you had discovered.'

'That's what I told Bruce . . . Mr Ingram . . . but he pointed out that we hadn't really discovered anything. He wanted us to get hold of some concrete evidence by substituting a copy of the *Gazette* for one of the . . .' For a moment, she thought Harris was going to explode and her voice died away in a fearful whisper. It would not have taken much to make her break down. 'Then . . . all this happened,' she finished and lowered her head to avoid Harris's gaze.

There was another long silence. The sergeant flexed the muscles in his neck and fingers. Iris murmured something about coffee and stole out of the room. Harris loosened his collar and dragged at his tie. He looked weary; the lines on either side of his nose and across his forehead seemed to have deepened and the whites of his small eyes were speckled with red, as though the colour had seeped in from the surrounding flesh.

'You seem to have had a very lucky escape, Mrs Craig,' he said at last, speaking more gently.

'Yes, I know. I suppose, when I realised what Dick's message meant, I should have called the police right away, but it was nearly three o'clock in the morning and by the time they got here it might have been too late. I had no idea when the plane was due to arrive—for all I knew it was down already. As it was, I only just got there in time.'

'Just the same, you took a very foolish risk.'

'I know,' Melissa repeated. She felt exhausted, dishevelled and badly in need of a bath and some rest.

'I shall have to ask you to come down to the station later on today and make a full statement. I may need to see you again, and an officer from the Drugs Squad will certainly want to take a statement from you. We shall want to see Mr Ingram as well. Do you have his phone number?'

'Here.' Melissa flipped open her personal directory that lay by the telephone and pushed it towards Harris. 'He may not be at home . . . he said he was going away for the weekend.'

'Perhaps we'll be lucky. May I?' He was already dialling the number. Melissa glanced at her wristwatch; it was half past eight. Outside, it was broad daylight, the early sun lay soft and golden on the valley and the grazing sheep were scattered like creamy mushrooms over the sloping pasture. Dick's sheep, the flock that he had watched over so carefully, day after day. Someone else would tend them now but who would care for Jennie and the children?

Rage and a desire for vengeance lit a slow fire inside her. It was the kind of fire that she had sensed in Bruce when he spoke of the drug dealers and their victims. If some of the responsibility for Dick's death could be laid at her door, at least she could claim to have done something to bring his killers to book. Even if the actual hands that had held him down while he choked his life out in some filthy stagnant pond were never identified, there was a good chance that their owners would be in the net when it closed on the evil organisation that employed them. One way or the other, they would be made to pay for what they had done.

Harris had succeeded in rousing Bruce from his bed and seemed to be concluding some arrangements.

'That's fine. Thank you, Mr Ingram, and my apologies to you and the lady for any inconvenience. I can rely on you both to say nothing of this to anyone for the time being? . . . Thank you. Goodbye.'

'You caught him then.'

Harris's grin was as good as a wink. 'I caught him all right. I'm afraid we're going to upset his weekend arrangements but he took it very well.'

The implication was clear. Melissa wondered if the girl was Rowena and she was surprised to realise that she did not mind although she was glad that Iris had not been there to hear. Iris had guessed how close she had been to getting her fingers burned over Bruce.

'He's as anxious as anyone to see drug dealers smashed,' she told Harris. 'It's like a crusade to him.'

'Maybe he knows someone who's been hooked, someone close to him.'

'Yes, it's possible. He's never actually said so but I know he feels passionately about it.' Her thoughts went back to Dick. 'And so do I.'

They were all on their feet and it seemed that the interview was over for the time being. Then Iris appeared with a tray of fresh coffee and a plate of bread rolls filled with goat cheese.

'Thought you might be peckish.' She had obviously been home to raid her own freezer; the rolls were of her own make, still warm from the microwave.

Harris, a half-eaten roll in one hand, was making a second call.

'That you, Medhurst? Harris. Sullivan and I are leaving now. Any news of the PM? . . . Yes? . . . Yes, I see . . . well, keep that quiet for now. Have you broken the news to the widow? What? Any idea where she's staying? Right, when you see her, don't say anything about foul play at this stage. Death was by drowning. That goes for the press boys too, and no names to be released, okay? And I want to talk to a senior man in the Drugs Squad the minute I get back.' He replaced the receiver, took another bite from his roll, chewed and swallowed. 'The post-mortem would seem to support your theory, Mrs Craig. Death occurred between approximately ten o'clock and midnight and it looks as if there was a clumsy attempt to make it look accidental. For the time being there'll be no public statement to the contrary. I must ask you . . . and Miss Ash, of course . . . not to mention your suspicions to anyone else. Our Press Officer won't reveal who found the body so you shouldn't be troubled by reporters and Mr Ingram has promised to keep quiet about what he knows.'

'Can we trust him, sir?' Sullivan's surprising intervention made everyone turn round. He was looking anxiously from one to the other. 'I mean, he is a reporter, isn't he? This is hot news!'

Harris's eyes swung back to Melissa. They had lost something of their accusatory stare. 'Mrs Craig knows him better than we do. Let's ask her.'

'I think you can trust him to do whatever you ask, Chief Inspector. He's far more interested in seeing the ring smashed than in getting a story.'

'Hardly a typical newshound,' commented Harris drily.

Melissa smiled. She had come to this conclusion some time ago. 'You could say that. The one you might have trouble with is his colleague, the girl who helped us track the couriers. She's dead keen to get a scoop . . . but Bruce seemed pretty sure she'd have the sense to keep quiet if something big was about to break.'

'Thanks, I'll bear that in mind. Well, we'll be going. I'll be in touch as soon as I can arrange a meeting with the Drugs Squad. Meanwhile, I suggest you try to get some rest. And thanks for the breakfast.'

At three o'clock that afternoon, Melissa and Bruce stepped out of the headquarters of Gloucestershire Constabulary. It had been a mild, pleasant morning but thin cloud was beginning to drift in from the west and a chilly breeze blew dust and last year's dead leaves across the forecourt. Rain had been forecast for the rest of the weekend.

Together they walked across to the visitors' car park.

'You okay to drive?' said Bruce. 'That was your second grilling of the day . . . you look pretty washed out.'

'My head feels like a heap of bones in the desert . . . picked clean,' said Melissa wearily.

'How about going somewhere for a cup of tea?'

'Not for me. I'm marinaded in tea and coffee already, thanks all the same.' She unlocked the door of her dark green Golf and he held it open while she slid into the driver's seat. 'Has your weekend been a complete write-off?'

There was a twinkle in Bruce's eye as he shook his head and replied, 'I told you the other day, that girl is a jewel!'

So it was Rowena. 'Has she found out yet that your yarn about collecting for the Intensive Therapy Unit was a load of codswallop?'

He chuckled, totally unabashed. 'She never did swallow it. Tore me off quite a strip the first time she rang me. I had to take her out to . . . well, to put things right. It sort of went on from there.'

'So she has some inkling of what we've been up to?'

'Oh yes . . . but she's very discreet.'

'I'm sure she is,' said Melissa drily. 'Were there ever any suspicious enquiries about Clive?'

'No. We seem to have been barking up the wrong tree there.' The merriment faded from his eyes. 'I'm very much afraid Clive is in big trouble.'

'That reminds me. I was thinking of getting in touch with his father and maybe going to see him. Perhaps I'll do that later on today. Now the other business is out of our hands . . .'

'Won't know what to do with yourself, will you?' said Bruce wickedly. 'No more Sultry Sam and Gorgeous George . . . life will be very dull!'

Melissa shot him a withering look. 'There is a small matter of a novel I'm supposed to be writing.'

'Of course . . . well, cheer up, the past few days have given you plenty of material for it!'

'The trouble is, what has been going on is too close to my plot . . . no one will believe I invented it.'

'Does that matter?'

'Of course it does. I can just imagine some fork-tongued reviewer silkily suggesting that Mel Craig seems to be losing her flair for originality. Do you realise, even my villain is an antiques dealer, like one of the partners in the Benbury Park consortium!'

Bruce chuckled. 'I remember . . . Gregory something or other. No problem! Make him a bishop!'

'Oh, brilliant! I suppose he smuggles stolen church art treasures out of the country in the helicopters that bring his fellow clerics to the Palace garden party!'

'Right! He needs the money because a country rector is blackmailing him on account of his illicit relationship with a stripper—see how easy it is!'

'You are an idiot!' Melissa laughed at the nonsense and felt better. 'Well, I'll have to get down to it. As soon as this lot breaks I'll have my agent breathing down my neck.' She fastened her seat-belt and turned the key in the ignition. The engine responded instantly and Bruce gave a nod of approval at its smooth tickover.

'Nice motor. GTI, isn't it? Lively little beast, so I'm told!'

'It was Simon's actually—my son's. He was getting rid of it when he went to the States so I bought it from him.'

Mild surprise flickered across Bruce's face. It was the first time she had mentioned Simon.

'I didn't realise you . . .' He checked himself and for a moment seemed embarrassed. His eyes went back to the car. 'Can it do the ton?'

'I dare say it can but I've never tried. I suppose it's a bit ridiculous for a middle-aged woman but it's fun to drive. Well, enjoy the rest of your weekend. My regards to Rowena.'

'Sure. Be seeing you.' In the mirror, she saw that he was watching her as she drove out. Perhaps he too had come within an ace of making a fool of himself.

Twenty-two

'MR SHEPHERD?'

'Who is that?' The voice was high-pitched, patrician, slightly imperious. Melissa pictured silver hair, an upright carriage and aesthetic features.

'My name's Melissa Craig. You won't know me . . . I'm a friend of your son's.'

There was a pause, barely perceptible, before the man said, 'I presume you are aware that my son is at present recovering from a serious motor accident, Miss Craig?'

'Mrs Craig, actually.' The correction was mechanical, part of a defence system built long ago. 'Yes, I do know. As a matter of fact, I went to see him yesterday. I'm afraid he's in rather serious trouble.'

'Indeed?' It seemed that a touch of frost had crept into the carefully modulated voice. 'I find that difficult to believe in the circumstances.'

'I . . .' She had known it was going to be difficult. How does one break it to a complete stranger, particularly one so obviously unfriendly, that his only son is liable to be accused of murder? 'I know that you and Clive aren't very close . . .'

'Please come to the point.'

'It's very difficult to explain over the telephone. Could I possibly come and see you? I won't take up too much of your time,' she added, fearing that he was about to refuse. There was the suspicion of a sigh of exasperation at the other end of the line and she could have sworn she heard the sound of impatient fingers drumming on a table.

'Very well,' the man said grudgingly, 'if you consider it necessary.'

217

'Would tomorrow afternoon be convenient?'

'I suppose so. I can spare you a few minutes at three o'clock.'
It was plain that he considered her request both inconvenient and
impertinent but she could hardly back out now.

'Thank you very much. Please, can you tell me how to find
you?' His tone, as he gave directions to a house on the outskirts
of Stow-on-the-Wold, was curt to the point of rudeness and he
cut short her thanks by putting down his receiver. It was plain
that her reception would not be cordial.

Oaklands Park was an impressive house of grey stone set about
a hundred yards back from a quiet country road. The entrance
reminded Melissa of Cedar Lawns, with tall pillars flanking the
entrance to a tree-lined drive which ended in a circular gravelled
forecourt. Yet it lacked something of the hospital's welcoming
aspect. In bright sunshine it would doubtless be a picture straight
out of a glossy magazine but today, under a chilly drizzle from
clouds the colour of old army blankets, it had a depressing, faintly
hostile air.

Melissa backed the Golf against a low hedge to the right of the
entrance. On the opposite side, in front of a row of outbuildings
which had evidently once been a stable block, an elderly man
was polishing a white Rolls-Royce. When Melissa got out of her
car he came across the courtyard to meet her, a grave and rather
dignified figure who wore his dark green overalls like a livery.
Evidently he had been told to expect her.

'Mrs Craig? Please come this way.' She followed him to the
front door, which had been left on the latch. He held it open
for her, his head bent in the deferential yet dignified manner of
an old-fashioned family retainer. She felt he would be more at
home in a black coat and carrying a silver tray of wine-glasses,
an impression which was confirmed as he said, 'Mr Francis is in
the library.'

He was delightful, a period piece, pure Agatha Christie. Melissa
would have been prepared to bet that he still referred to his employ-
er's son as 'Master Clive'. The depressing nature of her errand
had not suppressed her writer's capacity to observe characters and
surroundings, and as she followed the man across a large square
hall with suits of armour in the corners and huge, gilt-framed
pictures on the walls, it became clear that the place belonged to
someone with a discriminating eye backed by substantial means.

If, as Clive had bitterly claimed, his father worshipped Mammon, then it was obvious that Mammon had not been ungenerous in return. The paintings were originals and there was nothing mass- produced or modern among the carefully arranged pieces of porcelain and bronze. It was almost like visiting a stately home.

The manservant led her round a corner, tapped on a door leading off a passage and opened it without waiting for a reply.

'Mrs Craig,' he announced, ushering Melissa inside.

The thin, grey-haired man who rose from behind a large mahogany desk had the same high forehead and prominent cheekbones as his son but he was not so tall and there was nothing friendly in his demeanour. His well-fitting flannel suit, silk shirt and tie were, like his surroundings, expensive and in perfect taste. There was no warmth in his pale eyes and his mouth had a downward twist. Whatever his worldly success, Clive's father was not a happy man. He took Melissa's proffered hand with evident reluctance, brushing it briefly with chilly fingers before waving her to a chair facing him.

'Thank you, Preston. When you have finished cleaning the car, kindly drive into Stow and fill it up. I may need it later.'

Preston's respectful nod was almost a bow. 'Yes, Mr Francis.' He went out and closed the door.

'Now, Mrs Criag, perhaps you will be kind enough to tell me why you are here.' Without actually glancing at his watch, her host managed to make it clear that the interview was to be brief.

'It's . . . not easy to explain,' she began. She had spent most of the drive rehearsing what she would say without coming to any satisfactory conclusion. 'As I said on the phone, I know that you and Clive are not on good terms, but . . .'

'My relations with my son are no concern of yours.'

It was an unpromising start. She tried again. 'I expect you know about your son's association with a girl called Babs Carter?'

'I know nothing of my son's associates. Who is this girl?'

'She is, or rather was, a . . . that is, she worked at a nightclub called The Usual Place.'

The pale eyes hardened and the thin lips registered distaste. 'You led me to believe that my son was in some kind of trouble. Do I understand that this . . . person has something to do with it? Has she had a . . .' He seemed unable to bring himself to utter the word and Melissa, thinking to save him embarrassment, said it for him.

'A baby? Oh, no! I only wish it was as simple as that.'

'Then kindly come to the point.'

It was the moment Melissa had dreaded. She drew a deep breath.

'Mr Shepherd,' she said quietly, 'Babs Carter is dead . . . strangled. There is a chance that Clive may be charged with her murder.'

There was a long silence, accentuated rather than broken by the steady ticking of a long-case clock in a corner of the room. The man behind the desk stared at Melissa with an intensity that made her uneasy. She braced herself for an outburst of rage and a furious order to leave the house, but nothing came. Instead, he stood up, went to the window and stood for several moments staring out in silence at the rain. He held himself as straight as a guardsman but the hands that hung at his sides were clenching and unclenching as if he were keeping time with the clock.

Melissa glanced round the room. The books that lined the walls were obviously valuable, the paintings above them were masterpieces, the carpet, furniture and ornaments must be worth thousands of pounds. The broad window gave on to a spacious, well- tended garden with an uninterrupted view across the rolling Cotswold Hills. It was the dwelling of a rich and successful man whose wealth had erected a barrier between him and his only son. No doubt the father had had dreams and ambitions for the boy and had grown bitter as he watched them fade over the years. Now they were in danger of being destroyed for ever.

The silence became unbearable and Melissa said timidly, 'I . . . I'd like you to know that I don't believe that Clive is guilty.' There was no reaction but she would not be discouraged. She was here and so long as she was not ordered to leave she would say what she had come to say. 'But he's in a strange state of mind and is saying some very odd things.'

'What do you want of me?' Still he did not turn his head.

'I want nothing,' said Melissa. 'I thought you should know how things were so that if it became necessary you could arrange for Clive to have the best possible legal advice.' Now the stance was less rigid than before, the iron-grey head less erect. He seemed somehow more approachable and Melissa got up, took a step forward and reached out a hand. 'Mr Shepherd, I . . .'

'Kindly don't keep calling me that!' He rounded on her and she backed away at the sight of his glittering eyes and flaring nostrils. Never in her life had she seen anyone look so angry.

'I'm sorry, I don't understand,' she said. She could feel her voice shaking. 'You are Clive's father, aren't you?'

'Yes, yes, yes!' The voice dropped to a harsh growl. 'I am his father and he is my only son. After his mother died, I dedicated my life and my fortune to him. He had the best of everything that money could buy. Nothing, nothing was too good for him. He rejected it all . . . his home, his father . . . even his name!'

'His name?'

'That was supreme insult, rejection of his father's name. Clive Francis became Clive Shepherd.' He spat out the final word as if it burned his lips. 'But there was worse to follow!'

Melissa shook her head in bewilderment. 'So you are really Mr Francis? I'm sorry, I had no idea . . .'

So much, she thought grimly, for her cozy image of the old family retainer using the style of address of a bygone age. She should never have come. Nothing would be achieved by her visit but the tearing open of a wound whose depth and pain were beyond her understanding. She would have given anything to be able to slip quietly away but Mr Francis went on speaking in a voice thickened by emotion.

'He left his home with hardly a penny in his pocket. He left everything behind, everything I had given him . . . his car, his pictures, horses . . . even his books. He walked . . . yes, walked . . . out of this house with one suitcase and I never saw him again. And all this was to be his!' Standing with the light behind him, his head thrown back and one hand extended in a symbolic gesture, he had the air of a medieval architect in a stained-glass window, proudly holding a model of his masterpiece. A lonely, disillusioned man, he inspired both pity for his suffering and despair at his blindness.

'He lived like a pauper!' The eyes were still directed at her but she had the uncanny feeling that they did not see her. Behind their rage was a kind of blankness. 'He refused even the pittance I was prepared to allow him. And then, as if he had not humiliated and disappointed me enough, he became entangled with a whore!'

'I can understand how upset you must be feeling,' Melissa murmured, conscious of the triteness of the phrase, its total inadequacy in the light of the message she had brought. Sooner or

later, of course, he had to know what kind of girl his son had
loved. She only wished she had not been the one to tell him.

'She was after money, of course! The young fool had let slip
that he had a wealthy father. Everyone knows that women of that
sort are not above a little blackmail!' Slowly, he returned to his
chair and sat down, his jaw set and his eyes glittering.

Despite the warmth of the room, Melissa felt a chill at the
back of her neck. There was something indecent about the way
the man's polished exterior was peeling away, layer by layer, like
the veneer from a piece of cheap furniture, revealing the worm
that was eating away at his soul. She didn't want to hear any more.
She had done what she set out to do and now it was time to leave.
She half-rose but he continued speaking and she felt compelled to
hear him out.

'She telephoned me, asking for five thousand pounds to leave
the county, go where he wouldn't find her.' His bark of laughter
was like a howl of pain. 'A miserable five thousand! I would have
given ten, twenty thousand! Sums like that are small change to
Gregory Francis! All I wanted from her was her undertaking
never to see my son again. I had a document prepared for her
to sign and I got Crane to bring her here. That was a mistake,
I'm afraid.' His voice became a frantic mumble, he seemed to
be speaking to himself. 'Once she saw what Clive's inheritance
was to be, a few thousands were no longer enough. She wanted
everything. The young fool had actually asked her to become his
wife and she announced that she had changed her mind about
leaving him. She had the effrontery to tell me she had decided
to accept. That little slut would have been mistress of all this!'
His voice rose to a shriek and he gazed wildly round the room,
flinging out both arms in an attitude of outraged dignity like an
actor in a grotesquely over-played black comedy.

Melissa listened, almost frozen with terror. In a far corner
of her memory sounded an echo of the Rector's voice as he
spoke about the members of the consortium that owned Benbury
Park. 'Gregory Francis . . . a local businessman . . . an antiques
dealer . . .' Was this man so obsessed with the acquisition of
wealth that he had turned to the more lucrative trade of drug
trafficking? The contents of his house were worth a fortune, far
more than the most successful dealer could normally amass by
legitimate means. And the irony was that they had brought him
no joy; he dwelt alone, eaten up with bitterness against the son

who had turned from him, appalled at the thought of his treasures falling into the hands of a girl like Babs. The prospect seemed to have brought him to the very edge of reason.

'I offered her fifty thousand pounds and she laughed at me. Imagine it—that common, painted little harlot, laughing at Gregory Francis! I ordered her to be quiet and she only laughed the more. I took her by the shoulders and she called me "Father" and invited me to kiss her. I took her by the throat . . . !' Like a burned-out firework, the madness in his eyes died out and he leaned back in his chair with a calm, almost satisfied expression. He contemplated his hands as they lay on his desk, a little apart, the fingers curving gently upwards, fingers that would handle a precious piece of porcelain with reverence or fasten round a girl's neck and snap it like the stem of a flower.

The heavy desk was between him and Melissa and the door was behind her, ten feet away. The key was on the outside; she remembered noticing it when Preston showed her in. He, with luck, was in Stow getting petrol for the Rolls and the place seemed otherwise empty. Praying that Francis would be slow to react, she made a dive for the door, wrenched it open and slammed it behind her, clinging with all her strength and weight to the heavy brass handle and managing to turn the key just as Francis, shouting obscenities, began tugging from the other side. She yanked the key from the lock and raced back towards the front door, dropping the key into a huge porcelain vase that stood on an oak chest in the passage. That should delay things a bit.

She was halfway across the hall when she heard the sound of a car in the drive. That must be Preston coming back. He would hear the disturbance and come running to investigate. For a moment, she thought of trying to find another way out, then realised that the muffled shouting and hammering from the library would be unlikely to reach him from the other side of the courtyard. Forcing herself to move naturally and composedly, she opened the front door. There was no sign of the Rolls but a white Mercedes had just been parked a few feet from her own. Out of it stepped a big man in country tweeds and a woman in a Burberry outfit complete with hat and scarf. In their unfamiliar costume it took a moment for Melissa to recognize Pete and Annie Crane.

For the second time in thirty-six hours, she felt a trap was about to close on her. She stood, physically and mentally paralysed, on the top step as the couple turned from the car and came hurrying towards her. Then something clicked in her brain and it sprang into life.

Come on, girl, you've got Nathan Latimer out of tighter corners than this. Those two look het up about something and anyway they won't recognise you without your U.P. Club warpaint. Just take it easy, keep your cool! With her head upright and her right hand firmly closed over the car key in her pocket, she descended the steps and went to meet them.

'Preston is out and the door is on the latch,' she informed them briskly. 'Mr Francis is in the library.'

'Thanks!' Pete strode past her with barely a glance but Melissa felt Annie's hard green eyes sweep over her face as she went by. She met them with a cool nod, fighting the rising urge to break into a run. She reached her car, got in and fastened her seat-belt. As she started the engine and engaged first gear, she glanced back at the house. Pete and Annie were standing at the top of the steps, looking at her. Annie seemed to be saying something; they were hesitating. The front door was wide open and they must surely by now hear the pandemonium from the library and realise that something was wrong. Any minute now, the heat would be on. Melissa let in the clutch and sent the Golf hurtling towards the entrance.

At the same moment, the Rolls turned in from the road and began a slow, majestic progress along the middle of the drive towards her. In normal circumstances she would have waited for it to pass but this was no time for knight-of-the-road tactics and she kept her foot firmly on the throttle. The Rolls made an undignified swerve to its left as Preston jerked at the wheel but the drive was too narrow for both cars and Melissa had to put two wheels on the grass. She shot past, narrowly missing a tree and with barely the thickness of a coat of paint to spare, leaving Preston goggle-eyed with fury and amazement.

At the bottom of the drive, a quick glance in the mirror before she turned out into the road revealed the Rolls still moving ponderously forward but no sign of anyone else. That meant nothing. It could only be a matter of minutes, seconds perhaps, before someone gave chase. As she accelerated away, racing through the gears along the empty road, she imagined what might be going on in the house.

Gregory Francis had, in her presence, as good as confessed to murdering Babs. Whether or not, in his unbalanced state of mind, he was aware that he had betrayed himself, it would not take long for the Cranes to realise that Melissa was a threat that must be eliminated. The hesitation on the doorstep, the staring back at her as she prepared to drive off, indicated that Annie had recognised her. The snapping green eyes that had examined her so thoroughly at their first meeting had seen through her amateurish efforts to change her appearance and registered the features beneath the make-up. It would have taken no more than a few seconds for Annie to place her in the U.P. Club.

What then? Seeing her come away from the house, they might assume at first that she was working for Gregory Francis, was perhaps there to report on the distribution system at the U.P. Club, even to check on the loyalty of the manager and his wife. A policeman friend had once told Melissa that drug dealers mis-trusted one another almost as much as they feared the law. Annie would remember finding her alone among the coats and shopping trolleys at her last visit and their first reaction might be resentment and indignation. But employees do not normally lock their masters up in their own libraries and whatever garbled story the agitated Francis was shouting through the door, it would not take long for the message to get through that Melissa had to be pursued, caught and silenced.

She remembered the road from her drive out; it had long straight stretches, interrupted by sweeping curves and some nasty sharp bends. There were a few minor intersections and a sprin-kling of farms but no villages, not even a cluster of houses or a country pub, for several miles. On this dull, drizzle-soaked Sunday afternoon, she had it to herself.

Except for the white Mercedes. It appeared in her mirror after she had been driving for no more than a minute or two and it soon began gaining on her. She trod hard on the accelerator and the Golf responded with a surge of speed but still the big car drew closer. A bend was approaching; with clenched jaws and her stomach knotted with fear she braked as late as possible before hurtling round, praying that the tyres would keep their grip on the wet road. Once, Simon had proudly demonstrated how good the little front-wheel-drive car was at cornering but she had never put it to this kind of test. For one petrifying moment it seemed that she was losing control. Then, miraculously, they were on the straight again and the gap between the two cars had widened a shade. Almost immediately came another curve, another teeth-gritting, stomach-churning battle with brakes, throttle and steering-wheel.

The Golf was holding its own but it couldn't last. On every straight stretch of road, the more powerful car began eating up the distance between them and the few yards the Golf gained on the bends could only delay the inevitable outcome. The Mercedes was near enough for her to recognise Pete at the wheel. Any minute now and he would be close enough to run her off the road. Was that how Clive's accident had been caused? She would never know the truth now, never learn whether the crazy risks she had taken would bring about the destruction of the drugs ring that she was now certain was centered at Benbury Park. The terror that had ridden on her back during the whole reckless, nightmarish chase dragged from her throat a dry, despairing sob.

As they came out of the next bend, the Mercedes was barely fifty feet behind and the road ahead seemed to run, straight as an arrow, into infinity. A final, frantic glance in the mirror showed Pete looking almost relaxed, as if he was enjoying himself, his big hands gripping the wheel and his fleshy lips parted in the loathsome, sensual smile he turned on for the women at the U.P. Club, the smile that never reached his pebble-brown eyes. He pulled out as if to pass; in a moment he would be alongside.

She saw the smile vanish and the thick lips mouth an obscenity as he fell back behind her before she realised that there were cars ahead. Two of them, approaching fast. White, with blue lights flashing on the roof. Police. They must be in a hurry but somehow she had to attract their attention. She switched her headlights on full beam, put a finger on the horn button and stamped hard on the brakes.

In her panic, she forgot for a crucial moment to steer and she found herself heading for the verge. The nearside tyres lost their grip on the loose gravel, sending her veering back on to the road just as she wrenched the wheel to the right. Overcorrected, the Golf slewed round and screeched to a halt in the middle of the road with the Mercedes heading straight towards it. Melissa had a glimpse of Pete sawing frantically at the wheel as the big car swerved, catching the rear of the Golf as it hurtled past. There was a deafening bang and she felt the shock of the impact crashing through her body. Hedges, cars and trees spun madly past her windscreen. Paralysed with fright, she sat staring ahead, vaguely aware that there were men all over the road and that the rear end of the Mercedes was sticking skywards out of the ditch like the stern of a sinking ship. Then she passed out.

TWENTY-THREE

'THE HEADLINE WRITERS REALLY WENT TO TOWN,
didn't they?' said Melissa, showing Joe her press cuttings. ' "Dawn
Swoop on Jet-Setters' Playground"! "Cotswold Manor Concealed
Drugs Laboratory"! "Local Antiquarian and Prominent City Figures held in Murder and Dope Scandal"! This one's my favourite
though: "Crime Writer Gives Tip-off in Real-Life Thriller!" '

Three weeks after the 'Benbury Bust', as Bruce insisted on
calling it, Joe sat drinking tea and eating fruit-cake in Hawthorn
Cottage while listening to the story behind the newspaper reports.
By the time Melissa had finished, his normally deep-set eyes were
almost bulging from his head.

'You're mad!' he spluttered. 'You need a minder! You shouldn't
be allowed out alone!'

'You wanted me to get some publicity,' she pointed out.

Joe exploded. 'Oh, so it was my idea! That's a good one! "Lit-
erary Agent Goads Writer into Deadly Research Project"—how's
that for a screamer?' He got up and began pacing up and down.
'You could have been killed, Melissa. Hadn't you any idea . . .'

'. . . of the risks I was taking?' she interrupted. 'Now don't
you start. I've had all that from everyone from the chief constable
downwards.'

'I'm not surprised. What the hell possessed you to go tearing
off like that on your own?'

'You mean to call on Clive's father? I was only trying to do a
little peacemaking. You don't suppose I'd have gone if I'd known
who he really was, do you?'

Joe sat down again and gazed at her with a troubled expression.
Anxiety had drawn deep lines on either side of his normally
humorous mouth.

228

'Nothing would surprise me after the way you went tracking that plane. I shan't sleep for a week, thinking of you being hunted by those thugs. And as for that murdering bastard in the Mercedes—if the police hadn't happened along when they did . . .'

'They didn't just happen along.'

'No?'

'They were on their way to Oaklands Park after a tip-off.'

'Who from?'

'Bruce. Well, Rowena really. You see, when she gave me Gregory Francis's telephone number, we both referred to him as Clive's father. She was on the phone to somebody else at the time and never thought to mention that Clive was using a different name.'

'So what made her realise . . . ?'

'Now that *was* pure chance. She was with Bruce that Sunday afternoon. He'd heard from Sophie—his colleague on the *Gazette*—that she'd spotted someone she recognised as a plain-clothes copper chatting to the driver of the Hanger Hill delivery van, round the back of The Usual Place. Evidently Pete had seen this as well and didn't like the look of it. He called the driver over and they exchanged a few words. Then the chap got into the van and drove away. Sophie said Pete looked distinctly edgy and I imagine that was why he and Annie went to Oaklands Park, to persuade Francis that it might be as well to suspend the Tuesday trolley-run for the time being.'

'So it was Francis who was masterminding the operation?'

'Yes.'

'And the drugs were being distributed along with the fruit and vegetables?'

'Right. They were getting them to outlets all over the county. The Drugs Squad are rubbing their hands . . . it's been one of the biggest clean-ups on record.'

'You still haven't explained why the fuzz were heading out towards Oaklands Park.'

'Bruce thought I'd be interested in Sophie's report and tried to call me. When he got no reply, Rowena said, "She's probably gone to see Mr Francis." '

'And Bruce picked it up and put two and two together?'

'That's right. He remembered my telling him that one of the members of the Benbury Park consortium was a Mr Gregory

Francis. Bright lad, Bruce. He should do well in the police force.'

'Police force? You mean he's giving up journalism?'

'He thinks he's found a more direct way of helping to clean up society. He'll probably start writing crime novels in a few years' time. You'd better sign him up.'

Joe rolled his eyes upwards. 'If I had two like you to deal with I'd be a nervous wreck! I'd rather stick to agony aunts.'

'How's the steamy novel coming along, by the way?'

Joe grinned. 'Getting more salacious by the minute. Talking of things salacious, what about the porn racket that was supposed to be going on at that model agency? Was there any connection with the Benbury Park set-up?'

'No . . . that was all very small beer. Just the agency photographer doing a little moonlighting, using the firm's models. Twenty pounds apiece that poisonous little creep paid Babs and her partner for that session.'

'Squalid trade!' agreed Joe. 'Hope he gets sent down for a good spell.'

Silly kid, Melissa thought, degrading herself for such a paltry sum. Yet who could blame her? At a stroke, society had in its wisdom robbed her of a loving—all right, an all-too-loving but also a well-loved—father and thrust her into an alien environment where she had quite possibly been exposed to even more corrupting influences. No wonder she had sought the company of older men and gone to desperate lengths to make a secure future for herself. The day she was taken to Clive's old home, she must have thought she was driving through the gates of Paradise. Instead, she was going to her death.

'What about that hairdressing salon?' asked Joe. 'Were they involved?'

'Apparently not . . . Bruce was very disappointed! He was convinced they were all tied up together in some huge, devilish conspiracy.'

Joe frowned as another thought struck him. 'Gregory Francis must be a cold-hearted devil, killing that girl for what you might call purely snobbish reasons. I suppose Crane organised the heavies from Benbury Park to dispose of the body. It's a miracle none of Francis's domestic staff saw what was going on.'

'There was only old Preston there at the time and he's been with the family for nearly thirty years so they were confident he'd keep his mouth shut. Just the same, it must have been a severe test of loyalty for him. The poor man was broken-hearted when Francis was arrested but thankful to be able to unburden his own conscience.'

'And then to order his own son's murder . . . !'

'No, that was Pete using his initiative. He was terrified Clive wouldn't give up until he'd found out what had happened to Babs. Then the whole set-up would have been blown open. Of course, he had no idea at the time who Clive really was. When he did find out, he must have been scared stiff that Francis would find out he was the one who'd caused his son's accident. He left Annie in charge of the bar that night to go after Clive. It's ironic, isn't it? The police picked up Clive's trail right up until he left the pub at closing-time but never thought to check that Pete was at The Usual Place all evening.'

'What about the note? The one Babs was supposed to have written?'

'Annie left that when she went to get Babs's things. They had the wind behind them that day . . . it was early closing, Petronella's was shut and no one saw her.'

'So Pete and Annie have been singing?'

'Not Pete. Annie. He's been fooling with other women for years and she'd had it up to here. She sang and sang until her voice cracked.'

'Aha! Hell hath no fury . . . I suppose the heavies who buried Babs also killed that farmer friend of yours?'

'That's right.' Melissa got up and went to look out of the window. The year had moved on and the May blossom had made way for creamy masses of elderflowers. Lambs ran about the sunlit pasture, bleating pathetically as they sought their shorn mothers. 'Poor Dick! That's something I shall never quite forgive myself for.'

'You mustn't blame yourself,' Joe said gently.

'It was so diabolically callous. He'd been seen near the laboratory—the police think someone must have been careless and left it open—and then he was overheard talking to me on the phone. They must have thought he'd found out what was going on and was going to shop them.'

Joe's face grew grim. 'It's lucky for you they didn't have the nous to make him tell them who he'd been speaking to . . .' he began, and Melissa jumped as his meaning dawned on her.

'I never thought of that,' she whispered. 'You mean, they might have come after me?' Her veins seemed to run with ice-water. 'I suppose I was lucky . . . they could only have overheard bits of the conversation and not realised he'd told me anything significant.' She closed her eyes for a moment, overwhelmed by the horror of it all. 'They kept him at the Park, giving him drinks and pretending to be friendly until about the time he'd have left the Woolpack. Jennie was staying at her mother's with the children, you see, and he simply wasn't missed. And then . . . then they . . . took him out to the ornamental lake and . . .' Her voice cracked and the tears began to flow. Joe got up and put an arm round her shoulders. She leaned against him for a moment, thankful for his comfort and sympathy. 'If only I'd tumbled sooner to what that message meant . . .'

'I doubt if it would have made any difference to Dick,' said Joe. 'Even if you'd been able to convince the police that there was something fishy going on, and they'd mounted some kind of operation, it would probably have been too late to save him.'

'Perhaps I could do something for Jennie and the children . . . set up a trust fund or something out of the proceeds from the novel . . . if there are any.'

'There will be,' Joe predicted. 'It'll make a bomb on both sides of the Atlantic! Should be good for a TV series too.' He gave her shoulder a squeeze before taking his arm away. 'Now all this is over, you'll be able to get down to it.'

'It'll never be over for some,' said Melissa sadly.

'You mustn't be too pessimistic. People do get over these things in time.'

'But there are so many casualties. Apart from Babs, and Dick and his family, and the Rector, there's Clive. He's lost a year of his life and now he's got all this trauma to live with.'

'He's young, he'll be all right. Didn't you tell me he's left the clinic? How's he getting on?'

'He left as soon as he found out his father had been paying the bills. Actually, I suppose things are looking up for him.' She reminded herself that as well as tragedy there was hope. 'He's going back to work part-time . . . his firm has been very good and they're finding him a desk job until he's fit to drive again. Bruce and Rowena have taken him under their wing, and he and Dawn are seeing quite a bit of one another, I hear.'

'Well, there you are then. I'm sure Dawn is much better for him than Babs could have been.'

'I'm sure she is.'

'And what about the Rector?'

'He's been given leave by the Bishop to spend some time in retreat. At least, his wife has been very supportive although I don't suppose she's got the faintest idea what's really behind his breakdown. She thinks it's overwork and goes round uttering reproaches against everyone from the PCC to General Synod for making too many demands on him. And there's one other bright spot amid the gloom.'

'Oh?'

'Stanley Parkin—Gloria's husband—is in the clear . . . at least, as far as the drugs racket goes. He knew nothing about it . . . it's his partner who's the dealer. He's got two sites for his second-hand car business and the one he looks after himself is clean as a whistle . . . give or take one or two dubious "low-mileage-one-careful-lady-owner" cars!' Melissa managed a tremulous smile. 'Gloria might have to hock a few earrings to pay his fine but she'll take it all in her stride. Her Stanley can do no wrong in her eyes.'

'How nice it must be to have a loyal partner,' said Joe with unmistakable meaning.

Melissa got up and began clearing away the tea-things. To respond to that kind of remark could lead to dangerous ground. Maybe some time in the future . . . but not yet. As if he read her signals, Joe glanced at his watch and stood up.

'I'd better be leaving,' he said. Before getting into his car he put both hands on her shoulders, kissed her on the cheek and brushed his head against hers. 'No more amateur sleuthing, mind!' he said softly. 'Promise?'

'Don't worry. I'll be in touch when the book's ready. Drive carefully!'

Iris emerged from the garden of Elder Cottage as the Audi drove away. 'Nice man!' she observed. 'Pity he's married.'

'He's getting a divorce,' said Melissa absently, returning Joe's wave as he turned into the lane. 'Nothing to do with me,' she added in response to a keen look from the steel-grey eyes. 'I told you, it's just a professional relationship. I must go and finish my letter to Simon . . . I want to catch the evening post.'

'When's he coming over?'

'In a couple of weeks. There are one or two things I want him to bring for me.'

Iris gave one of her witch-like cackles. 'Wonder what he'll say when he hears?'

'About the murder and so on?'

'Have a fit when he knows what his mother's been up to!'

'Probably. At least I've proved I can take care of myself.'

'How are you going to bear it here in the winter?' Simon wanted to know. 'It's cold enough in July to freeze the ass off a jack-rabbit!' They were standing at the top of the bank near Daniel's hut after Melissa had given him a conducted tour of the village. The sky was a pearly grey and a cool breeze flattened the long grass.

'You've become soft!' she teased him. 'Anyway, I may not be here for the entire winter. Iris has invited me to her cottage in Provence for as long as I like to stay.'

'You could always come over to Texas for a while.'

She looked up at him, laughing happily. 'I do believe you've grown . . . you seem enormous! Does it ever snow in Dallas?'

'Not since I've been there.'

'I'll think about it. I've never been that far south.'

'Do that. I don't like to think of you stuck out here on your own.' He looked down at her with concern on his young, tanned, unlined face. 'You need someone to look after you, Madre.'

'Do I, dear? Well, we'll see.'

MYSTERY WITH STYLE ⬜

__LAY IT ON THE LINE by Catherine Dain ─────
0-515-10926-6/$3.99

A great new mystery series for fans of Sue Grafton

Reno's cat-loving, Keno-playing, plane-flying P.I. Freddie
O'Neal helps an ex-chorus girl whose elderly father is
being conned by his caretakers. The case seems easy
enough—until murder and family secrets have Freddie
gambling with her own life.

Look for the next Freddie O'Neal mystery,
<u>Sing a Song of Death</u>, in 3/93!

__A COLD DAY FOR MURDER by Dana Stabenow ─
0-425-13301-X/$3.99

With her loyal Husky, savvy investigator Kate Shugak goes
back to her roots in the far Alaskan north...where the
murder of a National Park Ranger puts her detecting skills
to the test.

Look for the next Kate Shugak mystery,
<u>A Fatal Thaw</u>, in 1/93!